The Samurai Revival Trilogy (Vol. 1)

BITTER TRUTHS

Rheagan Greene

Hamon Publishing

Authors note:

Although predominantly accurate geographically, this story is a
work of fiction. Any resemblance in this story between people or
events and real life is unintended and purely coincidental.
Furthermore, use of the Japanese language and historical references
have been simplified; a Glossary is included at the back of the book.

ISBN 978-0-9573040-0-0

Cover concept and design by: Rheagan Greene
With inputs from: Danny Keay & Tom Gordon

Printed and bound in the UK by TJ International Ltd., Padstow

Hamon Publishing
Suite 55, 28 Old Brompton Road, London, SW7 3SS, UK
www.hamonpublishing.com

Dedication:

To my mother and brother, and in fond memory of my father – their support made life's worst bearable and its best something to be shared with gratitude and pride.

Acknowledgments:

My sincere thanks to all those who have encouraged me to complete these books. Notably: Andrew, Anna, Anne-Marie, Helen, Rob and especially Jo and my editor, Lynn Curtis.

Also, my thanks to Simon King of Inside Japan Tours Ltd. His knowledge of Japan and advice concerning my intricate location requirements enabled me to travel Japan effectively and experience first-hand much that has influenced this story.

BITTER TRUTHS

CHAPTER 1

Japan, August 2023...

The remote town of Iga Ueno lay sweltering beneath a burning sun and clear blue sky. The searing heat stopped even the adventurous from visiting the first Ninja castle and the birthplace of the renowned haiku poet, Matsuo Basho; remnants from the town's prestigious past. But the one truly remarkable association of which Iga Ueno could still boast stayed hidden, as it had for centuries.

Deep within the inhospitable mountains to the north, craggy hillsides came together to leave a narrow gully through which most people thought only a stream passed. But there was a footpath too. It started inconspicuously on the plains below, zigzagged up the steep forested incline and scrambled over the brows of several hills before finally squeezing into the secluded valley beyond. With its fertile plateau cradled by thickly wooded slopes, the valley was sublimely peaceful. Indeed, its owner's right to this serene solitude had been enshrined in law many generations earlier by the Emperor of Japan.

The path meandered up the valley. It passed through a cluster of wooden cottages where the farmers lived, eventually petering out by another huddle of buildings. Beside the largest, a massive old water wheel dipped rhythmically into the fast-flowing stream. But today, the forge it powered was silent.

At the head of the valley, central within a walled enclosure, stood an archetypal samurai house, its ancient timbers and graceful scalloped roofs with grey glazed tiles testament to the builder's supreme craftsmanship. A mulberry-coloured flag fluttered listlessly from a nearby pole. It bore a distinctive emblem comprising a black-and-gold scene of a tiger in a bamboo tree and a stylised gold chrysanthemum flower.

A flagstone path led from the roofed gateway across the front courtyard. Where it reached the house, lattice doors had been slid apart to reveal a substantial audience hall. However, in an alcove to the left was a smaller, more private, ceremonial room. Its walls were of beautifully finished sandalwood, with intricately carved beams punctuating the subtly panelled ceiling. The atmosphere inside was one of timeless sophistication, charged with assured expectation.

Thick tatami mats covered the floor, in the middle of which was an exquisite, highly polished, low black lacquer table. On it stood two ornate gold stands, proudly presenting a newly made samurai sword, the graceful beauty of its slender curved sheath masking the deadly blade within.

The master sword-maker sat on a mulberry-coloured *zabuton*, dressed in finest hand-painted silk. Without a sound, strong but sensitive hands lifted the sword reverently off its stands. One last time the end result of many months' hard work was scrutinised.

Twelve hundred years before, Keitaro Amakuni had discovered this valley and its unique sword-making materials and conditions. He had built a forge and settled down, and his ancestors had made weapons here ever since. For a thousand years, Amakuni swords had been accepted as the undisputed best in the world. Nobody had ever been able to produce weapons of comparable quality, or artistry. Admittedly a couple had come close, one workshop near Kyoto and another in Toledo, but apart from them, other weapons were vastly inferior.

Formal recognition came in the late-1860s after Amakuni weapons helped return the Emperor to power during the civil war that culminated in the Meiji Restoration. As a reward, their family, together with one other, earned the right to incorporate the Imperial chrysanthemum within their family crest.

The sword-maker's right hand moved to the hilt and, with an agile flick of the wrist, unsheathed the weapon. Rejoicing at being released, the blade glistened and hummed with anticipation, keen to follow its calling…

"Patience," murmured the sword-maker. "All in good time."

Although not shiny, the grey blade possessed a remarkable sheen; deep enough to display the reflection of the sword-maker's smile. The wavy misted line of the hamon marked the boundary between the toughened body and the thousands of incredibly sharp hardened cutting edges at the front of the folded steel blade. Unusually, a second hamon ran close to the back edge of the blade. Although pointed, it was not surgically sharp. Unlike the first edge, its task was to cut through steel and stone rather than flesh and bone.

With a noise like a sigh, the blade was slid back into its sheath and carefully returned to the stands. For several minutes, its maker gazed at the weapon with the same pride, satisfaction and sense of anticipation with which a mother adores her new-born child.

The sword-maker smiled, reflecting on how times had changed. After much global turmoil, guns, explosives and weapons of mass destruction had been banned; day-to-day law enforcement was once more maintained by samurai sword-wielding Peacekeepers. High-quality weapons were in demand again; but the Amakuni had always been very selective about their swords' owners.

Kimi Amakuni stood up and walked to the open window. The view down the sun-drenched valley was magnificent. She sighed and turned back to face the sword, pulling a thin mulberry-coloured mobile phone from behind her kimono's obi. She flipped it open, entered a number from memory and pressed the call button. It was answered in seconds.

"It is done," she said, "the sword is ready."

"Kimi-san," answered the softly spoken man at the other end of the line, "I am grateful. I accept this is an unusual commission, but I am sure it will be a force for good and benefit both our clans."

"I understand. I feel it too," she replied quietly. "Nevertheless, do not forget our agreement. You will not let the sword out of your care until its true owner claims it; and even then, if that person is not of sound character and an expert, you will return it to me?"

"Yes, I promise. Kimi-san," continued the man tentatively, "are you pleased with it?"

She paused as her eyes lingered on the elegance and brutal artistry of what she had created.

"Oh, yes," she replied with a proud smile. "This is the finest sword I have ever made. It is the finest blade any Amakuni has ever made. Few swords will even dare threaten it. This weapon is certainly capable of ending the feud, provided its owner wields it skilfully … and can be persuaded to do what needs to be done."

The man breathed out, relieved and encouraged.

11

"Thank you, Kimi-san. Thank you very much indeed. You have done all you can, the rest is up to us. I will make the necessary arrangements for the sword's arrival here, and will inform you when the owner comes to collect it."

CHAPTER 2

London, two weeks later...

In a well-appointed mews house in affluent South Kensington an internet radio clicked on quietly. Tessa Pennington heard it because she'd hardly slept; she had too much on her mind. The business she owned and managed was being sold. So far, she had confined the stress of the transaction to the daytime hours, but now it was invading her nights too. However, there was a lot at stake for her, not least financial security for life.

She groaned and waited for the farming report to start; shortly afterwards a woman cheerily began describing the ins and outs of inoculating battery chickens. In an hour Barry would arrive with his taxi to take her to Heathrow. She needed to get going. Bleary-eyed, she staggered into the bathroom and stood in front of the mirror. She stared at the reflection of the shapely young blonde woman studying her from the mirror with steely blue-grey eyes, and smiled. After years of being shocked by the face that met her gaze, everything was in order now.

She showered, dressed and went downstairs for a hasty breakfast. Then she gathered her papers, threw them into a bag and added her lap-top. As she closed the zips she heard the gentle rumble of Barry's taxi reversing slowly down the cobbled mews. Boy, he's good, thought Tessa. At 5:30 a.m., most taxi drivers relished the opportunity to wake all the residents by thundering over the cobbles. But not Barry. He would drive into the mews, carefully turn round and quietly reverse down, ready to make a speedy but discreet getaway.

She grabbed her bag, switched off the lights and armed the house alarm. As she went out, the back door of the taxi swung open.

"Morning, Barry," said Tessa brightly. "How's your back?"

"Bloody awful, luv, 'urts like 'ell. I'll have to see 'quack again. What terminal?"

"Oh, number one, please. So those new tablets aren't helping then?"

"Nope, not a bit, luv. They just make me wanna puke," he replied as the taxi started up the mews.

Concluding that cheery conversation would be wasted on Barry at the moment, Tessa studied some papers until it was time to pay at Heathrow.

Penny Reid was a confident, eye-catching young woman who dressed as she felt every Chief Executive should – smart. Today she was wearing a dark grey designer suit with black patent shoes; her turquoise blouse contrasted perfectly with her neatly styled blonde hair. She checked in for her early-morning flight and went to the Executive Lounge in search of an espresso.

Thirty minutes later, she settled into her usual Business Class window seat. She glanced at the empty seat beside hers and shook her head.

Not long afterwards another smartly dressed young woman arrived.

"Hon, one day you'll miss the flight," Penny chided her.

"Morning, babe," laughed Tessa. "Suffice to say, I remain a dedicated exponent of *just in time*."

"So I see."

Tessa opened the luggage compartment and put her bag next to her friend's. But as she sat down an unnatural hush spread throughout the plane. An impressive-looking Asian man wearing a samurai sword had just boarded. The weapon was slipped through his wide black belt to which it was tied with a violet cord. Like everyone else, Tessa and Penny watched him with considerable curiosity.

"Excellent! The probability of us being hijacked just plummeted," remarked Penny contentedly.

"Hardly likely anyway after all that airport security," goaded Tessa.

"You wait, in a few years when there are more Peacekeepers around, I bet all security will be relaxed, and not just in airports. The armed police in flak jackets are already gone, aren't they?"

"True, but since when have Peacekeepers been acting as air marshals?"

"Oh, they don't. It's too difficult to draw a sword within the confines of an aeroplane."

"Great! And why don't they wear anti-stab vests?"

"Because they're either too cumbersome to be practical, or too light to be effective. Apparently the best protection is a modern take on traditional samurai armour, but hardly anyone wears it."

Tessa pulled a face.

"I daresay this model for peace-keeping worked well in Japan four hundred years ago, but the world's a very different place now. Look what's been achieved so far." She held up her newspaper which announced: *"New Crime booms as Calver Cats tighten their grip on London's criminals, often living up to their name by disembowelling their victims alive..."* "Aren't you worried when even the FT fills its front page with the machinations of a bunch of alliterative thugs who treat people the same way the Japanese prepare live fish?"

"Well, we're not the only ones in a transitional phase. The world's changed incredibly quickly. Criminals have adapted faster than expected."

Tessa responded by pointing to an article in Penny's paper. *"As Special Forces struggle to maintain control, New Crime continues to capitalise on the shortage of trained Peacekeepers and reduced weaponry for Police."*

"I accept we live in troubled times," conceded Penny. "But too many people have invested too much in the International Peacekeeper Treaty to let it fail..."

"Maybe, but the world isn't facing the same challenges that the Samurai were up against. Our problem today is the way new technologies are being applied by politicians and religious fanatics. Are you sure these so-called fundamental changes to global peacekeeping are really going to fix that?"

"Yes, absolutely. Ever since the Three Tragedies, people have rejected the old weapons stand-off. Remember how horrified everyone was when millions died in that North Korean nuclear catastrophe? Not to mention the Iranian Taliban attempt to explode dirty bombs in London and Tokyo, and the Al-Qaeda plot to release Sarin gas on the New York and Chicago subways. Well, the Peacekeeper Treaty is designed to deprive all those who would be violent of their weapons, and it will. But it's early days yet..."

People had indeed had enough. Exasperated by politicians' duplicity, greed and overt distancing of themselves from the needs and values of the population they were supposed to represent, virtually everyone had wanted an end to violent feuding between nations and religions. More than three billion people united via internet petitions and, after a year of intensive lobbying by peace activists and global political stalemate, the UK and Japanese governments took the initiative. They jointly proposed the banning of all guns, explosives and weapons of mass destruction together with the reintroduction of capital punishment for those carrying arms illegally. Funds previously set aside for national defence were to be invested in the environment. Only the revamped, and at last effective, United Nations for World Peace would have an army and it would source weapons components from all over the world in UNWP-controlled factories. Individual countries could only have a small fully armed Special Forces division and Police armed with truncheons; not even Taser stun guns. Furthermore, it was proposed that day-to-day law and order would be maintained by independent samurai sword-wielding International Peacekeepers. These were effectively a cross between the marshals of the American Wild West and the Samurai of Ancient Japan.

Amazingly, these ground-breaking proposals received almost universal support. The International Peacekeeper Treaty was drafted and soon signed by most governments. Countries with endemic gun cultures, notably America, Israel and Switzerland, resisted doggedly. However, even they acquiesced when faced with virtually world-wide trade and financial embargoes.

The impact of these changes was dramatic. Free trade blossomed and traditional crime syndicates disintegrated as they struggled to obtain firearms to bolster their power. Initially crime levels fell dramatically, but there were too few Peacekeepers. Organised crime quickly adapted and filled the vacuum caused by the rapid disappearance of guns. They trained their own people to use swords, and New Crime was born.

The authorities encouraged more people to enrol on the arduous Peacekeeper training courses. However, not many were able to meet the stringent requirements, which no one wanted to relax since Peacekeeper powers were so far-reaching, not least with regard to their licence to kill. The number of Peacekeepers in circulation only increased slowly and soon they themselves became targets...

Five minutes later, Penny whispered to Tessa, "I'm not being bitchy, but are you all right? You look shattered."

Tessa twisted round to face her with an aggrieved expression.

"Thanks, but I'm fine. It's the disposal. It's been full on for weeks now. Getting there though."

"We're letting life get too serious, hon. We've missed catching up for two weekends. How about dinner at the Falcon on Saturday?"

Tessa smiled, "I'll put it in my schedule now – and I promise not to blow you out."

Although barely thirty, Tessa and Penny had both been extremely successful; each owned and managed a significant business. Penny's, Schrauben and Mutter, had headquarters near Stuttgart and made a wide variety of nuts, screws, washers and bolts, a product portfolio which never failed to amuse, as did S&M, the abbreviation of the company name. Tessa's business, Druckmaschinen + Service, made printing machines. It was also based in Germany, but at the other end of the country in Düsseldorf.

"So how are you getting on now your investment bank's been taken over?" asked Tessa.

"Could be a lot better. Although I control the majority of S&M's shares, BNYI also has some now. Far from ideal for all sorts of reasons, but swapping banks would be very difficult at the moment." Tessa nodded; she knew the Beijing New York International bank didn't have a particularly good reputation. "At the moment we're keeping our head above water, but it isn't much fun; and BNYI is beginning to flex its muscles. I'm sure we're not the worst of their problems, but we're not one of their favourites either."

"Who's your contact there?" asked Tessa.

"Blaise Collins-Clarke."

"Oh, I've heard of him, it's not exactly an easy name to forget. Slimy, pompous two-faced git was the way I heard him described."

"Actually, that's rather unfair on all the other slimy, pompous two-faced gits; they're probably bearable in small doses. But Collins-Clarke is pure poison, believe me," replied Penny with disdain. "I certainly don't want Schrauben & Mutter to go under, so I'm doing my best to keep him on-side. But I'm beginning to wonder whether what we both had to do is compounding the situation."

"Fixing a birth defect shouldn't make any difference to anyone, especially BNYI," retorted Tessa.

"No, it *shouldn't*, but perhaps it's unrealistic to expect otherwise. Hardly anyone even tries to understand. It's easier to ignore what's perceived as a problem and take refuge in narrow-mindedness."

"Yes, that's how most people react when something unfamiliar confuses or scares them," agreed Tessa. "It's just a shame they don't realise that eventually the solution's not a choice, it's a necessity, whatever the cost. It's no fun going against convention, but all things considered I haven't been disappointed so far."

"Me neither," agreed Penny, "though it does add an unusual dimension to things..."

The plane landed and, once the Peacekeeper had left, the other passengers stood up. Tessa offered to hand Penny her luggage. As she opened the door to the overhead compartment Penny's jacket fell out, together with the top and body of an expensive fountain pen. Letting go of the locker handle, Tessa instinctively caught the jacket with her right hand and the pen top with her left. Then she quickly scooped up the pen in its top and screwed the two together with one hand as she passed the unblemished jacket to Penny.

"Tessa!" gasped her friend. "I do wish you wouldn't do things like that."

"Sorry. Can't help it. I've always had quick reactions. I caught a full glass of wine last week, didn't spill a drop!"

"Well, those aren't quick reactions, they're phenomenal! I've never seen anyone move that fast."

Tessa smiled.

"All part of the unorthodox package. Anyway, are you sure you don't want to stay at my place tonight?"

"No, thanks, I've got to go on to Switzerland."

"OK. I'll call you this evening then."

CHAPTER 3

After a short taxi ride down the A3 autobahn, Tessa arrived at the Druckmaschinen headquarters. Her office, a large corner room on the third floor with ultra-modern furniture, emanated an atmosphere of controlled discipline, efficiency and professionalism. People tended not to go in there without good reason. Tessa liked that; it reflected the way she ran her life. Although not exactly impatient, she never could abide people who wasted her time.

A distinguished white-haired gentleman knocked quietly and stood in the doorway, hesitating to interrupt. Tessa looked up at her loyal, long-standing finance director.

"*Guten Morgen*, Herr Schneider," she said warmly, in German.

"Good morning, Frau Doktor," he replied, with due deference. "Do you have time to talk?"

"Of course. What can I do for you?"

"There are some details of the disposal I would like to discuss…"

"Ah. Yes, I saw their e-mail about the completion schedule…"

Tessa beckoned Schneider to take a seat at the circular meeting table and they were soon engrossed in conversation. Their meeting continued long enough to ensure that, despite the best endeavours of Stefanie, her highly efficient PA, the day became the hectic rush to which they had both become accustomed.

Only at 8 p.m. did Tessa finally stop working. She drove from her private garage beneath the offices to a local Chinese restaurant for dinner. Forty minutes later, she had eaten and returned to her flat opposite Hochdahler Markt. Here, she poured herself a glass of chilled German beer and picked up her *Cloud Based Communicator*. It was her newest gadget and the result of many years of technological progress following on from the now humble *pda*.

"Hi, babe … Oh, are you in a meeting?"

"No, I'm on my own, but in a restaurant."

"Right. How was your day?"

"Mediocre," replied Penny, with a note of frustration in her voice.

19

"For some reason several key accounts have taken their business elsewhere. It's strange because they'd all declared their loyalty before we went to the States, and when I phoned them, they wouldn't even say why they'd changed their minds."

"Weird. Can you replace them?"

"I think so, but it is odd, very odd... Anyway, how are you?"

"Oh, fine thanks," replied Tessa. "No problems of any consequence really. Just tons of work and not enough time to do it."

"I take it you've launched your profile on WebIntroz?"

"Yes, babe, as ordered. Although I'm still not convinced internet dating is for me."

"Understood, but we've got to get some experience somehow and WebIntroz is probably as good a crash course as any."

"Sounds like a recipe for disaster to me."

"We'll see. Anyway, how about taking all Saturday off? It would probably do us both good. We could start with breakfast at Antonio's?"

"Why not? It's been so long I suspect I'm suffering from Antonio withdrawal symptoms. I'll see you there at nine."

It turned out that Antonio, the effervescent gay Italian owner of the patisserie, was so pleased to see them that their breakfast lasted all morning and marked the start of a weekend in which neither of them did much work.

On Monday, Tessa and Penny were amongst the last passengers to board the flight to Düsseldorf. They enjoyed travelling together and revelling in the admiring looks they received from the male passengers on the plane. Few could resist watching the two attractive young women. Tessa was slightly taller than Penny, but both had blonde hair meticulously styled in pageboy bobs. Tessa's face was exquisitely crafted with high cheekbones and a pleasantly pointed chin. Penny's face was a bit rounder with a softer chin; both had smooth white skin, were well made-up and expensively dressed.

Tessa, renowned for always listening to music of one sort or another, made a selection on her *cbc* which, even with a Bluetooth earpiece, could be used on the plane.

"Another new gadget?" asked Penny.

"I've had it a couple of weeks, actually. It's a Cloud Based

Communicator … *cbc* for short. It's essentially a very clever user-interface – the software and data are all stored on a cloud system." She put the grey phone-like box on her fold-down table, opened it and pressed a key. Immediately, a holographic image of a computer screen appeared behind the device with a full keyboard in front.

"Wow!" exclaimed Penny.

"It'll do anything you want … well, just about … and if someone pinches it, it's useless. It's user-specific, like those new guns the UNWP issued to the Special Forces. The registered owner must be holding the *cbc* when entering the password. Do it wrong and it's rendered inoperable. Early on some were stolen, but the thieves just threw them away. They couldn't even sell them."

"That's fantastic."

"I hoped you'd say that." Tessa smiled. "Here's yours."

She took another *cbc* from her from her bag and handed it to Penny.

"Oh! Thank you, hon. That's so sweet," said Penny, leaning over to give Tessa a hug. "I love it."

She grinned and started reading her newspaper, much of which was devoted to yet another depth exposé of New Crime. *"Bent on expansion, the Calver Cats now openly target Peacekeepers…"* People had become all too familiar with this relatively new and previously insignificant gang, which had taken devastating advantage of the changes in international law. Many traditional crime organisations had been absorbed or eliminated by the Calver Cats who chose to meet fire with fire, fighting Peacekeepers on their own terms with swords and knives.

Her reading was again interrupted by the arrival of a lone International Peacekeeper, this time a young Asian woman with two swords slung over her shoulders.

"Thank goodness for small mercies," muttered Tessa sarcastically. "Now at least we know we're travelling in a bubble of peace and tranquillity, while all hell breaks loose outside."

Penny chuckled. She watched the Peacekeeper with admiration and envy.

"I think she looks really cool. She must be incredibly fit; there aren't many women with an OCL. I wonder which countries backed her. Mind you, it does look as though she'll have her work cut out. I bet

Peacekeeper life expectancy isn't high at the moment, and the poor sods only get paid a pittance." She paused, ignoring Tessa's expression of abject boredom. "You know, carrying swords over the shoulder is extremely rare. She can only do that because they're Ninja short swords ... otherwise it would be physically impossible to draw them."

Tessa took a deep breath and switched off her music.

"I suppose I'm going to regret this, but ... what's an OCL?"

Penny looked at her with a mixture of astonishment and anticipation. "You don't know?"

Tessa shook her head and waited for the snowball to gather momentum.

"Oh, hon, now you've asked for it! Well, if you want to be an International Peacekeeper the first thing to do is to enrol at a licensed Peacekeeper training school and, amongst other things, learn how to fight properly with a samurai sword. By all accounts it's very difficult – technically, physically and emotionally. If you're good enough, the next step is to take the Samurai Proficiency Test. It's incredibly tough – lots of questions, some technical and others to assess one's character; then some really vicious combat situations against official experts. I've heard they're so demanding, some people are injured during them."

"Anyway, passing means you're graded either with an RCL or an OCL. RCL stands for Restricted Carrying Licence and OCL for Open Carrying Licence. OCL passes are graded A1 which is the highest, but nobody ever gets one of those, then A2 and B; then there's the RCL pass. If you get an RCL or any OCL pass, you're allowed to carry a sword in public provided it is locked in an approved case. But all sword licence holders may draw their swords to defend themselves, or the Police, or if asked by the Special Forces."

Tessa raised her hand in an attempt to interrupt, regretting she'd opened the floodgates to this torrent of over-technical information.

"I haven't finished yet! Only someone with an OCL pass is able to become an International Peacekeeper and for that they have to be proposed by two countries. It's not difficult getting a proposal from your home country but people often struggle to find a second. However, the dual country requirement is deemed key to ensuring Peacekeepers remain independent and are not influenced by, say, religion or politics. So, only full International Peacekeepers, like that woman over there, can wear their swords in public. They are obliged to assist the Special Forces in crime busting whenever and wherever reasonably called upon to do so. But they can only do so as part of a documented 'Mission', which has to be supported by two countries … not necessarily both the ones that proposed them, though.

"The consequences of misusing an OCL are draconian, but otherwise Peacekeepers are permitted to do pretty much whatever they feel is necessary in order to keep the peace and apprehend criminals. Not surprisingly, they tend to be revered and feared in equal measure. However, it has now been proven statistically that although sword inflicted wounds are gruesome, the scale of the carnage is always vastly less than would have been the case had guns or explosives been used. A gun or a bomb would kill or maim lots of innocent people; but a sword wielded by an expert, doesn't. The reduction in crime-related deaths has been phenomenal…"

Thankfully, Penny paused for breath here.

"Babe! Please, tell me you're done?" pleaded Tessa in desperation.

"You did ask."

"True. But I think I detected one or two slight embellishments to the concise answer I craved."

"Well, what did you expect? You know this is one of my favourite topics," replied Penny with a satisfied smile.

Her confidence in this new approach to law enforcement never ceased to amaze Tessa. She was willing to accept that the concept was theoretically appealing, but as a naturally pragmatic person, she doubted it would work in the real world. She had come to the conclusion that this enthusiasm of Penny's owed much to the catastrophe which had blighted her early life. When she was eight and spending the night at a school-friend's house, her parents and sister had been murdered in a burglary that seemed to have escalated out of control.

"These Peacekeepers with their swords might be an interesting approach," said Tessa, quickly continuing when she saw Penny's eyebrows rise. "I only said might. But they're already struggling to hold back New Crime. This says global drugs sales have risen fourfold because no one has the wherewithal to go after the dealers; and the black market for guns has grown tenfold."

"Yes, I read that article too. There still aren't enough Peacekeepers. Even so, it must be better than having all that old religious-inspired terrorism, gun crime, and testosterone-driven politicians invading other countries. It will take time, but I'm sure it'll work. Eventually..."

Forty minutes later they were parting company in the bustling modern airport.

"Well, I suppose I'll have to let you go," said Penny. She always hated goodbyes. Denied security in her early life, she now set great store by her friendships, particularly the one with Tessa. The two of them had shared so many experiences, and had so much – apart from a love of Peacekeepers – in common.

"So, when's your flight to Stuttgart?" Tessa asked.

"Forty minutes."

"Would you like me to wait with you?"

"No, of course not. You get on with it. Besides, I might get chatted up by some hunk in the departure lounge."

"Good luck with that!" laughed Tessa.

As the weeks passed, Tessa found herself working all hours on the sale of Druckmaschinen and was frequently in the US with Chicago Engineering. Meanwhile, Penny was grappling with Schrauben & Mutter's inexplicable sales decline. But, apart from mentioning that the situation was worsening, she made it clear to Tessa that she did not want to discuss it. Although they found it increasingly difficult to meet, they tried to make up for lost time whenever they could.

During one evening together, snatched in Milan, Tessa was surprised to discover that Penny had become uncharacteristically fanatical about her fitness, to the detriment of any other leisure pursuits. Tessa wasn't sure she was in a position to criticise since she'd become extremely focused herself. Apart from continuing her fitness regime, she hadn't had time for anything else either. But to add to the mystery, Penny wouldn't say much about what she was doing, only that she was attending a club somewhere in South Kensington.

"If you're so curious, why don't you come with me," suggested Penny.

"I've no time; it's difficult enough squeezing some Karate in."

"And whatever it is you do with that wooden pole," added Penny, laughing.

"Kenjutsu," replied Tessa.

"Quite. So, how many years have you been into closet violence?"

"Ha-ha! It's only for self-defence, and to keep mind and body in trim … off and on since I was fourteen, actually."

"… and you call yourself a pacifist. What on earth inspired you to start?"

Tessa frowned. "My brother, remember? I told you in America, the night before we…"

"Oh, God, I'm sorry." Penny bowed her head in contrition. "Of course … I'll never forget that time we spent together. We bared our hearts and some, didn't we?"

Not only had they talked about Penny's own tragic past, but also the baleful shadow that had haunted Tessa's childhood and youth. She had been forced to endure violent assaults from her handsome, charming and secretly sadistic elder brother, Beauchamp, whose favourite method of torture was to half-drown her. But when she was twelve his physical bullying became more perverted and sinister. Penny had been shocked to the core when Tessa confessed she had only taken up martial arts to defend herself from ever again being raped by her own brother. Her parents knew nothing about it, and she had spared them the shock and disillusion of needing to find out by learning to fight off her brother's unwelcome attentions on her own. The self-confidence that being able to defend oneself brought had, in later years, empowered her to take some very tough personal decisions. In doing so she had met Penny, who was facing a similar dilemma. It wasn't long before they became best friends and inseparable soulmates.

"And still you've never even held a sword?" queried Penny in disbelief.

Tessa rolled her eyes.

"Nope. Give me a long stick and I'll beat the hell out of anyone, but with a sword *I'd* be petrified… Anyway, how are you getting on with WebIntroz?"

Penny smiled. "Not brilliantly. I was chatted up by one chauvinist twit who introduced himself by asking whose PA I was."

"No? I blame the testosterone," retorted Tessa dryly.

"Indeed. He became somewhat more flaccid when I told him I

owned my own company. And you?"

"Oh, my most intimate experience was nothing to do with WebIntroz. I had my bum pinched on an overnight flight back from Chicago. The guy said I filled my pyjamas beautifully. I told him he should have seen how I *used* to fill them, and suggested he get some sleep. Heaven only knows what conclusion he jumped to!"

They both burst out laughing.

"Frustrating as it is, we'll just have to be patient. I'm ready though, aren't you?"

"After all this waiting?" pined Tessa. "Absolutely! But it's going to have to be someone pretty special."

CHAPTER 4

The following week, Tessa had a meeting in London with John Denton, a partner with McAllister's, Druckmaschinen's corporate lawyers. John was young for his position; quiet and efficient, with cropped black hair and dark-framed spectacles, and an unflappable, knowledgeable approach to his work. Like him, his office was modern, relaxed and purposeful; he and Tessa got on well. At the end of their meeting, John mentioned that he'd heard Blaise Collins-Clarke had imposed harsh credit restrictions on Schrauben & Mutter.

"What can you tell me about BNYI and Collins-Clarke?" asked Tessa.

"Well, Beijing New York International is an enormous bank, with its European headquarters here in London. Collins-Clarke rose to Executive Director a while ago and is responsible for Corporate Finance. Rumour has it he's out of his depth. Although the recent upheavals in international law have benefited world peace, they've had a mixed economic impact. The opening of markets to free trade has not suited everyone, especially Collins-Clarke. Too many of his companies are the ones being compromised by, rather than benefiting from, this new climate. This has been aggravated by his unorthodox strategy of buying up small German and Swiss finance houses. Apparently it's these banks' holdings which are now causing him most grief.

"Of course, BNYI can always take control of troublesome companies if the situation merits. But that usually achieves very little, as they're unlikely to run businesses any better than the incumbent management team. Furthermore, if BNYI forces the companies to close, an asset sale never recovers much, while the bank simply earns a reputation for lending during the good times and pulling the plug when the going gets rough. His job is probably on the line..."

Tessa was shocked that Penny hadn't mentioned any of this to her and resolved to tackle her friend about it as soon as she could. They met the following Saturday in Penny's flat. Tessa brought a bottle of fine port with her in an attempt to ease her way into a discussion.

At first Penny refused to talk about it. But Tessa was insistent and eventually managed to extract from her the admission that the difficulties stemmed from the substantial, and still unexplained, drop in sales. Tessa immediately offered to help but Penny wouldn't hear if it, insisting the Druckmaschinen sale was more important. Only when she became uncharacteristically irritable did Tessa finally let the matter drop.

Soon afterwards Tessa assumed sole responsibility for the Druckmaschinen sale, with John Denton handling the legal side. This represented the beginning of the final phase of her transaction and a period of hard negotiation to settle outstanding details. For two weeks she was so deeply engrossed in work she didn't even speak to Penny.

One Monday evening, Tessa returned to her house in South Kensington after working through the weekend. She ate her takeaway sushi for dinner and settled down to work once again. She had a lot to do that night and was booked on the early flight to Düsseldorf the following morning. Nevertheless she was delighted when her *cbc* rang with a familiar tone.

"Hi, babe!" she said, eagerly. "It's good to hear your voice."

"Likewise," replied Penny. "How's it going?"

"Brilliantly. I'm whacked and there's still tons to be done, but everything's on course. How about you? You sound stressed."

"Oh, no, everything's fine."

"Good," replied Tessa. "Well, even with my pessimistic hat on, I'd say the chances of our signing on Friday are very high indeed. I've just got this mountain of trivia to sort first."

"I'm pleased for you," replied a weary-sounding Penny. "Look, I don't want to bother you now, but when you have a minute, there's something very strange going on with Schrauben & Mutter. It's been driving me crazy but I just don't seem to be able to get to the bottom of it. Anyway Collins-Clarke has asked to meet me on Thursday. I think it's likely to get rough, so I'm going to try and postpone it for a week. Then perhaps we could both go, assuming you still want to join my board?"

"Of course I do," replied Tessa. "But from now until Friday will be horrendous. If you let me sober up on Saturday, I'm all yours thereafter. Would that be OK?"

"Yes, I should think so. It's all a bit weird. I didn't realise how weird until I started to delve into the minutia myself... Anyway, I've hired some consultants to look into it for me. Would you mind if I e-mailed you a copy of my analysis, and some other stuff that's relevant? If you don't get to it sooner, we can go through it together over the weekend."

"Sure," exclaimed Tessa.

"Great! Then I'll stall Collins-Clarke until we've had a chance to meet. Here it comes. Give me a call as soon as you surface, and good luck for Friday."

"Thanks," said Tessa, concerned by Penny's melancholy mood. "Oh, the file's just arrived … Shall I have a quick look at it now?"

"No, that would be unfair of me, but thanks for asking. It's far more important that you concentrate on your own deal. You've too much at stake. Get that sorted first, then we can plan the future. I should have done this earlier, but now I'll wait my turn. How about dinner on Saturday night?"

"What an excellent idea," agreed Tessa quickly. "Let me take you to the Falcon and we can celebrate in style."

"Lovely, thanks. Oh, and by the way, hon, I know I've just missed your birthday but you were so engrossed I didn't want your present to distract you. It took me ages to get it, but finally it's here. It's rather special, so you need to be in an appropriately receptive mood."

"Oh, babe, you shouldn't have. I'm really curious now. I promise I'll be receptive."

"Good. See you Saturday."

The call ended and Tessa settled down with her papers. The next two days were frenetic, but by Wednesday evening she realised she had actually finished everything she needed to do. All that remained was for the lawyers to complete the final drafting. She returned to her flat in Hochdahl and poured herself a large gin and tonic.

"Cheers!" she murmured to herself. "I do believe you've cracked it."

She phoned the Chinese restaurant in Hochdahler Markt to order a meal. Then, with some background music playing, settled down on the sofa and sipped her drink. Remembering Penny's file, she put her laptop on her knee and started paging through the data.

At first she wasn't really concentrating; but as she focused more closely on the screen her mind started to register the contents of the complex spreadsheets. Her contented smile evaporated. She scowled and quickly scanned Penny's conclusions, nodding her head in agreement.

She telephoned her friend. But there was no reply and Tessa didn't feel it right to leave a message about such a sensitive subject. She decided to go and eat, and then study the file in detail. Later that night she again tried to reach Penny, but without success.

On Thursday morning she arrived at her office exceptionally early. Stefanie soon realised the intensity of the past few days was not easing off. There was another project in hand now: Tessa was going into overdrive concerning Schrauben & Mutter.

Although she still couldn't reach Penny, she did learn from her office that the meeting with Collins-Clarke had not been postponed as requested and was scheduled for early that afternoon. Time was of the essence and Tessa had already used up the advantage given her by Düsseldorf being one hour ahead of London. She had no other choice but to put a plan of her own into action.

She telephoned John Denton and described the Schrauben & Mutter situation. He listened unenthusiastically to what she wanted to do. Eventually, convinced she had considered all the risks, he undertook to do as she asked. Two minutes later she strode out of her office.

"Stefanie, I'm going to London. Get me a seat on the next flight, please; I'll use my open ticket. If anything really urgent crops up you can reach me on my mobile. And if Chicago Engineering asks what I'm doing, just say I've had to attend to some urgent private business but I'll be back tomorrow for the signing. No time for a taxi, I'll take my car. Phone me with the flight details."

"You're leaving now!" exclaimed Stefanie. But Tessa was already halfway down the corridor.

On the plane, she finalised her strategy. It was going to be tricky, and not without risk, but she had to try. John Denton met her at Heathrow with a chauffeur-driven limousine. As they travelled into London, he explained the papers which had been prepared and indicated where Tessa should sign.

"You are sure you want to do this, aren't you?" he asked seriously. "It's money you don't have as yet, and bridging alone will cost a small fortune."

"Yes, I understand, but Penny and I have been through far too much together for me to let her fail now. She'd do the same for me. Is there anything else I need to sign?"

John passed her some more papers with little yellow labels sticking out.

"I presume everything's OK for tomorrow?" she asked, returning the last of them with her signature.

He smiled.

"I'm pleased to hear you haven't completely forgotten about the little matter of your own company's sale. Yes, everything's fine. Well, there's nothing you need worry about at any rate. Chicago Engineering are annoyed you're not in your office, but I pointed out there was no need for you to be there now. Orla will prepare the papers in Düsseldorf, but you must be there for ten a.m. Has your life always been this ... busy?"

"Pretty much," she replied grinning. "Fun, isn't it?"

John didn't reply but simply raised his eyebrows, smiled and checked the papers before sliding them back into his briefcase.

"OK," he said, "we're nearly there. Be it on your head. I've done as you asked and not told anyone we're about to gate-crash."

"Thanks, John, you've been great. You always are."

"You're welcome. I just hope this all works out."

Their limousine pulled off the Embankment towards a large modern building near the Gherkin. A moment later they went round a courtyard and down a ramp into the large underground car park. It was 1:45 p.m. The meeting would already have started.

By being brutally persuasive they managed to get themselves shown to the appropriate office suite. Somewhat unenthusiastically, the secretary outside opened the door for them, and Tessa, followed by John, stepped into the large bright meeting room. The décor was extravagant, featuring a sumptuous red carpet, beautiful furniture and tasteful pictures. The end wall was made entirely of glass, giving a wonderful panorama of the City and a close-up view of the Gherkin. In the centre of the room stood a large rosewood table with Penny sitting on one side, looking harassed, and two men on the other. As the newcomers entered, everyone looked up in surprise.

"Tessa!" exclaimed Penny. "What on earth are you doing here?"

"Hi, Penny, sorry, but I have been trying to reach you."

Tessa turned to the two men sitting opposite her friend. Both were smartly dressed, but one was much younger than the other, and clearly junior. They stood up and Tessa approached the older man. He had taken off his black pin-stripe jacket to reveal a pink shirt and bright red braces stretched over his portly stomach. He had thinning white hair and a florid face. He looked tired.

"Good afternoon. Mr Collins-Clarke, I presume?" began Tessa, smiling sweetly and holding out her hand to him.

"Yes, indeed, nice to meet you. Who exactly…?"

"My name is Pennington," she replied, handing him her business card. "This is John Denton. He's a partner at McAllister's and handles all my legal affairs. I do apologise for joining you unannounced, but I hope you don't mind if we listen in for a while. I have a special interest in Schrauben & Mutter and might be able to help you and BNYI."

Collins-Clarke read her business card and gently inhaled, nostrils flaring in disdain.

"Hmm, well I'm not too sure what you think you can contribute, but if you would like to stay, I have no objections."

"That's most kind, thank you," she replied, looking questioningly at the other man.

"Oh, this is Narinder, one of my managers," continued Collins-Clarke dismissively. "Ignore him. He's just here to fetch and carry."

Tessa smiled and shook hands warmly with the younger man, amazed by the off-hand way in which he had been introduced. He appeared to be used to it. She moved round the table to sit on Penny's left. John Denton sat next to her. Blaise Collins-Clarke ordered some fresh tea and the meeting paused briefly in anticipation of its arrival.

"Tessa, what are you up to?" hissed Penny.

"Doing to him what he's trying to do to you," she whispered slyly, shocked to see her friend so upset and clearly on the verge of tears.

"… Right, I'll get on with it if that's all right?" said Collins-Clarke as they began to drink their tea. Tessa and Penny looked at him across the table. "As I was saying," he drawled, smiling at Tessa as if to say *before I was so rudely interrupted,* "I accept this dramatic fall in performance is unusual. Nevertheless, it is a remarkably steep decline which I regret BNYI can no longer support…"

His diatribe continued for nearly twenty minutes as he forecast a continuing irreversible deterioration in the fortunes of the business. He paused for dramatic effect, and took a sip of his tea. Tessa sensed Penny quaking inwardly.

"…Unfortunately, therefore, I have no alternative but to call in the loan. I have instructed Administrators to take control tomorrow morning and commence an immediate break-up."

"What!" Penny exclaimed, trembling with rage. "Blaise, you're being unnecessarily precipitate and you know it. Schrauben & Mutter has performed perfectly well for years. Something very strange is going on here and it's far from the normal commercial cut and thrust. I've retained some people to look into it. At least give them a chance to tell us their findings. Schrauben & Mutter has never asked you for anything of consequence before, and quite frankly I find it a little rich that the moment something goes slightly wrong, you threaten to foreclose."

"I hear what you say and, of course, I'm very sorry. But this is not a threat, it's my final decision. We can't afford to pour good money after bad. We intend to recover our loan as best we can with a sale of assets. End of discussion," said Collins-Clarke, eyeing Tessa with a mixture of curiosity and dislike. "Unless anyone else would care to say something?"

"If you wouldn't mind," she offered, interrupting Penny.

Collins-Clarke nodded and Tessa patted her friend's knee under the table.

"I am inclined to agree that BNYI is acting with remarkable alacrity, given Schrauben & Mutter's historically good performance and the unnatural characteristics of this decline. Also, I am surprised that you have already instructed Administrators. Surely it is hardly appropriate to initiate a break-up before it has even been discussed with the company's board and shareholders? But I suppose times are hard, and we all know banks have a reputation for never being there when they're needed, don't we? I presume you have cleared all this with your own board?"

Collins-Clarke was seething, but found himself having to nod agreement to the last comment, rather than respond to the subtle insults Tessa had smoothly let slip beforehand; nevertheless, he

33

started gathering his papers together contemptuously.

"I'm so sorry if I'm delaying you," she purred. "But I daresay you've had to convince your board to accept, what, three pence in the pound? After all, an Administrative recovery is unlikely to secure more than that."

Collins-Clarke's expression exuded boredom and irritation, but his body language suggested he was anticipating an interesting development.

"I don't intend to divulge our forecasts but you're not miles away. No one seems to want to purchase outright, and although many of the production assets are quite new, they are very specialised and unlikely to fetch a good price on the open market. But in case you were wondering, we have factored in the cost of a Social Plan to release the workforce."

Penny looked as though she'd just been struck. Like Tessa, she was highly committed to the welfare of her employees and hearing their future being discussed so cavalierly was torture to her.

"Of course you have," continued Tessa. "But I doubt your board is particularly happy to exit like this. No one ever comes out of such a situation smelling of roses, do they, Mr Collins-Clarke? And, at the end of the day, BNYI won't see much of its investment back?"

"Call me Blaise," he said, expansively. "My surname's too much of a mouthful. But you're right, it's not the best of outcomes; it is with utmost regret that I find myself without any viable alternative."

"So, if I knew a way to get you five pence in the pound, then that would be of considerable interest to you and your board, wouldn't it?"

"Well, it would be of some interest. But, as I'm sure you understand, once a decision to foreclose has been made, wheels are set in motion and I would be foolish to delay implementation, even by a day. So if you're considering some form of financial involvement yourself, not only would I expect to see far more than five pence in the pound, but I would need the transaction to complete today, which quite frankly is bordering on the impossible."

Collins-Clarke was clearly expecting to hear some yarn about White Knights rescuing Schrauben & Mutter at an indeterminate date in the future.

Tessa paused, making a point of looking at his business card, and

34

gently flaring her nostrils in disdain.

"Well, Blaise, here's the deal. I'll give you five pence in the pound, and buy out BNYI in full. If you're willing to accept, say so now, and the rest is up to me, isn't it?"

Collins-Clarke thought for a moment and looked at the clock. It was 3 p.m.

"Ten pence in the pound and it's yours," he said, with a disbelieving sneer.

"Blaise, don't be too greedy. We both know I'll be able to buy the business for four pence in the pound on Monday. I'll repeat my offer one more time. Five pence in the pound and I will buy out all BNYI's interests in Schrauben & Mutter GmbH."

Tessa stood up and leaned across the table towards Collins-Clarke with her hand outstretched.

"Five pence in the pound … and I get the money before four-thirty today?"

Penny sat back in her chair, feeling disgusted but confident that Tessa would be able to save Schrauben & Mutter, if Druckmaschinen had been sold.

"Agreed," replied Tessa. "But bear in mind, Blaise, once we've shaken hands in front of all these witnesses, the deal is done."

"All right. I accept, if you complete on time." He still didn't believe the deal would go through. "But if the money isn't here by then, the deal's off."

He and Tessa shook hands and she sat down again. Penny tried to attract her attention, but she'd already turned to John.

"Well, there we are, it's over to you."

He raised his eyebrows, opened his briefcase and took out several thick bundles of papers.

"OK. So, the deal was done at five pence in the pound?" asked John, looking questioningly at Collins-Clarke, who nodded. John smiled, and started sorting through the different bundles, theatrically.

"Right, so … we don't need this one … nor this one … nor this one. Ah, yes, here we are. The five pence in the pound papers," he muttered, looking up and smiling. "Right at the bottom of the pile, isn't that always the way?"

Collins-Clarke's lower jaw was in danger of hitting the table. He realised that not only had Tessa always been ready to do a deal, but also that she had been prepared to pay far more than she had got away with. He desperately craned his neck in an attempt to see how much more, although part of him thought it would be better not to know. He scowled at Narinder, who was having difficulty in not laughing.

"Please sign here, Mr Collins-Clarke," continued John. "It will formalise the agreement, although I will need to sort out the transfer of ownership with your legal department later. The deal will effectively be complete once I have given you this negotiable bond. If you are worried about its validity you may have Narinder present it now. But I can assure you, it is legitimate."

He handed the papers to Collins-Clarke who scanned them and passed each sheet he'd finished to Narinder for checking. Once they were both satisfied, the banker took out his pen.

"This seems to be in order," he said. "But it is unusual for us to accept a negotiable bond for so much at such short notice … however, in the circumstances, I am willing to bend the rules."

Once each party had a full set of signed documents, John handed the bond to Collins-Clarke. He gave it to Narinder, and told him to draw against it immediately.

"So," said Collins-Clarke, "would anyone care for more tea, or perhaps something a bit stronger while we wait?"

"Thank you, but not for me," replied Tessa, turning to Penny. "Could I have a word?"

They both stood up and went over to the window. They gazed out over the panoply of steel and glass so they could talk without being overheard.

"Have you gone mad?" whispered Penny. "That cost a fortune. Have you got the money?"

"Well, not exactly," replied Tessa, grinning, "but I will have tomorrow."

"You hope! What if the Druckmaschinen sale doesn't complete?"

"Ah, then we'll both be up to our necks in something very unpleasant, but that's not going to happen. Anyway, I'm sorry about the drama, but I really did try to reach you. I read the file last night and … why didn't you tell me? Someone's properly got it in for Schrauben & Mutter. Your sales didn't just wither away, customers dropped out almost in order of significance. It's not natural. Somebody must be orchestrating this."

"That's what I think," replied Penny as a tear ran down her cheek. "If I didn't know better, I'd say one of our key competitors is leaning on our customers, but I can't find out anything conclusive. I wanted to tell you, but you were so busy with your sale I didn't want to disturb you."

"Hey, don't worry, it's not your fault. It's both our faults for not communicating better. And whatever you do, don't cry, it'll ruin your mascara. In a few minutes, you'll be rid of Collins-Clarke and then you can be as beastly as you like to him. Just think. Once we've recovered Schrauben & Mutter, and we will, it'll be worth a fortune after Collins-Clarke has written off all the debt! He'll be hopping mad, and if you really want to wind him up you can tell him I was ready and willing to pay fifteen pence in the pound!"

They both laughed aloud.

"That's better," continued Tessa. "Don't worry, John's really good. He'll take care of everything, but you might want to hang around just to check the transfer of ownership goes smoothly. I've got to get back to Düsseldorf. Apparently they're peeved about me not being there, and we definitely don't want to delay tomorrow's signing! So, let's stick to our arrangement and meet for dinner on Saturday."

"Oh, Tessa, what would I do without you?" sighed Penny.

"Amongst other things you'd have gone to America on your own, and so would I. So, babe, what would I do without you?" replied Tessa as they hugged.

"Well, you've just demonstrated that ruthless streak of yours, which makes me doubly sure your birthday present is right for you," said Penny excitedly. "One good tiger deserves another."

"What on earth…?"

"I'll explain on Saturday," she interrupted. "Now, I know this sounds daft, but have you got a pound coin I could have?"

"Er … I think so, hold on." Tessa rummaged in her purse. "Yes, here's one."

"Brilliant, that's saved me a lot of trouble, thanks. I'll call your flat tonight."

"Make a point of it, will you? Although I'm not sure what time I'll be back."

Penny smiled and gave her another hug. Then Narinder returned.

"Everything's fine," he said, "the money transfer is going through now."

Tessa turned to John.

"Is everything fine?"

"Yes, it is. I'll go back to my office and liaise with their legal department from there. We should be able to finish everything this afternoon. But you don't need to wait, I can do everything else under your Power of Attorney. Also, I suspect Orla would be much happier if you were back in Germany."

"I'll stay until everything's done, just in case," interjected Penny, swapping business cards with John.

Tessa nodded and smiled.

"Well, Blaise, it's been a pleasure doing business with you. But I'm afraid I really must go."

"Then let me show you out," he replied, gesturing towards the door. After showing them to the lift, he returned to his secretary.

"Get me our external lawyers, will you? And the administrators."

Tessa and John were soon back in the limousine, driving along the embankment.

"Hopefully, congratulations are in order," said John. "But you know he's livid, don't you?"

"I sincerely hope so! He was being a real bully and now he understands he was the one who got stitched up. He's virtually given Schrauben & Mutter to me and Penny. I'd like to be a fly on the wall when he explains it to his board! However, I have to admit the *coup de grâce* was definitely you taking out all those bundles and going to the bottom one for the five pence deal. Lovely! He must have wanted to die..."

CHAPTER 5

Tessa didn't return to her flat until 3 a.m. the following morning. She was exhausted and although surprised not to find a message from Penny, collapsed into bed still revelling in her victory over Collins-Clarke.

Meanwhile, London's Blackwall dockyard was dark, dank and deserted. It was crammed with identical-looking shipping containers, like cells in a hive. One of them had been taken over by the Special Forces. Inside, the subdued red lighting and humming electronics heightened the air of tension in the cramped control room. At one end, three men stooped over surveillance displays. The tallest, a man in late middle age with a short beard and his hair tied back in a ponytail, straightened up.

"I don't like it," he muttered, shaking his head. "Why are they so late? What's changed?" He tapped his headset. "Flood, anything happening out there?"

"Not much, sir. I've had Hachiro move round to the north while Takara is to my right. It's her first Mission so I'll be watching her back. I'll let you know if the situation changes. Switching to team comms. Flood out."

"And we shouldn't have brought Takara," continued the first man to his colleagues.

"Well, we only found out yesterday that Hachiro would be in the UK, and Takara was keen to contribute. Her Peacekeeper training school did give her a glowing report," replied his balding colleague. "Technically she's very good."

"Maybe, but this isn't school. Flood and Hachiro are old hands. Takara's a novice: young, bright, pretty. I just wish she wasn't..."

"Here they come," interrupted Flood. "It is the Calver Cats."

Seven strongly built thugs armed with samurai swords entered the area between the containers and the dockside. They all looked ready for action in black three-hole balaclavas, black fleece jackets and blue jeans. Their female leader, nicknamed The Barb, was dressed in a black

39

leather jacket with a distinctive stylised 'EB' on it. She issued some orders and the others took up position. They drew their weapons and started practising combat situations.

"OK, Peacekeepers, headsets on continuous. It's time to tango," ordered Flood. "Hachiro, follow my lead. Takara, with me."

He broke cover and approached the gang. Takara stayed within a few yards. Hachiro advanced from the left. They drew their swords as floodlights illuminated the area. A megaphone boomed out.

"Peacekeepers! Drop your weapons. Stay where you are."

The Barb raised her arm and whirled it round three times. Then she pointed, first to her right and left, and then with both hands together to the centre. The gang split into two, and turned to face the Peacekeepers. More Calver Cats appeared from behind a container and they all ran forward in a co-ordinated attack.

"Ambush!" yelled Flood. "Takara, fall back."

But she stood her ground. She knew this was disobeying orders, but felt it wrong to desert her colleagues in such dire circumstances. Soon all three of them were embroiled in a vicious struggle. Flood felled two, and it appeared to be going well for the Peacekeepers. However, with him and Hachiro surrounded, Takara found herself being manoeuvred to one side. Then The Barb approached, and her colleagues blocked Flood and Hachiro from helping the novice Takara. She wiped the perspiration from her forehead, took a deep breath and raised her sword.

The duel started with a lightning-fast exchange of sword strokes. Then another. Takara moved back, struggling to defend herself against the onslaught of brutal attacks. She knew her opponent was the better fighter. But she didn't need to win; she could play for time. While she had a weapon in her hands, she would have the strength and skill to protect herself.

Suddenly The Barb aimed a strong sweeping blow at Takara's sword.

As the blades met, a loud *clang* echoed around the dockyard; followed by an abrupt *chink*. Takara looked in dismay at the stub of her shattered weapon. She gritted her teeth and braced herself for the inevitable.

"Presumptuous bitch," hissed The Barb.

She thrust forward, paused, and calmly pulled out her sword.

Takara's hopes of survival exploded in an instant as the blade passed through her heart. She sank to her knees as her sword hilt clattered to the ground. She could feel the warmth of her life blood draining away. She took one last look round, keeled over and died.

The Calver Cats started a quick, disciplined withdrawal by boat, with Special Forces vessels in hot pursuit.

Two hours later, a grey van sped through the City. It was following a carefully selected route between the thrusting tower blocks which housed the headquarters of many international banks and businesses. It avoided virtually all the surveillance cameras; those it did pass mysteriously malfunctioned. The van's tyres squealed as it accelerated past a particularly imposing office block and turned left towards the Gherkin.

Nobody heard the vehicle screech to a halt. Nobody heard the sound of the back doors being flung open, or the dull unnatural *thud* as something heavy was tossed on to the road. Seconds later the van sped away and a cold eerie silence engulfed the scene.

It was a while later when the sandwich delivery van approached. Its driver was distracted as he struggled to open the flask of coffee his wife had given him. So he didn't see the obstruction in the road. But he soon realised he'd hit something. He slammed on the brakes, swearing as his scalding coffee spilled. He'd run over a dog once and dreaded what he'd find this time. He got out of his van to discover it was much darker than usual as most of the street lights weren't working, but he always carried a torch with him. His heart was thumping. He hated the sight of blood and loved animals. Why hadn't he been looking where he was driving?

He walked hesitantly towards the back of the van and immediately froze when he saw the body with a trickle of blood snaking away from its head. How could he have been so stupid as to hit someone? The person's feet were resting on the pavement. His stomach churned. Trembling, he reached for his mobile phone and dialled the emergency services. As he put the phone to his ear, he summoned up all his courage and shone the beam from the torch on the body. As someone answered, he let out a cry. The body was that of a young woman, horribly mutilated.

41

The voice from the emergency call centre became more insistent. But he couldn't take his eyes off the woman's form. There were wounds all over it and her remaining clothes were covered in blood. Her arms were pulled awkwardly behind her, as though tied, and he noticed that her ankles were strapped together with a long black plastic tie wrap. The impact of his van's wheel had obliterated part of her face, but the driver could still see she had been very attractive. He vomited noisily into the gutter.

The driver's phone location was tracked and two minutes later several sets of blue flashing lights surrounded the scene. Not long after that, the area was cordoned off. As the sky brightened, people started arriving for work. They were forced to give the area a wide berth. A rumour soon spread that the battered body of a woman had been found. Onlookers stood by to see if they could catch a glimpse of the gruesome remains.

Eventually, the van driver noticed a dark blue-grey limousine arrive. Two men with an official air about them got out. One was wearing a strangely cut dark suit and had his hair in a ponytail; the policemen saluted him and raised the barriers. The other man was dressed in jeans and a thick grey pullover. He looked strong and alert, with a crop of thick black hair. He knelt down and lifted the blanket covering the body. With a sigh, he looked at his colleague and nodded. He replaced the blanket with what appeared to be an expression of remorse. A moment later they walked back to their car, issuing orders before leaving.

Crowds of people were filing past the cordoned-off area to reach their offices. They were pointing and whispering. But apart from the congealed blood on the road, all that could be seen of the corpse was some blood-stained blonde hair. Many of the people passing by were executives in smart pin-stripe suits. Most had newspapers tucked under their arms. But one didn't – the only one who was smiling.

CHAPTER 6

Tessa had slept so badly she again went into work early.

"*Guten Morgen*," greeted Stefanie, gesturing towards the coffee pot. "Is everything all right? You look dreadful!"

"Ugh! I just had a bad night, that's all," groaned Tessa. "Don't know why. I was incredibly tired. Anyway, coffee should help, thanks. Is everything arranged for the Works party this afternoon, and my flight back to London tomorrow morning?"

"Yes, and I've made a reservation for two at the Falcon for seven-thirty, tomorrow" replied Stefanie.

"Great, thanks."

Tessa poured some coffee and headed for her office.

"By the way," added Stefanie, "John Denton phoned late yesterday. He said the other deal had completed without problem and asked if you could call him as soon as possible this morning."

"Hmm, well, he won't be in yet. I'll telephone him from the car on my way to Düsseldorf."

Eventually, Tessa left for the lawyer's office where completion of the Druckmaschinen sale was to take place. She instructed her car-phone to dial London.

"Good morning, John. I understand you were trying to reach me?"

"Yes, morning, Tessa. The S&M deal went through fine, so that's all done. But there's something else... As soon as I got back to my office yesterday, Penny called from BNYI. She asked me to prepare an additional document for her. In fact, she insisted that I prepare it straightaway. She said it had to be completed before she left the bank and also told me not to mention it to you until it had been signed and witnessed. As you can imagine I wasn't enthusiastic, to say the least, but it was going to be to your benefit, and … well, she was adamant. She said if I didn't do it, she would get the first lawyer she could find and have them do it. So, to cut a long story short, I did what she asked."

"Which was?"

"She sold you sixty-seven per cent of the Schrauben & Mutter shares for the grand sum of one pound, which apparently you gave her yesterday. With the nine per cent you acquired from BNYI, you now own seventy-six per cent. She retains nineteen per cent and the remaining five are held by senior employees. According to the Articles of Association, you have a controlling interest, come what may."

There was a pause after John had finished speaking.

"Tessa, are you still there?"

"Yes, John, I'm here. Did she say why she wanted to do this?"

"She simply said you'd already agreed to join the board, and after what you did yesterday, it was the least she could do. I'm sorry if you're annoyed, but in the circumstances I didn't feel I had any choice."

Tessa sighed.

"Don't worry, you did the right thing. I know what she's like once she's made her mind up. Silly girl, that wasn't necessary, nothing was necessary at all; but I'll tell her myself later. Look, I've arrived and need to get on with the signing. But before we finish, have you spoken to Penny since? I've been trying to reach her and can't get through."

"No, I haven't," replied John. "I think she left BNYI as soon as we completed her paperwork, which was about five. Would you like us to try and track her down?"

"No, it's all right. I'll have another go, but we're meeting tomorrow anyway. Thanks again, for everything."

"You're welcome. Happy signing! Bye…"

Tessa parked her car in the underground car park, and took the lift to the third floor. Again she tried Penny's *cbc*, but still without success.

In the conference room, Tessa found that John's colleague Orla had everything extremely well organised. On the enormous table were eighteen neat stacks of paper, all with numerous blue and pink stickers showing where the two parties were to sign. It soon became clear the completion process would take several hours, but Tessa didn't mind. She knew she would still have ample time to celebrate with the employees back at her old office.

She returned to Druckmaschinen in high spirits. While she was being updated by Stefanie on the arrangements for the afternoon's celebrations, her private telephone rang. It was John Denton.

"Hi, Tessa. It's all done and the money is in your account. It's a little more than expected because our costs were lower than budgeted, but you probably won't notice the difference in all those digits. I've repaid the S&M bridging loan, and even after that, the sale proceeds make you very rich. Congratulations! You worked hard and you deserve it. Just make sure you enjoy it."

"Thank you, John," said Tessa with a satisfied smile. "You and Caitlín must come round for dinner with me and Penny sometime. I couldn't have done it without you and we ought to celebrate."

"We'd love to, but you get on with your party now. Take care. Hopefully see you again soon."

Three hours later, flushed and in high spirits, Tessa returned to her office. Herr Schneider was with her and Stefanie brought in a pot of coffee. Laughing and joking, Tessa started pouring. Then her private phone rang again. Stefanie answered it and her smile evaporated.

"Frau Doktor, I'm sorry but it's a Mr Sinclair for you. He says you haven't spoken to him before, but it's very important he talks to you now. He sounds … official."

Tessa put the coffee pot down. There was something in Stefanie's tone which caused a chill in the exuberant atmosphere. In silence Tessa went behind her desk and sat down to take the call.

"Hello, can I help you?"

"Am I speaking to Dr Tessa Pennington?"

"You are," she replied. "Who are you?"

"Am I correct in thinking you know a Dr Penelope Reid of Onslow Square?" continued the caller.

"Yes, but before we go any further, I want to know who you are?" answered Tessa. A slight tremor had crept into her voice. Although he hadn't said much, there was something about the caller's voice which made her uneasy.

"Oh, sorry," continued the man in a slightly softer tone, "my name is Sinclair, I'm a Private Investigator. Dr Reid hired me and a colleague, Mr Jones, to look into her affairs."

"She's never mentioned your names," replied Tessa, remembering that Penny had said something about consultants. "Anyway, what has this to do with me?"

"I'm sorry. There's no easy way to say this," said Sinclair, "but I'm afraid Dr Reid is dead."

Tessa was stunned. She couldn't believe what she'd heard.

"Mr Sinclair, I think there must be some mistake. I was with Penny yesterday afternoon and she was perfectly all right when I left her."

"Yes, we know. She phoned us from the bank. Amongst other things she told us what you'd done. But we believe that was the last time anyone heard from her."

"But … what happened?"

"We don't know yet," he replied. "Her body was found this morning in the City."

Tessa's throat went dry and all the colour drained from her face. The man sounded so certain. She wanted to protest that this was all a mistake, but found she could not. For a moment she was speechless, although she wanted to cry out in despair. Two minutes ago she had been on top of the world. Now her world was empty.

"How did she die?" Tessa forced herself to ask.

"I'd prefer not to discuss it over the phone. But they were not natural causes. We would very much like to meet you as soon as possible. You may have information which could help us piece together what happened, and why. We are working closely with the police. Also, and I'm sorry to have to ask you this, we were hoping you would be willing to make a formal identification of Dr Reid's body? She didn't have any relatives we know of, and it seems you were her closest friend. When were you anticipating returning to London?"

Tessa paused to remind herself to breathe and sat back heavily.

"Dr Pennington, are you still there?"

"Yes, yes," stammered Tessa, "just a moment, please."

With her left hand covering the phone's mouthpiece, she turned to Stefanie.

"Do whatever it takes to get me on the next flight to Heathrow. I'll go from Köln-Bonn if necessary."

Seeing the look of devastation in Tessa's eyes, Stefanie didn't wait for an explanation. She dashed into her office and started making calls.

"Mr Sinclair, sorry, hold on, please," mumbled Tessa. She desperately wanted to ask some questions, lots of questions, but wasn't sure she could speak for much longer without breaking down. She knew how efficient Stefanie was, so tried to keep a grip on her emotions by gathering some papers and her lap-top ready to put in her bag. A moment later Stefanie rushed back into the office and handed Tessa a note.

"Thanks. Taxi please."

"Already on its way."

Tessa tried to force a smile.

"Mr Sinclair, I'll be on the next flight from Düsseldorf to Heathrow. To catch it, I'm going to have to leave now."

"OK. What's the flight number? We'll meet you in the Arrivals Hall."

"BA941. It arrives at seventeen-fifty-five. Have a card with TP on it, so I can find you."

As Tessa put the phone down, she realised Stefanie and Schneider were looking at her in concern.

"It's Penny ... she's dead."

For a few seconds no one said anything while Tessa mechanically stuffed things into her bag.

"Oh, God, that's awful," murmured Stefanie.

"How?" asked a shocked-looking Schneider.

The sound of a taxi hooting outside the building could be heard.

"I don't know yet. He only said she didn't die from natural causes. Don't tell anyone else, we'll do that on Monday. I'm sorry you two had to find out now, but don't let it dampen the celebrations. I'm afraid I've got to go."

Tessa grabbed her bag and rushed out of the office. In the taxi, speeding towards Düsseldorf airport, she toyed with an endless stream of unanswerable questions. She couldn't understand why anything like this should have happened, why anyone would ever have wanted to harm Penny...

Two hours later she was walking briskly through Heathrow Baggage Claim towards the Arrivals Hall. She slowed briefly to take a copy of a free evening newspaper. While scanning the front page for Breaking News; two items caught her eye.

"Peacekeeper killed by Calver Cats in dockside ambush..."

"Private owner of large German engineering concern dies in mysterious circumstances. The death follows a steep decline in performance..."

In despair and disgust, Tessa tossed the paper into a bin and continued walking. She found her path blocked by a group of large American tourists whom she was obliged to follow as they ambled through the double doors into the Arrivals Hall. Impatient to get round them, she ducked under the rope barrier which kept the exit free. She had often done this with Penny when they wanted to avoid the crush. It brought her out behind the people awaiting new arrivals and allowed her to look for Sinclair and Jones without their realising she had arrived. She was curious to see what they looked like before announcing her presence.

She soon found them. Both were very well dressed, but not exactly what she was expecting for Private Investigators. One was slightly stocky and seemed somewhat older than his companion, probably in his fifties. He looked very healthy, with a tanned, weather-beaten complexion. His greying hair was gathered back into a neat ponytail and he wore a small pointed beard. Unusually, he was dressed in a dark silk collarless suit with a white collarless shirt beneath. Tessa had never been a fan of men with ponytails but his seemed to suit him. He emanated a sophisticated, almost oriental, air. He had a distinguished, confident look about him, and his eyes were warm.

The other man seemed more conventional and aged in his mid-forties. Sturdily built, he had short black hair and hands that were noticeably large. He looked strong and alert, his grey eyes studying the heaving crowds. He seemed extremely uncomfortable to be holding up a board with TP written on it in large black letters. The hired muscle, thought Tessa.

Suddenly there was a brief hiatus in the background noise as an International Peacekeeper walked by, followed by two police constables wearing no body armour and armed only with truncheons. Tessa froze for a moment at the memory of Penny and how fiercely she had believed in the Peacekeepers' role. Then, taking advantage of the distraction, she approached Sinclair and Jones from behind.

"Gentlemen, I presume you're looking for me?"

The two men spun round in surprise, so quickly that Tessa was forced to take a step back. Nothing was said for a moment as the three of them scrutinised one another. The two men saw an attractive blonde eyeing them suspiciously through steely blue-grey eyes. She was immaculately dressed and composed despite the recent shock she had suffered.

"Dr Pennington?" asked the man with the beard.

"Yes. And you are?"

"Sinclair," he replied. "We spoke earlier."

"You're Scottish?" observed Tessa, managing a weak smile in response.

"Yes, I'm originally from northern Scotland, but I've lived elsewhere for most of my life. The accent remains to remind me of my roots. Jones here is Welsh…"

Tessa realised the younger man was still looking at her; staring, in fact. She turned back to face him and pointedly let her eyes meet his.

"Oh, I'm sorry," stammered Jones, "it's just I wasn't expecting…"

"Neither was I," retorted Tessa, turning back to Sinclair. "Do you both have identification?"

They fumbled, eventually producing badges that identified them as Private Investigators.

"Thank you," said Tessa, having read them carefully. "You have a car?"

"Yes, of course," replied Sinclair. "We really are very sorry for your loss. We had come to know Dr Reid quite well, and respected her greatly. It…"

"Quite, thank you," said Tessa, feeling tears threatening again. "Me too. Let's just go, please."

As they set off in silence to the short-term car park, Tessa noticed Sinclair was limping. They got into a dark blue-grey limousine and set off for London with Jones driving. There was only one conversation of consequence on the way. Sinclair turned round to ask whether she would mind if they visited the mortuary first. Tessa wasn't expecting that. She had hoped she would have more time to prepare; but once asked, she nodded in agreement. She was terrified by the prospect of seeing Penny's dead body.

Forty minutes later, they stopped in front of a gloomy Victorian brick-built building in Lots Road. Tessa had not even known there was a Mortuary in Chelsea.

"Why isn't there a sign saying what it is?" she asked, as Sinclair held the car door open for her.

"Oh, it's a private facility," he replied. "We have some influence with the police and used it to ensure she was put here rather than … well, with all the others."

"Thank you," murmured Tessa, faintly feeling she was expected to say something along those lines. In fact his explanation had made her suspicious, but she decided to play along for the time being. She followed as Sinclair led the way into the uninviting foyer. She noticed Jones linger outside to check the street in both directions before coming in behind them.

A wizened old man behind a thick glass window nodded at Sinclair, but nothing was said. There was a loud buzz, and the door to their left clicked open. Tessa had never seen a dead body before, let alone been inside a mortuary. She was immediately struck by the sickly sweet smell, tainted with disinfectant. She started to shiver and tried to convince herself it was only because the air was unnaturally cold.

They walked along a number of poorly lit corridors and up some stairs accompanied only by the echo of their shoes clattering on the concrete floor. Clearly the building had been a hospital once; but it appeared to be empty now, and definitely not an active mortuary. Tessa swallowed nervously.

It was all like a horrible nightmare to her. She already hated this place and felt uncomfortable with Sinclair and Jones. Her legs began to tremble and she wanted to scream out loud that all this was wrong, a terrible mistake. She could not be here to view the remains of her friend. Penny could not be dead, she could not…

They walked up some more stairs, along another corridor and came to a halt outside battered green double-doors. Sinclair fixed Tessa with his eyes.

"I should warn you, this will not be at all pleasant. It's never easy seeing a dead body, especially if you're not used to death and it's someone to whom you were attached. However, on this occasion it's going to be even worse. I didn't want to tell you earlier, but Dr Reid died quite a violent death. She put up a fight, that is clear, but in the end she lost the war."

For a moment there was silence, except for the distant sound of water dripping.

"She lost the battle," whispered Tessa coldly, "not the war."

"Sorry?" said Sinclair.

"Nothing," Tessa murmured. "Let's get on with it, shall we? I'm not sure I can take much more of this."

Inside, the room was surprisingly big, although Tessa could only see the middle of it clearly. It was illuminated by a ceiling lamp which cast a clinical bright white light over a large circular area. Directly under it stood a new-looking trolley on which lay a body, covered completely with a clean white sheet. Sinclair walked towards it. Tessa followed with her heart in her mouth. She had never been so scared in her life. Her throat had dried and she could feel her heart thumping. When they reached the trolley, Sinclair motioned her to stay on the left while he went round to face her. Jones stood behind her. Sinclair took hold of the top of the sheet covering the body and looked over at Tessa.

"Are you ready?" he said with a sad and surprisingly compassionate expression on his rugged face.

Tessa didn't know what to say. How could one ever be ready for this? She simply swallowed hard and nodded; and Sinclair started pulling the sheet down.

Tessa's eyes widened in horror at what she saw. There was no doubt the body was Penny's, but it was only just recognisable as part of her face was missing. For a moment Tessa simply froze as she desperately fought to retain control. She managed to calm herself, with difficulty.

"What happened to her face?" she gasped.

"She was killed late last night, and left in the City early this morning. It was the delivery van that found her body which caused that injury," replied Sinclair.

Tessa motioned him to continue lowering the sheet. He hesitated, so she looked at him insistently.

"Mr Sinclair, I must see it all. I need to understand what she went through, so that I can remember everything when those responsible face justice."

The sheet started moving again. More and more of Penny's battered body was revealed, with cuts and bruises everywhere. A number were clearly defensive wounds, but her genital area was also badly bruised. However, Tessa's attention was drawn to a deep incision from one side of her abdomen to the other. Involuntarily she gripped the side of the trolley.

"Oh, no!" she wailed. The sheet stopped moving. "Who on earth would do this ... to anyone ... and why Penny?"

Neither Sinclair nor Jones answered.

"What actually killed her? Was she raped...?"

Tessa's voice petered out. It required a superhuman effort to hold back her tears; but she was determined not to cry, not here.

"The wound to the abdomen killed her. It was inflicted with a sword by someone left-handed. It will be possible to obtain the weapon's signature later," replied Sinclair. Adding after a short pause, "And, yes, I'm afraid she was raped, by at least two men."

He started to pull the sheet up again, but Tessa reached over and lifted Penny's hand. She held it for a moment, taking in the softness of the skin and the broken, blood-stained nails. The unnatural coldness was distressing, but Tessa was determined to let her friend know she was there for her now. She cupped the cold hand in hers and caressed it, bending down to whisper words of comfort. Then, with tears rolling down her cheeks, she kissed Penny's hand and finally put it down. As the sheet started moving again, Tessa kissed her own hand and reached over to lay it on Penny's pale lips.

Sinclair cleared his throat.

"Are you certain this is Dr Penelope Reid?"

"Yes, of course it is … was … Penny. But you must know that, you said she hired you?"

"Indeed, but a relative or close friend must formally identify her. Dr Pennington, I'm very sorry to have had to put you through this ordeal." He handed her an immaculately pressed white silk handkerchief.

"What will happen to her now?" asked Tessa, dabbing away her streaming mascara.

"There will be a post-mortem, after which her body will be released to whoever is going to take care of the funeral arrangements."

"I'll do that. Can you let me know as soon as her body can be moved somewhere … else?"

"Of course. There are some forms to sign confirming her identification, but after that we can go."

Tessa was in a daze as she signed them. She couldn't even be bothered to read them although she did ask for copies. Shortly afterwards she was relieved to find herself sitting in the car once more, although the thought of leaving Penny alone in such a horrible place reduced her to tears again. Jones started the car and turned questioningly to her.

"I'd like to go home, please," she said weakly.

Jones looked at Sinclair who nodded, and ten minutes later the car stopped outside Tessa's house. She was still wondering how they knew where she lived when Sinclair opened the door for her.

"I understand you're upset," he said, as she got out, "but we do have some questions. You may know something which could help us find whoever did this."

"Not now," replied Tessa. "I'm sorry, my brain's not working any more. We can meet tomorrow if you like, but for now I need to be on my own."

CHAPTER 7

The following morning, Tessa struggled to accept that Penny wouldn't be calling. The person with whom she'd endured so much was gone forever. Penny's wise counsel, her creativity, her laughter and her quizzical looks had all been snatched away. Their weekend of joyous celebration would never happen now.

She phoned her mother and told her what had happened and they both broke down. But Tessa refused the immediate offer of support. She had things to do; a funeral to organise, and probably a Will to track down…

She was sure Penny had mentioned the name of her lawyer once, and searched through the e-mail history on her lap-top. She found him, a Mr Coyle who ran a practice in High Holborn. It was Saturday morning, but Tessa tried telephoning him anyway, and was both amazed and pleased to find him working. She told him what had happened and made an appointment for the following Wednesday afternoon. He thought by then he would be able to discuss Penny's Will. He also undertook to liaise with the police concerning Penny's body.

Tessa changed into a smart but sombre suit and set off for Antonio's where she had arranged to meet Sinclair and Jones. Throughout the brisk fifteen-minute walk from her house, she was deeply engrossed. Every conceivable shade of grief, injustice and loneliness welled up inside her, together with an increasingly intense anger at her soulmate being so cruelly deprived of life. She tried to console herself with the knowledge that she was in the enviable position of having more than sufficient resources to ensure that whoever was responsible for Penny's death would pay dearly for what they'd done. Indeed, she soon concluded that there was very little else which mattered to her now.

Antonio's Patisserie was one of Tessa's and Penny's favourite haunts, a bustling upmarket café which served an eclectic mix of Italian and French food and drink. As usual, Tessa was greeted histrionically by Antonio, but the atmosphere soon changed when she explained what had happened. He had come to know them both well and was genuinely upset by the news. Eventually Tessa settled down at a corner table. She was still staring disconsolately at her low-fat latté when Sinclair and Jones came in. She waved them over to her table and Antonio took their orders. The coffee arrived shortly afterwards.

"Mr Sinclair," said Tessa in a menacing tone, her eyes narrowing, "you said Penny retained you to investigate whether someone was maliciously targeting her? Well, clearly there was. So what have you found out about them, and what was the motive for her murder?"

With a jolt Sinclair and Jones realised it was they who were being questioned rather than the other way round. Jones shifted awkwardly, promptly sweeping his cup and saucer off the table with one of his enormous hands. Tessa moved like lightning and caught them both, barely rattling the spoon. Jones looked at her dumbfounded.

"My apologies," observed Sinclair, smiling, "I'm afraid Gareth is renowned for doing such things. But that's the first time I've ever seen someone catch a full cup and saucer."

Tessa shrugged and returned them, looking expectant.

"Penny…," he resumed, "…she asked us to call her that … approached us about three months ago. She felt someone was targeting both her and her business. She even suggested that it was lucky for her that she had started self-defence classes."

"Self-defence?" muttered Tessa. She hadn't known Penny had enrolled for anything of the sort, though she had only known she was training hard in a gym. "Sorry, carry on."

"We soon confirmed her suspicions," continued Sinclair. "But we couldn't find out who was responsible; nor how or why her business was being compromised. It was clearly very well planned and carefully orchestrated. So, we began to wonder whether there might be some connection with organised crime, or New Crime as the media calls it. It takes a lot to damage a big international concern like Schrauben & Mutter. But try as we might, we couldn't establish a motive. I'm afraid that's about as far as we got."

Tessa thought for a moment.

"Hmm. Let's see if I've understood this correctly. Penny hired you some time ago to confirm she and her business were being targeted. This you did quite quickly, say, in a week or two?" She looked up at

Sinclair and then Jones who nodded, somewhat unwillingly. "Since then she has been paying you to find out how and why her business was being attacked and by whom, which you have failed to do?"

As Tessa scrutinised them, Sinclair and Jones felt distinctly uncomfortable. They knew she was right and weren't particularly happy about it.

"Now, do you think it unreasonable of me to assume Penny was also paying you to keep her alive? After all, if you failed to do that, how could she continue to retain you?"

A wry smile passed fleetingly across Sinclair's face and he sighed.

"Unfortunately, that is correct."

"You failed her in every material respect. Haven't you proved to be rather a poor investment on her part?" asked Tessa, her voice hardening.

There was brief silence from the two men.

"That remains to be seen," murmured Sinclair. "But we have failed her. We know that, and we're not proud of it. We thought we had done enough to protect her, but clearly we hadn't, and that is something we will regret for a long time..."

He realised Tessa was close to terminating their involvement.

"Could we have done more? Truly, I don't believe so. But rest assured, we have been asking ourselves that ever since her body was found. Whoever organised this had already finished planning her death before we were called in."

This stoical admission of responsibility brought Tessa back from the brink. His frankness impressed her although not enough to diminish her anger, a fact which did not go unnoticed by either man.

"Thank you. With me, honesty is always the best policy. But it's a bit late for Penny, isn't it? The question I have to answer now is, do I retain you? While I'm considering that, I would like you to forward to me a written report of all your findings to date. I want to understand precisely what it is you have achieved so far. You can send it to me electronically, if you like. Here is my e-mail address." She slid a business card across the table. "Also, I'm sure you were issuing regular status reports to Penny. I would like to see them all, please, preferably today. I have some catching up to do. On Monday I will be taking over at Schrauben & Mutter, so if Penny was targeted because of her business interests, I will be next in line. Presumably it wouldn't be good for your reputation to lose another client? Finally, I suggest you add a few words explaining why you think I should retain you. Is that all clear and reasonable?"

Sinclair smiled and looked at Jones, who nodded.

"Good. I'll postpone deciding whether or not we should meet again, but either way I will honour your account for the time being. And don't worry, the coffee is on me."

With that Tessa got up, grabbed her coat and left Antonio's.

Jones turned to Sinclair, and breathed out noisily.

"Wow! So much for *us* asking *her* questions. I don't think we've had a dressing down like that for years."

"We deserved it, and some," his boss replied disconsolately. "Penny was relying on us, and we let her down. Unfortunately, it is as simple as that. I have to admit, I rather like this friend of hers; no wonder they got on so well. Penny was special, but this woman … well, she gives a new dimension to the word. One's first impression is of sweetness personified, but there is immense underlying strength. She's sharp and good-looking too, with reactions and control the like of which I've never seen before."

Jones nodded.

"True. How could one ever be prejudiced against that package? However, we need to make sure she continues to retain us or things will get much more complicated. Somehow we've got to rescue our credibility, and we do still need to ask her some questions … I suppose we'd better start with me getting her all those reports?"

"Yes, and while you do that, I'll keep a discreet eye on her. But we'll need to come up with something rather more creative for the long-term."

"OK. I'll take a taxi back to the office and catch up with you later."

At home, Tessa first turned her attention to finding a funeral parlour to which Penny's body could be transferred. That done, she decided to check her friend's flat. She considered asking Helen, her friend and neighbour, to come with her. But then she thought that if something untoward happened, it would be dreadful to have another person involved. Also, she thought it likely that if anyone else had wanted to search Penny's flat, they'd probably have done so by now.

She took the keys to Penny's flat from her safe and made a mental note to retrieve hers from Penny's. They had swapped keys and the combinations to each other's safe and alarm systems a long time ago; Tessa changed her codes straightaway.

She walked to the flat feeling distinctly uneasy, despite having decided to take her Kenjutsu staff with her. Penny had moved there some six months ago, to ensure they lived closer together. Tessa stopped outside the large Victorian house in Onslow Square which contained Penny's flat, and looked round. But she didn't see Sinclair sitting in the dark blue-grey limousine parked further down the road. He smiled to see her staff, sure that soon it alone would not suffice.

In the flat, everything was just as Tessa expected to find it: clean, neat and sophisticated. She opened the safe, its contents were undisturbed. She quickly found the envelope containing her own keys and put it in her handbag. Then she looked through the mail and other papers to see if anything needed urgent attention or might have some bearing on Penny's murder. But there was nothing. She checked the desk and filing cabinet, but found nothing relevant. Most of the documents were business-related although she did find some unusual receipts headed SKS. They were very basic, without any address or telephone number. Tessa wondered whether they were from the place where Penny had recently been spending time. She switched on Penny's PC and checked her e-mails for SKS, but found nothing. Then she searched on the Internet, again without success. She resolved to find this mysterious place. Maybe the people there could shed some light on this sorry affair.

She went into the kitchen and filled several refuse sacks with perishables. In Penny's bedroom there were many clothes, most of which they had bought together. Tessa knew the majority would fit her as their build was so similar. For a while she looked for Penny's *cbc* which Sinclair had said was missing, but couldn't find it. She went back into the familiar lounge and looked around. Memories flooded back of the many happy times they had spent there together, but Tessa refused to cry. Instead, she clenched her fists, willing herself to get through this. She made a vow to find out what had happened to her best friend and why; and then to pay back those responsible, with interest.

Tessa checked the flat was in a secure condition and closed the curtains. Then she left, taking the refuse sacks with her. Again she didn't notice Sinclair watching as she walked home.

That evening an e-mail arrived from Jones with a number of reports attached. Tessa ordered a Japanese takeaway and settled down to read them. There was a lot of information, but nothing of consequence. However, they did give the impression Sinclair and Jones had been working quite hard. For now, she decided, they could stay on the payroll.

On Sunday evening, Tessa returned to Germany full of foreboding; she wasn't looking forward to having to tell everyone at the factory that Penny was dead. In Stuttgart, she spoke first to the directors and then addressed the workforce. There was stunned silence as she made the announcement and several employees broke down. Tessa explained that all their jobs were safe, and that as majority shareholder she would become Chief Executive. Later, she went to Penny's flat in Tübingen. Again she looked for papers which might give an indication as to why her friend was murdered, or the whereabouts of SKS, but found nothing. With Penny's apartment secure, she went to a local *gäststatte* to plan. She knew she was going to be incredibly busy over the next few months, with work and winding up Penny's affairs. So she would just have to pressurise Sinclair and Jones for some fast results…

Back in London, Wednesday turned out to be a day of wonderful weather, which only served to depress Tessa further. She surfaced from her dark mood as the taxi stopped in High Holborn. Coyle's offices were luxuriously appointed and spread over three floors, much larger than she had expected. She was shown into his office where she found a rotund man in his early-sixties, with thinning grey hair and a sanguine expression. He had a competent, distinguished air about him. Greeting her warmly, he beckoned her to sit opposite him while he settled back into his green Chesterfield armchair behind a large antique mahogany desk. He spoke in a calm relaxed voice which exuded confidence, experience and sympathy.

"Dr Pennington, it is a pleasure to meet you at last. I only wish the circumstances were different. I have heard many good things about you. Penny and you were clearly very close. Please accept my sincere condolences."

"Thank you, Mr Coyle," Tessa replied. "I shall miss her terribly. This untimely death has come as a great shock."

Coyle nodded in melancholy agreement, before deftly steering the conversation to business.

"Well, I suppose we'd better get down to it. I've been in touch with the Police and the various other authorities involved. Everything is progressing administratively and I see absolutely no reason why I should not tell you the provisions of the Will since you are the sole beneficiary. Are you ready?"

"Yes, I suppose so. It seems odd there's no one else concerned?"

"The only friend Penny ever mentioned to me was you, and to the best of my knowledge there are no surviving members of the Reid family. I have been acting for her ever since her parents were killed. I am quite sure there is nobody else who should be here."

Coyle smiled and nudged a box of tissues towards Tessa. Then he purposefully put on a pair of gold-rimmed half-glasses and, using a silver paper-knife, opened the sealed envelope that contained Penny's Will. Tessa had been dreading this moment. He started reading. '

"'I hereby state that to the best of my knowledge I have no living relatives, dependants or friends whom I wish to benefit from my Estate apart from herein mentioned.

"'Subject to the payment of my debts, funeral expenses and testamentary expenses, I wish my body to be cremated after a private funeral and my ashes spread over the Pentland Firth; a magical place. I bequeath all my worldly goods, regardless of form, function or location, to Dr Tessa Pennington of South Kensington. Her friendship has made the last few difficult years fun. I owe her a great deal and feel this bequest will be only small compensation for everything she has done for me.

"'I have been attempting to purchase a smallholding in Orkney called Mardykes and have instructed Mr Coyle on how to proceed. If successful, I would like Tessa to continue these endeavours and build the cottage we discussed together.

"In fact," interjected Coyle, "the bidding closed last Friday and I used the existing Power of Attorney to purchase the property. It was quite a contest with the local laird, but Penny had prepared well and won."

"Excellent! I'm delighted," said Tessa. She was pleased she at least would be able to honour Penny's dream of living on Orkney.

"'Finally,'" continued Coyle, "'I would like the enclosed sealed letter to be given to Tessa on the occasion of the reading of my Will.'"

The solicitor held up a lilac-coloured envelope.

"Penny made this Will a few weeks ago. She came here herself and dictated everything. I will, of course, let you have a copy. There is absolutely no doubt as to its authenticity or that she wanted you to have everything. As such the Will is straightforward. If you agree, I would be pleased to arrange the transfer of her estate."

Tessa nodded and grabbed several tissues. Initially she had worried her mascara might run, but now she didn't care.

"Thank you, that would be most helpful. Please keep me informed as to your progress."

Coyle nodded and handed her the sealed envelope to her.

"I think I'll read this now, if that's all right?"

He nodded and Tessa carefully opened it and took out the three sheets of delicate notepaper, handwritten by Penny.

Darling Tessa,

It doesn't bode well if you're reading my Will! I do hope my passing didn't hurt. Mind you, I doubt anything could be worse than what we've already been forced to endure. Anyway, presumably I've died under suspicious circumstances because that's why I wrote this.

I've no idea why anyone should want me dead but I've been worried for months. I hired a couple of PIs (Sinclair and Jones) to see what they could find out, and instructed them to contact you if anything untoward happened to me. I think they're quite good; much better than first impressions would suggest. Mind you, they never did tell me why or by whom I was being targeted, and it seems they failed even to keep me alive.

Coyle is a good man; expensive, but worth every penny. I recommend you let him do what he can to help you take over my Estate. He knows where everything is, so he's well positioned to handle the transfer.

Now, there's just one more thing. If I've already given you your birthday present, ignore this bit; but if I haven't, then I'm really peeved to have missed that and you've got a challenge on your hands!

This present is something I decided to get you a long time ago. I knew it would be perfect, and now that I've seen it, I'm even more thrilled. When you find it, I'm sure you too will be captivated by its extraordinary beauty. It is truly unique, and of incredible quality. It is immensely valuable, not only as an artefact in its own right, but also because, regardless of all my other possessions, it is the thing I value most.

You are probably wondering what on earth it is. Well, unfortunately, due to the enormous number of favours I had to ask in order to be allowed to commission it, I had to accept some restrictions with regards to your taking ownership. I particularly had to undertake not to tell you what or where it is. I could only bring you to it, and presumably that is going to be difficult now. "Weird," I hear you say. But you will understand what I mean when you find it; and call it sixth sense if you like, but I'm sure you will, when the time is right.

I know it might take you a while to get used to its purpose. So when you've got it, you must promise to try your hardest to learn how to use it. If for no other reason, do it for me. That's non-negotiable. I'm sure you'll be very good with it. Just use it wisely. It is truly awesome, and I don't doubt you will soon love it as much as I do ... well, did.

So, my dear, you'll have to work at it a little before my most prized possession comes into your hands. But don't bother looking for any clues about it amongst my paperwork. There aren't any.

Finally ... Tessa! Oh, Tessa ... how I shall miss you. You really did help me so much. After years and years in the wilderness, struggling alone with our common problem, I finally found a friend to help me overcome all the obstacles. I owe you so much and am deeply sorry I will not be able to share the future with you. I hope yours is good, very good. Live and enjoy it for both of us.

With all my love,
Penny xxx

"How strange," mused Coyle, when Tessa had finished reading the letter and showed it to him. "No wonder she wouldn't tell me what she'd written. She knew I would never have condoned anything like this. Well, good luck finding it, whatever and wherever it is! All that remains today is for you to sign these papers. Please read them carefully first, but there's nothing controversial. Incidentally, I don't know whether you are aware, but Penny was independently wealthy apart from her business holdings. She had inherited a substantial sum from her parents, most of which is invested."

"Mr Coyle," said Tessa, wiping her eyes, "I would gladly forego my inheritance and some, just to have her back."

Outside, she found a crowd of men jostling for taxis. In disgust, she walked to the nearby underground station, and, once on the train, decided to listen to some music. She clipped in her earpiece and selected some tracks on her *cbc*, soon losing herself in the music. As she got off at South Kensington, she suddenly felt something jolt against her bag. She looked down, and realised the handbag of a woman getting on to the train had brushed against hers. But then, just as the carriage doors slammed shut, her music was interrupted by the sound of a woman's voice, close at hand.

"It'll be your turn soon."

Tessa spun round to see who had spoken. No one nearby was using a phone, so she looked into the fast receding carriage. All she could see was the back of the woman who had bumped into her; she was putting something into her bag. Had she just threatened Tessa? Surely not? Maybe her own *cbc* had simply caught a snippet of someone else's conversation. Her music started playing again and she returned to wondering what Penny could have bought her which was so wonderful and valuable, and yet so secret. More importantly, how on earth was she meant to find it?

CHAPTER 8

The funeral arrangements proved depressing but straightforward enough to make. Tessa decided to have a formal public wake in Germany, to which all Penny's friends and colleagues could come; and a separate private event in England. She intended to spend this time alone with Penny, as that was how they had supported each other through their most difficult challenges. Having a good idea of what would have pleased her friend, she was delighted to find that, despite its being unorthodox, a funeral parlour was happy to oblige, albeit at a price.

The wake in Germany was organised for the following Tuesday and she closed Schrauben & Mutter for the day.

During the service Tessa tried hard not to show her emotions, but couldn't help crying on several occasions. She had flown her mother over, and it fell to her to try and console Tessa, although they were both distraught. The following day they flew back to London together.

On the plane Tessa, desperate to find something to occupy her mind, picked up a celebrity magazine. Its cover was yet another picture of a beaming King William and Queen Catherine standing on the steps of Balmoral Castle with their three young children and recently arrived twins. She flicked through the pages until one article caught her eye. She stared at the picture with disbelief. It showed a substantial Home Counties manor house with two people standing in front of it: her brother Beauchamp and his wife Caprice. Even Tessa had to admit they looked good together. Beauchamp always had been a handsome man; he was over six foot tall, in his early-forties, fit and strong with piercing blue eyes and thick curly blond hair. He had been an astute lawyer from the outset, but his career really took off when he joined a City firm managed by an old friend of his wife's and was soon made a partner. He was also much better dressed these days, another of the many changes that had followed his marriage to Caprice. She, with her brown eyes and long dark hair, was an eye-catching if intriguing woman, whose past remained predominantly a mystery. She was known to be extremely adept at furthering her husband's career, albeit with a spiteful temper, a sharp tongue and a domineering personality. Tessa read the article with mounting incredulity.

"...Beauchamp and Caprice Caille have been voted this year's most prominent Power Couple in Britain. Proud father Beauchamp is a hard-working senior partner with top-ten City legal firm Whicker Atkinson. Meanwhile, his fragrant wife Caprice ensures that family life runs smoothly ... and with three active, high-achieving children, that takes some doing! Nevertheless, she still finds time for local charity work and supporting her husband at the many formal functions he attends as Master..."

Tessa looked up to find her mother engrossed in an eReader. Her wrinkles and white hair betrayed her age, but the glint in her eyes was just as sharp as it had always been.

"Have you seen this?" said Tessa, passing over the magazine.

"Fancy," mused her mother with a wry smile.

"That doesn't sound like the family home I remember," retorted Tessa. "I always thought the place resembled a high-security prison. And there's no mention of the army of down-trodden third-world staff they employ for peanuts to do the real work."

"Yes, well, each to their own. The children have turned out nicely at least."

"Really? When did one of them last contact you?"

"Well, not recently, I admit, but they're teenagers now, grandparents won't be so important to them for a while ... and poor Adam's gone to the US for more medical treatment, apparently alopecia isn't his only problem."

"Well, I feel sorry for him, but that's still no excuse for neglecting you and Dad after everything you've done for them. And what about Beauchamp himself? He hasn't communicated with me in any way since I first told him what I was having to do and why, not even an e-mail. And that was well over two years ago, now."

"Well, dear, I'm sure he'll get used to it, eventually. We need to go easy on him. When we christened him Beauchamp Caradoc, your father and I didn't realise when that he would live up to his highfaluting names with such gusto! But he's all right really, he just can't adapt as quickly as you."

"He couldn't even be bothered to return the books I lent him about it," said Tessa bitterly.

"I'm sure he'll come round, dear, just try and be patient. He took us to a civic function at the Guildhall recently, though I suspect he only wanted his parents there for show. Anyway, as your father's mobility is somewhat restricted since the accident, Beauchamp even offered to have us picked up in his company limo. Bill the driver, a rough-looking sort, seemed devoted to 'the boss.'"

"How touching. And what about Caprice, any idea what she thinks about it?"

Tessa's mother looked coy, not wanting to dig herself any deeper into a hole.

"Come on, I can see there's something," persisted Tessa.

"She wrote a letter to your father. It arrived on the day of Penny's wake." Tessa's jaw clenched as her anger rose. "For goodness' sake, dear, coincidences do happen. We've never even mentioned Penny to them."

"OK, sorry. But I can't remember Caprice ever having written anything before. What on earth did she say?"

"Oh, it really doesn't matter, dear. I shouldn't have mentioned it."

"Come on, you've got to tell me now."

"Well, it was a bit odd, even by Caprice's standards. It said she and Beauchamp viewed what you've done with extreme disfavour, and that if we persisted in supporting someone who had brought such disgrace on the family name, they and their children would be obliged to sever all contact."

"What!"

"Yes, well, we didn't pay much attention to it. And neither should you," her mother said placatingly.

Tessa was immediately reminded of Beauchamp's reaction after she'd explained to his face what she was about to do. He'd simply gulped down his third malt whisky and said in disgust: "Typical! You've always been a bloody embarrassment to me. I just need to consider what difference this makes." The harsh response was hardly uncharacteristic for him, but Tessa had not expected to be openly ostracised by him and his family. And now it seemed her parents were to receive the same treatment, tainted in his eyes by their continuing association with Tessa.

"But that's disgusting!" she exclaimed.

Her mother gave her a warning look, tinged with kindness and resolve.

"We intend to carry on as though nothing was ever said."

"But … are they worth the effort?"

"Oh, yes, dear. As you know, we all have our issues. I haven't given up on them yet, and neither should you. The children will make their own decisions when they're old enough. Just remember, your father and I are as one on this, we support you completely and respect you for what you've done. You're still our child and we love you just as much as ever… We could see at once it was right for both of you."

"I know, and I'm very grateful. It was good of you to be so kind to Penny too. I know she appreciated it immensely, not having any close family of her own."

"She earned a special place in our hearts, dear, which makes this all the more terrible. We know how closely you supported each other, and she deserved more from life."

"Much, much more… By the way, I know you weren't in favour of my changing my surname, but I still believe it's for the best."

"Oh, we don't really mind, just so long as you didn't do it to protect us. It wasn't necessary you know, we're very proud of you. For everything you've done."

"Thank you," said Tessa, kissing her mother on the cheek.

"Now, we're not going to be able to fix the problem of Beauchamp and Caprice today, so why not concentrate on Penny this one last time?"

The following day Tessa found it difficult to concentrate on anything and ended up checking and re-checking the arrangements for the evening ahead. She and Penny had always enjoyed listening to music and drinking port together; and that was precisely what she intended to do for her friend's send-off. She had hired the funeral parlour for the entire evening, starting at 5 p.m. when a sound system would be set up. She had arranged for a car to collect her from home at 6:30 and take her there.

Tessa had already provided the funeral parlour with an exquisite Japanese Fukagawa Seiji blue urn for Penny's ashes. She had bought it in Japan several years earlier while in Hiroshima on business. She had spent the weekend sightseeing, visiting Kintai Bridge at Iwakuni and the Fukagawa porcelain works in Arita, where she'd found the blue chrysanthemum-patterned urn. It was one of only five. The short production run had been commissioned by someone close to the Emperor and in consequence the urn was very expensive. However, she had been so taken by the design she had bought one and had it shipped back to England. She hadn't expected it to be used so soon, but was sure Penny would have approved.

When Tessa arrived she found everything laid out as requested.

The intimate oak-panelled room had a deep-pile dark red carpet that muffled her footsteps. At the far end stood Penny's immaculate white lacquer coffin displayed on a pedestal before a pair of grey velvet curtains. Between the coffin and the door was a very comfortable looking two-seater sofa. The sound system was nearby, and on a table to the left of the sofa stood two fine crystal glasses and a decanter containing the contents of a bottle of rare vintage port, Taylor Fladgate 1924. There were also some biscuits and a small selection of cheeses, together with a Thermos of coffee. Tessa thanked the manager and confirmed she expected to be finished by about 8 p.m. She would press the remote when she was ready. With that she was left on her own.

With a sigh she dimmed the lights and poured two glasses of port. She placed one on the side table next to where she intended to sit and the other on Penny's coffin. She stood there for a moment, lost in thought, and tears started to trickle down her cheeks. She said a prayer. Then she loaded the CD she had prepared and helped herself to cheese and biscuits as she settled down to listen, eat and drink, just as she and Penny had done so many times in the past.

As time and memories passed by, she drank many toasts to her friend. Occasionally she smiled; but more often she wept. Later on, she heard someone enter, but couldn't be bothered to see who it was, concentrating on reminiscing and drinking the rest of the port.

Tessa was jolted back to hazy reality by the start of the penultimate track of music, the soulful Lacrimosa from Preisner's Requiem for my Friend. This only served to exacerbate her feelings of injustice, loss and intense loneliness but she forced herself to stand up and walk over to the coffin. She laid both hands on the coffin and swore a solemn oath.

"Penny, I promise that those responsible will pay dearly for this; no matter how long it takes and, once more for us, no matter what the cost."

Then she gently tipped over Penny's full glass of port; it broke with a splintering crash, sending streams of red liquid over the pristine white coffin. As the final track began she hesitated, took a deep breath and pressed the button on the remote control.

The curtains opened with a subdued hiss and, almost imperceptibly, the coffin started to move. Tears poured down Tessa's cheeks as she watched her friend depart. It felt like an age, but eventually the curtains closed behind her. A moment later the music stopped and Tessa slumped back onto the sofa. It was several minutes before she finally stood up unsteadily, and turned round. She found Sinclair and Jones sitting in the dark at the back of the room. She had drunk so much she staggered slightly as she walked over to them.

"Gentlemen ... I'm sorry I didn't ... I was otherwise occupied," she said, trying unsuccessfully not to slur her words.

"It was the least we could do," replied Sinclair, sympathetically. "I hope you don't feel we were intruding?"

"Not at all," she continued, trying to force a smile to her tear-stained face. "Thank you for coming ... from both of us."

"Are you all right?"

Tessa glared at him.

"No, Mr Sinclair, I am not all right." Her voice shook with emotion. "I'm not sure I ever will be."

"Time does heal even the deepest of wounds," he replied. "We've both been there; we know how difficult it is to get over a loss such as this. But we must, and we do. You never recover from the fact that there is a void where once there was vibrant life, but you do learn to live with the new reality, I promise."

"Perhaps, if those responsible for Penny's death had been brought to justice," Tessa replied dejectedly. She was swaying slightly and Jones tentatively reached out to support her; but she ignored him and continued speaking. "I have decided to continue retaining you ... for now. But you need to do better, a lot better. So, while I appreciate your coming here, and I'm sure Penny does too, what we both want is for you to find the perpetrators of this crime. Do it ... and do it fast."

She tottered past them and through the door which Jones held open for her. She muttered some words to the manager of the funeral parlour and walked unsteadily into the street.

Sinclair turned to his partner.

"Grief exhibits a different dynamic in everyone; this is her way. We need to find whoever killed her friend quickly or I suspect she'll take things into her own hands."

Jones nodded.

"I just wish she'd rant and rage a little to release all that tension. But I don't suppose she's the type. The quieter she gets, the more dangerous she's likely to be. But at least she's agreed to keep us on. That should enable us to stay closer than might otherwise have been possible... That was certainly one hell of a send-off!"

They left the funeral parlour just in time to see Tessa being driven away.

"Did you see the logo on that limo?" asked Sinclair thoughtfully.

"Yes. It's South Kensington Sedans. Heaven only knows why she chose such a rinky-dink outfit, but I did check them out. They're fine."

"Hmm, perhaps she doesn't know where it is," mused Sinclair, but Jones, busy looking for his car keys, didn't hear.

A week later, with the funeral behind her, Tessa found solace of a sort in the challenge involved in taking control of Schrauben & Mutter. Occasionally she thought about the mysterious missing bequest. She felt sure finding SKS was key, but no matter what she tried, she came up with nothing.

Slowly her life began to regain a semblance of normality. Coyle completed the transfer of Penny's estate and Tessa sold her flat in Hochdahl, and Penny's in Onslow Square and Tübingen. She had monthly meetings with Sinclair and Jones and reluctantly accepted that they appeared to be doing all they could to track down Penny's murderers, although their progress was frustratingly slow.

Meanwhile Schrauben & Mutter was experiencing an unexpectedly rapid recovery. Tessa didn't understand why, but the defection of customers had reversed and the company was once again amongst the industry's leaders. However, deep down, she no longer felt comfortable running the company; it wasn't the same without Penny to discuss things with. So she was delighted when one of Schrauben & Mutter's competitors offered to buy her out. Tessa was able to negotiate an extremely good deal and a quick completion was agreed. Weeks later, and the second sale had made her a multi-millionaire all over again.

It was a week after completion when Tessa finally extricated herself from the company. She'd invited Herr Schneider down to a celebration dinner, and he took her to Stuttgart airport the following morning. They arrived early and stood by his car to say their farewells. They'd put boxes containing all her things in the boot of his car; he was going to ship them back to the UK so Tessa only had to carry a handbag.

"What will you do now?" asked Schneider. "Attractive, intelligent, very rich, and with time on your hands."

"I'm not sure. Once everything's sorted at home, I'll go and see the property Penny bought on Orkney, and then maybe I'll travel for a while. I've always enjoyed visiting the Far East, and haven't been for several years now. We'll see. Anyway," she continued, "thank you again … for everything."

"Frau Doktor, it's been a pleasure," he replied, "most of the time. This past two years have been truly memorable, and I'm pleased, indeed honoured, to have been a part of it all. I only hope you find whatever it is you are seeking."

Tessa went up to him and kissed him lightly on both cheeks.

"You're blushing!" she observed, grinning.

"I'm not in the least surprised. *Auf Wiedersehen*, Frau Doktor."

CHAPTER 9

Tessa intended to spend the plane journey reading the newspapers. There were articles about successful Peacekeeper actions, albeit won at a high price; one about recycling flak jackets, and another in which a manufacturer of armour-plated vehicles complained about the limited market for Peacekeeper cars. But Tessa lost interest when she found that most of the editorials were devoted to the rise of New Crime, led in the UK by the now notorious Calver Cats. She discarded the papers and started evaluating her options for the future.

Not unused to being described as an intense, direct person, she wasn't sure how she'd adjust to not having a business on which to focus her energy. It was one thing to be free, with an embarrassingly healthy bank balance, but it was quite another to know what to do next. Especially since she didn't particularly want another full-time job just yet. She needed a rest first; or a change at least.

At Heathrow the high-speed train was suspended so she caught the Underground into London. At South Kensington, she climbed the stairs to street level and waited for the pedestrian lights. It was a gloriously uplifting sunny day and her gaze rested idly on the sleek Italian sports cars in the showroom across the road.

The pedestrian lights changed to green and she crossed, pausing briefly on the traffic island as her mind turned to more pressing matters. How about an extravagant celebratory lunch at the Falcon? She was certainly hungry and knew she would enjoy it from the numerous times she had eaten there with Penny. But would it be the same without her? She doubted it.

Continuing down Old Brompton Road, she passed a small shoe repair shop, and stopped abruptly as she noticed a narrow alley leading off to the left through a brick archway set between two tall buildings. In all the years she had lived in South Kensington, she'd never realised there was a street here. Tessa read the rusty sign on the wall and found it was called Barnaby Mews.

She strained her eyes to peer down the alley, but it was so dark she couldn't see far. She could just make out a pair of ornate wrought-iron gates barring access through the arch. But one of the gates was slightly ajar, left just wide enough for someone to pass through. Feeling curious, and with nothing better to do, she decided to investigate. Once past the gates, Tessa found her eyes grew accustomed to the poor light, and she saw that the path in front of her was cobbled. She saw two more rusty plaques screwed to the wall. These proved to be even more difficult to read than the street sign. However, one appeared to say 'Private – No Admittance'; the last word of the second was illegible, but it started with 'South Kensington S...'. Sedans? she guessed. Maybe this was where they were based? With her curiosity heightened by this oblique and unexpected reference to SKS, she decided to continue despite the 'private' warning.

The silence and the poor light were quite intimidating though. As Tessa continued into the darkness she began to question her decision to investigate this place. Although she had not come far from the noisy bustle of Old Brompton Road, she could hardly hear it. Occasionally she saw people walking past the top of the alleyway; but, just as she herself had done so many times before, they were acting as though Barnaby Mews did not exist.

But then it widened slightly and the light improved enough for her to make out another rusty weather-worn sign ahead of her. It was hanging from a wrought-iron bracket set high on the wall of a large brick building to her right. There was just enough of a breeze to make the sign swing, its eerie creaking cutting through the pervasive silence.

Tessa paused just short of the sign. On it she could see three familiar letters – SKS. She took a deep breath and walked on. Gradually she began to relax. Although the place still felt strange, it no longer felt threatening. Furthermore it looked remarkably clean, with no litter and no unpleasant smell of neglect. She became aware of a display window to her right, just before an arched doorway. On the wall, between the display window and the door, was yet another sign. It was much clearer this time, but written in Japanese. "Now that is weird," she muttered. "Perhaps it's South Kensington Sushi?"

Reaching the window, she stepped closer to peer through. Although the glass was spotlessly clean it was still difficult to see into the display. She waited for her vision to adjust and found herself staring at her own reflection for a moment before she could look through the glass. First she noticed a robust security grille. Then she saw the luxurious burgundy-coloured silk draping the display area. She blinked in surprise and moved closer to the glass. She was looking at a vertical rack holding three sheathed samurai swords. Despite her own martial arts hobbies, Tessa was no sword expert, but even she could tell that these were very fine examples. The artistry of the decoration alone was stunning. Nevertheless, the swords themselves were subtly menacing and looking at them sent a shiver down her spine.

She concentrated on the sword at the top of the rack. It was the shortest of the three. Its sheath was a dark bronze colour with the entire surface subtly speckled in gold. There was a single fine gold ring round the top of the sheath. The hilt was bound with dark brown threads in a regular diagonal pattern over a mottled cream-coloured material, with a fine emerald set near the centre. Although the design was relatively plain, the overall effect was wonderful.

The lowest sword was the longest of the three. It had a black mottled finish with a number of sets of shiny black bands passing round the sheath, arranged alternately in groups of three, four and seven; dazzling in its simplicity. The hilt was also bound diagonally but this time in dark red, again with a cream mottled material underneath. A fine ruby glowed from near the middle of its hilt.

Finally her gaze fell on the sword in the middle of the rack. It looked rather drab in comparison. Its sheath was finished in matt black with some fine shiny black lines running lengthwise along it. However, she was intrigued by the elegant simplicity of its design which set it apart from the other two. Its dull lustre had an incredible depth, and whereas the hand guards of the top two swords were brightly decorated with intricate, almost gaudy patterns of gold and silver, this one appeared to be of a simple undulating black finish. Although the top and bottom weapons were undeniably beautiful, Tessa thought they were perhaps just a little too flamboyant. The middle sword exuded a winning air of calm, confident, unstoppable purpose.

She read the sign at the base of the display area and had her suspicions confirmed. SKS stood for South Kensington Samurai. She had wondered whether that was what the Japanese sign had said, but hadn't been confident in her translation. Was this where Penny had been spending her time? She had always been infatuated with the concept of International Peacekeepers. But to join one of the few licensed clubs in the UK was going much further than Tessa would ever have expected of her friend.

"Surely not?" she muttered, shaking her head.

"Why's that?" asked a compelling voice from right behind her.

Startled, she spun round to find herself looking at a Japanese man.

"Goodness! I didn't hear you coming," she exclaimed. He smiled and bowed slightly. Without thinking, Tessa bowed in response. The man smiled again and for a moment they studied one another. She saw a wiry upright man in his fifties, with greying hair and a tanned face. He wore sandals, baggy burgundy-coloured trousers and a loosely fitting collarless shirt, gathered at the waist with a violet cord. He saw an attractive young blonde Caucasian woman, dressed in a blue suit which highlighted the steely light in her blue-grey eyes.

"I'm sorry, I didn't mean to startle you," continued the man softly. "They are beautiful, aren't they? All works of art in their own right; made by masters, extremely valuable and very dangerous. That is why they must be kept behind this unattractive, but effective, grille. As I'm sure you know, there are many rules and regulations as to who is allowed to own such weapons, so we are obliged to keep examples of this quality safe and secure at all times. But SKS is a registered Peacekeeper training school, and within our own four walls, we have much more freedom."

Tessa found the man's matter-of-fact tone strangely reassuring. She had to struggle to remind herself he was talking about deadly weapons and a school where people trained to use them.

"You seemed unsure of something," he continued. "Perhaps I can help?"

"Well," stammered Tessa, thinking how unusual it was for her to be the one trying to gather her wits and not sound wrong-footed, "A friend of mine spent a lot of her time at a place she called SKS. But I don't think she can have meant here."

"Is it so hard to believe that swords as beautiful as these can attract people? And learning to use them is an excellent way to get fit. Being able to wield a sword expertly is a goal which many enjoy pursuing, although few attain it. Indeed, I think you would be surprised to learn how many wish to be exponents of the ancient Japanese art of Samurai, which extends far beyond swordsmanship and combat. It is a surprisingly rewarding and absorbing pastime for those who are suited to it."

With a gesture of a sinewy hand, which epitomised strength and control, he indicated the three swords. Tessa had no choice but to look at them again.

"Surely you are not going to tell me these wonderful weapons don't intrigue you in the slightest?" He paused for a moment to let what he had said sink in. "With the ban on firearms, there is now considerable interest in swords and learning to use them. If you are still uncertain as to whether your friend came to SKS, I can assure you there are no other similar clubs around here."

Tessa stood still, irritated to discover how nonplussed she was by the situation, and the fact that she was indeed fascinated by the swords.

"So would you like to come in, or would you prefer to continue considering your options outside? " he murmured. "However, if you like looking at swords such as these," he gestured again towards the window display, "perhaps you would enjoy making a closer inspection?"

For a moment Tessa was unsure what to do. But deep down, she knew she was too inquisitive to resist the temptation to go in. To find out what this place was like on the inside, even hold the swords from the display, was too good an offer to refuse.

"Well, maybe just a quick look. I wouldn't want to inconvenience you. But first, who are you … if you don't mind my asking?"

He laughed.

"No, I don't mind at all. My Japanese name is a bit difficult to pronounce in English, so I use the name Lee, although my students call me Master Lee, or Sensei. I founded this establishment many years ago when I first came to England from Japan. Now SKS is one of only five schools in the UK licensed to give lessons on how to use samurai swords and prepare students for the Samurai Proficiency Tests."

"OK, let's go in then. However, I do have some other commitments this afternoon, so I mustn't stay too long."

"Of course, I quite understand."

With another graceful sweep of his hand, Master Lee beckoned

Tessa to lead the way. Two large burgundy-painted wooden doors filled the imposing archway. As Tessa turned to face them, the left-hand door swung open to reveal a muscular teenage boy. He was sweating and appeared not to have shaved for several days. He was dressed in a burgundy-coloured tunic tied with a red cord. She smiled at him, but he simply looked past her and bowed, saying respectfully, "Good afternoon, Master Lee."

The door closed behind them and Tessa saw that they were standing in a sizeable, if dimly lit, room. There was just enough light for her to see that the walls were of exposed brickwork. The original old timber rafters were visible high above and the floor was of well-worn wooden blocks.

"Yes, it is a bit dark, isn't it?" observed Master Lee. "But we teach people how to fight to survive, and they are not always able to choose the conditions of conflict. So, without warning, we vary the environment between extremes. Let me give you a quick tour. This is our main practice area…"

Tessa watched several youths sparring. Suddenly one of them outsmarted an opponent and yelled "Yield!" as his sword hovered in a threatening position. The defeated combatant took a pace back and bowed. It made Tessa think of the wounds on Penny's body, and she shivered.

"Are you all right?" asked Lee.

"Yes, of course," she replied indignantly, surprised he had noticed the slight reaction.

"Very well. Obviously, to ensure safety we have strict rules as to how many students may be active with swords at any one time. All must wear tunics in our school colour, which is also that of my clan. The colour of their cord belt indicates their level of training. There are seven levels, starting with red and finishing with violet, but we don't tend to see many of those. There are none in the UK at the moment, apart from mine."

As he continued talking, Tessa's eyes became accustomed to the light and she looked round in amazement. Positioned at the edges of the room, in order to leave as much clear space as possible in the centre, were examples of every conceivable type of exercise equipment. Opposite the entrance was a slightly raised podium, in the middle of which stood a luxurious rococo armchair, beautifully upholstered in thick burgundy velvet.

"Yes," continued Lee, "that is where I sit. From there I can watch how people are progressing and assess their frame of mind. It is that which is most important in shaping a successful Samurai. Physical fitness and prowess with a weapon are indeed taught here, but we take those for granted. It is the warrior's mind-set and ability to sense their enemy's weaknesses which makes the real difference, and it is that which is the most difficult thing to learn. At least, that part which is not instinctive."

"Are you suggesting it isn't possible to teach people to achieve beyond the skill level they are born with? Isn't that elitist?"

"To a degree, yes," he replied with an enigmatic smile. "But only insofar as one would not expect everyone to be capable of becoming a virtuoso violinist or a world-class mountaineer. Often people's true capabilities only become apparent after a considerable amount of teaching, training and sacrifice; although one can sense when innate skills are present. Call it elitism if you like, but that is how it is in most aspects of life, no matter what people say. I teach fighters to recognise and develop their skills to the maximum extent possible, honing both their instincts and their intuition. Fortunately, if perhaps surprisingly, it is easy early on to test the likely level of skill which someone will be able to attain in our discipline."

He looked at Tessa with a query in his eyes. This time she knew precisely what he was thinking and was quick to respond.

"No way! We never discussed that. I only agreed to come in for a quick tour and to hold those swords." She glanced towards the display window, which she noticed was obscured behind thick burgundy velvet curtains. "I didn't agree to sit any test, or to let you make a fool of me."

Lee roared with laughter.

"So you do have opinions after all! Well, I am sure you will not be made to look foolish. In fact, I suspect quite the opposite. Concerning the swords … actually, I didn't say you could hold those in the display. I simply said, swords such as those."

Now it was Tessa's turn to laugh.

"Oh, now, that's not fair! You know perfectly well I came in expecting to hold the swords in the display, but you wanted me to come in and sit your test. It seems we have a stand-off."

"Indeed," said Lee, clearly enjoying the exchange.

"Well, not to worry, I'll just leave while I'm ahead."

He laughed again.

"Wonderful ... and you would too, wouldn't you! Such resolve. But please don't go. I thought you wanted to find out whether your friend was spending time here?"

"I did. But there are other ways."

"All right, how about a compromise? I will let you hold one of the swords from the display if you agree to take my test?" suggested Lee, holding out his hand, clearly hoping to seal the deal with a handshake.

Tessa grinned as her confidence began to return. She kept her hands firmly by her sides.

"Tell me more about the test first."

He chuckled.

"Very well! It's very simple and doesn't take long at all – less than ten minutes, in fact. You just have to use a sword to demonstrate your speed and manual dexterity in a way which shows how instinctive and intuitive your reactions are. I'm sure you'll enjoy it. Everyone does."

Tessa looked doubtful.

"This test involves using a real sword?"

"Yes, but don't worry, it's not dangerous. In fact, it is best done by those with no previous experience," continued Lee, convinced he had won her over.

"Hmm. OK, I will take your test, *provided* I can use one of the swords in the display. After all, you did say it wasn't dangerous."

Lee realised there was more to this woman than had first been apparent. He hesitated for a moment, and then smiled.

"You know, it never used to be this difficult. How about this? The swords in the display are extremely valuable. But I will let you use one for the test if you choose the only sword in the display which is the correct length for you. Otherwise I will select another sword, possibly not from the display. That should avoid unnecessary damage to either you or the sword. Agreed?"

Tessa was beginning to grow bored with his prevarication.

"One in three sounds lousy odds, but let's just get on with it, shall we?"

"Excellent," said Lee, as they finally shook hands. "So, which sword would you choose?"

Tessa fixed her eyes on him and, without hesitation, replied, "Oh, the quietly confident one in the middle of the rack, please. I know it's the plainest of the three, but somehow it's still the most elegant."

He chuckled and, graceful in defeat, bowed his head.

"An inspired choice. I will get it for you."

A spontaneous hush spread throughout the practice room. While Tessa wondered why, Lee glanced round imperiously. This was enough to prompt everyone to resume their training.

He walked over to the display and pulled the curtains aside, revealing a grey slatted security screen. He pressed some buttons on a small keypad and there was a loud metallic *clunk* as the screen unlocked and started to rattle slowly upwards. One by one the swords became visible. Tessa thought how much more beautiful they looked when viewed unobstructed by the grille. Apart from Lee, everyone seemed transfixed by the sight. As the screen reached the top, there was another noisy *clunk* and it stopped.

Lee leaned over and gently picked the black-sheathed sword off the rack. As he moved back from the window area, he pressed another button and the security screen started to close. He walked purposefully over to Tessa, handling the sword with what appeared to be something close to reverence as an old Japanese man closed the curtains.

Lee stopped in front of Tessa.

"I am not surprised this sword spoke to you. It does not have a long history, but was commissioned by someone who knew it was not their own destiny to use it. However, I suspect they would be very pleased to see you holding it now."

Tessa wasn't listening, completely absorbed in studying the sword which she now realised she was desperate to hold in her own hands. She tore her gaze away from it and looked at Lee. Holding it horizontal in both hands, he stretched out his arms and offered it to her with a bow.

"Are you sure I should be doing this?" murmured Tessa. "I'm not exactly correctly dressed and this sword is so incredibly beautiful,

80

I would hate to damage it … And besides," she continued, glancing round, "everyone seems to be watching."

"Ignore them, just take the sword. Let's see if *it* also likes *you*."

Very carefully, Tessa took the sword from him. She immediately knew her initial assessment of the weapon's beauty had been wildly understated. True it appeared plain, but its very simplicity was intoxicating, and although the sword didn't feel heavy, it didn't feel light either. It felt just right. The sheath did have a matt black lacquer finish but, as she had noticed earlier, this possessed an uncanny depth. Looking at it was like staring into a mirror but seeing no reflection. There were six narrow black shiny ridges running along the length of the sheath. Four of these were located in pairs near the rounded corners of the sheath, while the other two ran up the centre of the front and back respectively. However, while the line on the back of the sheath ran from end to end, the one on the front stopped for about six inches near the top. She wondered whether she would ever be able to give the sword back.

"This is so beautiful … I can't find words to describe it!"

"Indeed," replied Lee, in a soft tone. "It is a very special weapon. Please unsheathe the blade and check it for length and weight. But I think you will find it is very comfortable to hold."

He moved away and Tessa took a deep breath before slowly unsheathing the sword. As she did so there was a gentle hiss as finely made surfaces slid over one another until the blade was fully drawn. Immediately a soft yet menacing ringing sound pervaded the room. The sword felt perfect in her hands. It could be moved through the air with ease, and yet stopped with consummate accuracy.

Lee smiled as though something important had just happened. Tessa looked at him quizzically, but he didn't say anything, so she carefully re-sheathed the blade. She turned the sword over in her hands, quickly becoming familiar with its weight and balance. He had been right; it suited her well. Then she noticed some black film obscuring the top part of the sheath and also part of the hand guard.

"Ah, you noticed," he said with a smile. "Let's have a look underneath, shall we?"

He reached over and peeled off the lower of two pieces of film on the front of the sheath.

Tessa's eyes widened. Beneath the film was the most beautiful black-and-gold scene of a tiger in a bamboo tree, together with a resplendent white and gold chrysanthemum flower. The intricate designs were beautifully worked and a wonder to behold. She hesitated to speak, and Lee looked at her curiously.

"Are you sure you're all right?"

"Yes, yes. Sorry, I was miles away… This is gorgeous," she continued. "What fantastic workmanship, and such a wonderful decoration! It's so life-like. The tiger looks as though it's sizing up its prey."

Lee smiled.

"It is the maker's mark. The family which forged this weapon has been making swords for many hundreds of years. They always label their swords this way. The design above is the signature of the family member who made it."

"You mean, there's more decoration?"

"Yes, a lot more," he said, peeling off the next piece of film to expose the most exquisite golden flower. Tessa had never bothered to learn much about flowers, she simply admired them. But compared to all the flowers she had seen before, this one was truly stunning.

"Oh, my!" she exclaimed. "That's magnificent. So vibrant."

"Indeed. It's a depiction of a rare orchid, *Masdevallia norops* to be precise. It is found only high in the mountains of Ecuador and Peru."

"I'm lost for words," replied Tessa, holding the sheath closer so she could study the detail. "It's a remarkable combination of beauty and menace; sublime, sinister, and … well, just a little bit seductive. Almost in an erotic sense."

Lee laughed.

"How interesting. My wife said much the same the first time she saw it."

The flower design was about one and a half inches in length. Again it protruded slightly from the side of the sheath, although it felt smooth to the touch. Tessa discovered that the more she looked at it, the more intricate she found it.

"It's quite something, isn't it?" continued Lee. "Different types of gold are used for the flower's petals while the stem's green colour is made from fine particles of emerald suspended in gold. Quite unique. And that is the care she was willing to take with just her signature."

Tessa's ears pricked up. He smiled.

"Yes, that's right; the maker of this sword is a woman. Shall we continue? There is more to discover."

Tessa nodded, desperate to see what other secrets the sword would reveal. Lee removed some more of the black film from underneath the hand guard. That exposed yet another exquisite design, this time of a golden eagle swooping down with talons outstretched, one either side of the back edge of the sword blade.

She shook her head in disbelief.

"Goodness, this is so fantastically beautiful and terrifying all at the same time. And I thought this sword plain in comparison to the others! In fact, its beauty far outshines theirs."

"I will let you remove the last piece of film yourself," said Lee. "I think you will find beneath it the most interesting design of all."

"Shouldn't we keep the pieces, so we can put them back later?" suggested Tessa. "The designs are so wonderful, surely they should continue to be protected?"

"It is not necessary for you to do that."

She turned the sword up to reveal the remaining piece of black film on the upper surface of the hand guard. It was shaped like a rounded, slightly inflated square.

"That is called the tsuba," said Lee. "Its purpose is to stop the holder's hand from accidentally slipping on to the blade, while also offering protection from an assailant's blade, should one slide down the sword. However, the tsuba is often highly decorated, as testimony not only to the skill of the sword-maker, but also to the quality of the weapon."

Tessa found herself hesitating as she wondered what further example of the maker's sublime artistry would be exposed. She looked at Lee, then summoning all her courage, carefully peeled away the final piece of film.

As the design on top of the tsuba was revealed, Tessa couldn't stop herself from sucking in her breath. She saw another superlative design, this time of a female Samurai warrior, wielding in her right hand what was presumably the sword Tessa was now holding. The warrior woman was riding a fearsome dragon which was swooping down through storm clouds into battle. Again the design was in black metal embossed with yet more gold in a variety of subtle shades. As

Tessa looked more closely, she started to admire the black-and-gold detail on the woman's kimono and raised the sword slightly so she could study it more closely. She looked at the woman's short flowing golden hair. Then she looked at her face – and jumped in surprise. She stared hard at it.

"Mr Lee," she said, "this woman looks a bit…" She stopped abruptly, thinking how impertinent it would be to suggest that the warrior's face bore a resemblance to her own.

"Remarkable, isn't it?" he observed. "Anyway, enough of admiring the sword. Now you have to keep your part of the bargain."

"I'm sorry, I can't use this," said Tessa, shaking her head. "It's too … well … too everything."

She was petrified at the thought of damaging the sword, which was clearly an extremely valuable work of art. For a moment she wondered whether she should change her mind completely and beat a hasty, if undignified, retreat. But Lee radiated reassurance.

"I am sure you won't damage it … but in all fairness you should honour our bargain by taking the test seriously. So, may I suggest you first take off your jacket? It will allow you to move your arms more freely. Then clear your mind of all distractions and focus on winning. If you were fighting a battle, there would be plenty of sights and sounds, and probably none of them would be particularly pleasant. You would have to ignore them all, just as now you should ignore everything else here. Simply perform the test to the best of your ability."

"Hmm, well, just for the record, I'm not into fighting. Quite the opposite, in fact."

Lee smiled as Tessa carefully handed the sword back to him and slipped off her jacket, revealing her bright red silk blouse. He motioned to the old man who was watching quietly from a seat near the door. He came over and with a bow took Tessa's jacket and handbag, placing them carefully by Lee's chair on the podium.

Lee himself moved forward and bowed again as he offered the sword back to Tessa. She took it with both hands and bowed back to him.

She followed him to a far corner of the room, to the right of the podium, entering an area which, much to her relief, had a high wall round it. But then she found it contained a large caged space, which made her feel nervous again.

"Don't worry, it will be fine. Let me show you what to do."

Lee turned and in Japanese addressed the old man who had followed them. He returned carrying a wide black canvas belt with some buckles and cords on it. Lee took it from the old man, unlatched the gate and led Tessa through; she kicked her shoes off by the entrance, and removed her knee-high stockings.

"Excuse me," said Lee as he knelt down to strap the belt around her waist. "The sword will be slid through this and tied to it. Beginners' belts are a bit cumbersome, but provide protection if, in the heat of the moment, you miss the sheath."

Tessa swallowed as a combination of thoughts flowed through her mind. The incredible beauty of the sword was intoxicating; she felt honoured to have been allowed even to hold it. But it was still a weapon of violence, which she abhorred, especially after having seen the sword wounds which had killed poor Penny. To use such a weapon to perform a beginner's test seemed madness, even if the confidence Lee exuded appeared limitless. Nerves began to get the better of her and she wished she'd gone for lunch instead of letting curiosity take over. Nevertheless, she had given her word, so she would have to go through with it. And besides, no matter how strange, the test was intriguing; her competitive side wanted to know whether she would be any good at it.

Lee helped her attach the sword to the belt and explained to her how its position and height could be adjusted.

"Now, when you draw the sword, grip the top of the sheath with your left hand and rotate it outwards a little, so the blade edge moves away from you. At the same time, push the tsuba up slightly with your thumb to break the seal and present the sword hilt to your right hand. Then, taking care to keep your fingers out of the way, simply draw the sword as quickly as you can. When you return the sword to its hilt, line up the back edge of the blade against the hole in the sheath. If you want, you can cup the thumb and forefinger of your left hand to help guide the blade, and then slide it back. You will find twisting your torso away from the sheath will help. Don't underestimate the difficulty of re-sheathing the blade; it is nowhere near as easy as drawing it."

Lee moved towards the old man standing just outside the cage.

Tessa interpreted this as an opportunity for her to practise drawing the sword. As quickly as she could, she drew it and held it out in front of her. There was a loud ringing of steel. With surprising speed and agility, Lee sprang away from her. Without looking, and using her left hand only to steady the sheath, she nonchalantly re-housed the blade.

"Sorry, wasn't I meant to do that?" she asked.

"Not really … there is something else you should recognise about this sword. It is sharper than anything you have ever known. If you just touch the blade, no matter how lightly, it will cut you."

The old man gave Lee a flake of gold leaf and he gestured for Tessa to unsheathe the sword a second time. Again a gentle hissing sound ensued, creating an air of foreboding as prelude to the menacing ringing. She noticed this time that the blade was not shiny; it was a dull grey with two subtle wavy lines running up it. But it had a lustre so deep she could see her own reflection in it. When her arm reached a comfortable degree of extension, the blade left the sheath and the ringing started.

She carefully moved the sword out in front of her, holding it only with her right hand. Gripping the hilt about a third of the way down from the tsuba, she put her left hand on it too. The sword felt perfectly comfortable when held with only one hand, but with two she could exert much more force. She was amazed by how relaxed she felt and was only jolted back to reality by an exclamation from Lee.

"Excellent! As I suspected you have a strong natural talent for this. Anyway, hold the blade upwards and perfectly still."

She complied with a quick flick of her wrist which made the blade twang in response. As it came vertical Lee reached over and, peeling the flake of gold leaf off its backing tissue, let it gently float towards the blade. The gold leaf was so thin and so light it wafted from side to side as it slowly fell. Tessa stood completely still and was convinced the blade was not moving, although try as she might she could not stop it ringing. Finally the gold leaf gently drifted on to the cutting edge and instantly became two pieces. Tessa watched in amazement.

"Wow, that is sharp," she acknowledged. "Are you sure I won't hurt myself, or anyone else for that matter?"

"Quite sure," said Lee with a smile. "Besides, if all goes well, I expect to be on the outside of the cage soon. Now," he continued before she could say anything else, "return the sword to its sheath, please."

Tessa dutifully slid the sword back, surprising herself by the ease with which she was able to handle it and get the point of the blade into the tight-fitting hole at the top of the sheath. She sighed. It seemed the sword possessed an enthusiasm all of its own to be out.

"Hah," chuckled Lee. "I was going to demonstrate how to re-sheathe the sword correctly, but it seems you already know. Do you like holding it?"

"Like is not the right word, it's a wonderful sensation," she admitted. "It's fantastic! The weight, the balance, the artistry are all perfect. Please thank the owner very much for letting me use it. I hope they won't mind."

"Trust me, they'll be delighted to have it so appreciated. By the way, are you still all right for time?" he asked, grinning. "You mentioned some other commitments."

"Oh, yes, don't worry, they can wait," replied Tessa, forgetting that she was hungry and not even looking at him as she spoke. She was too busy savouring every moment she held the sword.

"Good," he said, smiling as he watched her adjusting the way the weapon was slung with remarkable ease. "Let me tell you more about the test: it is little more than a race against the clock. I'll describe what you need to do and, while you think about it, I'll fit the sword's sheath with a sensor to detect when the blade leaves and returns. When you are ready, simply draw the sword to start the clock, and after the test, return it to the sheath to stop it.

"The test is very simple. All you need to do is to strike the seven pieces of rolled straw and bamboo which you see on the stands over there. You will need to move forward to reach them. The first four are in pairs, to your left and to your right. The final three are at the end. All the rolls are of different heights. You should try to cut them where they are marked with a white band, and not to knock any of the stands over. After the last roll has been struck, return the sword to its sheath and the test is over. Is that clear so far?"

"Yes … but what do you mean by *so far*?"

"Ah, well, we wouldn't want to make it too easy. You see, you will be blindfolded. Also, once you can't see, we will move the stands holding the bamboos. But you will hear the noise of them being moved, so you should be able to work out their new positions."

"Oh, no!" said Tessa in disbelief. "This is madness! What happens if I miss them all?"

"You accrue time penalties against your score," Lee told her with a smile. "As you will if you cut a bamboo outside its white band."

She took a deep breath, already starting to plan how she would move.

"Blindfolded?" she repeated in a trembling voice. "Wielding a two-foot-something razor blade?"

"That's right. Now, any more questions?" asked Lee. "If not, I'll fit the sensor and the blindfold, and leave the cage. Once I am out, and we have moved the bamboos, you can start the test whenever you like. But take all the time you want, there is no rush whatsoever. Start only when you feel ready."

"OK. But I'd like to practise drawing the sword a few times, if that's all right?"

Lee nodded and stepped well back while she drew the sword and replaced it several times. It didn't seem too difficult, so Tessa nodded, and he strapped the sensor to the sword sheath. Then he tied a thick burgundy-coloured blindfold over her eyes.

"How do you know I can't see?"

"We would know," he told her. "Just empty your mind of all other thoughts. Relax and listen carefully when we move the bamboos. Then just concentrate on cutting them all at the correct height."

"Right," replied Tessa, swallowing, realising the blindfold was very effective.

She heard Lee walk out of the cage and the *c-clunk* of the gate closing. She concentrated on the mental picture she had constructed of where the bamboos were located and listened carefully to the grating sounds of them being slid into new positions. She updated her mental map and was convinced she could see in her mind where all the bamboos now stood. She started taking deep breaths and tried to relax. Her thoughts were only of the sword by her side and of the bamboos.

She gripped the sword hilt and smiled as she convinced herself it also wanted her to excel at the test. In her mind's eye she again checked the distances between the bamboos and their heights from the ground, and took a final deep breath in preparation.

Drawing the sword as quickly as she could, she took a pace forward. The blade immediately started ringing as it swished through the air. A click announced she had hit something to her right, so she quickly swung the sword back to the left as she moved forward slightly. Another click resulted and she took two paces forward. She swung the sword to the right again and then back to the left. Surprised and overjoyed, she heard two more clicks in rapid succession. The sword continued to move effortlessly through the air, ringing merrily as it sped on. Feeling more confident, Tessa ran three steps, looping the sword round in the air as she moved. She brought it down to the left and, with an upward diagonal motion, swept the sword round. She felt three faint judders. She moved her right arm quickly up and slipped the sword straight back into its sheath. Like it or not, good or bad, she had finished.

With adrenaline coursing through her veins, she was still panting as Lee loosened her blindfold.

"There you are," he said, smiling. "It's all over and you didn't have any trouble returning the sword to its sheath."

"Oh," she said, looking down at the sword hilt. "Thank heavens for that. But I have to admit, I'm exhausted now."

"It is exhilarating, isn't it?"

"That's one way of putting it."

Tessa took a deep breath and smiled with relief. She was hesitant to survey the damage she had done but curiosity forced her to look at the bamboos. The first four had been cut and fallen to the floor, but the last three appeared to be intact. She remembered she had not heard any clicks as with the first four; presumably she had only nicked them.

"OK, tell me the worst. How bad was it?" she asked.

"Interesting actually," said Lee, as he led her to the cage door. "You will probably not be surprised to hear the fastest time we have recorded here is mine at 2.67 seconds. Our best student recorded a time of 2.83 seconds, but that was only after considerable training. In fact, anything quicker than 3 seconds is excellent, but we would not normally expect a student to be able to achieve such a time. Furthermore we would not enrol somebody if their time was slower than 4 seconds."

Tessa was hanging on his every word.

"So?"

Lee looked into her eyes and she felt as though he was scrutinising her soul.

"How difficult did you find the test?" he asked.

"Well, not as difficult as I thought it would be," she replied. "In my mind's eye, I could see where I thought the bamboos were, even after you'd moved them; and the sword was surprisingly easy to wield."

"I thought as much. You're no amateur, are you?"

"With a sword, yes, but I have studied Kenjutsu."

"And I'm sure you excelled, being so fit and supple. You managed to sever all the pieces of bamboo within the white bands so there are no penalties, and you managed to re-sheathe the sword quickly, first time. That is all very good and extremely unusual."

"Thanks, but I only seem to have cut the first four bamboos," Tessa replied, worried she was about to accrue lots of penalties.

"Really?" said Lee with a smile. "You need to take into account the fact you were getting much faster and more confident towards the end. Also the sword you were wielding so competently is a truly remarkable weapon. Watch."

He stamped his foot hard on the floor and both of them looked towards the end of the test area. The final three pieces of bamboo wobbled and then all the tops fell to the floor with a clatter.

"Now there's a thing," observed Tessa proudly.

"Quite so," continued Lee. "You recorded a time of 2.79 seconds, which is very fast indeed, especially for a first attempt."

Tessa looked at him dumbfounded. Part of her had wanted to do well, the part that always drove her to succeed at anything she tried. But she'd never expected to achieve anything as good as that and wasn't even sure it was wise to have done so. She looked for the clock to check.

Lee chuckled.

"I'll show you the clock on the way out, but there were no tricks. You can't be that surprised, surely? You must know you have quick reactions – very quick in fact – and that, of course, is essential for a good outcome. However, a result such as yours indicates considerable innate talent. With training it is normally possible to improve on an initial test result by between ten and twenty per cent, so you could be much faster than me one day."

Tessa laughed nervously.

"That sounds a little far-fetched"

"Well," continued Lee, "I told you it was a special sword, and in the right hands capable of remarkable feats. You just proved that, and a few other things besides. If you have the time, why don't I ask my wife to make us some tea? It will help you relax, and then, if you are interested, I could tell you about this sword and the person who made it. But you should take it off now, please."

Tessa nodded and with great reluctance removed the weapon. In just those few minutes, it already seemed to have become a part of her.

CHAPTER 10

Lee led Tessa through a door to the left of the podium and along a corridor. As the noise and light of the practice room faded behind them, she began to feel more normal again, and wondered why she had agreed to go with him. Then they entered a room decorated in traditional Japanese style. Here the whole atmosphere was of calm, order and consummate beauty. Tatami mats covered the floor, helping to emphasise the exquisite lines of the sparse but functional furniture. Automatically, Tessa kicked off her shoes by the low step at the entrance and slipped into one of the pairs of sandals neatly lined up for guests. The wall to her right comprised a full-length window looking out on to a carefully manicured Japanese garden. She had always felt very much at ease with Japanese culture. Its long history, prizing of ordered neatness and emphasis on personal honour, all attracted and intrigued her.

"I would never have expected to find such a lovely Japanese home in the middle of South Kensington," she said, smiling.

"Thank you," replied Lee.

Tessa knelt down by the low black lacquer table, first resting one knee on the *zabuton*, then the other, and finally shifting round to face Lee. To her left was a decorative alcove with a bonsai tree in it, above which hung a scroll inscribed with Zen calligraphy, reading: *Reason and hope – tools of dignity.* She could hear the burbling of a miniature waterfall flowing into a pond outside where she could see flashes of gold and orange as several large fish darted beneath the surface.

"Koi?" she asked in amazement.

"Yes. Japanese *nishikigoi* to be precise."

Then Lee spoke softly towards a closed door behind him.

Soon afterwards a Japanese woman entered the room via the sliding door. Dressed in a beautiful hand-decorated yellow kimono, her black hair gathered tightly behind her head, she carried a tray on which stood two finely decorated Japanese cups and a matching teapot. She bowed as she put the tray down to the left of Lee, and smiled at Tessa.

"This is my wife," he said.

"I'm pleased to meet you," said Tessa, her rusty Japanese prompting a polite smile from Lee, and a bow from his wife.

"Please, forgive the informality but my wife will prepare the tea for us," continued Lee.

Tessa nodded as his wife knelt down in silence and placed in front of each of them a plate with a Japanese red bean sweet on it and a narrow wooden fork. Then she whisked two cups of powdered green tea, setting them down carefully in front of Lee and Tessa. Finally, she bowed and gracefully reversed out of the room. Tessa waited for Lee to indicate she should start. As he nodded, she followed his example and ate the sweet. Then she placed the cup in her left palm and gently gave it two quarter turns clockwise with her right hand, to ensure the design was facing Lee. She lifted it with both hands and took a sip. She liked *macha* tea, especially when hand-made from powder. This tasted particularly good, although she still struggled to make a convincing slurping noise as she took her third and final drink.

"I see you know how to drink Japanese green tea," mused Lee. "Are you hungry?"

"A little," replied Tessa, still admiring the room and garden.

"Do you eat sushi?"

"Oh, yes, I love Japanese food," she replied.

Again Lee gently spoke in the direction of the sliding door. Soon his wife reappeared, carrying a tray with glasses of water and two wooden boards with a variety of sushi arranged on each.

"Will this be sufficient?"

"Most definitely, it looks wonderful. Thank you," replied Tessa, waiting for Lee to pick up his chopsticks before she picked up hers. She was delicately biting through the first piece of fatty tuna when the old man entered. He bowed and started to set the samurai sword which Tessa had just used in the middle of the table. He stood it on a beautifully carved black wooden stand which supported it lengthways with the sheath designs facing Tessa. He bowed again, and left the room.

Lee carried on eating as though nothing had happened. But Tessa couldn't resist admiring the sword again. It was as though she was hypnotised by it. The more she studied it, the more she appreciated the mastery of its maker. She forced herself to continue eating her lunch, serenaded by the gentle gurgling of the waterfall in the garden. When they had finished eating, their trays were removed and a pot of green leaf tea left on the table with two fresh porcelain cups.

Lee looked up at her and smiled.

"So you were wondering whether your friend comes here. What is her name?"

"Penny Reid," replied Tessa, concentrating on returning her cup to its saucer without making a noise.

"I thought so … Yoshino," he said with a satisfied smile. "Like Peacekeepers, all SKS students are addressed only by a single Japanese name. My wife's father chooses the names here according to his instincts concerning the student. How is Yoshino? I haven't seen her for a long time."

"I'm afraid you won't be seeing her again," said Tessa as, much to her annoyance, her eyes started to water. "She's dead."

Lee looked shocked.

"That's terrible. How did she die?"

"She was murdered several months ago. It wasn't widely reported in the media but she was brutally killed and no one really knows why. The police think she must have been attacked by a gang, due to the number and severity of the wounds she suffered. In the end, she was killed by a single sword cut across her abdomen."

Lee sighed and for a moment looked down at the table to hide his grief.

"I am sorry. Despite not being a particularly gifted student, Yoshino demonstrated considerable commitment and enthusiasm in her studies here. But, as time went by, it became clear that something troubled her. She started focusing on self-defence, and what she lacked in instinctive skill, she tried hard to compensate for through determination and persistence. She would never give up trying to learn something, no matter how difficult she found it." He hesitated. "I presume you are Tessa?"

"Yes," she replied, reaching into her handbag for a tissue.

"Yoshino talked about you a lot," said Lee, as she dabbed her eyes. "I know you were very close and had shared, and overcome, many adversities together. For her to be so cruelly deprived of life is indeed a terrible crime. I will grieve for her also…

"However, as I said earlier, ability such as you have just exhibited does not often occur. The test is a surprisingly accurate predictor and you have just recorded the fastest time of any student who ever joined this school. You have considerable potential. I hope you appreciate it would be a waste for you not to develop your skill. The correct training will not only provide you with a stimulating and rewarding way to keep fit, but will also enable you to harness your newfound prowess for a purpose. If you wanted that."

He paused while Tessa, unmoved by his steady gaze, returned it with steely determination. She was quite capable of giving as good as she got.

"I'll come straight to the point," continued Lee. "I would like you to join one of my classes. It would be purely on a trial basis, but it would at least give you the opportunity to find out whether you like sword-fighting. Personally I am sure you would enjoy it, and you would learn some new skills and disciplines as well as getting fit. It would not take too much of your time."

Tessa smiled at him.

"Look, I'm extremely grateful for the warm hospitality shown to me by you and your wife. But, although this test of yours was *interesting*, and I admit it was wonderful to use the sword – and please don't forget to thank the owner, by the way – I have absolutely no desire whatsoever to enrol on a training course. Penny was into all that, and look where it got her. As for the purpose you referred to, I presume that would involve hurting people, and I prefer to leave that to others."

Tessa had been expecting him to try and enrol her but, much as she liked the sword, this was the end of it for her. Although she did understand better now why Penny had been attracted to this place, she would be more pragmatic. The life expectancy of International Peacekeepers was ludicrously short, especially when compared to that of rich pacifist cowards such as herself. She had worked hard to be successful in business, and intended to enjoy the fruits of her labours. Besides, she remained unconvinced as to the validity of the test.

"But you already keep fit, don't you?" parried Lee.

"Yes, I have my other activities like Kenjutsu and I run round Hyde Park whenever I can, usually for an hour or so."

"OK. Then instead of spending time in the park, why don't you spend it with me?"

"I run when it is convenient for me. Sometimes very early in the morning, and other times when I can fit it in."

"Then my contribution to this arrangement will be to ensure I am always available whenever you wish to spend time here," he countered. "That way you have absolutely nothing to lose, and possibly something to gain."

"That was a good try. But playing around with an incredibly sharp long knife doesn't sound anything other than extremely dangerous to me."

She reached for her handbag in anticipation of leaving.

"It is not playing," retorted Lee, a touch of indignation in his voice. "Using a sword such as this is many things, but it is *never* playing."

"I'm sorry, I didn't mean to trivialise your art. It's just that I am not a violent person. And besides I can't for a moment believe the owner of this wonderful weapon would be willing to allow me to use it for training."

She was trying hard to smooth over an awkward situation with a response which she hoped would curtail the conversation.

Lee nodded.

"I see. But what if I said I was sure the owner would allow you to use this sword for training?"

Tessa chuckled as she realised her attempt to evade further conversation had been frustrated. She enjoyed these verbal tussles with Lee; he wouldn't let her get away with anything. However, the time had come for her to be more brutal. Then her gaze fell on the sword, and suddenly she wasn't so sure. After all, she did want to invest some of her now plentiful free time in getting properly fit, and the prospect of something new did attract her... What he proposed was appealing, and might be a bit of a laugh if nothing else.

"Well, that sounds very generous, but as a beginner I wouldn't be using the sword much anyway, would I?" she said, realising she had unwittingly given away considerable ground.

"With your instinctive skills, you wouldn't be a beginner for long."

"Do you really think the owner would let me borrow that sword? It's so beautiful, it must be extremely valuable. Suppose I damaged it?"

"Ah, yes, I promised to tell you all about the sword, didn't I? But I think we should decide on your training first. It looks as though we need another of your *deals*. How about if I ensure you have unlimited use of the sword, and you agree to train with me for at least ten hours a week, for ten weeks?" He looked at her expectantly.

"I don't know whether I can make such a commitment," she faltered. "I wouldn't want to start something and not finish it."

There was a pause as he appeared unsure what to say next.

"Well, do you intend to train with me or not?" he asked finally. "I would like to know before I continue."

Tessa gave him a wry smile.

"I feel as though I'm being ambushed again."

"If you were ambushed before it didn't turn out so badly, did it? Serendipity alone did not bring you here, of that I am sure."

"I'm sorry, I just don't feel…"

Tessa was on the verge of demurring when she looked at the sword again. Her whole body and soul were overcome with a yearning to hold it, and without thinking she reached over and picked it up. She marvelled at the feel of it but couldn't understand why a weapon, a means of violence after all, could exert such a powerful influence over her. She studied it closely, shaking her head as she admired the flawless detailing of its decoration. Her right hand started to pull the sword from its sheath. Lee sat motionless, watching her every movement. A moment later the blade was drawn and the confident ringing sound filled the room. Tessa shook her head from side to side in wonder.

"Wow! I wish I knew why I'm so attracted to this," she mumbled, not talking to anyone in particular. She re-sheathed the sword and reluctantly returned it to the stand. "It is an absolutely incredible thing, but …" She paused to consider how best to decline Lee's offer. Then all at once it seemed as though Penny was whispering in her ear: "Tessa, do this for me, please."

"Well," started Lee. "How about if…"

"All right, I agree," interrupted Tessa, almost surprising herself with the speed of her outburst. "If I can use this sword, I'll sign up for ten hours a week, at my convenience, for ten weeks."

"Excellent," replied Lee, surprised by her abrupt pronouncement but delighted nevertheless. "I am sure you have made the right decision.

What's more, I am sure Yoshino would be pleased too. Very pleased indeed, in fact."

"Well, I hope you're right," whinged Tessa, still reeling from having agreed to commit herself to ten weeks of something she wasn't sure she wanted to do. But at least she'd get fit; and Lee still had to secure permission for her to use the sword.

"Now I will tell you about this remarkable weapon and its already remarkable history."

He paused for a moment to refill their cups.

"More than a thousand years ago in Japan, Keitaro Amakuni started making samurai swords. He took on an apprentice, Tatsuya Amafuji; but as soon as Tatsuya thought he had learnt enough, he left and set up the Amafuji forge. Both families' swords quickly became acknowledged as the best one could buy anywhere in the world. However, much to the consternation of the Amafuji, it was always accepted that Amakuni swords were the absolute best. Originally, both families had forges near Iga Ueno, close to Nara. However, when the capital moved to Kyoto, the Amafuji followed, re-establishing their forge in the hills to the north-west. But the Amakuni felt their process, which remains secret to this day, and their local materials, were so unique they preferred to stay near Iga Ueno."

"I've been there," interjected Tessa as Lee sipped his tea. "It's not the easiest of places to get to, but well worth the effort."

"Indeed it is and the Amakuni family still thrives there. The current Master is Kimi Amakuni and she has two apprentices. But I suspect the Amafuji family will soon stop making swords as the last of their long line is old and has no apprentices. The final swords he made were a matching pair commissioned by an American woman on the occasion of her marriage. Those swords, generally accepted to have been his finest, have since been lost..."

"They're probably buried in someone's private collection," mused Tessa.

"I doubt it. Those swords are far too good to be just trophies. It is more likely they're being used, we just don't know by whom. Anyway, the Amakuni family has always been very selective about whom it will allow to commission a sword and Kimi Amakuni is no exception. The same cannot be said of the Amafuji. They fell out of favour after the

Meiji Restoration in the late-1860s, mainly because they supported the previously ruling and eventually defeated Tokugawa Shogunate. The Amakuni, however, supplied their weapons to the victorious Satsuma-Chōshū Alliance and the Emperor. In assisting him, their family secured a very special status, shared by only one other who fought with and protected the Emperor during this dangerous time. Even today these two families are revered throughout Japan and are alone in being able to include the Imperial chrysanthemum within their family crests. It is the stylised flower which stands with the pouncing tiger logo on that sword.

"At the time there were two million Samurai in Japan, but only the most influential secured weapons from either the Amakuni or Amafuji families. When the fighting finally stopped, industrialisation helped bring about the abolition of the Samurai class. This prompted some families to resort to crime in order to maintain their high standard of living and they found that only the Amafuji were willing to supply them. The others were determined to uphold the law, and obtained their weapons from the Amakuni. This only helped fuel the feud which had already developed between two of the most powerful Samurai families in Japan. That feud still continues today…"

Lee paused for a moment, lost in sad reminiscence.

"It is an Amakuni tradition that the Master makes the entire sword; each one takes a long time. This makes the swords very rare and very expensive – assuming one is permitted to commission one in the first place. Most people fortunate enough to have such a sword would never dream of parting with it, or at least not of their own volition."

Lee smiled and took a deep breath as Tessa waited expectantly, totally absorbed in his story.

"Suffice it to say, Amakuni and Amafuji swords have earned their reputation by being the supreme examples of their kind. They are weapons of violence but, as you see, they are also works of art…"

Tessa nodded in agreement.

"Now, one day Yoshino came to me saying she wanted to purchase a sword, a good sword, the very best money could buy. I remember the conversation well. As gently as I could, I pointed out that since she didn't even have a Restricted Carrying Licence, she wouldn't be allowed to take the sword home. We almost argued about it, but eventually I acquiesced and promised to help her. I asked her what sort of weapon she wished to purchase… Hah! It is not easy to surprise me, but Yoshino did that day. She told me she wanted an Amakuni sword. I was amazed she even knew the name as it is hardly ever mentioned, even among experts, and I still don't know how she came across it…

"Anyway, with the recent changes in international law and the creation of International Peacekeepers, the problem of weapons supply has become exacerbated. Sword-fighting experts appreciate only too well that a skilled person armed with one of these swords can become extremely powerful. So, given Yoshino's unknown status and relatively low skill level, there was no doubt in my mind Kimi Amakuni would not normally consider making a weapon for her. I told Yoshino all of this, but she was not in the slightest deterred. She understood she would never be proficient enough to justify owning such a sword herself, but assured me she knew someone who would. But she wouldn't tell me who that person was. The more I asked, the more she reiterated I would just have to trust her judgement for once. Well, I don't know why, but I decided I would…"

Tessa was beginning to get a bad feeling about the direction this story was taking.

"It just so happens the Amakuni family has been friends with mine for many generations. So I contacted Kimi Amakuni and asked if she would make a sword for Yoshino. I described the situation and, not surprisingly, Kimi-san refused at first. However, eventually I managed to persuade her; but only after I promised to keep the sword here and never give it to anyone who was not responsible and skilled enough to wield it with honour. Shortly afterwards a deal was done and Yoshino transferred the funds to Japan."

"So how much did it cost?"

"Oh, a lot. An awful lot! Yoshino wanted some refinements; the armoured sheath for example, and the rather special decoration on the tsuba. Beautiful, isn't it?"

Tessa nodded, her sense of unease growing exponentially.

"I don't know the final price paid, but I do know it was quite a bit more than the three million initially discussed."

"Three million Yen?" asked Tessa. "Fifteen thousand pounds doesn't

100

sound much for a work of art like this.

Lee rocked slightly with amusement.

"Pounds sterling *not* Yen," he said quietly.

Tessa's eyes widened in disbelief.

"What! Three million pounds? That's a vast amount of money."

"Well, for an ordinary sword maybe, but for a sword such as this, it is not at all unreasonable. You need to understand there are swords, good swords, and excellent swords. But Amakuni swords are in a totally different league from even the most excellent of excellent swords. When used correctly, they can even shatter another weapon. In fact, there is not much they will not cut through. Each one is unique. Each one is a combination of superlatives which defies comprehension."

Tessa shook her head.

"Please tell me you're joking. Please tell me Penny didn't really spend so much on that sword."

"Oh, but she did," replied Lee. "What's more, since Kimi Amakuni was not able to meet the ultimate owner, Yoshino had to provide her with a great deal of information about that person. Height, weight, build, arm length, leg length, and of course what she looked like."

Lee paused for all this to sink in, while Tessa struggled to stave off her worst fears.

"After the sword was delivered," he continued, "Yoshino promised to bring the person she had in mind to SKS. But then she stopped coming so I had no alternative but to keep it safe and wait… Do you want me to go on, or will you just believe me when I say there is no doubt in my mind that she intended you to have this sword?"

"No! Please, no," was all Tessa could blurt out. "She must have been mad to buy this for me. I have never held a sword in my life before. I can't stand the sight of blood, and don't have any faith in the concept of International Peacekeepers. How could she ever have thought I would want to own something like this?"

"Maybe she knew you better than you realised; certainly, she has procured something very special for you. As soon as we met I suspected you were this sword's true owner. But I wanted you to take the test first, and in so doing you proved Yoshino correct in her assertion that you could do this weapon justice. So in response to your question of whether or not you may use it for training, the answer rests with you… This sword is supreme in terms of both form and function. Its value far exceeds that which can be measured in monetary terms. The sword feels so comfortable in your hands because it has been made for you, and I can prove it."

As Tessa continued to shake her head in disbelief, he smiled at her.

"May I have permission to draw your sword, please?"

"Yes, of course."

With slow reverential movements Lee leant forward, picked up the sword and gently unsheathed it. He smiled as the blade glowed in the now fading sunlight. But Tessa realised immediately that something was missing.

"You've noticed, haven't you? It will not ring for me. No matter what I do, it will never ring for me, or for anyone else," said Lee with a smile. He returned the sword to its sheath and handed it to Tessa.

"Now you unsheathe it again."

She did, several times, and no matter how slowly and gently she withdrew the sword from its sheath, it would ring. She carefully returned the sword to its stand in the middle of the table.

"It rings only for you because it is tuned to you. No doubt Yoshino tested some tuning forks on you at some time?"

Tessa nodded.

"It is tuned to you in every respect. If you are angry, its ringing will reflect your anger. If you are happy, it will have another tone. The more alive you are, the stronger it will ring, and if you are more dead than alive, it will stop ringing. With training you can learn how to draw the sword without making it ring, because sometimes that will be important…"

Lee's words tailed off into silence.

"This is an extremely valuable personal gift to you from your dear friend Yoshino. I am sure she is pleased to know you have it in your hands at last."

He leant forward once more, picked up the sword with both hands and gracefully offered it lengthwise to Tessa with his head bowed.

She swallowed, accepted it from him, and laid it gently on her lap, running her hands over it. She sat for what felt like an eternity, overcome with emotion. Tears started rolling down her cheeks. Speechless, she fumbled in her handbag for another tissue.

"I'm sorry," she sobbed. "Penny meant so much to me. She didn't have anyone else, and we had come to trust each other completely … and I miss her … and the last image of her I have is of her body lying in the mortuary…"

Lee studied her with a determined expression on his face.

"This sword's destiny lies with you. Make Yoshino happy by accepting it with pride. I will teach you the art of using it wisely."

Tessa looked at him and lovingly stroked the sword in her lap. Despite its radiant beauty she thought how much she would rather have had Penny with her instead. Pent-up fury welled inside her as tears trickled down her cheeks. She drew the sword, prompting a remarkably loud, angry and menacing ringing. Even Lee looked taken aback. His wife's father burst into the room to investigate.

"What a thunderous noise," he said with a wry grin. "The sword is home at last."

Lee smiled at him.

"It seems we have a new student," he said. "You had better choose a name for her."

"Easy! If the sword is willing to make a noise like that for her, then she must be called *thunder*. Nariko shall be her name," replied the old man. He bowed and left the room.

Forty minutes later Tessa emerged from SKS, having agreed to start lessons the following morning. Lee closed the door behind her and, smiling broadly, went to make a telephone call.

"Kimi-san, I have excellent news. The sword has found its rightful owner and she has more than enough potential to wield it well."

"And wisely?"

"I believe so."

"Does she understand what must be done?"

"No, not yet. Now is not the time to tell her of the darkness on the horizon."

"Don't delay too long. If something goes wrong the sword must still be returned."

"Of course."

"Very well, let us see how the future develops. But be careful. You and your brother are playing with fire…"

After that, Lee made another call.

"Isamu-san?"

"Oh, hello, I'm in a meeting."

"No problem. She has found it at last and agreed to let me guide her. But you must keep the path here clear for her."

"Understood. I will take care of it."

CHAPTER 11

The following morning soon saw Tessa questioning the wisdom of her decision. As she ran round Hyde Park at her usual brisk pace, she found Lee waiting at various points to insist she run faster. By the time she reached SKS she was exhausted, but he still had her do all sorts of other physical exercises. By lunchtime she was completely worn out and aching all over. She pointed out that after she had begrudgingly allocated him two hours, he had taken her entire morning. But he simply asked what she would have been doing otherwise, and she knew there was nothing of consequence.

Tessa laughed and asked if she could at least hold the sword for a while. She wanted some time with it, to show it the respect it deserved as the most valuable single item Penny had left her. So Lee gave it to her and explained the purpose of the different components and showed her how to clean it without cutting herself. This proved to be a surprisingly difficult art to master. Fortunately none of her injuries were serious but, like paper cuts, they stung mercilessly. Lee told her that she would need to practise until she could clean the sword quickly in complete darkness, and suggested she come back one afternoon to learn just that. Tessa readily agreed. Indeed, she soon found she'd committed herself to a number of extra lessons and even found herself looking forward to learning about *Iaidō*: the art of drawing the sword quickly in a smooth controlled action, striking an imaginary opponent, flicking the blade clean, and speedily returning the sword to its sheath.

Despite continuing to question the appropriateness of what she was doing, Tessa soon established a routine with Lee. She would get up early and run for at least an hour and a half. Then, after a quick healthy breakfast, she would spend the next two hours at SKS. This meant she was finished by mid-morning and able to attend to other matters; although in fact she often returned to SKS during the afternoons. She knew she was spending far more time there than she had intended and even visited the British Library several times to learn more about the Samurai, their swords and combat techniques. There was no denying she was enjoying it all, and there was also no doubt she was fitter than she had ever been in her life. At first she took lessons with other pupils. However, after she mastered the thirty-five basic sword strokes in a matter of days, Lee started teaching her on her own...

One day, she had just put her tunic into the washing machine when her thoughts were interrupted by the ringing of her *cbc*.

"Good afternoon, Mr Sinclair. I take it you have some news for me at last?"

"Hello, Dr Pennington. Alas, nothing conclusive, but we are due to give you an update. I know it's short notice, but would this afternoon be convenient?"

"As it happens, I am free. How about Antonio's at three?"

"Perfect. Thank you."

Tessa changed, did some paperwork and left her house to walk to the café. She arrived early. After the usual over-the-top greeting from Antonio, she settled down at a corner table with a newspaper, coffee and a large piece of decadently moist chocolate cake, only crumbs and smudges of which remained when Sinclair and Jones arrived.

"Hello," replied Sinclair, sounding unusually cheery as both men pulled up chairs.

"You look pleased with life," observed Tessa.

"I am," he replied, "for all sorts of reasons."

"Good. I can hardly wait to hear all the progress you've made."

Their teas arrived and Jones described in detail what they had been doing since the last meeting. Once again Tessa found herself believing they were working hard for her, but remained frustrated by their slow progress.

"...It's disappointing for all of us," Jones was saying. "We've invested a considerable amount of time and effort in this but we keep on coming up against brick walls. Mind you, that in itself is of significance since we can learn from the obstacles." Tessa looked puzzled. "The difficulties we're encountering are complex and substantial. Which means whoever organised Penny's death must have had the influence to erect them, and not only within the criminal world. Her murder certainly bears all the hallmarks of a professional hit..."

"But why on earth would Penny be of interest to organised crime?"

interrupted Tessa.

"That's a very good question … and unfortunately one to which we still don't have the answer," sighed Jones. "However, you did take over S&M, and the two of you were very close. There's a possibility you could be in danger too."

"I doubt it. Especially now that I've sold the business."

"Even so, you should be careful," interjected Sinclair. "As a precaution, I would strongly recommend you vary your routine. Don't always run at the same time, alter the routes, and hide the fact that you attend SKS. But there's no reason for you to stop going. We'll be keeping an eye on you, in the background of course, but if anything strange happens, give us a ring."

"Right," said Tessa in disbelief; she hadn't told them about SKS, and she hadn't been aware of anyone watching her…

Eventually, with her hopes dashed once again, she walked home feeling despondent. She desperately wanted Sinclair and Jones to find Penny's killers and get them behind bars. Maybe then she could stop feeling haunted by the loss of her friend.

Meanwhile, back in their car, Sinclair turned to his partner. "She's definitely not taking us seriously. I do want you to make quite sure she can't be traced to SKS, it's important nobody knows she's going there."

"OK," replied Jones, intrigued. "But as I said, it's going to take a lot of resources: cordons, decoys…"

"Just do what you need to do, and plan to do it for a long time, surreptitiously. Also, if you think she's being tracked, leak her training name as Yoshino."

"That was Penny's name."

"I know. She'd be delighted to be used as the decoy in this cause. I'll tell SKS."

CHAPTER 12

Slowly, Tessa grew accustomed to being called Nariko at SKS. At first, they used wooden swords to practise combinations of blocking and attacking techniques. However, they soon started to train with metal swords and she learnt to use her sword as an extension of herself, rather than simply a weapon she was holding. But she rarely used her Kimi sword, as she called it, because it was too dangerous even when they wore anti-stab vests. Occasionally, Lee would challenge her to a duel. At first Tessa always lost, but she improved quickly, and then, suddenly, she won…

"You see," said Lee, rubbing the place where she had hit him, "it is not always the best swordsperson who wins; it is the swordsperson who is best at the crucial time. But now that well-earned victory of yours is in the past. What counts is next time!"

Tessa was amazed to find herself enjoying the training so much. Lee's patience seemed boundless and she found herself spending more and more time with him. She knew it was distracting her from other things, notably finding a man and a new job. Not that she needed the money; she just felt it was too soon for her to retire.

After her fourth week, Lee needed to go away for a few days. This suited Tessa since she wanted to visit the land Penny had bought in Orkney, and scatter her ashes.

Mardykes was a smallholding on the island of Burray, located on the northern slope of a hill overlooking Scapa Flow. It comprised twenty acres of rough grazing land with a crofter's cottage in the middle. This had collapsed a few years earlier and now was little more than a pile of lichen-covered stones. But from the pictures Penny had shown her, Tessa thought it looked wonderful.

Penny had been determined to purchase Mardykes. She had not only submitted a generous bid to secure the property, but also carefully planned the reconstruction of the cottage and how to use the land; Tessa intended to respect her wishes.

It would take her twelve hours to drive from London to Orkney, so she decided to hire a car rather than use the ageing one she owned. When the day arrived, she programmed the car's Sat-Nav for Watergate in Kirkwall. It was a narrow street between the Bishop's and Earl's Palaces opposite St Magnus Cathedral. Parking there would leave only a five-minute walk to her local solicitors.

Tessa set off after lunch, with the Fukagawa urn containing Penny's ashes safely strapped into the passenger seat. She drove through the night and arrived at the Scrabster ferry terminal to find the *St Ola* car ferry docked and loading.

With the car safely on board, Tessa carefully slid the urn into her rucksack and went on deck to watch the ship cast off. She was hoping to spread the ashes as the ship passed the Old Man of Hoy. She knew Penny felt a deep association with this lonely sandstone pillar jutting out of the rough Atlantic seas, so it would be a fitting final resting place. Coyle had obtained the necessary permissions for her to scatter the ashes from the ship and told her to ask for the captain if she ran into any difficulties.

Tessa went to the lounge and sat drinking a cup of coffee lost in melancholy reminiscences. As the *St Ola* started to pitch and roll, she saw that Hoy was nearing and went back on deck. Using a little flag to test the wind direction, Tessa found to her dismay it was gusting strongly and blowing towards the ship. But as she stood supporting herself against the handrail, she marvelled at the beauty of the sight before her. Hoy, the second largest island in Orkney, glowed in the early-morning sun. She could see countless birds noisily circling the Old Man. Its silhouette appeared orange, in striking contrast with the turquoise water and rolling green hills of Rackwick Bay. Awestruck, Tessa couldn't help but smile to see such wild natural beauty.

Then the ship slowed and altered course slightly. Now the conditions were ideal. Tessa glanced round to check she was on her own. Then she took a deep breath, unpacked the urn and rested it on the handrail, holding the lid on with her hand.

"Penny," she shouted, "I miss you. I will always miss you. I promise that all those responsible for your death will be brought to account. And you're right … this is a truly magical place!"

Full of sorrow, she lifted the urn up and turned the spout towards the Old Man. Then she took a deep breath and slowly eased the lid open. Penny's ashes poured out in an orderly light grey plume, collecting and swirling briefly some ten yards away from the ship before heading off in the direction of Hoy – first as a dense stream, then a slowly dissipating cloud. When Tessa could no longer see the ashes, she shook her head in wonder and awe. Satisfied the urn was empty, she replaced the lid and, with the urn safely stowed back in her rucksack, stood watching the Old Man of Hoy disappearing into the distance. As the St Ola neared Scapa Flow, she stood up straight.

"Good-bye, babe," she whispered, and turned away.

When she went inside, she almost bumped into the captain.

"Morning, miss," he said, in a thick Scots burr. "I just wanted to make sure everything went all right?"

"Er, yes," confirmed Tessa. "I didn't realise you knew I was there?"

"Of course, miss, it's my job to know. I promised Mr Coyle I'd look after you. I'm very sorry for your loss, miss… We'll be docking soon."

"Thank you," she replied with a smile.

The captain touched his cap and walked away. Tessa quickly found a women's cloakroom and did her best to rescue her make-up.

The *St Ola* docked with ample time for her to have an unexpected but welcome breakfast at the Hakon Hotel. Afterwards, looking and feeling refreshed, she drove the last few miles to Kirkwall. As she walked into town, she admired the imposing cathedral with its walls of local red and yellow sandstone. It amazed her to think it was contemporary with Angkor Wat in Cambodia, and yet so completely different.

Tessa continued to her solicitor's office. This turned out to be in a set of dour wood-panelled rooms with worn green carpets. A far cry from the subdued luxury she was accustomed to in London, but respectable enough. After a few minutes she and her solicitor were joined by a large strong-looking man wearing a tweed jacket and kilt. He had unruly red hair and a dense matching beard; Jim Nurqwoy was the local laird's right-hand man, it seemed.

"Mr Nurqwoy," said Tessa, once the introductions were over. "I have a proposal for you to consider. But first, please note that Mardykes is now called Pennysview, in memory of a friend of mine who died recently. Now, as I understand it, Pennysview stands in the way of sheep transfers from one side of the laird's property to the other?"

"Indeed it does, miss," replied Nurqwoy, surprised that she knew.

"OK," said Tessa, unfurling a large-scale map with Pennysview in the middle. "Then, in certain circumstances, I might be willing to lease parts of my land to the laird."

"Which parts, and in what circumstances, miss?"

"Well, I suspect you could do with free access to these areas for transit purposes," said Tessa pointing to several parts of the map. "While these would be useful for additional grazing. Correct?"

Nurqwoy struggled to hide his amazement.

"Yes, miss, that would be most helpful."

"Good. Then I would be willing to lease these lands for a peppercorn rent on a renewable triennial basis, paid quarterly in advance. However, in addition to allowing you to remove temporarily the dry-stone walls here, here and here, I would like you to maintain the dry-stone walls here, and construct new ones along here. When the lease is eventually terminated, the removed walls would need to be reinstated while in the meantime the leased land would need to be well maintained."

"That sounds very fair to me, miss," replied Nurqwoy without hesitation. "I will need the laird's permission before I can sign anything, but I don't think there'll be a problem. When would the agreement be ready for signature, miss?"

"Later today, if you like. I've already approved the final draft, so if you care to have your solicitor look through it, we could sign this afternoon. Would that be too soon?"

"No, that should be fine, miss. I'm sure the laird will view this as most acceptable."

"Excellent. I look forward to perhaps meeting him sometime."

"I'm sure he'd be pleased to meet you too, miss. He'll be at Burrody Castle this weekend."

"Oh, I'm afraid I'm going back to London today. Maybe next time. Now, I hope you'll excuse me, but I have some other business to attend to. May I suggest we reconvene here at three-thirty to sign our agreement?"

"I'll be here, miss, thank you," replied a bemused Nurqwoy.

Tessa went straight to the Town Hall. There she received assurances that her plans for rebuilding Pennysview were not controversial and were likely to be approved at the next Planning Committee meeting. Given this broad acceptance of her ideas, she visited the builder/ architect Penny had selected and discussed in detail what was to be built and arrangements for third-party supervision. However, being an automation expert, Tessa had incorporated some new sophisticated technology into the design. Therefore, although the majority of the construction would be carried out by local contractors, her additions would be installed by specialists from the south.

Delighted she had been able to complete everything before lunch, she walked down to the quayside and along to the Balkie Hotel. She sat down at the table in the bay window and ordered some sandwiches 'to go'. As she waited, she drank coffee and watched the *Earl Thorfinn* roll-on-roll-off ferry leave for Westray...

Thirty minutes later, she was turning left off the Burray coast road on to the narrow track which climbed up to Pennysview. She was grateful her car had four-wheel-drive as otherwise she would have had difficulty getting up the muddy track which grew rougher and steeper as it climbed. Eventually, it petered out on a flattish patch of grass in front of the remains of the cottage.

Tessa switched off the engine and opened the window. The only sound was from the wind rustling through the grass. It was brisk and blowing strongly, but smelt gloriously fresh. She got out and, with her back to the ruins, admired the panorama before her. She was standing about two-thirds of the way up the northern slope of Burray, which extended right down to the water, and immediately understood why her friend had fallen in love with the place.

"Penny, this is fantastic!" she exclaimed, grinning. "It's even better than the pictures!"

Pennysview enjoyed uninterrupted views over Scapa Flow to many of the other Orkney islands. To the north-west were Flotta, Hoy and Graemsay, with Stromness far in the distance. To the north and north-east were Mainland and three of the Churchill Barriers. She could even see over Graemshall to Tankerness, Deerness and Copinsay. She shook her head in awe and walked round muttering 'wow' repeatedly as she ate her sandwiches and drank some water.

Feeling elated she reluctantly got back into her car and returned to her solicitor in Kirkwall. Arriving punctually, she found Nurqwoy waiting, and the agreement was soon concluded. He even made the first lease payment.

It was four-fifteen when she left and she had ample time to catch the last ferry back to Scrabster. The return journey was long and tiring and she was forced to take several extended rests. But Tessa arrived back at South Kensington late the following morning buoyed up by the beauty of Pennysview and the satisfaction of having honoured her friend's last requests.

CHAPTER 13

Surprisingly quickly, the day of Tessa's final sword lesson arrived. This prompted her to think seriously about what she should do next and whether her life would seem empty without SKS. Training had given her a new sense of purpose, and although not keen to admit it, not only did she relish holding the sword more than she would ever have imagined possible, but she was also getting quite good at wielding it. However, as yet Lee had not changed the colour of her belt. He'd insisted he wanted her to improve because she wanted to and not to attain a belt of a different colour. Nevertheless, at the end of her final lesson, Tessa wasn't surprised to be invited by him to drink some green tea. She was sure he would want her to continue training. She sat down in his artfully simple room and admired the fish gliding around the pool.

"So, Nariko, we have reached the end of your ten weeks," declared Lee. "As I expected, you have excelled. Indeed, I know of no one else who has learnt so much, so quickly. Are you enjoying yourself?"

"Yes, very much indeed," replied Tessa, taking a sip of her tea, "far more than I expected."

"Good! I am pleased. Now, I have taken the liberty of putting your name forward for a little demonstration tomorrow. I hope you're free?" he said, sipping his tea.

"I can be," replied Tessa, without thinking. "What do you have in mind?"

"Well, there are two other students involved too. All of you are enrolled for the Samurai Proficiency Test. It will take place here and will be judged by some Special Forces people. The tests are quite gruelling and typically last for about four hours. This is split between examinations, interviews and practical challenges. I think you will find it all fairly straightforward, and you'll be able to use your Kimi sword. If they think you're good enough, you'll be granted an RCL."

Lee said all this in a relaxed soporific tone which endeavoured to lull her into a false sense of security. But Tessa wasn't having any of it,

114

and nearly banged her cup down in surprise.

"You're joking?" she exclaimed. "I can't do that! I don't want a licence to hurt people. I'm a pacifist … well, mostly."

"Quite so," replied Lee, "and that is why you should take the test."

"When are you going to stop springing traps for me?" replied Tessa, trying not to show her anger. "I really don't want to do it."

Lee smiled.

"Well, you are entered now and all the paperwork has been done. So, if you didn't turn up, we would both be in trouble. Don't worry, I'm sure you will do well."

"That's exactly what I'm worried about!" Tessa retorted. "How could you do this to me? I trusted you."

"And rightly so," he replied. "When we first met, you said you didn't like swords, but now you do. You also said you wouldn't enjoy learning how to use a sword, but now you do. So, I thought you would enjoy taking your Kimi sword home with you."

Tessa's attitude changed to one of exasperated curiosity.

"Oh, so that's the sweetness in the sting, is it?"

"It is unusual for a student to take the test after such a short time, but I think in your case it's worth a try. One either fails the test or passes with either an RCL or an OCL grade. All you need to take your sword home is an RCL pass. I believe you can win one if you keep your wits about you. You'll need to carry it in an approved case, of course, and have a sword safe installed."

"Very clever. Or should I say devious?" replied Tessa, shaking her head. "You've done it again haven't you? I presume you've been planning this for weeks."

"More tea?" Lee asked, without answering her.

The following morning Tessa arrived at SKS already wearing her tunic. Lee met her at the door and immediately asked her to remove her red cord belt.

"I should have done this before, but never quite got round to it."

He held out a violet-coloured cord.

"But that's level seven?"

"Yes, you earned it technically some time ago but I thought it might be bad for your ego if I told you." He laughed as she raised her eyebrows in mock annoyance. "Now, you will all sit the written exams together.

Then there will be individual oral and practical examinations, and finally the combat challenges. You will be last for these. You can meet everyone now, but afterwards you should go to the library for your theory and character tests."

Tessa swallowed and put on her new belt, then she followed Lee into the practice room. It seemed unnaturally quiet, without the usual group of students. All the training equipment had been moved to one end, leaving an enormous empty space in the middle. She was joined by two other students and together they went to meet the four visitors. Two of them were in suits: a balding, sharp-looking man in his early-forties and a somewhat younger woman with bleached short curly hair. With them were two men in dark blue fighting tunics.

"Good morning," said the suited man. "My name is Potter. I am the chief adjudicator and will be judging with my colleague, Ms Crick. These two gentlemen will be your adversaries for the combat challenges. As they are active members of the Special Forces, we do not give their names." Tessa bowed to Potter and Crick and looked at the other two. She had never seen such enormous muscular men. They towered over her. She bowed to them but said nothing. They bowed back and smirked. Nice, she thought. No doubt all part of the psychological challenge.

The other two candidates were both male and younger than Tessa. They tried to put on a brave face, but she was sure they were equally as daunted. The three of them were ushered into the library and sat the theory examinations. They had to describe weapons and components, write about defences to various attacks and show they understood the law. Then they split up for the oral and practical examinations and she had to demonstrate how she cleaned her sword, blindfolded. After that she found herself waiting alone in the library. Eventually Potter popped in to say she had passed the other examinations with distinction and had a couple of hours before her combat challenges. In fact, it was only an hour later when Lee knocked at the door.

"Nariko, it is your turn now."

"Wonderful... Wasn't that a bit quick?"

Lee nodded, his face downcast. It had obviously not gone well for her predecessors. She stood up, breathed out noisily and flexed her shoulders.

"This is madness," she muttered as she followed him out, but he didn't reply.

In the practice room, Lee's podium looked even more austere than usual. It held a large oak table, behind which sat Potter and Crick. Each had three sets of papers in front of them. Potter was busy flicking through one of these. Tessa knew the combat challenges were a variety of mock duels. However, since none of those involved would be wearing anti-stab vests, no sword contact was permitted. As Lee returned to the podium, Potter raised a sheet of paper. Then he looked it over and afterwards studied Tessa. He seemed puzzled and perturbed.

"Nariko, I presume there's some mistake ... how long have you been learning?"

"Ten weeks," she replied.

"Only ten weeks!"

Tessa nodded and Lee smiled as he sat down to observe.

"Master Lee," said Potter, "I must say it is highly irregular to ask us to test such an inexperienced candidate... However, she's here now and I suppose her Kenjutsu might help. OK, Nariko, these seventeen cards show the various challenges which you need to undertake against our two experts. You must win at least fourteen to be eligible for a grading. The challenges are precisely the same for male and female candidates internationally. The first is always one and the last is always seventeen, but I will select the others at random. Are you ready?"

Tessa took a deep breath and nodded.

"Let's see how far we get this time then. Challenge number one. Speed."

Potter's tone exuded boredom and irritation. The first two students had clearly not done well and he didn't expect her to fare any better. This heightened Tessa's sense of isolation and she considered fumbling the first tests to avoid having to do the others. But she decided to persevere since this represented the final instalment of her commitment to Penny; and it would be good to be allowed to take the Kimi sword home even if she planned to do nothing else with it.

She looked up at the adjudicators to see them talking to each other but was quickly snapped back to the task in hand on hearing a loud sneering yell from behind, presumably intended to unnerve and provoke her. She turned to find one of the burly Special Forces experts striding confidently towards her.

As she bowed politely, the man responded by going for his sword. He hoped to secure an early victory while she was preoccupied with the niceties. But before his hand had managed to unsheathe his sword fully, Tessa had drawn hers and brought it up ready to strike a blow to his neck. As her blade rang out confidently the man paused, shocked by the speed of her draw. Then he stepped back and bowed with more respect.

The babble of conversation on the podium stopped abruptly. Potter raised his eyebrows and Crick put her papers down. Clearly now they were both fully engaged in the trial before them.

While all this was going on, the second man was creeping up from behind. But Tessa had heard him. As he drew his sword and raised it to strike, she spun round. With her sword still drawn, it was easy for her to move quickly to her left and block his swing. A lightning-fast exchange of sword strokes followed. Initially the two of them barely moved, but then she attacked hard and persistently, and slowly the man was forced back. The contest lasted for a couple of minutes but ended as quickly as it had begun. As the sword-fighter prepared to renew his attack, Tessa suddenly yelled, "Yield!" He looked down in surprise and found her sword poised to strike a blow at his undefended waist. He stepped back immediately and bowed to confirm he had stopped fighting.

Potter and Crick were now both sitting bolt upright. They made some notes and Potter shouted out the number and name of the next challenge.

Slowly the minutes passed. Tessa kept winning the challenges. But her victories only served to intensify the Special Forces experts' determination to beat her. There was barely a break between the challenges, but she still managed to sneak a glance at Lee. He was clearly having difficulty in restraining his amusement. Fifty minutes passed and, although she had started to tire, Tessa remained undefeated, much to her opponents' consternation.

Finally, challenge seventeen started. Tessa would have to fight both experts simultaneously, free-form. This meant there were no rules, apart from not harming anyone. Shrieking loudly, the two men rushed at her from opposite sides of the room. A furious exchange of sword blows ensued. They were determined to win this challenge so the thought of fighting cleanly did not enter their minds. Tessa had to move continuously to keep as narrow an angle as possible between her opponents. It was extremely taxing fighting two such strong and determined aggressors. Soon the struggle was progressing round the training area, and the fierce clashing of their sword blades could be heard outside in Barnaby Mews.

The combatants were so evenly matched, it began to look as though the challenge would have to be adjudicated before exhaustion set in. But then Tessa managed to force a mistake from one of her opponents. He attacked, but she fought him off so fast and hard he stumbled slightly while stepping back. He rolled sideways to recover, giving her the opportunity she wanted. She turned on the other man and, with a combination of speed and ruthless precision, quickly drove him away from his colleague.

She forced an incredibly fast exchange of strong sword blows. Desperate to regain the initiative, the man took a pace back and raised his sword over his head to attack Tessa as he ran at her. He hoped brute force would break through her defences, but if not she would at least be delayed sufficiently for his comrade to recover. However, as he struck, she neatly side-stepped, defending the blow with such ferocity he had to pass her. As he did, she spun round and followed him, aiming a blow at his back. He turned to find himself looking down at her sword.

"Yield," she panted. He lowered his sword, relaxed and moved away.

Then Potter and Crick watched aghast as Tessa re-sheathed her weapon, closed her eyes and took a deep breath. She stood motionless with her back to her final assailant. He thought she'd forgotten the challenge would only end when one combatant remained standing. But she had practised responding to an unexpected attack from behind, many times; and this was hardly unexpected.

The man neared and raised his sword, preparing for a powerful downward stroke. Tessa knew all this from listening to his approach. At the very last moment she spun round, drawing her own sword, and took a step backwards. As her Kimi sword sped upwards and round she flicked it over so the back edge of the blade faced her attacker's sword. The room filled with the loud *whoosh* of the two swords flying towards each other. They met with a mighty *clang*, followed by an abrupt *chink*. But while Tessa's blade continued swinging upwards, her opponent's snapped off near the hilt.

She looped her sword round and thrust forward aggressively. Wide-eyed, Potter and Crick looked on aghast until she stopped the blade an inch from her opponent's heaving chest. Shocked, he continued to stare at the stump of his broken sword.

"Yield!"

For a moment the room was utterly silent with only the confident ringing of the Kimi sword cutting into it. The second expert stepped back and bowed.

"Absolutely outstanding," he acknowledged, with a surprisingly friendly grin. "Incredible, in fact. That's some weapon you have there. I've only ever seen a sword shatter another once before."

Smiling, the two experts convened in front of her and bowed deeply. Tessa returned the compliment.

Potter and Crick conferred briefly and then summoned her to come forward.

"Very impressive, Nariko," said Potter. "Very impressive indeed. Our judgement is unanimous. We grade your performance OCL A1 … the highest grade possible. This entitles you to be issued with an RCL immediately and also qualifies you for a full Open Carrying Licence once you have secured two international sponsors. Master Lee will no doubt tell you all about that if you don't already know. Well done, and thank you for what was admittedly an unexpected but nevertheless extremely fine demonstration of swordsmanship. Crick will be here tomorrow morning at nine to complete the formalities and issue the necessary documents for you to carry your sword in an approved case."

"We already have one," interjected Lee, "so it can be marked at the same time, if convenient?"

"OK. Well, thank for your hospitality, Lee," said Potter. "You certainly have a very fine student here. I hope we'll be able to count her amongst the Peacekeepers soon. Congratulations to you both. I'm sorry your other two didn't make it, but they weren't so bad. Maybe next time…"

CHAPTER 14

Initially, Tessa celebrated her success as enthusiastically as Lee. However, she soon began to consider the wider implications. Having an OCL A1 licence would attract considerable attention, which she did not want. Consequently, she spent most of the night tossing and turning, chiding herself for not sensing the danger when Lee gave her the violet belt. He probably knew all along that she would achieve better than an RCL pass.

She went for her usual run trying to analyse which of three issues currently troubled her most. First, without doubt, was the matter of the sword and all that owning it entailed. Second, the lack of a man's company was a continuing source of frustration and disappointment to her. Third, she needed to find another job to keep her occupied.

Resolving her man issue would simply require her to devote more time to finding one, which would mean spending less time at SKS. Securing a job should be much the same. However, despite her enviable CV, it was clear that many senior executive recruitment decisions were not made purely on the basis of competence, but were, in fact, still influenced by prejudice against people like her.

Back home, she showered, ate some fruit and set off for SKS. She felt slightly churlish for being so fed up while on the verge of what most people would regard as a remarkable achievement. However, as she walked along Old Brompton Road, the all too obvious question floated up from her subconscious. Why am I doing this? Is it to bring a sword home which I would never have owned if I had had any choice in the matter? Is it to collect a licence to hurt people? Or is it purely because I've been too lazy to find something better to do? Frustratingly, she concluded she had allowed herself to behave like a feather, blowing in the breeze of Penny's bequest.

So, even though she knew it would make her late, Tessa crossed the road to the Starbucks coffee shop opposite Floyds bank and bought herself a low-fat latté. She flopped down by the window, lost in thought. Penny had given her the sword for reasons unknown and she had somehow managed to stumble across it. But surely she had done her duty by her friend now? Not only had she trained to use it, she had become a licensed owner. However, it was generally accepted that anyone who obtained an OCL pass would convert it to a full OCL. That would give her obligations to help maintain law and order, quite possibly leading her into situations where she would have to use the sword in earnest. This behaviour was nothing remotely like the Tessa she had striven so hard to be. She sipped her coffee and continued deliberating.

Should she refuse the licence? If she did, then she wouldn't be able to take the sword home. That would be a shame, not only because the Kimi sword was so beautiful, but also because Penny had given it to her. But if she accepted, where would that lead?

Somehow she had to take control of the situation, or risk being at the behest of others for years to come. "Hold on a minute," she muttered to herself. "If I accept the RCL, I would have several years during which to decide what I really want to do. It could get Lee off my back in the short-term which would give me time to consider everything more carefully. Maybe the answer will make itself plain in due course. So it's obvious what to do for now: accept the licence, get the sword home, and adopt a low profile. Then focus on my other burning issues *instead* of SKS. Decision made!"

Elated, she finished her coffee and walked over to SKS, arriving fifteen minutes late. Crick was already there, looking impatient. Lee was clearly annoyed.

"You're late, where have you been?" he asked, in an unusually direct manner for him.

"Sorry, I had to sort something out first," she replied noncommittally.

"Let's just get on with it, shall we?" snapped Crick. "Right, the first thing you have to do is to sign the Sword Licence Agreement. By signing, you will relinquish your right to vote at any election or align yourself with a political party or any other movement, religious or otherwise. Your RCL status will be noted on your driving licence centrally but not on the licence itself. The same applies to your passport, so you will be able to travel without people knowing you are a sword licensee..." Crick continued for an age, telling Tessa what she could do and what she couldn't. What would be noted where, and what would not. Tessa was barely listening until she said, "...now I'll mark your sword carrying case with your RCL number."

Lee passed her a smart black elliptical sword case made from glass-reinforced fibre with a flip-top lid held closed by three locking latches. Inside there was room for one sword, a knife, a belt, and a cleaning kit.

"I had Kono-san, a friend of mine, prepare this for you," he said to Tessa who nodded, embarrassed that he should have taken such trouble on her behalf. Crick produced some stencils and acid-etch equipment but continued talking.

"Now, the first line is 'RCL-44' to show you are a UK Sword Licensee. When you convert to a full OCL, the 'O' is simply etched round the 'CL-44', so the case won't need to be changed. The second line is 000625. This is your unique licence number. The numbers are allocated at random so no one knows how many licensees there are. But it's not very many at the moment."

"Twenty-five squared," muttered Tessa.

"What?" said Crick, momentarily distracted.

"625 ... it's twenty-five times twenty-five," replied Tessa, grinning.

"Fancy that," muttered Crick uninterestedly. "There, all done. So, now you may carry your sword locked in this case throughout the UK. Personally, I don't recommend you do so unless you have a specific purpose in mind. You'll find a sword case attracts considerable attention, most of which you probably won't appreciate.

"If you wish to take your sword overseas, you'll need to obtain the appropriate approvals from the Special Forces. The contact details are shown in this document pack, together with a full explanation of the rules, responsibilities and entitlements. Here are your RCL certificate and identity card; it is wise to carry your card at all times. Don't forget, you are only allowed to take your sword out of its case in public if invited to do so by the Special Forces, or if your life or that of a policeman is in danger. In those cases you are permitted to do what you can to ensure innocent people are not hurt. However, after any such event, you must complete an incident report explaining why you felt it necessary to draw your sword and so on. If you draw your sword in public without just cause, it is likely your RCL will be revoked, and it will be very difficult for you to get it back. Of course, you are allowed to unsheathe the sword in your own home, to clean it and such like. Now, do you understand everything I have just said?"

"Yes, thank you," said Tessa, trying to smile politely and not look bored.

"Good. The only other thing I should say is that to convert your RCL into an OCL will take proposals from two governments. Generally speaking, how you obtain these proposals depends entirely on your own canvassing skills. However, if you assist our Special Forces to resolve a couple of incidents, a proposal from the UK is almost guaranteed. Obtaining the second proposal is more difficult, but I understand you're fluent in German so you could try offering your services to Germany."

"What would happen if I hadn't secured the backing of two governments within the allotted time?" asked Tessa, seeing Lee stiffen out of the corner of her eye.

"Well, we've never had that happen before. I suppose the RCL status of the licensee would be reviewed and possibly continued, possibly not. It is likely your availability would be circulated to any countries interested, and… But, having seen what you can do, I really don't think that's likely. I'm sure you'll achieve OCL status with the minimum of effort; probably in much less than three years, never mind five. Have you any plans to get a sword safe installed in your home?"

"Oh… well…" stammered Tessa.

"Kono has agreed to fit one," interjected Lee. "I think you're familiar with his work. He could do it this afternoon, if Nariko is interested?"

"Yes, please, this afternoon," continued Tessa, embarrassed again.

Once Crick had left, Lee turned to his pupil.

"So what was that all about?" he demanded. "I've never known you be late before, and you weren't listening to what she…"

"Master Lee," interrupted Tessa, "since you didn't even do me the courtesy of discussing the test before enrolling me, why should you be surprised if, after it, I don't react with boundless enthusiasm? The only reason I took the test at all is because I do want to take the sword home, but I definitely do not want to progress to full OCL status. I have no idea why Penny bought me this sword, but it is truly mine now. I've earned it. I will always be grateful for your help – I couldn't have done this without you – but I am not a naturally violent person.

Violence scares me … as do the people who employ it; as does what I have learnt to do with this sword. I only started this because Penny gave me an astonishing gift. Why on earth would I want to progress any further? A licence to kill? No, thank you! I'm a girl who dreams of leading a regular girl's life. I'm sorry if you're disappointed, but now I am going to take my sword home and consider my position." She bowed deeply and thanked him formally. "*Domo arigato gozaimas*."

She had never seen her sensei so close to losing his temper. But even with his eyes clouded by anger, he could see the stubborn defiance in hers. He took a deep breath and bowed back to her.

"Nariko-san, you are not a regular girl and you never will be," he said, sounding annoyed and saddened in equal measure. Tessa glared at him, furious that he might be referring to her past. "Your God-given gifts with the sword will always conspire to prevent you from attaining the regular life you crave. However, you will be able to find fulfilment in honourably wielding your sword so as to prevent violent people doing terrible things." He paused and looked her in the eyes. "No matter how hard he tried, King Knut could not stop the sea from advancing. In time, you will learn it is the same for you and this sword. I would be grateful if you would train with me tomorrow."

Tessa was moved by Lee's use of "Nariko-san". It was the familiar, respectful form of her Japanese name, the predominantly male suffix always being used for Peacekeepers, regardless of their gender. But it was not enough to persuade her. Furthermore, the suggestion that she should be content to use her sword rather than make a new life for herself with a man did not sound appealing in the slightest.

"I'm sorry. I need a rest."

An awkward silence followed as Lee pondered the situation. Tessa studied the RCL logo adorning her sword case and waited for his counterattack. She knew he could be very convincing, but she had made her mind up.

"I understand. Perhaps it was wrong of me to push you so hard. Maybe your mind needs time to catch up with your new skills. But please, believe me when I say your ability is unique and your mind will catch up. Abilities such as yours will not allow themselves to be repressed. They gather their own momentum. But you are right to take some time to consider the situation. When you are ready, come back. I will be waiting, and as pleased as ever to see you."

He bowed to her, turned and walked towards the door leading to his private rooms.

"Kono-san will arrive at your house at three today to install the sword safe. He is a good man, I am sure you will like him. He can make and fix anything to do with swords."

Alone in the practice room, Tessa looked round feeling pangs of guilt. She hadn't wanted to offend Lee, especially after all he had done for her, but she did need to call a halt to all this before it really got out of control. She picked up her sword and slid it into the shiny new case, locked the top and slung it over her shoulder. Then she smiled, took a deep breath and walked out of SKS.

As she strolled up Barnaby Mews she resolved to keep running each morning, and maybe even to practise a little with her sword at home … purely because she wanted to. She knew this would mean she hadn't completely relinquished her training, but perhaps she had changed; hopefully, not so fundamentally that she could not return to her previous life.

She turned left into Old Brompton Road and bright sunlight. Within seconds her satisfied smile had evaporated. Two policemen approached and touched their helmets respectfully. Shocked, she realised other people were staring and even avoiding her by crossing to the other side of the road. Bustling South Kensington ground to a halt because of Tessa and her sword. Crick was right; carrying a sword case in public attracted far too much attention.

She quickened her pace and began to consider how to approach her house without anyone seeing. She crossed Cranley Place and went left at the traffic lights towards Neville Terrace. Then she turned left into Onslow Gardens and stopped to check that no one was watching. Just as she was trying hard not to be noticed, a blue sports car with the top down stopped alongside her. It was her neighbour Helen. She had beautifully cut auburn hair, and, as usual, was stylishly dressed; she and Tessa had always got on well.

"Hello," said Helen cheerily. "My! Is that what I think it is?"

"Probably," replied Tessa, unenthusiastically. "I had my test yesterday and thrashed a couple of enormous hunks. So now I'm allowed to bring it home with me."

"Wow, fantastic, well done! What does it feel like?"

"Awful! Did you see the effect it had on Old Brompton Road? Policemen saluting and everyone else crossing over to the other side of the road!"

"Ah, that was you, was it?" mused Helen, laughing. "You do always make an impression one way or another, don't you?"

"Hah! Thanks."

"You're welcome. Want a lift?"

"Yes, please. Perhaps I could cower in the footwell," Tessa replied, climbing into the car. "Are you sure you don't mind being seen associating with a licensed sword carrier?"

"Not at all! Quite the opposite. I can't imagine *White Van Man* messing with me when he realises I know you!"

"Oh, great," muttered Tessa. "Look, whatever you do, please don't tell anyone I've got a Sword Licence?"

"My lips are sealed."

A couple of minutes later the car stopped outside Tessa's house.

"You must be really pleased to be bringing Penny's sword back with you?" Helen commented.

"Well, it's my sword now. I fought hard for it and won. But, yes, I am pleased to have it with me … euphoric in fact. Mind you, seeing how everyone reacts makes me wonder what it is I've really achieved. I was just having fun focusing on training before. Now, especially given that I don't intend to progress to gaining a full licence, I have the unenviable prospect of living with the consequences of what I've done."

Helen smiled.

"Well, wasn't it you who told me it's only practical to plan one's life in manageable steps? You said, identify an obstacle, overcome it, and then move on to the next one. Maybe you should just give it some time, and the next obstacle for you to surmount will make itself known."

"Hoist by my own petard," sighed Tessa. "Fancy a cup of green tea? I'm having a sword safe fitted at three, but in the meantime some down-to-earth conversation might help me unwind."

"Well, tea would be nice, and I'd love see this legendary weapon. Not sure we'll manage the rest though…"

As Helen drove the short distance to her own house, Tessa went into hers. She put the RCL document pack away, opened the case and took out the sword. Its beauty was even more sublime than when she had first laid eyes on it. She unsheathed it and couldn't help smiling as the room filled with a proud, confident ringing sound.

"I wonder who's controlling whom?" she muttered, returning the sword to its sheath.

After Helen had left, Tessa moved her furniture and created space for the sword safe in the cupboard under the stairs. She had just finished when the front doorbell rang. Kono clearly took as much pride in being punctual as he apparently did in his work.

He was Japanese, in his early-sixties, with a surprisingly large face for a man of such short stature. He cut a distinguished if friendly figure. His thinning grey hair betrayed his age, but a younger man would have been proud of his strength and agility. They talked and drank green tea as he worked, soon becoming friends.

Tessa discovered he had known Lee since childhood. Kono evaded her questions about whether he had ever wielded a sword, although he did say that centuries ago in Japan, his family had been influential on Shikoku. His business focused on providing every conceivable accessory and service someone with a sword might require. Not surprisingly, following the formation of the International Peacekeepers, his expertise was much in demand. He had postponed a prior engagement in order to install her safe that afternoon. This made Tessa feel even more guilty about disappointing Lee. But she didn't say anything to Kono, and if he knew about their unhappy parting, he didn't mention it.

Two and a half hours later she was the proud owner of an extremely sturdy sword safe. She thanked Kono profusely and paid him generously. They had one final cup of tea together during which he admired her sword. Eventually he left after telling her to contact him if there was anything else he could do for her.

During the next weeks Tessa's life slowly settled down; she approached some executive recruiters, without much success, and had a series of unsatisfactory encounters via WebIntroz. She continued to run each day and found a way to train with her sword at home. It wasn't ideal, not least since in avoiding the low ceilings, she managed to slash several cushions, and was still finding feathers several days later.

She even started designing a harness mechanism to allow her to carry and draw the sword over her shoulder, the viability of which had intrigued her ever since Penny had said it wasn't possible. Her sword's blade was a fairly standard twenty-seven inches long, a couple of inches less than the distance from her right hand, when it was hanging by her side, to the ground. It was physically impossible to draw a sword of that length from behind with the sheath top at shoulder height; and slinging it lower made it difficult to reach the hilt and compromised the wearer's agility. However, if her mechanism worked, she would be able to draw the sword quickly over her shoulder... Not that she'd ever need to do that, of course.

Eventually, she decided to go to Pennysview for a couple of weeks. She had hardly spent any time there since the building works had been completed. And she felt some fresh air and an opportunity to think, unencumbered by the pressures of London life, would do her good.

CHAPTER 15

As usual, Tessa enjoyed herself in Orkney, not least since Pennysview was proving to be a delightful place to live; indeed she hoped to retire there one day. However, after a week of dreaming about her sword, or rather its absence, she decided to return to London. She caught the late ferry and drove through the night.

Back in South Kensington, she went for a run and, after a light lunch, walked to Chelsea to buy some new bedding. An hour later, she was clutching a fine goose-feather pillow under each arm. Since it had started to rain, she looked for a taxi, but finding none walked instead to Sloane Square underground station. As she waited on the westbound platform, a scruffy-looking man in a black fleece jacket marched directly at her from the right. Tessa was quite taken by the beautiful bouquet of amaryllis he was carrying. But while she was wondering who the lucky recipient was, he stopped rather closer to her than she would have preferred. Moments later, as trains approached from both directions, the man thrust the flowers towards her.

"For you!" he sneered.

Surprised, Tessa looked at the flowers and immediately noticed a suspicious red glow deep within them. Instinctively she raised the pillow under her right arm up against his chest to push him back. But he grabbed the top of her jeans, determined to thrust the flowers into her face. She responded by ramming the pillow higher, shoving the bouquet back towards him. Suddenly there was a muted explosion from within the flowers and a cloud of acrid white fumes enveloped the man. He staggered back, choking, and his grip relaxed. Tessa pushed him away, leaving him teetering on the edge of the platform. But out of the corner of her eye, she saw a man in a brown leather jacket moving towards her, brandishing an identical bouquet. He was a large strongly-built person, and approaching quickly and purposefully. Tessa was sure he intended to push her on to the track now that she was aware of the danger the flowers posed. But if she wanted to escape, there was only one direction she could go.

Dropping both pillows, she checked her distance from the trains and jumped off the platform. As the first man stumbled and lost his balance, Tessa landed between the middle two rails and took two quick paces forward. From the gravel mound between the two sets of tracks, she started a series of fast cartwheels diagonally away from the on-coming train towards the opposite platform, carefully avoiding the electrified rails. As onlookers screamed and both trains' brakes squealed, there was a flash from behind her as the first man toppled off the platform and was electrocuted; followed by a horrible crunch as the train hit him. Then Tessa slapped both hands on to the platform opposite and boosted herself up, rolling away just as the other train arrived. She looked back and caught a glimpse of the man in the brown leather jacket. He had a crew cut and a distinctive sculpted chin-strap beard. His eyes caught hers for a moment, and darkened. Discarding the bouquet, he disappeared into the crowd.

It was pandemonium all around as Tessa sat up. Bystanders were panicking, desperate to get away, and several people on the other platform had collapsed. Meanwhile, she realised she had hurt her arm; it had been a hard boost up and a long quick turn solely on her left wrist. Eventually, order was restored and the station manager came to her aid. Tessa was still sitting on the platform, leaning against a pillar, nursing her arm.

"Are you all right, miss?" he asked worriedly.

"Yes … I think so," she replied, coughing and watching disconsolately as feathers from her abandoned pillows fluttered around. The manager helped her to his office.

"The Police are on their way, miss," he said, offering her some water.

Tessa nodded, and took out her *cbc*. She was pleased she hadn't brought a bag with her that day. She phoned Sinclair.

"Hello, Dr Pennington, this is a pleasant surprise. How's Orkney?"

"Delightful," she croaked. "But I'm already back in London."

"Oh, I wish you'd told us."

"Well, you know now. Are you busy?"

"Yes, but why do you ask?"

"Well … someone just tried to kill me."

"Are you hurt?"

"Not seriously…"

"Where are you?"

"I'm in the manager's office at Sloane Street underground station; the Police are coming."

"Stay where you are," replied Sinclair. "We're on our way."

Ten minutes later, through the glazed panel in the door, Tessa saw him and Jones hurrying along the platform. Jones spoke to the policemen gathered outside and their stance immediately stiffened. Sinclair came in alone, asking the WPC to leave them.

"Thanks for coming," said Tessa, wondering why the policewoman had been dismissed. "I hope you didn't mind my calling, but…"

"Not at all," he said, pulling up a chair. "Tell me what happened." Tessa took a drink of water then told him about the two men.

"You've had a very lucky escape," said Sinclair, after she'd finished. He noticed her massaging her wrist which she'd wrapped in a damp tea towel. "What's the matter with your hand?"

"It was a tough boost up, I twisted it."

"Hmm. May I have a look?"

Tessa offered him her hand; his touch was gentle and sensitive.

"It's only sprained," she mumbled.

"I agree, but we should get it X-rayed. How's the other one?"

"Not so bad."

"OK. You will need to give the Police a full statement, but Jones should be able to organise a postponement for you. First I'm going to take you to the hospital."

Tessa looked at him in surprise.

"Surely I need to go to the police station first? A man died. Admittedly not a very nice man, but…"

"Indeed, and at some stage you will need to talk to them. But you're injured and in shock; that white cloud you alluded to was a cyanide derivative. Fortunately, none of the people on the platform were seriously hurt, but we need to get you properly checked over. Have you eaten?"

"Er, no, it's too early."

"It won't be by the time we leave hospital. What do you fancy … sushi?"

"Well, yes. I love sushi."

"Excellent, so do I. And Jones won't touch it."

Tessa looked at him, with his neat ponytail and immaculate collarless suit.

"Sinclair, do you always dress like that?"

He smiled at her uncharacteristic bluntness.

"It's extremely comfortable. Don't you approve?"

"Oh, yes, you always look very smart. Just different, that's all."

"Well, it's our differences which define us as individuals. More often than not, they should be a source of pride. People who are prejudiced against the differences of others are only demonstrating their own inadequacy. Wouldn't it be boring if we were all the same?"

"Very," murmured Tessa, surprised to hear him express such an opinion.

He smiled and moved towards the door, beckoning her to follow. As she left, she saw the trains had been backed away and a number of people in white suits were studying the gruesome remains of the man who had fallen on to the track.

"Jones," said Sinclair. "I'm taking Dr Pennington to hospital for a check-up, she's hurt her arm. Please clear it with our friends here and organise for her statement to be taken tomorrow. I'll vouch for her being there."

"Will do. By the way, all the security cameras went down just before the attack. Convenient, huh?"

It was evening when Tessa returned to her house. She had been examined and, although her wrist would need to remain bandaged for a few days, had been given a clean bill of health. Sinclair had treated her to an extraordinarily good dinner and she felt much better. She found she enjoyed talking to him.

"Thank you," said Tessa as the taxi stopped outside her house, "and for dinner."

"You're welcome," he replied. "Jones will collect you at ten tomorrow for your appointment with the Police. Sorry about the pillows."

When Sinclair returned to his office, Jones was waiting and handed him a small piece of paper with a flower-like emblem on it.

"So, it *is* the Calver Cats?"

"Is she all right?" replied Jones, nodding.

"Badly sprained wrist, but she's fine – thanks to her incredibly quick reactions. How many people would jump on to an electrified track rather than be pushed?"

"Only someone confident of their own speed and gymnastic abilities with the presence of mind to choose the unexpected option."

"Quite," agreed Sinclair. "However, the Cats reacted faster than we did to her early return. We're lucky they were so clumsy. Presumably it had to be a rush job when she decided to travel back by underground."

"We recovered DNA from both bouquets. The chap who went under the train was a known felon. However, the other one is a bit of a mystery. According to Lamper, there are no matching records on file."

"Hmm," mused Sinclair pensively. "The question is, given that Tessa and Penny looked alike, and indeed were similar in so many other ways, who was the real target ... or is someone after both of them? Clearly we need to keep an even closer eye on her. However, she's no fool; we won't be able to keep the truth from her for much longer..."

Not surprisingly, the attempt on her life had a significant impact on Tessa. She started paying a lot more attention to her surroundings and was very careful when she went out. She took to running with a hood obscuring her face, and wore a hat and scarf when out shopping. One day, she slunk surreptitiously into Antonio's for a coffee. She had just settled down when a man stopped by her table.

"Good morning," he said. "Please don't get the wrong impression, but I've often seen you here and you're always sitting on your own. Since I do too, I was wondering whether I might join you?"

Tessa's immediate reaction was to say no. Strangers weren't welcome in her life at the moment. She was also prompted to think of her WebIntroz experiences; all the men who had chatted her up, the dates she'd been on and the numerous frogs she'd kissed in her search for a prince. Could she really be bothered to go through it again, only to watch this one sprint for cover after she'd told him everything she'd done? She looked up; as potential frogs went, this was without doubt a remarkably good-looking and well-spoken one.

"Sorry," he continued, with a charming smile, "that probably didn't sound too good, did it?"

"Not terribly."

"Well, I meant no offence, I just wondered if you'd care for some uncomplicated company."

"I didn't realise there was such a thing," observed Tessa.

"Oh, yes, definitely. And with your permission, I'll prove it over a cup of coffee."

This man exuded a mixture of warmth, openness and confidence. He was just over six foot tall, in his mid-forties, and with what looked likely to be an athletic, well-toned body. His square-jawed face boasted a healthy tan and his thick jet black hair was neatly styled. His sideburns were trimmed closely, showing just a few white hairs, while his blue-green eyes were bright and friendly. He was dressed in a superbly tailored suit, making Tessa pleased she had taken the trouble to dress well that day too. Her defences crumbled; she smiled and gestured for him to sit down with her.

"Thank you. My name's David ... David Kensington."

"Tessa."

"Well, Tessa, I'm pleased to meet you, finally. What brings you to Antonio's?"

"I like it here ... and then there's the coffee."

"Oh, yes, good point." He waved to Antonio, who took their orders, winking at Tessa as he walked away.

Tessa and David started talking and soon discovered they shared an avid interest in business. It wasn't long before they were discussing the effect that removing trade barriers was having on different industries and markets. She also learned he had spent many years in the army, only leaving when his wife was diagnosed with cancer. She had died two years later, some nine months ago. After two hours of very amicable conversation, David announced he had to leave.

"Well, it has been delightful talking to you," he said, preparing to go, "and that wasn't too complicated, was it?"

"No, it wasn't. It was a very pleasant change, thank you," replied Tessa, smiling demurely.

"And what would happen if I asked you out?"

Tessa had been both hoping and dreading he would say that. The truth was her experience with men was still strictly limited, but she liked David and decided to throw caution to the wind.

"I would agree to think about it, and to give you my phone number," she said, writing it on a napkin.

"Thank you," he said, smiling and giving her one of his cards in return.

"Oh, how grand, you've a seat in the House of Lords."

"Well, nobody's perfect. I will be in touch, soon. Goodbye for now."

As he left, Antonio bustled over to her table.

"Hah! You-a come-a to Antonio's for a coffee, and catch-a a man... And a very handsome man too!"

"Indeed. What have I got myself into now?"

The following morning, David telephoned Tessa.

"I wondered if you'd care to join me for lunch in town on Friday?" he asked.

"I'd love to, thank you."

"Excellent. Fish all right?"

"Perfect."

"I'll call you when I've made a reservation. Shall we say twelve-thirty?"

"I shall look forward to it."

Tessa spent much of the next day with Helen, discussing what to wear, what to say and how to react. She felt surprisingly nervous when her taxi dropped her outside the Viking restaurant in Devonshire Street at 12:30. But at least she knew the place well. It had a traditional, sumptuous ambience and served excellent, if pricey, food. She went in to find that David had already arrived, and joined him in one of the old-fashioned wood panelled booths.

"Care for an aperitif?" he suggested, with a smile that sent a thrill down Tessa's spine.

"Yes, please. Tanqueray and tonic."

"We'll make that two then."

They proceeded to enjoy an outstanding lunch accompanied by very fine wines. They talked throughout, revelling in finding out more about each other. Eventually, Tessa looked at her watch, and, following Helen's advice, decided to end the meeting before he could.

"Heavens! It's nearly three. I'm afraid I need to go."

"Is it? I hadn't realised how long we've been talking. Let me settle up."

Tessa surveyed the empty wine, port and brandy glasses.

"You really don't need to pay for all of this..."

"Oh, but I do," replied David, grinning. "I haven't enjoyed myself so much for ages. But if it bothers you, there's always the possibility of treating me to a rematch."

He glanced at her questioningly.

"All right. When?" replied Tessa, with a smile which made David want to lean over and kiss her.

"Hmm, you said you like Mozart. How about coming with me to *Die Entführung aus dem Serail* next Thursday?"

"Oh, yes, that would be wonderful. But I thought it was meant to be my treat?" replied Tessa, with mock disappointment.

"Well, how about if I let you buy me dinner beforehand?" said David, typing his pin number into the credit card machine.

"I think I owe you more than that, but I suppose it's a start. Covent Garden?"

"I think so," replied David, still concentrating on the little grey machine as it slowly spewed out a receipt.

"You think so?"

"Well, yes. I only noticed it in the paper this morning … evening dress too."

"You mean, you don't have any tickets yet?"

"No, not quite. Well, not at all really. But I will have by next Thursday."

Laughing, they stood up and went out to their taxis. David was clearly unsure how he should say goodbye to her. Tessa resolved his dilemma by putting her hand on his shoulder so that he had no alternative but to kiss her on the cheek. They parted, feeling warmed by the time they had spent together and keen to meet again. Tessa in particular was relieved as well as excited. She thought the first date had gone well.

CHAPTER 16

Thursday couldn't come soon enough for Tessa. She wore a gorgeous black hand-embroidered Caroline Charles dress with a matching shawl. The wine bar where they were meeting, at the top of the Strand, turned out to be an extravagantly furnished up-market place with dark-stained wood, frosted glass and plush leather seating. However, she was very nervous, having been worrying all afternoon about doing something which might put David off. She already liked him a lot and hoped her man issue was about to be resolved. She knew this would only create other problems, but decided to worry about that later.

As she went in, lots of people turned to look at her, making her even more nervous, but then she noticed David, standing up and waving to her. She smiled with relief, and delicately picked her way over to his table. He kissed her on the cheek.

"You look wonderful," he said as they sat down, "I think you've made a lot of men drool and the women jealous. You've certainly made me feel very special."

"Well, you look pretty good yourself actually," replied Tessa, blushing. "A DJ suits you."

"Why, thank you, that's most kind. Now, here's the menu … it's all good. What would you like to drink?"

"T&T, again, please."

David signalled to a waiter and ordered their drinks.

"Found something you fancy?" he asked, studying his menu.

"Oh, yes," she replied, looking at him and trying not to be distracted by how immensely attractive she found him. "I thought the salmon salad, how about you?"

"Clearly we have similar tastes. I thought I'd have that too."

They chatted happily together. Their drinks arrived and then their food. Once they had finished, Tessa insisted on paying and soon they were walking the short distance to Covent Garden. She had taken the initiative and gently linked her arm through his. He had given it a gentle squeeze to indicate that he approved.

When they arrived at the Royal Opera House they found a crowd blocking the entrance as the doors hadn't been opened yet. This didn't surprise Tessa, the reviews of the production were euphoric. But she did wonder how David had managed to get hold of a pair of tickets for what was obviously a sold out evening-dress performance.

David continued authoritatively towards one of the doormen. The crowd, surprised by his confidence, grumbled quietly but nevertheless moved aside. David was not in the slightest deterred and was soon whispering something. The man nodded and opened the door for them. With a smile he gestured Tessa to go through. David followed and offered her his arm and they started forward again, only to be stopped once more. But this time David produced two tickets. The concierge nodded obsequiously and gestured them towards the stairs leading to the boxes. Theirs was near the stage and they had an excellent view of the performers and most of the orchestra pit. Tessa hadn't seen an opera live for a long time and completely immersed herself in the occasion, determined to enjoy every minute.

"This is marvellous," she said enthusiastically at the interval. "I'm really pleased you brought me here, although I'd quite like to know how you managed to get these seats. A box to ourselves at short notice when the performance is sold out … very impressive!"

David beamed with a mixture of satisfaction and pride.

"I'm glad you like the seats. As for getting the box, shall we just say I have influential friends in the City? Now, I hope you don't mind but I took the liberty of ordering us some champagne and strawberries."

"Wonderful," she replied gleefully.

At the end of the opera, the cast and orchestra received several enthusiastic ovations. When the applause had finally died down, David turned to Tessa.

"Do you fancy a coffee? I know a nice café not far from here."

"Yes, that's just what I need, thank you. As for all of this, it was fantastic!"

"I'm so pleased you enjoyed it. I love opera, particularly Mozart, but hate going on my own. So having the most beautiful woman in the house on my arm made tonight doubly pleasurable."

Tessa looked at him doubtfully.

"Well, thank you, but I suspect that's a bit over the top."

"Not as far as I'm concerned, and you should know how truly lovely you look. So, thank you."

"Wow, you're a smooth operator," said Tessa, laughing as she took his arm again.

David led her down to the foyer which turned out to be a heaving throng of people chatting before leaving. Three times they had to stop as people he knew greeted them. On these occasions the conversations were generally an exchange of pleasantries, but clearly people were curious to know more about the woman on his arm.

"They're quite inquisitive, aren't they?" noted Tessa, as they walked back towards Covent Garden.

"Nice but *nosy* might be a better description. Sorry about that. They're used to seeing me with my wife or, since she passed away, not at all. So I suppose … well, I suppose they were wondering…" David was clearly struggling to find an appropriate way to finish.

"Natural enough," interjected Tessa, squeezing his arm. "I'm just not used to being in the limelight. In fact, I usually try hard to avoid it. Reporters and the like are only interested in writing what sells, which may or may not have anything to do with the truth. I suppose as a breed they're not quite as bad as politicians, but when one gets down to those murky depths, it's difficult to differentiate and rank them."

"My, what a cynic you are!" laughed David.

"More of a realist. Ultimately, the truth will always out." Tessa immediately regretted reminding herself of what lay ahead for her someday...

"Couldn't agree more. Here we are," said David as he stopped in front of a smart-looking café. "Inside or out, it's quite chilly?"

"Oh, I would much rather sit outside, if you don't mind. I have my shawl."

"Excellent. Outside for me every time, I like the fresh air too. Not that one gets much in central London, but one can't have everything."

They sat outside under a large umbrella until the café started closing.

"It's no good," observed David. "I think I'll have to let you go, for now."

"Well, I've had an absolutely wonderful evening. I can't thank you enough," said Tessa, putting her hand on his.

"What about the other bit?"

"Ah, you mean the *for now* bit?" replied Tessa with a smile, picking up his hand in both of hers. "I'm surprised you need to ask. I'd love to see you again."

"Oh, good," he said, taking her hands and giving them a gentle squeeze. "Let me find an appropriate venue and I'll get in touch."

"I shall be waiting with bated breath."

He paid and they walked back to the Strand arm in arm. After crossing the road, he flagged down a taxi for her. As it drew to a halt they turned to face each other.

"Thank you. I really enjoyed myself tonight," said Tessa, putting her hands on his shoulders and kissing him close to his mouth.

David smiled back at her.

"So did I. More than I ever would have imagined."

For a moment they just looked into each other's eyes, but then he pulled her towards him and they kissed properly. Tessa closed her eyes, she didn't want to let go.

"Until next time then," she said, blushing, as they moved apart. David grinned and helped her into the taxi, closing the door behind her. She waved as the taxi pulled away.

David took a deep breath and pressed his bleeper. A few seconds later a Rolls-Royce stopped alongside him.

"Hello, Andrew. Sorry to have kept you waiting."

"Not a problem, sir. I hope it was a pleasant evening."

"It was very good. I had a wonderful time," replied David with satisfaction. "In fact, I'm rather worried by how wonderful a time I had. She's quite something."

"She looked it, sir, if you don't mind my saying," said Andrew, smiling into the rear-view mirror.

"She did look rather good, didn't she? They're right, she's definitely very special… Mind you, I do feel a bit guilty about it."

"I understand, sir. But I'm sure Lady Anne would be pleased for you. She wouldn't have wanted you just to sit at home."

"Well, I hope you're right there. But that's not why I'm feeling guilty... Anyway, time to get some sleep, I think."

"Very good, sir." The Rolls quietly glided off down the Strand.

After that evening Tessa and David met often, always enjoying themselves and finding each other's company relaxing and stimulating.

Their relationship was deepening rapidly and David began to think the time might be right for them to spend the night together. Tessa, meanwhile, worried more and more about precisely the same thing. She knew only too well that men who wanted to go to bed with you could change from amorous to downright rude if everything didn't go quite as they expected. She desperately hoped that wouldn't happen with David.

CHAPTER 17

Meanwhile, Tessa continued to run daily and practise at home with her sword. She also progressed the design for her over-the-shoulder harness to the point where she thought it might actually work. But the only way to be sure would be to ask Kono to make one. But she was concerned that if it *did* work, she might be drawn back into the sword-fighting world. She certainly didn't want to risk waking sleeping giants when her relationship with David seemed to be progressing so well. But practising at home was proving expensive as well as inconvenient; she had recently managed to slice through a lounge light fitting. At first, she'd laughed at her sword cutting through a metal light with such ease. However when she realised how much a replacement would cost, it didn't seem quite so funny. She wondered whether she should ask Lee if she could just practise at SKS, but didn't fancy the prospect of having to eat humble pie.

One afternoon, she decided to clean her sword case. She routinely cleaned the sword, but the carrying case had not been out often so it hadn't needed cleaning. However, she found one of the catches had jammed and it took her ages to get it open. The case would have to go back to Kono, so she phoned him. Delighted to hear from her, he suggested she visit him that evening and said he would replace the catch while she waited. She enthusiastically agreed, and decided to take her harness design with her.

She would need to leave South Kensington at 5:30 to travel to Kono's workshop in east London. The lateness pleased her. It would be dusk so fewer people would notice her and her sword case, although she had got into the habit of hiding it in a golf bag anyway. As for the prospect of walking through one of the roughest parts of London in the dark … with her sword to rely on, where was the risk?

As she reached the end of the mews, Tessa noticed a commotion in Cranley Place; a group of ruffians was being confronted by several police officers. She discreetly avoided the rumpus and went to the underground station. But as the youths were taken away, one of the

143

constables swore and took out his radio.

"Sir, I'm sorry. We've just lost her. We were busy sorting some hooligans near her house when she walked out… No, they weren't involved, but we've no idea where she went… Yes, she had a hood up, and apparently she was carrying a golf bag…"

Tessa caught a District Line train to Stepney Green, two stops short of the now derelict 2012 Olympic Park. She followed Kono's directions up Globe Road. She couldn't understand why he had his workshop in such a run-down part of town. Completely alone, she reached a railway viaduct and turned into a narrow side-street leading through a ramshackle industrial area. Deserted workshops filled the arches under the viaduct while crumbling factory buildings lined the other side of the road. All were quiet and, adding to the gloom, most of the street lights were broken.

"Nice," she muttered, wondering whether she should make her sword case more conspicuous.

As she walked, she noticed an executive limousine blocking the road. Its lights were off. A shiver ran down Tessa's spine; something was wrong here. A few steps further on she heard the sound of a violent scuffle coming from an alleyway near the car. Her worst suspicions were confirmed by the dull thudding sounds of someone being kicked, and their muffled cries.

Tessa stopped, trying to decide whether she should go on or turn round and get help. But could she bear the ignominy of calling for assistance while she was carrying a sword? She paused, just long enough to hear some more shouts of pain and protest; from a woman this time. Tessa bent down and opened the troublesome catch on her sword case, then another, leaving just one closed. After all, it would be illegal for her to draw the sword in public without just cause. Then she quietly carried on walking. The sounds of anguish grew louder, more frequent and in earnest. Clearly, at least two people were being beaten mercilessly.

"Oh, rats," muttered Tessa, pausing. "Why me?"

She unlocked the final catch and picked up the golf bag carefully so that the sword case wouldn't rattle open. She turned into the alleyway, carrying the bag in her left hand. On hearing more angry shouts, her heart started thumping quickly. She didn't want to be doing this, but

144

she couldn't ignore someone in trouble.

She stopped after about fifteen feet where the alleyway opened out into a small courtyard surrounded by high walls. A single wall-light illuminated the dingy area with an uneasy orange glow. The smell of stale urine was almost overpowering. To her left Tessa found two tough-looking youths standing over a policewoman who sat propped against a wall with blood streaming down her face. In the middle of the courtyard, a well-dressed man was lying on his back in a puddle of dirty water. He too displayed all the hallmarks of a brutal attack. His expensive suit was covered with footprints, and blood was oozing from his nose. Another youth was kneeling alongside, threatening him with a knife.

Tessa was incensed; for once she *would* do something. As she prepared to intervene, her heart-rate slowed and she felt strangely relaxed. She took a deep breath and stepped full into the light.

"OK, that's enough!" she yelled. "You, put the knife away! You two, move away from the constable… Now!"

The youths looked round in surprise.

"Bloody 'ell," exclaimed the youth kneeling by the prostrate man. "What' we got 'ere, posh cunt with golf clubs? What yer gonna do, darlin'? Take out a number nine iron and 'it us for six?"

"Sort of," replied Tessa, glad her sword case had not been recognised for what it was. "Please do as I ask, or I'll have to make you."

"Will yer now … all on your fucking little own?"

"Yes, that's right," continued Tessa, surprised by the confidence and menace in her voice. "Now, put your weapon down and all of you go and face the back wall. I won't ask again."

This provoked a torrent of abuse which subsided suspiciously abruptly. Out of the corner of her eye, Tessa saw a shadow move on the wall to her left. Someone had followed her up the alleyway. With a likely fourth aggressor arriving, it didn't seem sensible to hesitate. She'd have to worry about the consequences later.

She stepped quickly to her left and spun round, using the momentum to flick open her sword case. She found another youth approaching, brandishing a hunting knife. In a flash she'd drawn her sword. It rang enthusiastically, apparently rejoicing at the prospect of being christened at last. There was a brief whoosh and Tessa put a long gash across the young man's forearm. But she didn't want him to run away, so she put a deep wound in his calf muscle too. He shrieked in agony, dropped his knife and staggered backwards, sinking to the ground sobbing.

Putting her golf bag down, Tessa turned back to the others.

"Not golf clubs," she said. "Now, do as I say. Put your weapons down, and go and face the back wall."

"Fuckin' bitch!" yelled one of the youths standing over the policewoman.

He quickly drew a knife and threw it at Tessa. She considered putting out her left hand to catch it. But if she made a mistake and it cut her, the outcome of the confrontation might be jeopardised. So she ducked and the knife whistled past her, shattering against the wall behind her. Meanwhile, she had rolled to her left, picked up the knife the first youth had dropped, spun round and thrown it. Moments later, only the hilt could be seen, sticking out of the knife-thrower's thigh. Then the youth threatening the prostrate man shouted: "Drop yer fuckin' sword or this geezer's a goner!"

But Tessa had already started forward in anticipation. As his knife moved towards the man, she reached out with her sword and the blade passed effortlessly straight through his arm. In horror, he stared at the blood-soaked point. He dropped the knife which Tessa caught neatly in her left hand. She looked round at the fourth youth only to find that he too was drawing a knife. She threw the one in her hand and it sank deep into his leg. Shrieking in pain, he dropped his weapon.

Tessa stood up and moved away from the prostrate man, forcing the youth transfixed by her sword to follow.

"Bitch!" he shrieked. "We're Calver Cats. The Barb'll cut you for this!"

She looked at him, smiled and roughly yanked her sword from his arm. He screamed in agony and sank to his knees.

"Well, if you're anything to go by, I don't need to worry, do I?"

She checked around her. All her aggressors were incapacitated.

"OK, let's have another go, shall we?" ordered Tessa. "Go to the back wall and sit down facing it. And only pull those knives out if you want to bleed to death."

Her sword continued to ring as the dejected youths painfully

146

followed her instructions. Meanwhile, the policewoman slowly and painfully eased herself to her feet, and wiped her eyes.

"And no talking," added Tessa, turning to the policewoman. "Are you OK?"

"Yes, I think so. Thanks."

Tessa looked at the man who was sitting up and wiping blood from his face.

"How about you?"

"I'm fine, or I will be. Thought I'd had it, though."

Tessa continued to watch the youths as the policewoman found her radio and issued an *Urgent Assistance Required* call. Soon sirens could be heard in the distance.

"I suggest you cuff a couple together, WPC Woodley," said Tessa reading her name badge.

"I'll do the lot, I've plenty of straps."

With the four youths comprehensively restrained, Tessa decided it would be prudent to leave. She didn't want David to find out about her unorthodox hobby from a newspaper report.

"I'll be off then," she whispered to Woodley.

She walked back to her sword case, nonchalantly flicking the blood off her sword as she went. Surprised, the constable followed her. When Tessa reached the golf bag she had to pull the sword case out slightly to lock the catches. As she did, Woodley noticed the RCL number.

"You'll need to prepare an incident report," she said. "But there won't be any problems, and it could help you qualify for an OCL."

"Perhaps, but if you don't mind, I don't want any publicity," replied Tessa smiling. "You're both OK, that's the main thing. Those morons will think twice before trying anything like this again. Anyway, I'm late for an appointment. So I'll just make a quiet exit now and let you handle the paperwork."

Woodley looked doubtful.

"Look, I just did you a favour, didn't I?" said Tessa.

"Yes."

"Well, now you can do one for me. Please forget my RCL number. Say you didn't see me clearly. I don't want to have been here, it's better that way."

Woodley shrugged.

"OK, but I don't see how it could do you any harm. After all, if they are Calver Cats, you do need to be careful. The Barb has killed several Peacekeepers."

"Not my war," replied Tessa.

She walked quickly up the alleyway and disappeared into the darkness, occasionally checking behind to make sure no one was following. She chuckled as she wondered what Lee would say if he knew what she'd done. A few minutes later, she arrived at Kono's workshop.

"Hello, Nariko-san. I wouldn't have expected you to be late. Were my instructions unclear?" he asked, delighting her with his use of the familiar form of her Japanese name.

"No, of course, not. I am late, and I am sorry, Kono-san. It took slightly longer than I expected to get here," she replied, bowing. "I hope I haven't inconvenienced you?"

His nose twitched and he smiled, studying her over his thick half-rimmed glasses. He gestured her to come in, checked outside, closed the door and locked it.

"How intriguing. You can tell me about your journey while I fix your case. But why don't you make us some tea, first?" he said, waving in the direction of a kettle and a beautiful Japanese teapot. Tessa handed him the case. As she made the tea, various mutterings and tutting noises emanated from the workshop.

"This catch is no good," he said, joining her. "I will replace them all. I have a new design which I think you will like. Bring the tea into the workshop. While I'm changing the latches, you can clean the blood off your sword and tell me how it got there."

Tessa grinned.

"How did you know?" she asked, following him with the tea.

"It is subtle, but one can smell fresh blood on a blade," he continued.

"Well, I was forced to make a diversion," she confessed, handing him a cup of tea.

"Oh, you'll have to do rather better than that if you want me to change these catches."

So, as she cleaned her sword, Tessa recounted her adventure, prompting occasional nods from Kono. When she finished, he looked up at her.

148

"First blood?"

"Yes."

"And how do you feel about it?"

"All right really," she replied thoughtfully. "Much better than I would have expected. There's a part of me that's ashamed I hurt someone, but the rest of me is proud of what I did. They were dangerous thugs and before I met Lee, I would never have dreamed of getting involved. Tonight, I felt it was the right thing to do. I entered the alleyway with my heart in my mouth, but once I had decided to intervene I calmed down. Ultimately, I only meted out the punishment they deserved, and I did warn them first."

"Well, it seems to me that four young criminals will be off the streets for some time. A job well done, I would say – now, I have fitted a completely new lid. The latches on this one look the same as before but they do tricks. If you press on the side of the lid, here, all the latches release simultaneously, giving you immediate access to your sword."

Kono stood back, looking proudly at his handiwork.

"Oh, that's neat," said Tessa, trying it. "Is it legal?"

"It's not illegal, but I suppose it is right up to the line. Does that worry you?"

"After tonight, not really. If I hadn't unlocked my case before the fireworks started it would have made the whole episode a lot more complicated."

"Nevertheless, it might be a good idea if you try to avoid any further trouble on the way back," he said with a sardonic smile.

Tessa laughed.

"I'll do my best."

"So, Nariko-san, why did you stop taking lessons with Master Lee?" asked Kono, surprising her both with the abrupt change of topic and his directness.

"Ah. Because what I enjoy as a hobby seems to be something which Lee wants me to adopt as a way of life. I was worried that continuing at SKS would lure me into violence, which I abhor ... most of the time. However, the RCL enabled me to take the sword home, as I wanted to do in honour of Penny. But, I have to admit, practising there does have its disadvantages."

"I see. But doesn't what happened tonight put a different complexion on things?"

"I suppose so," sighed Tessa. "It seems if I find myself in a difficult situation with my sword, I have no qualms about using it to keep myself safe."

"And, more importantly, to help others?"

Tessa nodded.

"Mind you, I was annoyed when one of them threw his knife at me, I didn't feel confident I could catch it safely."

"You acted correctly. In a combat situation you can't afford to risk injuring yourself. But wouldn't you prefer to be sure you could catch the knife next time? Just in case there is a next time?"

"Yes," chuckled Tessa. "You're right. Perhaps I should resume my training."

"I am sure Master Lee would be pleased to see you again," continued Kono... "Anyway, let me show you a new sword safe I have developed."

He pulled a sheet off a safe which looked very similar to Tessa's.

"Now, normally you enter a code and the door swings open, like this..."

Tessa nodded, full of anticipation.

"But if you enter another code, with two more digits ... well, watch."

Kono typed in some numbers. There was a gentle *clunk clunk* from the safe as heavy locking bolts moved. Then a substantial portion of it glided forward and pivoted aside to reveal a second two-sword storage area.

"Admittedly, this is not legal, but it is very practical. For example, suppose you didn't want people to find your sword. You could simply hide it in the second safe, and place a clean copy in the front one."

Kono stood back proudly and crossed his arms.

"It's wonderful, and ingenious too," acknowledged Tessa, getting up to admire it more closely. "Just as I would expect from you, Kono-san. But one needs a copy of one's sword to make your story work, and I'm not sure anyone could copy this sword convincingly."

"Hah, Nariko-san! I would have thought you of all people would know one should never say *never*," he replied. "Now, it is customary to present a Samurai with a gift when their sword is first christened in battle. So here is my gift to you."

He opened a large safe in the corner of his workshop and took out a sword bag from behind several others. He walked over to Tessa, bowed and handed it to her with outstretched arms.

Tessa took it, bowing in return. Puzzled, she untied the bag.

"Kono-san, you are always so kind and generous to me. But you don't need to give…"

She stopped talking as she withdrew an extremely accurate copy of her Kimi sword.

"Oh, Kono-san, it's fantastic! How did you make it? You never held my sword for long."

"I had seen it before at SKS. After that it simply took time, and I enjoyed the challenge of making it. Of course, it is no Amakuni sword. However, without a detailed examination, most people would not notice the difference."

"I don't know what to say. Thank you, thank you, thank you," said Tessa with glee, bowing.

"Oh, that will do fine," he replied, beaming and nodding towards the safe. "Well, what do you think?"

"Oh, well, when can you install it?"

They agreed a date.

"Now, Kono-san, I have something to show you," continued Tessa. "We both know that the speed with which a sword can be drawn makes the difference between winning and losing. Equally important, however, is the time needed to deliver a winning blow. Now, with the sword by my side, I have to draw it and move it into a position to strike; all of which is complicated by the opponent's defence. However, if I could draw the sword from over my shoulder, it would be in an attacking position straightaway. But how can anyone draw anything longer than a Ninja short sword over their shoulder? The arm is simply not long enough to unsheathe it. Well, suppose my sword was in a carrier which, when triggered, would lift the sword hilt up and move the sheath down?" She spread the drawings of her shoulder-harness design on his table…

"Hmm. I understand the theory," replied Kono. "But it would all have to happen very quickly … and during the draw your torso would be undefended. If you were the slower, you would lose. I don't believe it has ever been done before, for which there is usually a reason."

Tessa laughed and nodded towards the modified sword case and the copy of her Kimi sword.

"Surely we both know that's no reason why it shouldn't be tried. In fact, maybe that's why it should be."

"I'm not sure," said Kono, stroking his chin. "The actuation mechanism would be very complicated, and reliability would be key."

"How about this?" continued Tessa, pulling out the bottom drawing.

"Hah! I see you have put a lot of thought into this... It's ingenious ... but won't be cheap with these exotic materials you've specified. I presume you would like me to make you one?"

"Yes, please. I've been playing with the design for ages. Initially I was simply trying to see if I could find a way of doing it. But now, I'd rather like to see if it works. I'm quite proud of it really. Rolling my shoulder to ready the sword will certainly surprise people."

"Indeed. I shall enjoy making it, the design is refined and innovative. I'll try and have a working prototype ready for when I install the sword safe."

"Wonderful," she replied with a smile. "Thank you. Oh, and just in case it doesn't work, don't tell anyone about it yet ... not even Master Lee?"

Kono smiled.

"I won't tell a soul."

Not long afterwards, Tessa left him to walk back to Mile End underground station. Although further away, this avoided the area where the incident had taken place in case the Police were still there. It was ten when she finally climbed the stairs to street level in South Kensington.

She'd spent the train journey considering the pros and cons of resuming her training at SKS. Try as she might, she had struggled to find a reason why she shouldn't. But she was determined to emphasise to Lee it was still only a hobby to her. It would also be more difficult to keep it a secret from David. But she felt this should be manageable, for the time being at least.

Kono had undertaken not to warn Lee so she knew her return would be a surprise. Despite its being late, she decided to visit SKS on her way home, before she changed her mind. Tessa walked up Old Brompton Road and turned into Barnaby Mews. She hesitated under the dim light by the main entrance, wondering how difficult Lee would make it for her. She took a deep breath and rang the bell.

After a while, she heard him unlock the bolts on the other side of the door.

"Hello, Nariko. How nice to see you. Would tomorrow at nine be convenient?"

She nodded.

"Good. Then please run for at least two hours beforehand, carrying a twenty-kilo weight, and be prepared to train all day. We need to check you haven't slipped too far back. Until tomorrow morning then?"

Tessa's nonplussed expression transformed itself into a broad grin.

"Thank you," she said. "By the way, I christened my sword this evening."

"Ah, I thought it might take that. I'm delighted, if not surprised, to see you are still in one piece. Welcome back, Nariko-san. Good night."

The door swung closed and Tessa smiled, knowing she had made the right decision. She was pleased and excited to be going back to SKS.

CHAPTER 18

Meanwhile, in a modern art deco-style building on the south bank of the Thames, lights were still on in several offices. Gareth Jones heard a knock on his door.

"Come in," he said, looking up. "Hello, Flood, you're here late."

"Yes, sir, so are you," replied Flood. He was a colossus of a man, thick-set and very muscular, with a remarkably cultured accent for one so physically imposing. "She's back home, safe and sound."

"Thank goodness for that. Any idea what she's been up to?"

"Oh, yes," replied Flood, grinning.

Jones raised an eyebrow.

"Well, I was browsing through this evening's UAR reports when one caught my eye. Four young Calver Cats had managed to stop a City executive in Stepney. They dragged him into an alley and started to give him a comprehensive beating. WPC Woodley intervened, but was overpowered before she could summon assistance. Things looked pretty grim until a woman turned up with a sword. According to Woodley it took less than three seconds for this stranger to take down all four of the ruffians. She said she'd never seen anyone move so quickly and deliver sword strokes so accurately. Anyway after the situation had been brought under control, this stranger left without filing an incident report. She said she didn't want any publicity; but Woodley managed to see her RCL number. The stranger asked her not to put it in her report, and she hasn't. But I know Woodley pretty well, sir. It was UK 625."

"So?"

"Well, 625 is Dr Pennington's RCL number, sir."

"Good lord, so it is!" replied Jones. "Hah! Well, I never."

"I fought in her Proficiency Test, sir. I like to think I'm no pushover, but she beat me and Rathmill fair and square, and at the end we were putting everything into it. Hell of a sword she's got too. She shattered mine with it, just like that bitch The Barb did with Takara. Anyway, I just thought you'd like to know."

"Absolutely right, Flood. Well done, nice piece of work. Did she kill anyone?"

"No, sir. They were all wounded one way or another, but nothing fatal. According to Woodley, she gave them quite a trouncing and wasn't even in a mild sweat. They admitted to being Calver Cats and threatened The Barb would get this stranger. Woodley warned the woman, but she said it wasn't her war."

"Hmm, we'll see about that. Anyway, at least everyone on our side's OK … and Dr Pennington has always looked so angelic."

"Well, sir, if she's got a sword in her hand, I'd want to be on the same side as her."

"You do hold her in high regard! Thanks for bringing this to my attention, I'll tell Sinclair. Please make sure her identity remains a secret, even from Potter. If he does find out, tell him to have a word with me. We don't want any official rumpus, it could wreck everything."

"Will do, sir. Good night."

Jones found Sinclair drinking a cup of green tea in his office.

"You'll never guess what Flood just told me…"

CHAPTER 19

The following afternoon, Tessa left SKS with every muscle in her body aching. Her legs were still trembling as she walked up Barnaby Mews. She stopped in the shadows just short of the wrought-iron gates and slumped against the wall.

"That'll teach me," she gasped as beads of perspiration trickled down her body. Meanwhile, back in SKS, Lee smiled and picked up his phone.

"*Konichiwa*, Hayasaka-san, are you all well...? Good. Is he there...?

"Matsumoto-san," continued Lee. "She's taking lessons again ... extremely gifted, a natural; her speed, grace, endurance and ability to control both arms independently are all quite remarkable. You must teach her... Yes, she is headstrong if pushed hard, and overly emotional on occasion — just like Yoshino. But maturity will come with knowledge and experience... I'll suggest it and she will no doubt refuse. We'll just have to wait until the path clears in front of her."

The hard training sessions continued but Tessa didn't dare complain. It had been her decision to go back and now she had to live with the consequences. Nevertheless, she couldn't understand why Lee seemed to be in such a hurry. She rarely finished before mid-afternoon and found herself completely exhausted by the time she returned home.

This meant she was still tired when she met David in the evenings. He even remarked on it. But she simply used Penny's excuse that she was suffering from the effects of going to a new fitness club. In fact, they had both separately concluded that slowing down their relationship would give them some much-needed time to take stock.

Finally, Kono arrived with the prototype of Tessa's sword harness and her new sword safe. They sat down with some green tea and she studied the harness.

"Well," he asked, "what do you think?"

"Kono-san, this is exceptional. It's a work of art. Have you tried it?"

"Oh, yes. It works, and well too. It has never failed to operate, so it seems the design is reliable. Whether it is faster is difficult for me to judge, but you can try it while I install the safe. I have brought some equipment so we can measure how long it takes to deliver fatal cuts with the sword slung traditionally and in the harness. Perhaps we should use your terrace? You'll be able to draw the sword without height constraints there. That is a drawback, you know, one does need more space to swing the sword."

They went up to the terrace at the rear of her house where Kono fitted the harness, slid the sword in and stood well back. "Now," he continued, "moving your right arm up and back will automatically trigger the mechanism, sliding the sheath down and presenting the sword hilt to your hand. But be careful how you swing the sword round. I've already managed to trim my hair. Bringing the sword forward moves the sheath up again and out of the way. Re-sheathing the sword is just the same. Aligning the blade takes practice, but it is not difficult."

Tessa raised her right arm and instantly felt the sheath shoot open. She grinned gleefully at him. They set up her target dummy and she started to practise drawing the sword from the harness. At first she found the new position ungainly, but she soon got used to it. After a while, Kono went downstairs to fit the new safe which already contained the copy of Tessa's Kimi sword. Two hours later he returned.

"The safe is finished. How is the harness?"

"Very good," she replied enthusiastically, "I love it. I'm getting quite good at drawing it, but need more practice with the re-sheathing."

Kono attached sensors to the sword sheath and the dummy.

"OK, now draw and strike the dummy … say, three times on the torso and then on the neck. I'll record the times and calculate the averages."

Tessa nodded and quickly delivered three blows to the torso, followed by three blows to the neck, returning her sword to its sheath each time. Then she slung the sword by her side with a traditional belt, and repeated the test blows. Kono raised his eyebrows in approval.

"Well, which was quicker?" she asked, burning with curiosity.

"I have to admit, Nariko-san, I'm surprised. But first, it would be remiss of me not to say you are already extremely fast, even with the sword slung conventionally. However, there is no doubt about it, you are faster with the harness. For the torso blows, the difference is small;

but for the neck blows, it is substantial. I believe the harness does give you a competitive advantage. Not that you need one."

"That's fantastic, Kono-san. I've always found carrying the sword from a traditional waist-belt cumbersome. This is much more practical, I could run completely unimpeded. Also, notwithstanding it gives a quicker draw, there would be a big advantage in people not knowing it could be drawn over the shoulder. Thank you for making it."

"Oh, you're welcome. However, having watched you using it, I would like to add some locking buckles to make it easier to put on and adjust, and also a leather sleeve to protect the sheath as it's more exposed across your back…"

Two days later, Tessa collected the improved harness and the black leather cover with Amakuni logos embossed in gold. She immediately started practising. She was keen to make using it completely automatic before she took it to SKS.

She soon got faster, but as Kono had warned there were risks. Once she drew quickly and, despite having gathered her hair back to keep it out of the way, felt her ear twitch. Then she heard something fall on the floor and looked down in horror. She thought she'd cut off part of her ear, but it was only the pendant of her earring…

A few days later she showed the harness to Lee. Being conventional, he made no secret of being sceptical about the design's practicality. But he soon realised it did have advantages and that its disadvantages could be minimised. Seeing Tessa was determined to use the harness as her primary method of carrying the sword, he worked her relentlessly to make sure she could use it effectively. This meant relearning much she had already learnt, but she didn't mind. She felt the harness represented her individual way of doing things. Together they developed some new techniques made possible by the sword's high position after having been drawn over her shoulder.

One afternoon, as she was packing up, Lee called her over to the podium.

"Nariko-san, forgive my curiosity, but what new car did you choose?"

"What do you mean?"

"Well, you said you needed a new car, and with an OCL pass you are entitled to purchase a Peacekeeper Equipment car," said Lee with a smile. "With your love of gadgets, I thought you'd be queuing up for one of those."

Tessa looked blank.

"You did read the documentation pack, didn't you?"

"Well, I wasn't in the mood at the time. So, what's a Peacekeeper Equipment car?"

"Oh, they have all sorts of high-technology gadgets in them. They're intended to help ensure Peacekeepers stay alive, and make it easier for them to get to Special Forces mission locations. If you want one we both need to sign the application papers; they are very expensive, but…"

"Sounds fun. I presume you have the papers ready?"

"By a curious coincidence," replied Lee, reaching down for an envelope by his chair. "Sign here, please."

"Do you always push home your attack when people are already on their knees?"

"Always. I thought you would have learnt that by now. If you have been forced to attack, you must continue until your quarry is rendered completely harmless. If there are a lot of them, then I'm afraid that is likely to mean dead."

Tessa grimaced as she signed, and returned one set of the papers to Lee.

"There is only one place you can buy PE cars in the UK," he continued. "It's on Stanhope Gate off Park Lane. But it is very low-profile as no one is meant to know what the cars look like. Have fun."

Walking home, Tessa smiled in anticipation, wondering what cars and gadgets would be available. She contacted the garage and made an appointment.

Two days later her taxi stopped outside a drab building in Stanhope Gate. Dressed in a expensive designer suit she strode confidently to the shiny black door. An enormous doorman in a top hat and a long green coat with highly polished brass buttons barred her way.

"Sorry, miss," he said in a deep voice. "Only people with a Sword Licence may enter."

"Oh, don't I look the type?" asked Tessa, invigorated by the man's apparent refusal to believe she might hold such a licence. He scrutinised her and grinned.

"Since you ask, miss, no."

"I'll take that as a compliment," she replied, and rummaged in her bag for her identification. The man watched impatiently. "Isn't it amazing what a woman can get in her handbag? Ah, here it is. Now, could you tell Mr Brown that Nariko is here to see him?"

The doorman took her RCL identity card, read it, double checked her picture, and smiled.

"Yes, miss, sorry for the delay."

Shortly afterwards she entered the showroom. It was brightly lit and surprisingly large with six cars in it: two four-door saloons, two SUVs and two coupés. A sharply dressed, middle-aged man approached her.

"Good afternoon, Nariko," he said, in a strong Irish accent. "My name is Brown … John Brown. We spoke on the phone." He led her over to his desk. "I'm afraid I will need to see your identity card."

"Of course." She gave it to him together with the papers Lee had signed.

"Excellent, this all seems to be in order. So, what sort of car are you looking for … saloon, SUV, coupé?"

"Coupé, I think," she replied, looking round. "Is there anything else available apart from these?"

"Oh yes, quite a few, we only keep a small selection here. I can show you pictures of the others. Do you have a budget in mind?"

"Nope. I have a nice car in mind."

"Oh, all the PE cars are nice. They look pretty much the same as their normal road-going counterparts except they are obliged to display PE badges so the authorities can identify them. Perhaps I can help you narrow the field a little. The British coupés tend to be quite large, while the Italian ones are very pretty but a little more, shall we say, extrovert? The German ones are arguably the most solidly built and generally lower profile. Well, apart from the Bugatti. Do you have any preferences?"

"Oh, solidly built and low-profile every time, and I do have a penchant for German engineering. But what's the Bugatti like?"

Brown passed her a glossy brochure which she perused in awe.

"Wow! I see what you mean about it not being low-profile. Mind you, it does look good. It says the engine is a W16 … have you some

160

more details?"

He nodded and passed her the technical datasheets.

"The Bugatti is an incredible vehicle. It's designed to be very fast, very safe and very comfortable. The top speed of the standard version is 259 m.p.h. However, the PE version is somewhat heavier and only manages 247. But that's still faster than just about anything else on the road. Its obscuration system is the best available and unique in having a partial stealth mode which makes the car resemble an Audi TT to the casual observer. I've never heard anything other than superlatives used to describe the Bugatti; but they are extremely expensive, even before the Peacekeeper Equipment is added. Apparently only one Bugatti PE has ever been built so far, and that was for the Asian market."

Tessa looked again at the brochures, glanced at the baseline price, and smiled.

"Then it's about time there was one in Europe. I'll just have to restrain myself if someone scratches it at the supermarket."

"Oh, the obscuration coating is highly resistant to scratches and the armour-plating means it's unlikely to dent. I suspect a supermarket trolley would come off worse if it rolled into one of these. But I'm afraid the car only comes in a sort of dark blue-grey; obscuration coatings have to be that colour."

"Then it's settled, I'll have a dark blue-grey one, please!"

Brown hesitated, not believing he could be on the verge of earning a very large commission.

"We are talking about a number well into six digits … I trust that's all right?"

"Absolutely. What extras are available?"

Brown raised an eyebrow and handed her several sheets of paper and Tessa carefully ticked the boxes by the options she wanted. Virtually all of them, in fact. She checked the sheets and handed them back.

"That should do the job."

"Heavens, what job do you have in mind? This will be the most comprehensively equipped vehicle we have ever supplied … Look, I am sorry, and please don't take this the wrong way, but this is quite a manly car and we are talking about a great deal of money?"

"Thank you, Mr Brown," she replied. "I will try not to take that the

161

wrong way. Meanwhile, I suggest you arrange the paperwork, and I'll organise the down payment."

It was another hour before all the details were finalised and Tessa had transferred the substantial deposit.

"When do you think it'll be ready?" she asked.

"I'll need to check with the factory, but I would guess in about four months. I can keep you informed of progress by e-mail, if you like?" said Brown, gathering his papers together and passing Tessa her copies.

"That'll be fine. Let me know when you've organised the high-speed driving lessons. The week after next would be good. Thank you, Mr Brown."

"On the contrary, Nariko, thank you."

The following day she trained as usual with Lee. At the end of the session, she mentioned she'd placed an order for a Peacekeeper car. He nodded, but much to her disappointment, showed no interest whatsoever in what she'd chosen. He only wanted to know when it would be ready.

"About four months? Oh, that should work out nicely," he observed.

"What do you mean, that should work out nicely?"

"Well, have you time for some tea?"

Such invitations were not unusual, but Lee's tone put her on guard.

"Nariko-san," he said, as his wife filled their cups, "I have a proposition which I'd like to put to you. But, please, let me finish before you respond."

Tessa bowed and thanked his wife for the tea. As usual she smiled, but didn't say anything.

"You are a remarkably gifted student. But if I continue as your only teacher, although you will still learn, your progress will slow as your skill level approaches mine. However, if you were to study with another teacher, a better teacher, then you would advance further and faster." Lee paused for a moment and noisily drank some tea. "From another teacher, you would learn different techniques and new ways of employing your knowledge. Also, a change of teaching environment would do you good. Always learning here, with me, does not expose you to the variety of situations you should experience. Finally, and most important of all, the teacher I have in mind is very

162

highly skilled. He will be able to teach you much that I cannot. I know him well and am sure you would not regret spending time with him. But the training would be hard, much harder than here, and he only teaches in Japan. Admittedly he is a trifle … eccentric. But nothing you couldn't handle."

"I have taken the liberty of describing you to him. Although hesitant, since he prefers to teach men, he is willing to take you on my recommendation. Or at least to meet you and assess whether he feels you could usefully spend time with him." Lee paused to pour some more green tea. "Nariko-san, I strongly recommend you accept this invitation and go to Japan for further training. I know we have not always seen eye to eye in the past, but I hope you will agree I have never let you down. Even if you have doubts about doing this, then please just trust me and go. I am convinced it is the right thing for you to do."

Lee was looking at her so earnestly she felt uncomfortable.

"I'm not sure how to respond," said Tessa, thinking events had evolved remarkably fast from the point when she didn't even want to train. "I've got quite a lot going on at the moment. I've met someone and, well, he's special and … how long do you think I would be in Japan? A week … two?"

Lee had prepared himself for a drawn out discussion, but Tessa's having started a relationship was an unwelcome complication.

"I'm not sure, but I would be surprised if it weren't longer. He teaches for as long as he feels a student can learn. Although, to keep the learning process as effective as possible, he prefers to teach in at least two tranches. He recommends a gap of a few months between them to allow what has been learnt to sink in. I have known initial training sessions be as short as six weeks and as long as fifteen. But never has a student left early once training has begun in earnest. You would have to regard the arrangement as a bit open-ended, although the training is absolutely full-time and residential."

Tessa desperately tried to find a way to decline gracefully, without either offending or disappointing Lee.

"Nariko-san, your eyes betray your thoughts and I can understand why. But, please, cast the short-term objections aside, trust me and go," he pleaded. "This invitation is a truly unique opportunity, and a great honour. If necessary, do it as a favour to me. Please."

His frankness unnerved Tessa.

"Now is a really bad time for me. I know this hobby is more important to me than I would ever have imagined, but I am not a violent person. I enjoy this as a sport, but I do not want it to become my way of life."

"Yes, yes, I know all that, Nariko-san. I was young and idealistic once too, but this is more important. I strongly, but respectfully, counsel you to rise above your immediate feelings in making this decision. I confess, I don't know all the answers; indeed it is important you work out many for yourself. But at the moment, I doubt there is anything which has ever been more important for you than this."

Tessa felt decidedly uneasy. She had acted too hastily once and didn't want to do so again. Clearly this was very important to Lee. Far more so than it was to her.

"You really want me to go, don't you?"

"Yes. More than you could ever understand. Something tells me you must go, and now. Please trust me, say yes."

She couldn't decide what to do. She respected Lee enough to feel it would be foolish to ignore what he said. But surely she didn't have to go to Japan for an indeterminate period? Just when she had decided to try and nudge her relationship with David forward.

"But you haven't told me any details," she continued. "You haven't said where in Japan I would be going, or who would be teaching me, what I would learn ... well, nothing, really."

"I cannot tell you more until you have agreed to go," replied Lee, feeling his control of the situation slipping away. "You will understand why once you have been there. I am sorry if that sounds mysterious, but it is a long and complicated story. Nothing you need worry about, though."

His voice faded, leaving them both listening to the sound of the water bubbling over the rocks in the garden.

"I need some time to think this over," replied Tessa quietly. "I understand what you're saying. But it's so unexpected and ... well ... different."

"How long do you need?" he asked Lee, unable to hide his disappointment.

"A week. I'm sorry, but that's the best I can do. If you must have an answer now, it has to be…"

"Don't say that, Nariko," interrupted Lee. "I don't want to have heard you say that. A week it is. But please consider this offer very carefully. As I said, I do not believe there is anything of greater importance in your life."

CHAPTER 20

Several days later, Tessa was at home when her *cbc* rang.

"Hello," said David cheerily. "What are we doing tonight?"

"Well, I thought I'd treat you to dinner. How about the Falcon, at eight? Aperitifs here if you arrive early."

"Italian. Perfect," replied David. "I'll come round at seven?"

During the time they had been dating, they had kissed and cuddled quite intimately on several occasions but had both shied away from discussing sleeping together. This suited Tessa, although she was surprised David hadn't raised the subject since the men she'd met through WebIntroz had all wanted to go to bed remarkably quickly. However, she liked David a lot and thought the time was now right. Nevertheless, she also felt an obligation to tell him some things about her past which might come as a bit of a shock. She didn't need to tell him, and understood all too well that leaving intimate disclosures to such a sensitive time risked hurt to both parties, but there was nothing to suggest David wouldn't be able to handle it. He exuded self-confidence and his not wanting children also simplified things, even if deep down Tessa knew she herself would love to adopt a child, one day.

When they eventually walked back from the Falcon, both of them were feeling relaxed after an excellent dinner. As they passed under the arch into the mews where Tessa lived, David stopped, gently pulled her to him and kissed her passionately.

"Mmm! Can't you wait? We're nearly home."

"No, one shouldn't wait with spontaneous urges … they lose their impact. That was a super dinner, Tessa, thank you."

"Oh, you're welcome. And here we are."

She opened the front door and switched off the alarm system. Soon they were comfortable on the sofa together, talking quietly. On the small Burmese lacquerware table near them, Tessa had laid cups of coffee, together with a brandy for him and a Cointreau for her. At 1 a.m. she looked at her watch.

"Goodness, look at the time," she whispered seductively. "It's a bit late for you to be wandering the streets of London. The ghouls might get you. Perhaps you should stay?"

David looked at her and smiled. Then he leant forward and kissed her fondly.

"That would be nice … very nice. Are you sure?"

"Oh yes, I'm sure," she replied.

"In which case, I would love to. But I should perhaps warn you, it has been a while, and …"

"Likewise," interrupted Tessa. "I'm sure we'll manage. But there's something you should know first."

"I suppose you haven't vacuumed or there are clothes all over the place?" replied David with a gentle laugh, running his fingers through her hair.

"No, it's a bit more fundamental than that…" Her words faded into a pregnant pause.

"OK," he said with a smile. "Obviously I don't know what it is, but if it's about your past, I don't care. I suppose you've been married before or something? I've come to know you as a beautiful, intelligent young woman. Nothing could change that. So whatever it is, you don't need to tell me if you don't want to. We are both old enough to have plenty of baggage. We should simply trust in our own judgement of one another."

Tessa swallowed.

"Thanks, but I think I'd better tell you all the same. Even if it turns out to be more for my benefit than yours."

"OK, but please hurry. I'd hate to fall asleep on your sofa."

"Oh, great." She laughed and playfully jabbed him in the ribs.

"Ouch! That hurt! You're stronger than you look, aren't you?"

"Oh, sorry. Told you I was working out," said Tessa, kissing his chest. "Right, well, here we go…"

Another long silence followed.

"So, what is it then?" asked David, trying to encourage her.

"Oh, dear, I don't know where to start … it's all so complicated." Tessa's conflicting emotions began to get the better of her and David watched in surprise as her eyes filled with tears. He hugged her.

"Tessa, this isn't necessary. I neither want to know nor care."

"Right," she replied, irritated with herself for being so apprehensive about describing her past. "You remember me telling you about my friend Penny? Well, we met while grappling with the same issue. In some ways it's what brought us so close together. Anyway, we knew that it would have to be resolved one day. So eventually we decided to fix it together."

She stopped and took a sip of her Cointreau while David drank some more of his brandy.

"My darling," he said gently, "shall we just go to bed? There's no need to put yourself through this for my benefit."

"No, I've started now and I want you to know. It all started a long time ago…"

When she finished speaking, some twenty minutes later, tears were rolling down her cheeks. David looked ashen. The atmosphere in the room had turned deathly cold. Tessa felt as though her stomach had screwed itself up into a ball.

"Surely not, Tessa? Please, tell me that's not true?" exclaimed David. The panic in his eyes made her dread what was coming.

"You said you didn't care what it was!"

Her heart was thumping, and for a moment she was worried she might be sick.

"But that was before I knew what you were going to say," he retorted. "You tricked me!"

"No, I did not! You said it didn't matter … wouldn't matter."

"Well, I'm sorry, but I'd underestimated the shock value of what you were about to confess. I'm stunned. How could you have left it so long before you told me something so… Did you lead me up the garden path on purpose? Did it give you a buzz or something?"

"Don't be ridiculous," replied Tessa indignantly. "How could you say such a thing?"

"I … I just can't believe it," he said, standing up angrily. "You…"

"I'm sorry you're upset," she interrupted. "But I'm not sorry about what I've done. And it wasn't a *confession*. We were getting on so well together … and…"

For a moment the two of them simply stayed where they were: David furious, looking down at her; and Tessa on the sofa, tearful, peering up at him, pleading.

"Goodbye, Tessa."

"David, no! Don't go. Not now, not like this. It's not fair. Let's talk about it, please?"

"I think quite enough has been said, thank you."

He grabbed his coat and headed for the door. Tessa struggled to her feet.

"David, please. Don't do this to me … to us."

He hesitated by the door, unable to face her.

"I'm sorry, but I … I've got to go."

He stomped out, closing the door noisily behind him. Tessa listened to him walking up the mews. Against all hope, she desperately wanted him to come back. She slumped against the door prompting David's footsteps to pause. But then he carried on.

He reached the end of the mews and stopped, standing by the arch for several minutes, thinking. Then he pressed his bleeper. Shortly afterwards the Rolls drew alongside.

"Good morning, sir."

"Hello, Andrew," replied David as he got in the back. "I'm sorry to bring you out so late."

"That's all right, sir, I was waiting up in case anyway," replied his chauffeur with a smile. He looked in the mirror. "If you don't mind my asking, sir, is everything all right?"

"No, Andrew, I'm afraid everything is not all right."

There was an expectant pause, and the Rolls remained stationary. Andrew wanted his employer to say more but didn't feel it appropriate to ask, so he waited on the off-chance.

"She told me something about her past which I didn't expect and couldn't handle."

"I see, sir. Something that was really important or just a shock to hear?" asked Andrew quietly, wondering how far he should go.

"Fundamentally important … and a shock. It's very private, Andrew. But, well…" David recounted what Tessa had said.

"I see. May I speak freely, sir?" Andrew requested.

"Yes, of course."

"Well, I have some experience of this, sir. A close relative of mine was similarly afflicted and had no choice but to endure the same treatment."

Now it was his turn to talk for a while.

"…So my instinctive reaction was similar to yours. Of course it's a shock to find out something like that, especially if it's come out of the blue. But ultimately it really isn't important, for all sorts of reasons. If anything, I suspect you'd find she's more of what you want, rather than less. She's had to walk through all sorts of hell to get to where she is today. Most people just aren't that strong … I suppose the real question is what do *you* think, sir?"

"Hmm," replied David with a thoughtful smile, "all these years and I didn't know you were a philosopher as well as everything else. I must admit, you make a strong case. But this so-called straightforward recce contract has become very complicated. In fact, I'm not willing to do it any more, and that's not because of what I heard tonight. Let's go home, Andrew. And, thank you."

"You're welcome, sir," he replied, as the Rolls moved quietly away.

Meanwhile Tessa had sunk on to the floor by her front door, sobbing. After a while she moved back to the sofa and continued to cry, curled up with a cushion. When she finally sat up, still weeping, it was 4:30. The gates to Hyde Park would have been opened. She went upstairs, changed and left for a fast and furious run. Her rage continued throughout the day, making it difficult for Lee to conduct an effective training session.

As the days passed, Tessa was forced to accept that David wouldn't be coming back. She missed him terribly and her fury with him for walking out, and not even being willing to talk to her, refused to go away.

Eventually, she wondered what to do with a pair of tickets she'd bought to attend a choral concert at the Albert Hall which included a performance of Allegri's *Miserere mei* sung by natural castrati. She offered them to Sinclair but he declined, although he had surprised her by proving to be highly knowledgeable about such music. He'd also told her not to go on her own. However, on the day of the concert, determined to reassert her independence, she decided to go anyway. She sold her extra ticket at the door to an Iranian woman who turned out to be excellent company for what proved to be an incredible performance. Tessa was still lost in the moving music as she walked home. But, as she passed under a lamp-post, she saw from

170

the shadows on the pavement, that someone was following her.

The whoosh that came from behind was an immediate trigger for Tessa. She instinctively ducked and the blow narrowly missed her. She spun round and stood up to find herself facing another woman. She was wearing blue jeans and a black fleece jacket with a three-hole balaclava; in her hands was a long staff. She twisted a grip on the staff and knife blades sprang out from both ends.

The woman spun the staff round and jabbed it forward. Tessa deftly sidestepped. Another jab followed, then another, then a high sweeping stroke. But Tessa had studied Kenjutsu for long enough to be able to evade the poorly aimed blows with ease. Her assailant was clearly furious, and tiring; Tessa started laughing.

"Is that really the best you can do?" she mocked. "Let me show you how it should be handled."

She advanced menacingly towards her attacker, who backed off and reached into her pocket. Thinking she might have a gun, it was Tessa's turn to retreat. The woman produced something and hurled it down in front of her. A cloud of acrid, foul-smelling smoke exploded between them. By the time it had cleared, the assailant was getting into a grey van some distance away.

"Hmm," muttered Tessa, "an amateurish attack and a stink bomb, used by someone who didn't want to be recognised … but why me? Anyway, I got the message. However, no harm done, so I think I'll keep this one to myself."

The following day, she went for her usual run. It proved to be an irritatingly nervous affair as she spent much of the time looking over her shoulder and studying those approaching her. After the attack at the underground station, it had taken her a long time to regain her self-confidence. Now it was gone again, and she no longer felt safe in London. Sitting on her doorstep, drinking water from a bottle and thinking, she made a decision.

She had a shower and prepared for her session at SKS. All she had to do now was to swallow her pride, yet again, and tell Lee.

They finished training mid-afternoon and, as Tessa wondered how to broach the matter, Lee spoke to her.

"Nariko-san, it was a good session, but anger doesn't enhance technique, it compromises it."

171

"I know, sorry," replied Tessa.

"I don't know what is troubling you," he continued, "but if I can help, I would like to."

Tessa forced a smile.

"I've been let down, badly, and it's really upset me."

"Why don't we have some tea?"

She joined Lee in his private rooms. His wife had barely left when Tessa broke the silence.

"I promised to give you my answer about training in Japan," she said. Lee looked up surprised, he hadn't expected her to begin with that topic. "You've been very understanding in not pressing me, especially since I've taken much longer than I said I would."

"Yes, I suppose I have," he replied, smiling in an attempt to hide his unease, "but I didn't want you to give the wrong answer. I thought it best to leave you to think about it."

"Well, Master Lee, you have been patient with me on several occasions. I would like to thank you for that, and indeed for having faith in me from the outset." Tessa looked at him, noting the anxiety in his eyes. "Perhaps now would be a good time to press home your attack concerning this issue." Her voice faded away and she looked down at the table.

For a moment only the sound of the water from the pool broke the silence. Then Lee let out a huge sigh of relief.

"What brought you to this conclusion?"

"Well, I doubt one should make such an important decision when one's angry, but it forced me to think differently. It's made me realise I need a change, something to distract me. That's not a good reason to go, is it?"

"It's certainly not the best reason. But in this instance I believe it is so important you do go, I don't think it really matters why. I am absolutely delighted. What's more, I am sure by the time you come back, the pent-up emotion which I see in you now, will be completely gone."

"I am still not convinced I wish to hone my skills in order to hurt people, but I have always enjoyed visiting Japan. Maybe if I do this I will understand better how my abilities fit in with my future."

Lee smiled.

172

"I am sure you will find out many things about yourself. But believe it or not, I am pleased you are hesitant to use your skills. If you were more enthusiastic, I would be concerned about your motives. Sometimes it can be difficult for us to live with skills that were given to us for a reason we do not comprehend. But everything becomes clear eventually, given time... Now I can tell you that your teacher will be Master Matsumoto. But a word of caution; it is prudent never to speak of your teachers to others, especially of one such as him. The fact that you will be training with him should remain a secret between us. Is that understood?" Tessa nodded. "I believe Matsumoto is the best samurai teacher in the world. Admittedly he does have a unique way of imparting his knowledge, but you will find out about that later. He will ask why you wish to train with him; you would be wise to have a good answer ready by then.

"He will start by spending some time, usually a couple of days, assessing your abilities. Then he will decide whether or not he wishes to train you. This is not something you can influence in any way other than by being yourself and doing your best. His decision will be final. If he concludes it is inappropriate for him to train you, then you should come home, or do whatever else he says. Indeed you should always do *exactly* what he says. He is a little eccentric, but he is a very good and very skilled man. I trust him completely, and so should you..."

Lee spoke for nearly an hour. Tessa listened intently, nodding occasionally, and becoming increasingly apprehensive as she realised Matsumoto was no normal teacher. But she still felt that one way or another the trip would be a welcome change. For her part she could decide during the assessment period whether she liked him or not. If she didn't, she would simply leave...

It took quite a while to obtain all the paperwork necessary for her to take her sword with her; only Potter could authorise it. However, once she'd tracked him down, things progressed more quickly. He appeared completely uninterested in her reason for taking her sword to Japan, which surprised her, but she wanted his signature not his approval.

The days passed quickly as Tessa made her preparations. She decided to pamper herself and bought First Class plane tickets. Lee assured her that someone would be at Tokyo's Narita airport to meet and guide her. However, she was still worried that she didn't know much at all about what she would be doing, not even her ultimate destination or the name of her escort.

Eventually, she had to tell Sinclair and Jones she was going away. She purposely left this until late since she wanted to keep pressure on them to find Penny's killers. She sent Sinclair an SMS requesting a meeting at Antonio's, receiving a reply by return suggesting later that day. She was already settled in the café when he and Jones arrived.

"Good afternoon, gentlemen," said Tessa, catching Antonio's attention so he could take their orders. "What progress have you to report?"

"Ah," said Sinclair, "good news and bad. We think we're zeroing in on the perpetrators and it does seem to be organised crime, but we're still not sure which gang or what motivated them."

Sinclair paused as the coffees arrived. Tessa looked irritated.

"But isn't this precisely where we were last time?"

"Well, I understand it might look that way," he replied, "but, I assure you, we are working hard on this and making progress. It is difficult and slow work and we would ask you to be patient. We will find out who did this and why. We will not give up."

"Especially while I'm continuing to pay you."

Sinclair breathed deeply.

"You know it's more than that."

"What exactly have you been doing since we last met, and have you brought the usual report?"

Sinclair looked at Jones who put down his coffee cup to pick up his briefcase. He knocked the table clumsily and found that Tessa had pre-emptively raised his cup. He smiled apologetically and removed a few papers, stapled together.

"Here it is. I'm sorry it looks so thin, but that's not a reflection of the amount of time and effort invested in our research. I'm afraid you'll just have to bear with us."

"No, I don't," retorted Tessa pointedly. "I take it you understand that?"

There was an awkward silence which Jones eventually broke.

"Let me tell you what we've been doing," he said in a placating tone of voice.

He spoke for twenty minutes, describing some of the complex

banking transactions they were tracing as well as the various rather unsavoury characters they'd approached. What he said did go some way towards alleviating Tessa's concerns but she didn't want to show it.

"I'll read the report later and let you know if I have any questions," she said noncommittally. "Frankly, I am very disappointed and feel you should have something material by now. However, I have some news of my own. I'm going away for a few weeks ... maybe a month, or even longer if I'm having fun. I would like you to continue pursuing your investigations in my absence. But I would also like to make it absolutely clear that, when I get back, I shall have high expectations of a breakthrough. If you can't report real progress then ... well, shall we just say, I'll consider my options?"

"Fine," said Sinclair with a relaxed smile. "Don't worry, we'll be working hard, even without you breathing down our necks every few weeks."

She looked at them both, puzzled that they hadn't asked where she was going. Jones realised that and clattered his cup against its saucer in his haste to redress the situation.

"Where are you going?" he asked, feigning interest. Tessa noticed Sinclair smile. "Somewhere nice ... in the sun maybe?"

"The Far East," she replied pensively. "I've always enjoyed holidays in that part of the world."

"Will we be able to reach you?" continued Jones.

"I'm not sure. You can send me an SMS, but if I end up in Burma or Bhutan your message might not reach me. So send me e-mails as well. With a bit of luck something will get through, eventually. I'll reply as soon as I can."

She was keen to avoid saying precisely where she was going and started readying herself to leave.

Jones looked at his boss who nodded. They both started to get up.

"Thank you for the coffee," said Sinclair. "Hopefully we will have something more positive for you when you get back. In the meantime, I'm sure a break will do you a power of good."

"Please, Sinclair, don't just *hope* you have something positive for me when I get back – have something conclusive," Tessa insisted. "This has gone on for long enough and my patience is nearly exhausted.

I want to see the guilty ones pay, so I can draw a line under this and move on with my life. Penny's death has haunted me for too long."

"I understand. We will get them. But try not to think about it while you're away. Concentrate on … having a good time."

Tessa smiled as she got up.

"I'll certainly try."

As she settled the bill, she couldn't help wondering why they weren't fazed by her saying she intended to go to the Far East. She would have expected them to be more concerned, especially since Burma was known not to be safe. In fact, the more she thought about it, the more she felt they must have known her destination already. But that would suggest they knew Potter; certainly a possibility if they were well connected. But they'd never mentioned they had contacts within the Special Forces. Furthermore, the movements of Sword Licence holders were meant to be confidential. She decided she would probe that further when she got back.

A few days later, she set off for Heathrow with her sword case, her carry-on suitcase and a not inconsiderable amount of paperwork.

She checked in for her flight and put her sword case in the regulation shipping crate. She was given one of the two keys; the other would be kept by the captain until the plane arrived in Tokyo. She would be allowed to check the crate was on the plane, but would not have access to it during the flight.

"Oh, well," she mumbled, as she watched London disappearing into the distance, "here goes nothing … hopefully."

CHAPTER 21

The eleven-and-a-half-hour flight to Japan felt frustratingly longer to Tessa. Desperate to disembark, she was delighted to find Immigration almost empty. She only had to wait five minutes instead of the usual half-hour; she never had been good at queuing.

Relieved finally to be on the short escalator down to Baggage Reclaim, she chuckled remembering the way the immigration clerk had not reacted by so much as a flicker when she had produced her RCL documents instead of a passport. He had simply stamped her papers and let her pass, wishing "Nariko" a pleasant stay. She had always liked visiting Japan, and, apart from her jet-lag, was pleased she'd come. It was bound to be interesting, one way or another, and perhaps even fun too.

Tessa headed for the Special Packages area to collect her sword. An impeccably dressed official and an equally well turned-out, obsequious-looking female assistant stood watching as she approached.

"*Ohayou gozaimasu*," said Tessa, wishing them a good morning in her broken Japanese.

"Good morning," responded the man, bowing to her with a glimmer of amusement on his face.

"I would like to collect my sword case, please. It arrived with me on BA005 from London. It is marked RCL-44 000625."

Their surprised expressions made her smile.

"*Ah-so*," he grunted. "We do have some packages from that flight. Confirm your name, please?"

"Nariko," she replied.

The man looked at his assistant and, as if in response to some unspoken command, the young woman rummaged through a file of papers, handing some to him.

"Hmm, your documents, please?" continued the man gruffly.

Tessa passed him her papers. He looked at them, then at her.

"Wait here, please."

He went into an office with a large window looking on to the hall.

Tessa could see him talking to his colleagues, all of whom looked at him, then at her, incredulous and curious. She found the whole process quite comical.

"Not the sort of thing a woman normally carries with her handbag then?" she said to the female assistant.

"No," replied the woman nervously, adding with a quick smile, "not yet."

Eventually the discussion in the office abated and one of the men disappeared. He returned with a baggage cart carrying the crate containing Tessa's sword case. The official came out with it and the envelope containing the captain's key.

"We do have your crate," he said unenthusiastically.

"Indeed you do," replied Tessa, trying to hide her relief at seeing it again. He stooped down to open the first lock and checked that two guards with long wooden staffs were nearby. "Please open the crate now. You may check that your sword is undamaged."

He stood back and watched Tessa comply.

"You understand we have strict rules about carrying such weapons in Japan?" continued the man abruptly.

"Yes, your Embassy in London explained them to me."

"I am still obliged to make clear that in Japan it is forbidden to draw a samurai sword in a public place. If you are found to have done so, then your sword will be confiscated and your RCL cancelled. In addition, you will be required to pay a substantial fine before being expelled from Japan. Do you understand?"

"Yes," said Tessa, tersely; quickly becoming bored. She slung her sword case over her shoulder in preparation for leaving.

"Enjoy your stay," the official grunted.

Tessa nodded and took hold of the handle of her small suitcase. Then she turned back, bowing respectfully to the man and his assistant.

"Thank you both for your kind and efficient assistance with this matter."

Surprised, they both bowed in response; the woman smiled.

When Tessa arrived at the Customs desk, the clerk looked at her sword case, then at her, and waved her through. She heaved a sigh of relief and strode into the Arrivals Hall.

However, within seconds, she realised that almost everyone was staring at her. She had grown accustomed to a degree of nervousness when carrying her sword case in London, but here everyone appeared far more uneasy. She wondered whether several civil wars with samurai swords very much to the fore was to blame. Perhaps it made this modern return to the sword even more scary for the Japanese.

Feeling distinctly awkward, she found the down escalator and descended to the mezzanine floor. She knew there was a Starbucks coffee shop there. She bought herself a large low-fat latté, and sat at an outside table to savour her caffeine fix. She watched the efficient bustle and couldn't help but smile. Japan was always neat, clean, ordered and on time; without drama, everything just worked. She loved it, even if many Westerners perceived it as alien. Nevertheless, she still thought it ridiculous she didn't know anything about the person hopefully meeting her; no name, no description, nothing. But at least she had a cup of coffee to keep her company.

"Don't look round, Nariko," a man's voice murmured from behind her. "It would be better if we were not seen talking. We are going to travel to Kanazawa. First, we will take the Skyliner Express to Ueno. There we will catch the Max Shinkansen from platform nineteen to Echigo-Yuzawa, and finally the Hakutaka Limited Express to Kanazawa, where a car will be waiting for us. The journey will take about seven hours. I have your tickets. Please go down to the platform. As you pass through the ticket barrier, I will insert your first ticket. Retrieve it yourself and get on the train waiting at platform two. I will not sit with you, but I will not be far away. I will make sure you do not get lost."

Tessa took a large gulp of her coffee, chiding herself for not having bought it to go. She glanced at the departures screen and saw they had three minutes to get on the train. Since this was Japan she knew it would leave on time; not early and definitely not late. She took another long gulp of her coffee, wondering why she hadn't been asked to make her own way to Kanazawa and why this part of her journey had to be shrouded in secrecy. Surely she was just another student visiting one of the several sword teachers in Japan? Certainly, the prospect of a long train journey after her overnight flight did not fill her with enthusiasm.

"We must leave now," said the voice insistently from behind her.

179

Tessa sighed and took two final defiant gulps of coffee. Then she slung her handbag and sword case over her shoulder and, dragging her carry-on suitcase, set off in the direction of the escalator down to the trains.

At the ticket barrier a slender tanned hand reached round from behind her to put a ticket in the machine. She collected it from the other end of the reader and studied it as she stood on the escalator. She was to sit in carriage 4, row 7, seat A; presumably by the window. She found her seat, stood her sword case beside her, wrapping one of the straps around her wrist, and settled down for the fifty-minute trip to Tokyo. As soon as the train started to move, an envelope dropped on to the seat beside her. In it were the tickets for her onward journeys.

She gazed out of the window and started to build a mental picture of her mysterious escort. His voice didn't sound powerful, but did possess an air of calm self-confidence. She thought he would probably be about 5' 3" tall, of slight build, mid-fifties, with a healthy tan and neatly cut greying hair.

A ticket inspector passed through the carriage and Tessa dozed off, only waking as the intercom heralded the train's arrival at Ueno. Tessa grabbed her luggage and went in search of her next train. She found she would have to walk to the nearby Japan Rail station. It took ten minutes, but was well signposted so she didn't need any prompting from her shadowy guide. She negotiated her way through the busy concourse towards the Shinkansen platforms. Everywhere she went, an uneasy hush followed. Even the inspector at the ticket barrier was more interested in her sword case than in her.

She went to the train and found her seat on the upper deck. Relieved to be out of the public eye, she put her suitcase on the rack above her seat and again twisted the sword-case strap round her wrist. Then she settled down for the doubtless wearing journey. She heard someone sit down behind her, but had already closed her eyes. She decided her escort would have to wake her if he wanted to say something.

At Echigo-Yuzawa she had a long and boring wait while changing trains. To her dismay she found the station didn't have a Starbucks. So, after eating sushi for lunch, she wandered aimlessly among the station stalls selling Japanese sweets and trinkets. She even found a sake-tasting shop, one entire wall of which comprised a vast number of neatly labelled little cubbyholes. In exchange for 500 Yen a customer received five tokens and a glass. Putting the glass in one of the cubbyholes and inserting a token resulted in the glass being filled. Having a liking for sake, she was sorely tempted, but thought it unwise to drink alcohol before reaching Kanazawa.

On the next train Tessa soon dozed off again. Occasionally she woke up and looked out of the window. Sometimes the train would be speeding through a town or industrial area, but more often through mountainous wooded countryside. She had her ticket checked once, but after seeing her sword case, the inspector was so nervous he seemed desperate to get away. She next stirred when the train stopped at Takaoka. From behind, the disembodied voice spoke again.

"Good evening, Nariko. Kanazawa is the next station. When we arrive, please go down to the main hall and turn left after the ticket barriers. I will then move in front and lead you to the car."

The train slowed and Tessa stood up to reach for her suitcase. As she did, she glanced back surreptitiously at her guide to verify her mental picture. He wore a well-pressed grey suit with a white shirt and a burgundy-coloured tie. He had a decidedly friendly face and was slightly taller than she'd expected, but his hair was white and wiry, quite long and somewhat unkempt. However, he certainly appeared to be in his mid-fifties. She sensed he felt he'd seen it all before, and that to him she was indeed simply another of his master's students. As their eyes met she nodded, almost imperceptibly, but otherwise gave no indication there was any interest or recognition in her gaze.

Meanwhile Hayasaka, the man who had just been so closely scrutinised by Tessa, was battling hard not to show his amusement. He always wondered how long it would be before a potential student allowed their curiosity to get the better of them. He had to admit at least this English woman had looked at him discreetly. She radiated an air of containment and accomplishment; very different from the many other students he had seen, the vast majority of whom had been male. Maybe she would be good enough. Certainly Lee had been adamant that this woman possessed the necessary talent and potential. That itself would be a change since so few demonstrated they could achieve the high standards demanded by Master Matsumoto. Nevertheless, he couldn't help wondering why a woman like this wished to enrol for such arduous training. She appeared to be alert and energetic, but still looked out of her element here with her neatly styled blonde hair and expensive tailored suit. It had been a long time since they had had a student this pretty. He watched her lower her bag and lightly hoist her sword case on to her back. Clearly she would not easily be separated from her sword.

As the train stopped, Tessa glanced longingly at the fine hotel which towered over the station. She had stayed there before on a couple of occasions while visiting Kanazawa for business. The prospect of a hot bath, decent food and a good night's sleep in a comfortable bed beckoned invitingly. She sighed, stepped off the train and went down the stairs to the exit. She felt slightly rested, despite the long journey, but definitely not as sharp as she would have liked to be. She hoped things wouldn't become too difficult too quickly. She passed through the ticket barrier and turned left, walking slowly so her guide could overtake. Soon the two of them were standing in front of the station's west gate.

Tessa couldn't see much in the darkness beyond the brightly lit station precinct. But to her left a taxi rank snaked forward as new arrivals were driven away. To her right was a quieter area reserved for private limousines. Hayasaka discreetly flicked the newspaper in his hand. A spotlessly clean old black saloon glided forward. Its shiny chromium trim glinted in the station lights. As the car stopped quietly in front of them, both the back door and boot lid sprang open and the driver got out. Before he had finished bowing, Tessa had placed her small suitcase in the boot and taken a seat in the back of the car with her sword case. Hayasaka smiled and got into the front passenger seat as the driver shut the boot.

A moment later they were off, zigzagging through the heavy traffic into the centre of town. They queued briefly outside a Starbucks and Tessa wondered whether she could persuade them to wait while she bought a cup of coffee. But just as she was about to ask, they started moving again. Deeply disappointed, she tried to remember what she could about Kanazawa. She knew it boasted an extraordinarily beautiful park, a remarkable geisha district and a long proud samurai history.

Before leaving London, she had tried to find out what she could about Master Matsumoto. However all her efforts had proved fruitless, not helped by Lee's insistence that she should not mention the name to anyone. Under pressure, he had confessed that he, Master Matsumoto and Kimi Amakuni had been close friends for many years. Then he had repeated several times that Tessa's training would be hard, very hard. He had also emphasised she should show Master Matsumoto utmost respect and trust him completely, regardless of how she felt at the time. Above all, Lee had insisted she should never swear, crack jokes or make wisecracks. Matsumoto would interpret that as discourteous and a crude lack of self-discipline. Tessa was confident she could handle him.

The car turned right and sped along a short dual carriageway, stopping at some traffic lights. Tessa noticed a sign to the Kenrouken Park. A moment later, as the car passed through a shallow gorge under a bridge, she glimpsed a sign to Kanazawa Castle. Eventually they turned right into the Higashi Chaya geisha district, one of the few in Japan which had remained unchanged for more than two centuries. Tessa had eaten very well there once. She saw some kimono-clad geisha wearing wooden clogs welcoming businessmen to a restaurant for an evening of eating, drinking, and polite, if childish, games.

For a while, she tried to memorise the way they had come. But the car moved so quickly through the narrow winding streets that she soon lost track. So, as they sped on, she resigned herself to accepting that she had no idea where they were or how to get back to the station. Already beginning to feel uneasy, she noticed the driver looking in the rear-view mirror to check that no one was following them.

Suddenly the car swerved sharply left and shot out from between two rows of wooden lattice-fronted geisha houses. It rattled noisily over a wooden bridge and plunged into the dense forest beyond. Then the engine started labouring as the car struggled up a steep hill on a winding unmade track. The trees closed in, occasionally parting to present a view of the steep drop to the lights of Kanazawa far below. The driver had clearly followed the bumpy, rutted route many times before, since he expertly avoided the worst of the potholes – a feat made all the more impressive by the fact that he insisted on driving as fast as the car would go with the way ahead lit only by the moon and the sidelights. Tessa became more apprehensive. To what isolated place were these people taking her? What exactly had Lee let her in for?

She was just wondering, for the hundredth time, how long she still had to endure being thrown around in the back when the car suddenly lurched to the right. It started up an immensely steep slope with the rear wheels spinning as they struggled to find traction. Then the incline eased and they passed through some dense overhanging trees along an overgrown muddy track. Finally, the car nudged through some high bushes and stopped. They were in the middle of a flat, almost circular gravelled area surrounded by dense forest.

Tessa saw two wooden houses, one on either side of what she decided to call the car park. Both were single-storey, with wood-tile roofs and chimneys from which thin plumes of wispy white smoke snaked upwards. In front of the car, she could just make out the silhouette of a high stone wall disappearing laterally into the darkness to both sides. Built into this, symmetrically placed between the two houses, stood a large double-roofed gatehouse framing a pair of substantial wooden doors. By the light of two lanterns, hanging near these, Tessa could see that the gatehouse was quite ornate, typical of entrances to ancient prestigious castles. It looked both impressive and daunting. For the first time, her guide turned to face her.

"Nariko, welcome to Matsumoto Castle, ancestral home of the Matsumoto family. My name is Hayasaka. Please come with me."

Tessa smiled and bowed, trying not to show how nervous she felt.

They all got out of the car, but by the time she had reached the back her small suitcase was standing waiting for her. The driver bowed to them both, got back in the car and drove away through the narrow gap in the bushes. Tessa watched it disappear with a forlorn expression on her face. Oh, now, that's great, she thought. I've got myself into one hell of a mess this time and the limo just left.

Sensing her concern, Hayasaka bowed.

"This way, please. You will be staying here tonight. You will enter the castle grounds on your own tomorrow at three a.m."

Tessa gulped as she took in what he had just said. He really expected her to go into the grounds of a completely strange place, on her own, at three in the morning?

But Hayasaka was already walking towards the wooden house on the right. Tessa looked down at her bag, waiting on the ground, and picked it up with a smile. Welcome to Matsumoto Castle indeed, she thought.

She followed Hayasaka into the house and found it to be much larger and more comfortable than was suggested by its drab exterior. The internal walls were of white paper on slatted wood, some panels of which slid aside to form doors. She soon concluded that although modern creature comforts appeared few and far between, this place was tasteful, warm and welcoming.

"How nice," she mumbled, kicking off her shoes.

"I am pleased you like my humble home," said Hayasaka, smiling at her in an unexpectedly friendly manner. "Dinner has already been prepared for us. Your room is the second door on the right down the corridor. It has its own bathroom. My room is next-door. I suggest you make yourself comfortable. We will eat here in twenty minutes. If you wish, you may remove your sword from its case now. There are no restrictions here. You will find a tunic in your room together with some sandals. Besides your sword, that is all you should take with you in the morning. Once you have entered the castle grounds, you will not come out until your time with Master Matsumoto is ended. You may leave all your other possessions here, they will be perfectly safe. I will remain here until it is time for you to go."

Tessa thanked him and marvelled at the way their previously limited communication had evolved into a significant information dump. She went to her room and, in preparation for a hopefully early night, unrolled her mattress and made her bed.

Dinner proved uneventful: miso soup, sashimi, rice, fruit, mineral water and green tea. Tessa saw no one except Hayasaka, and he said little. Clearly, they were each trying to size the other up. However, at 8 p.m., when he stood up to indicate the meal had finished, neither of them was much the wiser.

"I shall wake you at two-fifteen," he announced. "That will give you plenty of time to get ready and have a light breakfast. The gates will be opened for you at three and you must reach the castle by dawn, which tomorrow will be at four-forty-five. Master Matsumoto does not like students to be late, especially on their first day."

"I understand. But, Mr Hayasaka, may I ask why I need nearly two

185

hours to get from the entrance to the castle? Is it a long way?"

He smiled.

"Please, do not be concerned. I have told you all you need to know."

"But surely there is only one castle in Kanazawa, and isn't Matsumoto Castle east of here, past Hida-Takayama?"

"Everything will become clear in due course. Now, I suggest you get some sleep. Good night."

Tessa nodded. After her exhausting journey she soon fell fast asleep. However, she woke up well before she heard Hayasaka's gentle tapping at her bedroom door. Already dressed in her tunic, she slid the door open.

"Oh, you are ready, good," he said, surprised he had not heard her moving about.

Tessa ate her breakfast of miso soup, herb-infused rice and fruit in silence. She tried to console herself with the thought that over the years she had amassed considerable experience of travelling rough in the Far East. However, she'd been feeling nervous since she woke up, and sensed that fear would not be far behind.

She considered asking Hayasaka for a little time to think things over. But, as she gathered herself to say something, he pointed out that it was 2:50 so she returned briefly to her room. Shaking her head in disbelief at her own stupidity for getting herself into this situation, she checked she'd left everything in good order. Then she put on her shoulder harness, slipped her sword in, and went back to Hayasaka. He simply bowed and gestured her to the front door. As she walked past him he looked at her sword. He knew Kimi Amakuni's work well and could tell this was a particularly fine example. No wonder she would not be parted from it, he thought.

Tessa walked out of the house into the darkness with as much dignity as she could muster given that her legs were shaking. She and Hayasaka scrunched their way across the gravel towards what Tessa guessed was a fourteenth-century gatehouse. The two lanterns now cast a stronger flickering light across the large doors, by which stood two men.

The cold, damp stillness, combined with the butterflies in her stomach, were almost unbearable. Hayasaka gestured to the men and Tessa gritted her teeth. With a *clunk* the doors were unlocked with a large iron key. Then, with a loud creaking and groaning from massive rusty hinges, the two men pushed one door open just far enough for her to walk through. Tessa stood transfixed, mesmerised by the black hole which seemed to have opened up in front of her. She couldn't even see the path which presumably lay on the other side.

"You have more than sufficient time to reach the castle before dawn," said Hayasaka, quietly, "but you should keep moving. Once through the gatehouse the path is quite clear. But be careful as you cross the river. The wooden bridge is slippery, and if you fall, you will be hurt. Eventually, you will enter the castle grounds. Go through the main gate and up the stone staircase between the two chinthes; you will find Master Matsumoto at the top. You may enter now."

"Right," said Tessa hesitantly, studying the ominous blackness in front of her. "Follow the yellow brick road…"

"Sort of," replied Hayasaka. "But this is not Oz, there is no wizard, and clicking your heels will definitely not get you home safely."

Tessa spun round grinning, delighted by this unexpected quip.

"That's a shame, Mr Hayasaka. But thank you anyway."

She bowed, turned back, took a deep breath and walked forward. She was barely through the door when she heard it bang shut behind her, followed by the *clunk* of the key being turned again in the lock.

She tried to see where to go, but couldn't make anything out; it felt too dark and musty for her to be outside. She tentatively picked her way forward, instinctively reaching out in front. To her surprise she found she was about to walk into a stone wall. Then she felt a slight breeze coming from behind her.

"Ah," she muttered to herself, "it's one of those staggered gatehouses to stop attacking armies charging straight through."

She backed out of the cul-de-sac she had entered, and turned to her left. Then she felt the breeze again and could see some light. She turned right and rejoiced at reaching fresh air, but realised it had started raining. Nevertheless, in the moonlight, she could make out the rough track ahead. To her left stood a group of enormous camellia trees. There were several varieties, and many were covered in flowers, white, pink and deep red. Not only did they look stunning, they released an almost intoxicating perfume. She breathed in deeply and looked back at the path.

"Well," she muttered to herself, "of all the daft things you've done, this is without doubt the daftest! Now, get going."

Tessa knew she'd be soaked before long, but if she went quickly at least she shouldn't get too cold. She jogged along the narrow path as it wound down through a forest. Although she suspected she didn't have particularly far to go, not knowing the lie of the land made pacing herself difficult. As her eyes became more accustomed to the poor light, she quickened her pace. She wondered who would find out if anything catastrophic happened to her while visiting this … castle. There was no doubt that if this early morning run was intended to unnerve her, it was. Over and over again, she mumbled rhythmically, "This is mad-ness, this is mad-ness."

Soaked, but settling down, she broke into a relaxed run as she descended into thick mist with her tunic and sandals squelching noisily. The track developed into a more defined path and levelled out. As she ran on over rough pastureland, the noise of quickly flowing water became more distinct.

Suddenly, the path stopped at the base of a narrow wooden structure. This must be Hayasaka's slippery bridge, she thought, as she strained to make it out. But the mist prevented her from seeing more than a few feet ahead. However, from what she could make out, it looked like a narrow set of unsupported wooden stairs leading into the swirling clouds. The river could faintly be heard some distance below.

"Definitely not a good idea to fall," she muttered. Then the mist parted briefly and she caught a glimpse of what lay before her. She stared in horror and swallowed hard. "I do believe ludicrously bad just got worse!"

The bridge appeared to be made entirely from wood. Apparently each substantial step was made from a rectangular plank which had simply been laid with its edge overlapping the previous one, as though forming a corbelled arch. The undersides of the planks had been smoothed off to form a graceful curve. But there didn't seem to be any nails or bolts supporting the structure. Instead it looked as though it was held together purely by wooden dowels. She wondered how many such arches she would have to traverse to reach the other side.

The bridge reminded her of the Kintai Bridge at Iwakuni. The construction technique certainly looked similar. However, whereas the twelve-foot-wide Kintai Bridge had sturdy handrails to either side, this bridge was barely three foot wide and had none. Tessa seriously doubted its stability.

She gathered her courage and nervously started climbing. The first few steps were very worn, and the rain had made them incredibly slippery. No wonder Hayasaka had warned her about it. The bridge groaned in protest as it took her weight. Slowly she inched her way higher. As she progressed, the steps became shallower and the bridge started to flex and sway sickeningly. Scared of falling, Tessa went down on all fours. Near the top, the stairs stopped altogether and she found the surface was completely smooth, forming a gentle arch, as underneath. She continued forwards and turned round to reverse down the other side, seeing that she had at least one more arch to surmount. When she reached the stepped section downwards, she began to worry she was taking too long. She stood up and turned to walk down to the stone pier. But then a gust of wind struck the bridge, making it shudder violently. In danger of losing her balance, Tessa ran the last few steps, then slipped and fell forward. Struggling to reach the pier, she landed heavily on her knees.

"Ouch! That bloody hurt!" she yelled in disgust.

She stood up, rubbing her knees, looking disconsolately at the second arch. She dearly hoped there were only two. She paused, took a deep breath and started up the narrow steps. By the time she reached the top she was once again on all fours. She wondered how long she still had before dawn.

After what seemed like an age spent reversing down the second arch, her feet finally stepped on to soggy, grassy ground. With her knees still aching, she set off as quickly as she could. The going became easier as the path led her across the narrow soil banks between paddy fields. However, the rain hadn't eased and her tunic was completely waterlogged. To add insult to injury, she felt cold now too.

She could see the sky beginning to brighten in the east and knew the mist would lift soon. However, for the time being, it continued to swirl around her in impenetrable clouds. Just as she began to worry she was following the wrong path, a dark shape loomed in the distance.

"I sincerely hope that's the castle," she murmured, quickening her pace.

Gradually the dark shape became more distinct and the path widened as it traversed flat fields. She crossed a stone bridge over another substantial stream and passed the ruins of a wall extending in both directions. Tessa slowed slightly to catch her breath.

"Outer moat … inner moat soon," she muttered. Then, through the mist, she saw part of a massive stone wall. It was made from enormous rocks piled high and smoothed on the outside to form a dizzyingly steep upward slope. When she visited Iga Ueno, she had been told that it possessed the highest castle *honmaru* in Japan, but this one had to be much higher. It was also big. Tessa was convinced it had been built around a hill protruding from the plain. She could even make out a substantial buttress protruding further into the wide moat, strengthening the corner of the wall and providing the foundation for a long-gone watchtower. Then she came to a wide stretch of still water which she crossed by an old wooden bridge that appeared to have been a drawbridge once. The planks rattled noisily as she sprinted over them, sure she was nearing her goal.

She passed through a roofed main gatehouse with its huge doors left ajar, to find the path turned sharply to the right. A minute later, she stopped by a set of stone steps leading up. Encouragingly, there was a weather-worn chinthe to either side. The lions had clearly seen better days, but she still marvelled at what had once been a very fine pair of sandstone carvings. But the sun would be rising soon so she started jogging up the stairs. She followed the path as it twisted and turned, through one impressive gateway after another. She had no idea where she was going as she was always surrounded by high walls. The path seemed to go on for ever. Occasionally, it would divide and she would have to choose which way to go. Once she made an incorrect choice and nearly fell into the moat when the path ended abruptly at a precipice above it. However, determined not to miss her deadline for reporting to Matsumoto, she pressed on past abandoned sentry posts, and numerous rectangular and triangular archer and circular musket holes. Eventually she rounded a corner to find a closed gate. She paused, puzzled and breathless. Then she realised there was another narrow gate hidden behind a nearby buttress.

"Janitor's entrance," she chuckled, and started up a passageway with stairs of unequal heights and lengths. In the darkness, she found just walking up them difficult, but continued as quickly as she could. She mentally congratulated the castle designers on having produced such effective defences. Soon she found herself concentrating on her feet so intently that she walked straight into a low stone beam, presumably positioned precisely for that purpose. The noise of her banging her head was so loud it reverberated along the passageway. Stunned, she stepped back, tripped and fell. Badly bruised, muttering expletives and thoroughly disheartened, she struggled to her feet and seriously considered going down rather than up. But then she gritted her teeth and went on more carefully. Completely exhausted, she turned a sharp corner and entered a small enclosed courtyard. At the opposite side was yet another impressive gateway, with an iron-clad timber door.

"The final defence," panted Tessa. She ran up some more steps and, to her great relief, found herself in one of the corners of the *honmaru*. It was much larger than she'd expected, and rectangular rather than square. She paused to recover and rub her aching forehead.

The edges of the *honmaru* were bounded by a white-washed stone wall topped by a tiled pitched roof. It was braced with stone pillars and wooden connecting beams and appeared to run round the entire perimeter. The surface underfoot was of trampled soil with patches of worn grass. Tessa went to one of the arrow slits in the wall and peered through. Although the sun still hadn't come up, the sky was brightening quickly, chasing away the mist to reveal a breath-taking panorama. The castle stood at the confluence of two rivers in the middle of a large fertile plateau, cradled by high hills. She could see much of the path she had just run along, and even the graceful arches of the narrow wooden bridge as it crossed one of the rivers. It was stunningly beautiful and she could quite happily have stood and enjoyed it all day.

She reluctantly pulled herself away and started along a wide stone-flagged path which bisected the *honmaru* and led towards a substantial wooden arch. This was made from two enormous round wooden pillars, one on either side of the path, spanned by two substantial square timbers. The lower crosspiece was horizontal, while the other curved up gracefully at each end. In the middle they were joined by a wide vertical piece of wood on which was carved a large chrysanthemum. The overall effect was both aesthetically pleasing and subtly intimidating. It resembled a *torii*, but Tessa doubted she was entering a religious shrine.

The path continued through an avenue of trees which had been trained to slope inwards, meeting overhead. At the end of the avenue, where by all accounts she should have seen a castle, Tessa found a traditionally built wooden samurai house. The proud and balanced lines of the building beckoned her on, soothing her apprehension.

She strode on, studying the structure more closely. It had been beautifully built and was in magnificent condition, with perfectly proportioned multiple scalloped roofs. The house occupied a substantial part of the *honmaru*, but still looked strangely incongruous in what had presumably been intended for a much larger structure. Nevertheless, the whole place exuded an air of dignity, sophistication and confidence – just about everything she lacked at that particular moment in time. The fenced off inner courtyard seduced her further with a tantalising glimpse of the decoration within. Only the faint smell of a fire, and a stray wisp of smoke, suggested the house might be occupied.

As she walked, her sandals made an embarrassingly loud, squelching noise and Tessa wished it would stop raining. She paused at the foot of the five stone steps leading up to the covered gateway and glanced at the wall extending in both directions to the edges of the *honmaru*. Here, the lower half was still of white-washed stone, but the rest was stained wooden latticework, again capped by a pitched roof. Then she marvelled at the intricate carving on the doors, shaking her head in amazement. According to what she had read there were no castles or samurai houses of significant architectural merit outside Kanazawa town. Yet here she was, standing in front of one of the finest examples she had ever seen.

Tessa turned her attention to the roof tiles. Along the edges would be a row of circular end-caps displaying the coat of arms of the family responsible for constructing the building. She found an unusually complex emblem with three samurai swords, all pointing upwards with their blades crossed. One was vertical with the others crossing it from either side. Completing the design on either side of the swords was a large stylised chrysanthemum, the Imperial flower of Japan.

Tessa climbed the five stone stairs and took a deep breath to calm herself before stepping down into the inner courtyard. The path was laid more elaborately here. It comprised smaller cream-coloured flagstones bordered with two rows of grey stones. On either side of the path stood three massive stone lanterns, all seven foot tall but of different designs. These were very imposing, adding to the already overbearing atmosphere. Across the front of the samurai house, just under the roof, hung a long burgundy banner. On either side were large white representations of the same sword-and-chrysanthemum motif she had seen on the roof tiles. The centre of the banner was gathered upwards at the middle, framing the entrance to the audience hall.

Cautiously, Tessa approached the house. Only the gentle hiss of dying embers disturbed the silence. The two large wooden lattice doors had been slid aside, allowing her to see inside. A warm glow radiated from within. She considered how embarrassing it would be if she had come to the wrong place. But in any event, it was a stunningly beautiful and interesting place to have visited.

The ground to either side of her took on an orange hue and Tessa realised the sun had started to rise. Perfect timing, she thought and wondered whether she could make herself more presentable before the meeting. A quick glance down confirmed she looked dreadful. The path ended in three shallow wooden stairs leading up to a narrow verandah.

Tessa gathered her courage and climbed them. The audience hall was a surprisingly large and grandiose room with intricately carved beams criss-crossing the ceiling, but virtually no furniture. The floor was completely covered with tatami mats except for a large hearth. Finely carved stones formed its edges and in the centre were the remains of a substantial charcoal fire. Above it hung a large iron cauldron, suspended from the ceiling by a heavy black chain. The height of the cauldron could be adjusted by catching the chain on hooks screwed into what looked like a large wooden fish halfway down the chain.

What a wonderful place to live, thought Tessa.

CHAPTER 22

As her eyes grew accustomed to the light, she saw a stern-looking man sitting to the left of the hearth with his legs folded tightly in the lotus position. He seemed to be slim and strong, with a tanned, weather-beaten face. She thought he was probably about 5' 8" tall, and, despite a small, greying beard, looked younger than Lee. His hair was tied securely at the back of his head in a short ponytail. Overall, he appeared neat, relaxed, warm and dry; everything she would have liked to be herself. Gazing idly at the fire, he puffed on a finely made long-stemmed clay pipe. He gave no indication he knew she was there.

Tessa bowed.

"*Ohayou gozaimasu*," she said, desperately hoping her voice wouldn't betray how nervous she felt. "I apologise for the intrusion, but my name is Nariko. Hopefully, you are expecting me?" Her voice tailed off uncertainly.

"You're late," grumbled Matsumoto in quiet but cultured English, continuing to study the embers on the hearth. Their shimmering light glinted in his deep-set eyes.

Tessa's expression changed from one of relief to intense irritation. She turned slowly and deliberately to check the horizon. Only a tiny fraction of the sun was visible. She had arrived, cold, muddy and wet, but not late. She fought to control her annoyance at his churlishness.

"I am sorry, Master Matsumoto," she replied in English, trying to sound contrite but doubting she had succeeded. "The inclement weather made the journey difficult. May I come in, please? I am rather wet."

She raised her right foot in anticipation of being allowed to kick off her sandal.

"So I hear, Nariko," replied Matsumoto, still staring at the hearth. "You walk like a hippopotamus dancing in a bog, and rumble over my bridges. The weather is no excuse for your tardiness. Dawn is when the sun starts to come up, not afterwards; that's morning. You had more than ample time to get here. You shouldn't have dawdled."

194

Shivering on the verandah, Tessa was now close to exploding. She gritted her teeth and slowly put her foot down again. Matsumoto turned his head and regarded her with piercing brown eyes.

"You even *look* like a hippopotamus which has just wallowed in a bog. You may not come in. I don't want you dirtying my mats."

He scrutinised her from head to foot and Tessa began to feel uncomfortable. Perhaps she should have gone home after all. Maybe she still could?

"Are you scared?" he asked softly.

"No, just cold and wet. Should I be?"

"Oh, yes," said Matsumoto, and, with a flick of his wrist, threw a knife at her.

It all happened incredibly quickly, but Tessa was proud of her super-fast reactions. Furthermore, Lee had trained her incessantly in the art of catching knives, following her exploits in Stepney. She confidently reached out her right hand and caught the blade. Matsumoto nodded.

"Lee told me you were good catching knives … now. But can you throw them as well as you catch them?"

Still holding his pipe in his left hand, Matsumoto produced a 50 Yen coin and put it on the floor, barely an inch away from him.

"Throw the knife so that the point of its blade passes through the hole in the coin."

Tessa squinted at the coin lying on the tatami mat. She could only just see it in the dimly lit room, and the angle at which it lay made the hole in the middle look miniscule. If the knife overshot, it would hit Matsumoto.

"Don't worry," he continued, sensing her apprehension. "If you are able to strike me, you may go home."

Tessa wiped the water away from her face, hoping it would help clear her vision. Then she swallowed, aimed and threw the knife. She thought she had thrown it well; fast and straight. But the point of the blade struck the mat just in front of the coin, nudging it slightly closer to Matsumoto. He had sat motionless throughout.

"It seems your aim is nearly as bad as your Japanese."

He carefully extracted the knife from the mat and laid it beside him. Then, still puffing his pipe, he started to play with the coin, passing it over the back of his hand by flexing his fingers. The coin darted backwards and forwards surprisingly quickly, eventually coming to rest between his thumb and first finger. Tessa stood watching him, entranced. Suddenly he glanced towards the back of the room. Instinctively, her eyes followed; but she knew immediately that she'd made a mistake. Out of the corner of her eye, she glimpsed Matsumoto flicking the coin at her. Even her finely honed reactions weren't quick enough for her to evade it. There was a loud *ping* as it struck her hard in the centre of her forehead, just where she had walked into the beam. Momentarily stunned, she stepped back and promptly fell off the verandah, landing on her side in a muddy puddle.

"Ouch, that hurt ... again," she grumbled. "Oh, but at least it's stopped raining!"

As her senses returned she propped herself up on one arm to find Matsumoto standing over her wearing a sword.

"Get up," he rasped, retrieving the coin.

With her forehead throbbing, and trying to suppress her annoyance, Tessa eased herself up.

Matsumoto stood a few feet in front of her, relaxed and confident with his arms crossed.

"Attack me with your sword. Strike me before I strike you. But this is not one of Lee's cosy training sessions, this is for real."

She hesitated, not feeling comfortable about attacking the man she'd come to learn from. Furthermore, although she knew she could draw her sword at least as quickly as Lee, it seemed likely this man operated on an entirely different level. She wondered what the consequences of not beating him would be.

"As I said, attack me ... whenever you're ready. But please, don't dawdle again. It's going to be a fine day and it would be a shame to waste more of it."

Tessa remembered Lee telling her "anger compromises technique". So, she looked at Matsumoto, smiled, and then went for her sword.

She'd barely unsheathed it when she heard the ringing of his blade and felt the humming as it hovered close to her neck. She froze and glanced along it. The noise was reminiscent of hers and the steel had the same sheen, and, close to the hilt, bore the same family markings. Another Amakuni sword, but not from Kimi Amakuni. As the blades throbbed in unison, she carefully returned hers to its sheath.

196

"Hah! The sound is much more menacing when it's being turned against you, isn't it?" jeered Matsumoto.

Tessa didn't move, not even nodding. She didn't want to get any closer to the blade which she knew would cut her deeply with only the slightest of touches.

"So, are you scared now?" he asked, purposefully re-sheathing his sword.

"Even less than before," she replied, firmly. "It is clear you could have hurt me a long time ago if you'd wanted to."

"True. So why are you here?"

This was the question Tessa had been dreading. She had tried to prepare a plausible answer, but still hadn't come up with anything remotely satisfactory. She struggled to find something convincing to say, even if it wasn't entirely honest.

"Surely that can't be too difficult?" asked Matsumoto, harshly. "Lee must have told you to prepare. Or have you lost your voice now as well as your dignity?"

Tessa desperately tried to control her anger but knew it was getting the better of her.

"I haven't lost either," she replied pointedly, surprised to hear her voice quaking. She liked and expected to be in control, to command respect. This unaccustomed role reversal both infuriated and unnerved her. "I wanted to give you a full explanation, but I'm afraid I don't have a finely crafted, articulate answer for you. I only wish I did."

"How pathetic. You are more afraid of facing yourself than of facing me. Your childish excuses are of no value here; they waste my time while you hide from the truth. Just tell me what you are really thinking," he snapped, impatiently.

Tessa glared at him. However, it didn't appear to bother him in the slightest, if anything it looked as if he rather enjoyed it.

"I came here for several reasons. Master Lee, whom I respect, felt strongly that I should spend some time with you. I know I have only limited knowledge of samurai techniques, but I have been surprised by how much I've enjoyed learning ... well, so far. Anyway, after recently suffering some disappointments at home, I felt a change of pace and scene would do me good." Tessa knew her answer had been verbose, but at least it was honest.

"*So far!*" bellowed Matsumoto. "Try this for *so far.*"

Tessa wasn't quite sure what happened next. She experienced a sharp stabbing pain in her stomach accompanied by a bright flash of light. She lost consciousness for a moment, regaining her senses to find herself crumpled clumsily on her hands and knees, gasping for breath, with stars swirling in front of her eyes. Matsumoto calmly reached over and drew her sword. She moaned in panic, realising what he had done; she felt naked, beaten and vulnerable.

"Hmm. Kimi-san certainly excelled herself with this, but you hardly look worthy of it."

As Tessa concentrated on breathing, her vision slowly cleared. She looked down and was relieved to see that she wasn't bleeding; presumably he had just punched her.

"Scared now?" asked Matsumoto, standing over her threateningly.

"Getting there," she gasped, steadying herself by putting both hands on the soggy ground.

"Only getting there?" he boomed. "In which case…"

"No, please, don't," pleaded Tessa. She hadn't been intimidated like this since the last time her brother had assaulted her. Desperate and defenceless, she glanced round, wondering whether she could outrun him.

"Nariko, consider. You kneel in the mud while I hold your sword. Don't think of running away, just mean your next words," he insisted calmly.

Still panting, Tessa bowed her head. They both knew she would struggle to utter the declaration he wanted to hear, the consequences of which would be far-reaching.

"I yield," she whispered weakly. She knew the hierarchy of their relationship had been established. He would dominate, completely.

"Good! Now we're making progress."

He returned her sword to its sheath, and, slowly, Tessa stood up.

"So, why are you really here?" he continued.

"Because Master Lee thought…"

Matsumoto's eyes widened, prompting Tessa to brace herself and take a step back.

"Have you no opinions of your own?" he challenged her. "I asked why you came here, not why Lee thought you should come."

"I don't know."

"Yes, you do!" he retorted, raising his voice. "You just don't want to admit it – to yourself, or to me. We really don't have all day! Just tell me what you are thinking, then maybe we can get on with some real fun."

This last remark brought a smile to Tessa's face.

"You're right," she said, looking him in the eye. "Lee did want me to come here, but I couldn't make up my mind. Then my boyfriend dumped me and I was so angry I wanted to get away. To come here suddenly seemed better than drowning in self-pity at home. I'm sorry if that's not good enough, but it is the truth."

"It isn't good enough, but it is better. Have another go."

Tessa shifted awkwardly from one foot to the other. Matsumoto raised his eyebrows expectantly.

"Well ... before that, my best friend was murdered with a samurai sword and I swore an oath to ensure that all those responsible would pay for their crimes. She left me this wonderful weapon and I started to train with it, initially in honour of her memory. But I found I enjoyed it ... a lot. I felt I needed to be better able to defend myself, and thought the skills I acquired here might be useful in honouring my oath."

Tessa felt relieved since there was absolutely nothing else she could say. But she did wonder whether she had just tried another tack to placate him or whether she had in fact been pressurised into telling the real truth.

Matsumoto smiled.

"Why didn't you say that in the first place? So revenge, not justice, is what motivates you? How conventional, how superficial! You wish to inflict retribution on those who have offended you..."

"Well, it's not quite like that," she interrupted. "I would never act outside the law."

He sighed and looked at her sternly.

"Do not interrupt me ever again. Revenge and justice are very different things. You will understand that one day ... if you live long enough. And what happens after your evildoers have been eliminated? What will you do then?"

Still aching from his punch, Tessa waited respectfully to make sure he had finished addressing her.

"I haven't thought that far ahead," she admitted, "and I suspect I'm a long way off having to worry about it. The men I hired to find my friend's murderers have disappointed me so far. But, throughout my life, I have always focused on advancing one step at a time, without allowing myself to become distracted. When I am closer to facing the murderers, I will consider the consequences of helping to bring them to justice."

"*If* you ever get there. Public school, Oxford degree, rich, pretty and closeted... What experience do you have of the ugliness which spawns true criminality? Presumably the people who killed your friend were professionals. What are you in comparison?"

Tessa glared back at him, stunned to discover he knew so much about her and furious that he underestimated her determination.

"I may be little more than an amateur. But I've come a long way in a short time, and this is something I intend to do. Perhaps I'm not as proficient as many you've taught, but I face up to challenges and don't give up."

"We'll see whether or not you give up. But if you do train with me, you will learn how to defeat those who attack you. However, you must consider the burden which accompanies acquiring such skills. Have you any idea what it is like to take the life of another human being, no matter how evil their deeds? Are you sure you will be able to face your own reflection afterwards?"

"I don't know," Tessa confessed. "I've been asking myself that ever since I first drew blood with my sword, and I only wounded then. I suspect I won't know the answer until… It's all very strange. A series of coincidences has led me away from my previous life to Master Lee, and now here to you. I don't feel I have chosen this path, it seems to have chosen me. I do have misgivings about the consequences of using this sword – serious ones. I still like to think I am not a naturally violent person. But Master Lee trained me to use my sword, and to use it responsibly, and I will endeavour to learn more of both from you. What I lack in skill and strength, I will compensate for with determination and persistence."

The silence that followed was broken only by some wind chimes clanging softly in the light breeze.

"You are correct that determination and training can compensate for certain physical deficiencies," continued Matsumoto, in a more conciliatory tone. "But perhaps you are stronger than you think. Your frame certainly looks sturdier than I would expect in a woman..."

"What do you mean?" interrupted Tessa sharply.

Matsumoto smiled.

"Precisely what I said, Nariko. Nothing more, nothing less. Anything else is of no relevance to my decision as to whether or not I train you... The true art of Samurai has nothing to do with the coarse animal ferocity which many use to kill. The original Samurai were fearsome warriors, but they were also Zen Buddhists and sponsors of the arts; the word itself means *to serve*. A true Samurai abhors violence, and only ever resorts to it when there is absolutely no alternative. A true Samurai, trained by me, is guided always by three overriding principles: conscience, patience, perfection. You should never do anything against your *conscience*... A modern Samurai regularly makes life or death decisions, and must always be free from blind trust in individuals or organised persuasions such as religion or politics. Politicians endeavour to limit free thought and impose restrictions on the conscience to suit their own aims, while most modern religions are intolerant and self-centred, all too keen to hide their own failings. But do not confuse being God-fearing over issues of conscience with any involvement in today's organised religions; regrettably, the two are entirely different things. *Patience* is synonymous with the true Samurai. A trained warrior will never act hastily or without carefully considering all the consequences of his actions. However, if all alternatives have been exhausted, then *perfection* must always be what guides his actions..." Tessa smiled as he said 'his', but if Matsumoto noticed, he ignored it.

"My method of training is hard and demanding, and definitely not for the weak-willed. It is not a stroll in an English country garden; it will hurt, a lot. That I can guarantee. Perhaps most important of all, regardless of how far you progress, this training will alter you forever. Your new skills will bring new responsibilities, awesome ones, which sometimes will be difficult to live with. Are you sure you want to continue?"

"Yes," replied Tessa, surprising herself with her lack of hesitation. "If

I'd wanted to turn back, I had plenty of opportunities earlier today."

"Really?" replied Matsumoto with a quizzical smile. He stepped back from her and studied her again, stroking his beard pensively. "So, do you trust me?"

"I have no reason not to trust you."

Masumoto raised his eyebrows and looked at her searchingly.

"Let me see your hands."

She obediently held them out. He studied her palms and then turned them over. She felt his touch; it was hard but gentle, despite the underlying strength.

"Your hands are soft and weak. I presume the rest of you is equally pampered?"

Tessa was tempted to respond with a cheery 'I hope so', but decided to opt for the less contentious, "Probably."

"Well, you must trust me completely if you are to have any chance of learning anything useful in the time we might have. You must be prepared to work long hours with barely any sleep. I will ask you to do things you would never have thought yourself capable of doing. However, if you always follow my instructions, you will learn, and will not sustain any permanent damage. Do you accept this?"

"Yes."

Part of her wondered what was stopping her from turning and leaving, but she knew that she never could resist a challenge.

"Very well. I will make my final decision as to whether or not I train you after I have seen enough to judge your potential. In the meantime, we will make a start with your hands."

Lee had warned her Matsumoto was likely to delay his final decision for a couple of days. But Tessa was still disappointed to learn that the painful and undignified interrogation she had just endured was little more than a preliminary exercise. Her exasperation showed and he scowled at her.

"Nariko, I suggest you learn *patience* very quickly. Come with me."

Matsumoto led her to a wooden rack to the left of the samurai house and pulled off the cover. She stared in horror at the rows of vicious throwing weapons in front of her, most of which she had never seen the like of before. Meanwhile he went to another rack and uncovered it, then another, then another. As he uncovered the last rack, Tessa mumbled to herself, "It'll be a miracle if I survive this."

"Stranger things have happened," retorted Matsumoto, looking at her over his shoulder.

She swallowed.

"I'm sorry, I didn't expect you to hear my mumblings." Then she quickly added, in what she hoped was a suitably reverential tone, "Master Matsumoto."

"I may be a little older than you, but that doesn't mean my ears don't work. In fact, to the best of my knowledge, everything else still does, too."

He spoke with a satisfied expression that left her unsure whether she should laugh or feel threatened. She turned back to the first rack of weapons and considered her situation, quickly concluding it was far from promising. She certainly got the impression Matsumoto knew what he was doing. But would he really be able to train her in using these, without doing her any permanent damage? Matsumoto watched her, intrigued to learn the outcome of her deliberations. When she looked up he was standing uncomfortably close to her. Tessa marvelled at the way he had moved across the courtyard so quickly without her hearing him.

"They focus the mind, don't they?" he said. "Here you will learn the stealth, evasiveness and fighting techniques needed to defeat twenty opponents attacking with swords. Usually you will only be fighting four simultaneously as more would have difficulty accessing you. But, in order to be victorious, your sword skills will need to be vastly superior, as will your agility and stamina. I will teach you all of this, if you are ready."

She thought of Penny. Memories flashed by: the good times, the bad times, and seeing her friend in the mortuary.

"Master Matsumoto, someone I valued has been cruelly wrenched away from me. I cannot bring her back, but maybe I can stop the perpetrators from repeating such atrocities. I have achieved many things in my world, though probably little of consequence in yours. In the knowledge that there is never any gain without pain, I will do everything you ask to the best of my ability. What would you like me to do first?"

Matsumoto nodded. He believed she meant what she'd said, but doubted she understood its true implications.

"I understand you have studied Karate?"

"Yes."

"Good. Well, let's see if you can break objects which move and resist progressively, rather than static brittle ones. By that rack are some sacks and some sand. Fill a sack and tie it to the wooden crossbar so that it hangs freely at torso height. Then burst the sack by punching it. Use only one hand. I don't mind which. I will come to see how you are progressing after I have had my breakfast."

Tessa moved to undo the buckles on her sword harness.

"Do not take off your sword! Never remove your sword while you are here unless I tell you to. It must become natural for you to wear it at all times, regardless of what you are doing. Even while you sleep."

Matsumoto had already started to walk away when she sucked in her breath, but he still heard.

"Nariko, you have a habit of making light-hearted quips when under pressure. Don't do it any more, I find it very annoying ... and you wouldn't want to annoy me, would you?"

Tessa nodded, stifling the nervous smile that threatened to annoy him even more.

"I also think we should use whatever time you spend here to improve your Japanese. We will not speak English again."

She wanted to say something but didn't dare, so she just watched him walking away, open-mouthed and wide-eyed.

"You may start now," continued Matsumoto in Japanese, smiling to himself.

She filled a sack with wet sand and, straining to lift the heavy weight, tied it to the crossbar. She looked at it, swinging nonchalantly in front of her. She had never done anything this extreme before.

Oh, well, she thought, how hard can it be?

She braced herself and punched the sack as hard as she could with her right hand. There was a dull *thud* and Tessa screwed up her face in response to the excruciating pain in her hand. But she didn't make a sound. Instead she watched the depression she'd made in the sack quickly dissipate, as it swung backwards and forwards. She took a deep breath and punched the sack again, and again, and again. After thirty minutes her hand looked as raw as it felt.

She jumped when Matsumoto suddenly spoke from behind her.

"I told you to burst the sack, not tickle it. Hit it like this!"

He took her place and punched the sack, grunting. It promptly exploded, showering Tessa with sand.

"Now, fill another and begin again. Also, you need to learn to sense when someone is approaching. We will work on that later."

Tessa started all over again, trying to hold her hand and arm like Matsumoto had. After a few minutes, he returned.

"Better, but still not right."

He took hold of her now bleeding hand and moved the fingers.

"Since you're hitting something soft, you need to clench your fist like this. It will increase the impact on the sack and reduce the damage you suffer; and move your arm more like this."

He altered her stance and, holding her forearm and elbow, traced its movement.

"Imagine your fist passing through the sack, not just hitting the surface."

She checked she was about to do as he'd said, and punched the sack. The impact was entirely different and the impression her fist left was enormous compared to before. She didn't look at him, or say anything, she just prepared her next punch. It was another fifteen minutes later when Tessa, much to her surprise and relief, punched the threadbare sack and watched it slowly spew its contents on to the ground. Her right hand had lost all feeling a long time ago, soon after tears had stopped rolling down her cheeks.

"Excellent" said Matsumoto from behind her. She jumped again. "Now we can move on. You see the water urn over there?"

He pointed to a large square stone tank standing on four short legs; it was conical with its top wider than the base. Although the urn was nearly as high as her, Tessa could see its wooden top had already been removed.

She nodded, apprehensive of what he was about to say.

"First, have a drink from it, and then fill it until it overflows. There is a well halfway down to the chinthes. You will find some buckets and a yoke over there. Oh, and don't meddle with the urn. I know it has some leaks, but it is still possible to fill it."

He walked away. Tessa looked puzzled and was about to sigh noisily when she forced herself to stop.

"That's better," said Matsumoto, as he went up the stairs to the verandah of the house.

This time Tessa smiled openly as she walked over to the urn. She had a drink and bathed her hand. Then she hooked two buckets on to the yoke and set off down the stairs. This proved to be extremely difficult, not least due to the uneven steps. However, she found the well, filled the buckets and started back, staggering under the weight and trying not to spill any water.

She made several journeys and could hear the level of the water in the urn rising. She had just tipped another two buckets in when she saw water spurting out from the stone side. At first she thought it was a crack, but between some carvings she found a circular hole. Puzzled, she set off again. But every time she emptied buckets in, more water leaked out. She stood back from the urn and did some mental arithmetic, soon concluding she would never be able to fill it.

"Giving up so soon?" asked Matsumoto.

"I'm not giving up, I'm thinking."

"What are you thinking?"

"Well, given how fast the water is coming out and the rate at which I can bring it up from the well, it would appear to be impossible for me to fill the urn. However, you said it is, and so … I must be doing it wrong."

She looked around. The castle mound had clearly been built hundreds of years ago and, if under siege, a secure water supply accessible from the top would have been needed. She smiled as her eyes alighted on a low square stone wall with a wooden lattice cover over it, marking another well.

"Silly girl," she chided herself.

She picked up the yoke and went over to the well, quickly filling the buckets. Not long afterwards, water started flowing over the top of the urn, despite the prolific leaks.

As Tessa stood back, admiring her handiwork, Matsumoto watched her from the verandah and clapped.

"Perhaps now you understand that it takes brains as well as brawn. Drink some more water, eat this apple, and then burst a sack of sand with your other hand."

206

It was only forty minutes later when the next sack obligingly burst. Much faster than before, but by now Tessa's left hand was throbbing too.

"Good," said Matsumoto. "Now we'll see how good you are at cart-wheeling and handstands, to cover short distances quickly and accurately. Then you can run round the castle three times. When you get back, we'll have lunch."

Tessa knew she would be good at the gymnastics, but soon discovered the castle mound was even bigger than she'd thought. She returned an hour later.

Matsumoto smiled.

"I presume you can gut a fish?"

"No," she replied, still panting from her exertions, "not yet."

At last he beckoned her into the samurai house. She shook as much dried mud from her tunic as she could and kicked off her sandals. Then she slipped on some clean ones and followed him along the network of verandahs which joined the various buildings comprising the house. In the kitchen, he laid out several different fish on a large wooden chopping board, and quickly gutted one of them. Then he passed her the razor-sharp knife and guided her as, grimacing, she gutted her first fish. While he handed her another, Tessa took a quick peek through the lattice window. She was amazed to find the most exquisite of Japanese gardens beyond. She hadn't realised how much of the *honmaru* was behind the house. There was a large pond with several islands joined by arched bridges, and a wonderful selection of trees and shrubs, all beautifully maintained. Mesmerised by the view, she suddenly felt a vice-like grip descend on her right hand. She started in surprise, not least since she found Matsumoto's touch thrilling in a way she felt sure she shouldn't. He smiled at her.

"I would like fresh fish for lunch, not fresh fingers," he said softly, and looked down at the chopping board.

Her eyes followed his. She saw her hand with the knife in it, poised to cut through her left index finger.

"Ah … thank you," she said bashfully, as he released her hand. "I was distracted."

"Very unwise when holding a sharp knife. So, what single word would you use to describe my garden? Any language."

He was intrigued to hear her answer. He had heard so many struggle before her. Usually people came up with fantastic, or wonderful, or even sublime. But in his opinion, no one had yet done justice to it.

"Oh, now, that is difficult," mused Tessa, completely relaxed for a moment, lost in thought. "Hmm, Ritsurin-koen and Kenrouken are magnificent parks, and the Genkyu-en garden near Hikone Castle is quite exquisite. But this … this is a challenge in which I see no dishonour in failing. I know of no single word which adequately describes such a lovely place."

Matsumoto nodded.

"Very well. You may continue."

Tessa couldn't believe how much she enjoyed sitting down for lunch. However, as soon as he had finished, Matsumoto gave her another task, even though she was still eating.

Under his guidance, she laboured hard throughout the long hot afternoon. As soon as she had completed one horrendous challenge, he gave her another. It was evening before he finally announced she could stop for dinner.

She was delighted, not only for the break, but also because she'd spent much of the last few hours questioning her continuing presence there. It had helped to take her mind off the pain. But it hadn't taken her long to conclude she should not stay. His challenges were interesting, and she did appear to have the strength and determination to surmount whatever he threw at her. But, in truth, she found it all rather puerile; more appropriate to enhancing action films than real life. Nevertheless, she didn't want to give him the satisfaction of hearing her ask to leave. Instead, she would wait until he asked her to stay. Then, and only then, would she announce her intention of leaving. 'Thank you, but no thank you,' she practised saying in her mind, and the prospect both consoled and invigorated her. Hopefully, stopping for dinner meant she had at least endured the first day and would have only one more to go.

Matsumoto had also been thinking. He had pushed her as hard as he had pushed anyone at this stage. He wanted to find her breaking point, but so far he couldn't. Lee was right, this woman did have considerable potential. Despite her rawness and immaturity, with the right training she could be formidable one day.

Tessa was so tired she staggered slightly as she joined him in the audience hall. He had already prepared the food and, at his command, they both removed their swords. They sat opposite each other at the low table in the dining alcove. She ate her food as quickly as she could, suspicious that he might tell her to do something else. Then she cleared up after them both, coming back as instructed with some green tea.

She knelt at the head of the table, just as she'd watched Lee's wife do, and placed a cup of tea in front of him before sitting down herself. He nodded.

"Thank you. Sometime I must decide whether or not to train you. What do you think I should do?"

Tessa put down her cup and inspected her battered hands which only recently had struggled to hold her chopsticks. Exhausted and aching, she looked back at him with the semblance of a smile.

"I trust you to make the correct decision without advice from me," she replied, softly. Then she picked up her cup again and continued to drink, eager to finish her tea.

"Good answer," he said, studying her carefully. "Normally we would carry on well into the night. But today is your first day so I will prepare you some special fish, which I am sure you won't have tasted before."

In a desperate effort to stave off the urge to keel over and fall asleep, Tessa drank more green tea. She lost track of time, but suddenly realised Matsumoto was sitting opposite her again. He smiled and held up a black lacquer tray with a small decorated porcelain plate on it. Tessa looked at it, and her eyes widened in horror. There were pieces of several different fishes arranged on it, coiled into delicate swirls so that she could see both sides. The scaly skins were all brightly coloured, which suggested poison to her. One piece was green with orange dots, another blue with yellow stripes, another black with patches of white. In the middle lay some gooey dark red fish organs and some rolls of what looked vaguely like thick polythene. She thought the organs were probably livers and the "polythene" Fugu. A dark green gelatinous substance, presumably seaweed-based, had been liberally dribbled over the food. Never in her life had she ever seen or smelt anything quite so disgusting.

Insistent, he nudged the tray closer. With more reticence than she had shown while approaching anything else that day, she took the plate and put it down in front of her.

"I won't bore you with the details, but this is a very special dish. Admittedly, it is a bit of an acquired taste. However, I'm sure you will find it an experience worthy of placing alongside your other accomplishments. Eat it all, Nariko, and eat it quickly. Don't play with it. It is a rare combination, best enjoyed when freshly prepared."

Refusing to admit defeat with this, she made her first selection; the blue fish with yellow stripes looked prettiest. She picked it up with her chopsticks and placed it in her mouth. The taste proved even more revolting than she'd expected. She swallowed it and quickly reached for her green tea. Her stomach rolled in protest and for a moment she thought she was going to bring it back up. She looked up to see how far he'd progressed with his; but he didn't have any. This worried her since she couldn't believe he really wanted to give her a treat, although presumably he wouldn't want to poison her either. Wishing she simply had to burst another sack of sand, Tessa took a deep breath, ate the remaining contents of the plate and gulped down some more tea. Incredibly pleased with herself, she looked up to find Matsumoto watching her closely.

"Good," he said, noting the way her pupils had dilated. "I have decided you may stay here for further training."

Tessa smiled with satisfaction and considered the tone of voice she would adopt to deliver the conclusion of her deliberations. Got you! she thought with glee.

"Well, Master Matsumoto, thank you. I'm sure I should feel honoured, but there is something I would like to say…"

"Really? Go on."

"It's … it's …" Tessa frowned; suddenly she couldn't remember what she'd wanted to say. Instead, she became aware of an annoying buzzing noise and looked round to see what could be causing it. She opened her mouth, but no sound came out. Meanwhile the buzzing had grown so loud she could barely think, and her vision had blurred. Vertical walls were rippling before her like waves. She looked longingly at her sword and saw it flexing as though made from rubber. Then the walls dissolved into swirling clouds which started to advance towards her.

Oh, hell, she thought, that fish really disagreed with me, I must be about to faint. How embarrassing! But then another thought crossed her mind. Maybe the fish had poisoned her. Perhaps he wasn't as good a Fugu chef as he thought. She tried to stand up, thinking she should at least try and get out of the audience hall before she started vomiting. But she couldn't move.

Finally, she blurted out, "I'm not well…" Verging on panic she struggled to regain control. Flashes of lightning and crashes of thunder ricocheted around her head. Then she heard Matsumoto's voice, booming and echoing.

"Don't worry, Nariko, you have done well. Everything is fine. I will look after you. It will be easier for you now."

"No, I …" she moaned. "I feel …"

Everything spun sickeningly in front of her. Her ears rang with something akin to excruciating tinnitus. She clasped her hands together so hard they hurt. He implored her to relax. But she couldn't and started hyperventilating. As she desperately clutched at the remnants of consciousness, an incredibly bright light filled her eyes and she heard a deafening *whoomph*…

CHAPTER 23

Tessa's next memories comprised a disjointed stream of incomplete events. Many were of intense physical exertion, exhaustion and pain; but these were interspersed with starkly contrasting interludes of reading, talking and warm relaxed contentedness. However, what she thought she saw appeared to be happening at a distance, disembodied scenes within dense swirling mists, almost as though her mind was taking surreptitious peeks into her own future, to test whether she really wanted to go there. Whenever an image materialised, it evaporated as soon as she attempted to grasp it. Just as in a dream, with her consciousness adrift, she lost all sense of time and place.

It was during one such experience that everything suddenly started to change. Instead of dissipating, the scene came into clear focus and rushed towards her with alarming speed. So swift was its arrival that her body twitched, as occasionally it would just before she fell asleep. As the fog cleared, she found she'd rejoined herself, the world and reality. She blinked in surprise and looked around.

Tessa found herself lying on a thin mattress in her room at the back of the samurai house. She had no idea how she knew it was her room, but she recognised everything, especially the old bookcase leaning cockeyed against one of the walls. She read the title of the first book: *Advanced Ninja Methods and Weapons*. She didn't need to look at the others, she knew she'd read them all several times. There were books on Okinawan Karate, Kyokushin Karate, Aikido, Wing Chun, Taekwondo, Savate, Judo, Ju-Jitsu, and many other martial arts schools – Japanese, Chinese, Thai and Burmese – not to mention many on swords, knives and samurai combat techniques and strategies. On the lower shelf were books on traditional Chinese medicine, natural herbs and remedies, bone-setting and acupressure, disciplining the mind and healthy diets. Alone on the top of the bookcase lay a very worn copy of the Samurai Bushido code. Excellent books, she mused. How come I know them all so well?

Then, in the corridor outside, she heard the most gentle padding of bare feet being placed carefully on the wooden planks. Someone was trying to approach unheard.

Instantly wide awake, she silently stood up and drew her sword. She looked at it in surprise, it wasn't ringing. She stood stock-still on the tatami mat, slightly further than a sword's distance away from the paper walls. But out of the darkness, she heard Matsumoto's voice.

"Ah, Nariko, you are awake. What can you tell me about the person who approaches?"

"*Ohayou gozaimasu*, Master Matsumoto," replied Tessa, returning her sword to its sheath. "I know the person is a man on his own without a sword. He is walking barefoot and is holding something light with both hands."

"Perfect!" he said, chuckling. "You have learnt well. Now, join me. I would like to talk to you as we drink the tea I am carrying."

She hurried into the audience hall to find him already sitting cross-legged in front of the hearth. She sat down in what she knew to be her usual position to his right. For a while they sat in silence, drinking the green tea. Occasionally he glanced at her, but she waited patiently for him to speak.

"Well, Nariko, it is time for you to leave," he said softly. "Your training is complete, for now."

Tessa looked up amazed.

"What? But, Master Matsumoto, I've only just arrived. You gave me that, er, colourful fish … last night, I think. Surely I wasn't so bad?"

"No, you have done well. You have learnt much and I am very pleased with your progress. However, you have been here for ten weeks; you should return to your world now. In time you could learn more, but first you should practise and grow accustomed to living with your new skills. Lessons can only be absorbed properly when a student has matured sufficiently to put the knowledge in context. Follow your instincts and, if it is so fated, that will prepare you for coming back here again one day. However, I would counsel caution. Do not let the rash enthusiasm your new knowledge will engender control your actions. Do not be over-confident. Your recently acquired skills have their limits, and so do you."

Tessa bowed, still having difficulty understanding how she could possibly have been there for ten weeks. Nevertheless, she sensed the room, and indeed the house, had a new deep familiarity for her. Then she became aware of a pronounced throbbing from both her hands. She put her teacup down and glanced at her right hand. It looked terrible, black and blue from bruises, with streaks of red from burst blisters. On the underside were a number of large hard calluses where she knew she gripped her sword. She found her left hand to be almost as bad.

"Don't worry," said Matsumoto. "I promised there would be no permanent damage and there isn't. All those marks will be gone in a week or so. The bruises on your body will probably disappear even more quickly."

She quickly looked inside her now bedraggled tunic. She could see large dark bruises almost wherever she looked.

"But how…? What…? I don't understand," she stammered.

He smiled.

"There is no need for you to understand everything now. But ever since one of my students tried to poison me, I have not allowed what has been learnt into the fully conscious mind of a student until they have earned the maturity to accept it. All that you have learnt is ready for you to use, Nariko-san, but you must do so wisely…"

She couldn't resist smiling with pride as he used the more familiar and respectful form of her name.

"If your conscience disagrees with what you are considering, the knowledge you require will not be there for you to use. It is a simple but nevertheless most effective technique, as you will see…

"Hayasaka-san has made all the arrangements for you to travel home. You will need to be at the perimeter gate at dawn, which still gives us a little time before you must leave."

"But I didn't want to stay," said Tessa, realising now she didn't want to go.

"Yes, that is correct. We discussed it at great length. You told me how fed up you were and, more importantly, that you weren't convinced you wanted to train to kill people. I was encouraged by this since it confirmed that your conscience remained active and intent upon exerting a healthy influence. By morning we had agreed it would be all right for you to stay."

"We did?"

"Absolutely. You and I together," replied Matsumoto.

"Oh, well, I suppose that's all right then," she said, shrugging her shoulders. "It just feels so strange to have lost ten weeks. But thank you, Master Matsumoto. No doubt these weeks have been an experience I shall never forget … assuming I can ever remember."

He smiled reassuringly.

"Don't worry. When necessary, you will recall everything you need to, and your wounds really will heal very quickly."

Tessa nodded, finding she was content to accept whatever he said, without question.

"Here is a selection of herbs and mosses which I would like to give you. These are some you can use on your hands. Grind a small amount into a paste as I showed you, add some warm water, and apply it at least twice daily until your hands are healed. Hayasaka has some gloves for you to use in the meantime. Here are some more herbs and mosses which are particularly useful in stemming the flow of blood. Their effect is not permanent, but the extra time they give the wounded can make the difference between death and survival..."

He continued talking for several minutes as she gradually accumulated a pile of polythene bags containing a variety of mosses, herbs, powdered roots and minerals.

"There, you can put them all in that excellent waist bag you made."

Tessa looked down to see a black leather pouch slung from a belt around her waist. She took it off to study it more closely.

"I made this?" she asked, incredulously. "Now that really is amazing."

"Yes, it's one of the best I've seen. It did take you many attempts before you were satisfied with it, but the end result is very accomplished. It should serve you well," replied Matsumoto, trying not to show how close he was to laughing.

She shook her head in disbelief and put everything he had given her into the bag.

"There is just one more thing I would like to say before you go. I do not train people to win medals as exhibitionists. I train people to fight for what is good and right, and to survive as they do so. However, as I warned you when you arrived, you must learn how to live with the consequences of applying your knowledge. In a fight to the death, some will live, but many will die. If you survive, you will have to live

215

knowing that you have ended the lives of others. This is a terrible responsibility, Nariko-san, and not one to be treated lightly. You will find that at times your skills and your conscience are not comfortable bedfellows. Do not forget, conscience, patience and perfection must always guide your actions."

He paused as she finished packing her bag.

"Whatever happens after you leave here will be real. Your new skills should not be employed unless absolutely necessary. You must work on a higher plane. Out in the real world, if you are hit, you will bruise. If you are cut, you will bleed. If you make a mistake during a sword fight, you will probably die. Although you are now well versed in the art of unarmed combat, you excel with the sword. Never be without it whenever you might need it. Sloppiness at any time will only lead to your undoing, or that of others. Go now, Nariko-san. Go quickly and go safely, and perhaps one day we will meet again."

"But, Master Matsumoto, if I cannot remember what I've learnt, how will I know whether I have the knowledge and skill to handle a situation?" she asked, pleased she had at least managed to come up with one sensible question following all his earth-shattering revelations.

He smiled.

"Do as you would have done before. If you find yourself scared, then discretion is the better part of valour. But, Nariko-san, there is not much which will scare you now."

He stood up, looked down at her and bowed.

"*Sayonara*, Nariko-san."

He turned away and disappeared into the darkness at the back of the house.

Tessa sat for a couple of minutes, trying to come to terms with everything that had happened. She felt very alone in the large room, with the silence broken only by the crackling of embers on the hearth. She wanted to say something but couldn't think what. She battled to marshal her thoughts. So much must have happened... How could she have *lost* ten weeks of her life?

She peered down the corridor after her teacher.

"Thank you," she murmured. She stood up and faced the back of the room, put her feet together and bowed deeply. "Thank you for everything," she said more loudly.

She checked her sword was slung correctly and that her waist bag was secure, and savoured gazing round one last time. She didn't know why, but she desperately wanted to stay. She sighed, and walked silently across the audience hall on to the verandah. She kicked off her clean sandals and glanced at her outside ones. She decided to leave them where they lay, ready for next time, and stepped down barefoot into the courtyard.

She stopped at the courtyard gates to look back at the samurai house; beautiful and proud, silhouetted against the star-filled sky. Then she turned and broke into an easy jog. Soon through the avenue and the wooden arch, she felt like one rejuvenated; stronger, faster, more aware than she had ever been in her life. Energy she had never known before coursed through her veins. She started to run down the awkward stone steps; no longer were their uneven heights and lengths a problem for her; she knew them too well.

It was a glorious night, dark but with the welcoming glow of a full moon illuminating her path. As she ran, she glanced up at the sky to admire the stars. If the wisps of mist over the paddy fields suggested a chill in the air, she was oblivious to it. For now, at least, she felt at one with the world around her. Exhilarated by her newfound confidence, she occasionally interspersed running with quick handstands. Passing from one large stone to another, she rejoiced at her own speed and how easily she could judge the distances.

She ran on as she realised she had many times during the past weeks. Faster and faster she went, and neither the speed nor the terrain was a problem for her. She could have found the way blindfold. When she came to the narrow Kintai-style bridge, her pace barely faltered. Completely surefooted, she ran over the arches with the bridge swaying from side to side beneath her. She continued up the winding path through the forest, eventually seeing the outline of the perimeter wall in the distance. As she drew closer, she saw the silhouette of the gatehouse. A couple of minutes later she stopped by the camellia trees. She looked at them, remembering how, both day and night, Matsumoto would suddenly tell her to fetch some blooms from here. He would time how long it took her, insisting she should return more quickly every time. She drew her sword and carefully took a healthy cutting from a particularly fragrant tree with small white flowers. She carefully tucked it into her tunic.

As she entered the gatehouse, she heard the tell-tale *clunk* of the doors being unlocked, followed by the creaking of the hinges as one of the doors was pushed open. She still couldn't believe it was ten weeks since she'd first heard that sound. Whereas then she had been worried by what lay before her, now... She smiled at the realisation that her fear hadn't gone away, it had simply changed, like her. Now she needed to worry about what she might be capable of doing to others.

She walked quietly and confidently along the zigzag path to the doors. As she passed through the opening she could see the two guards studying her with great curiosity. But she didn't return their gaze. She only glanced briefly at Hayasaka, hoping he wouldn't notice the solitary tear running down her cheek.

"*Ohayou gozaimasu*, Hayasaka-san. I'm back."

As she continued towards his house, she heard the *clunk* of the heavy doors being locked behind her.

CHAPTER 24

Hayasaka suggested Tessa freshen up before breakfast. In her room, she held up her threadbare and embarrassingly dirty tunic. She grimaced at the thought she had probably been wearing it for ten weeks, and happily discarded it in the basket. Then she stood under the wonderfully hot shower for several minutes. When she emerged she found the two outfits she had brought with her, hanging in the cupboard. Both had recently been cleaned. She put on her tight red tee-shirt and black leather trousers, thinking they would be ideal for travelling back to London casually. Finally, she looked at herself in the mirror: much fitter, much stronger, weather-beaten, and clean for the first time in months.

Breakfast was excellent but Tessa ate and drank in silence, lost in thought. She struggled to keep her eyes open as extreme tiredness threatened to seize control.

"Nariko-san," said Hayasaka quietly, "it is time we left. You can rest as we travel. Do not forget to remove your sword."

She chuckled, realising it hadn't even registered with her that she'd put it on again.

The car had already arrived and this time Tessa let the driver put her bag in the boot and settled down in the back seat with her sword case. Hayasaka sat in front.

"We will drive to Komatsu and catch a plane to Tokyo's Haneda airport," he said. "From there we will take a taxi to Ueno and catch the Skyliner Express to Narita. I will accompany you all the way. You may sleep now if you wish."

She smiled gratefully, and they set off down to Kanazawa. The car cruised through the still-deserted town and was soon speeding south-west along the toll road to Komatsu. Tessa frequently dozed off, waking occasionally to gaze out of the window in the dim morning light. Once, as they passed along the coast, she could make out the white plumes of waves splashing up against the sea defences to her right.

Tessa had only a vague impression of standing next to Hayasaka at the Check-in desk. She sensed people were staring at her, their curiosity aroused by her slim leather-clad figure and sword case. But she didn't care, although she did decide to cover her bruised hands with the black leather gloves Hayasaka offered. Ms Suzuki, the booking manager, smiled and bowed to Tessa. Then she wound some strong retaining straps round her sword case to ensure it could not be opened. This meant she could carry it on to the flight herself, which was normal practice in Japan for domestic flights. But Tessa remained in a daze throughout, grateful to have Hayasaka with her to take care of the formalities. Eventually they settled down in the aeroplane.

"Hayasaka-san," she said wearily, "are you going to be able to stay awake during the flight?"

He laughed.

"Yes, of course. You *should* rest. You have barely slept during the last week."

"No wonder I'm tired. It would be very nice if I could have a cup of green tea just before we land, please."

"I will arrange it for you," he replied, as she leant back and fell fast asleep.

A few minutes later the flight attendant wanted to put Tessa's sword case in the coats compartment by the galley. However, seeing how tightly the straps were wound round the sleeping woman's gloved hand, she decided to follow Hayasaka's advice, and left.

Tessa slept throughout the flight, until she became aware of Hayasaka offering her a steaming cup of green tea. She drank it quickly and surprised herself by asking the stewardess for another, in perfect Japanese.

At Haneda the straps round her sword case were removed and they caught a taxi to Ueno station. She was feeling much better, although she sensed a lot more sleep would be necessary before she recovered completely. As Hayasaka purchased their tickets, she stood nearby with her sword case slung over her shoulder. Still with a feeling of detachment, she watched everyone rushing by on their way to work. Gradually, she began to feel more enthusiastic at the prospect of returning to her own world. Hayasaka came back with two tickets in his hand. Tessa smiled as he gave her the single.

"We have reserved seats on the nine-twenty," he said, returning her smile. "It leaves in seven minutes from platform two. There are only a couple of stops before the airport, so we will be at Narita in an hour."

"Oh, dear, no time to go shopping here then?" she remarked, picking up her bag.

"Not really," he replied. "What was it you wanted?"

"Some green tea and a rice cooker," she replied. "It's almost impossible to get the fuzzy-logic cookers in London and they seem to be the standard here."

"Absolutely. But I'm sure you will be able to purchase both in Narita."

Ignoring the escalators, they walked down the stairs to their platform, taking care to avoid the gaze of the ever-watchful security cameras. As they reached the platform, Tessa became aware of some people following them: five men, slightly built, young and fit. The first two were empty-handed, while the others each carried something fairly heavy. She knew all that without looking back. As the men's steps quickened, Tessa's suspicions were aroused. Apparently Hayasaka hadn't noticed them.

Their train had already arrived and seemed to be empty. But as they walked down the platform, she listened to the purposeful approach from behind. Unless she was mistaken the challenge would come…

"So, the blonde Caucasian buys a souvenir and thinks she's a Samurai?"

Hayasaka stopped and looked at Tessa. But she shook her head and motioned for him to continue towards their carriage.

"Not even brave enough to turn round and face us?" continued the sneering voice. "Nor your servile old Japanese guide?"

Tessa noted they had four minutes before their train departed. She also judged that neither of the two surveillance cameras on the platform could see her or Hayasaka.

A warbling noise announced the rapid approach of a missile from behind. Tessa sighed, but Hayasaka turned in alarm. She spun round and stuck out her right hand, catching the can of Coke six inches in front of his surprised face.

She looked at him and winked.

"Did you order something to drink?" she asked loudly in English.

"Er, no, actually," he replied, grinning. "Besides, that's not Diet, it

221

can't be for me."

"Thank you, gentlemen, but we didn't ask for this."

Tessa deftly tossed it into the "Cans" litter bin within a set of four some distance away. As it rattled noisily, she turned to Hayasaka and made a show of dusting off her hands.

"Excellent shot," he observed, with a glint in his eye.

"Thank you."

Then one of the men threw a baseball at Tessa. It was a good throw, but she nonchalantly reached out and caught it. She started playing with the ball, tossing it from one hand to the other, a confident smile on her face.

"Gentlemen," she continued loudly in English, "we don't want any trouble, and I don't believe we have done anything to offend you. However, if we have, I apologise. Now, please let us continue our journey."

She watched one of the men pick up two mops from some bags of cleaning equipment which had been left on the platform. He handed one to a colleague and they smashed the surveillance cameras.

"Please, leave us alone," Tessa repeated, continuing to play with the baseball. "We just want to go in peace."

She could now see that the three men at the back were all carrying RCL sword cases like hers. The one in the centre replied in a gruff belligerent tone.

"It was too late when you, a Western woman, had the audacity to come to our country souvenir hunting!"

The men split into three groups. The spokesman remained slightly behind, near the stairs. The two with mops started to approach Tessa and Hayasaka from the right, while the remaining two took up position to her left, a few yards from the spokesman.

A number of conflict scenarios played out in Tessa's mind.

"Hey-ho," she sighed, standing her sword case on the platform.

"Perhaps you should get on the train with my bag," she whispered to Hayasaka. "This won't take long."

He bowed, turned and left.

"Gentlemen. For the last time, please don't do this. Let's just go our separate ways," she said, in a final bid to stop them.

"No way, bitch. Everyone has got to pay someday," yelled their leader. "Today's your day."

As he finished he bent down and started releasing the catches on his sword case. Tessa heard Hayasaka get on the train.

"So, you're the boss are you?" she asked, continuing to toss the baseball from one hand to the other, watching the two men with mops advancing.

He looked up at her and nodded with a confident smile. However, the moment she had eye contact, she looked to her right. Automatically, his eyes followed, as did his colleagues'. Then, with a flick of her wrist, just as Matsumoto had propelled the coin towards her, she threw the baseball at the leader. The throw was hard, fast and accurate. He didn't even see it coming. It struck him on the forehead with a loud *crack*. Without making a sound, he toppled forward, unconscious. The ball started rolling back towards Tessa.

"Ouch, I bet that hurt," she observed, trying not to laugh.

The remaining four looked at their friend, and then at her with rage in their eyes.

"Look, boys, trust me, you really don't want to do this, it'll only get worse."

The two men with the mops stopped advancing some fifteen feet from her.

"Hah!" snarled one of them. "Let's see what you're really..."

He hadn't finished speaking before Tessa took a pace forward and dived down on her hands, covering the remaining space in two quick cartwheels. The next moment, she was upright in front of the nearest man with her right hand on his mop. Even though he hadn't let go, she slammed the top back into his head. It hit his temple with an abrupt *thud*. His eyes rolled upwards and his grip on the handle slackened as he fell back senseless. Tessa stepped over his prostrate body, spinning the mop horizontal as she moved. She used it to jab the second man hard in the stomach. He doubled up in pain, winded, and she thwacked him on the back of the head. He fell forwards, allowing her to take his mop in her left hand. Calm and collected, she whirled both mops round and stood them on end. The remaining two men were hurriedly drawing swords from their now-open cases. She had less than a minute before her train departed.

The men ran towards her with their swords drawn, one slightly

223

ahead of the other. Tessa brought the mops horizontal and, throwing underarm, launched one between the legs of each man. The man behind jumped away to avoid the missile, but the man leading tripped as the other mop lodged between his legs. He landed face down on the platform, sliding to a halt not far in front of Tessa. In a moment, she was standing over him. As he tried to get up and raise his sword, she trod on the blade and knelt down. She chopped him on the back of his neck with the edge of her hand, and he collapsed unconscious.

By now the final assailant was within striking distance and aimed a sweeping sword stroke at her. She rolled away to her right to avoid it, passing over the baseball which she picked up. As the man ran forward she flicked it at him. There was another loud *crack* as it found its target a second time. He dropped his sword and crumpled in a heap to the ground. Meanwhile the baseball bounced back towards Tessa. She caught it, stood up and started sprinting for the train. On the way, she tossed the ball into the "Miscellaneous" rubbish bin. When she was still some ten feet from the train, she heard the warning buzzer sound. She grabbed the strap of her sword case and leapt into the carriage as the doors slid shut. She looked round at Hayasaka.

"Well, it seems I have learnt something useful," she said with a smile, in Japanese.

"Indeed," he replied, "and learnt very well it would seem. Perfectly planned, perfectly timed, and perfectly executed."

"And what's more, I was patient, and my conscience is completely clear."

Hayasaka laughed.

"Master Matsumoto will be very pleased to hear how you handled this unfortunate incident. Only their egos are seriously wounded. Thank you for catching the can."

"Oh, you're more than welcome. But I wonder who will carry the can? This incident will be reported and people will be on the lookout for a blonde Caucasian woman with an escort. How long have we got before the train stops?"

"The next station is Nippori in five minutes."

"So, I have until then to change, and you should get off. There is no point in both of us getting into trouble. Could you hand me my other clothes, please?" said Tessa, as, much to Hayasaka's surprise and embarrassment, she started to strip. He couldn't help blushing as first he passed her the red silk blouse and then her smart suit trousers.

"Excellent," she said, adjusting the new clothes. She flicked open her lap-top and switched it on. Then she put her sword case by the window. "Could you put my leather suit in this polythene bag and take it with you, please?"

She carefully adjusted the position of her camellia cutting before closing her bag.

"Oh, what a fine specimen. I hope it adjusts well to life in London," remarked Hayasaka.

"So do I," replied Tessa, grinning.

While she draped her jacket over her sword case, he put her leather suit in the bag.

"*Sayonara*, Hayasaka-san," she said as the train stopped at Nippori. "Good luck, and thank you."

"It is I who should thank you. *Sayonara*, Nariko-san," he replied, handing her the various tickets and papers she would need.

They bowed to each other and he got off.

Tessa watched him hurry along the platform and on to the escalator up to the exit. When she had lost sight of him, she sat down and adjusted the position of her jacket to make sure it completely hid her sword case. Then she undid one of the buttons on her blouse and picked up her laptop. She started verifying a spreadsheet she had created during her flight to Japan…

Some ten minutes after the train stopped at Funabashi, Tessa saw two policemen questioning passengers in the next carriage. As they came towards her, she continued to work as though unaware of their approach. They stopped by her row and one addressed her in Japanese.

"Excuse me, madam, there was an incident at Ueno station. Did you see anything out of the ordinary?"

She looked up at him, smiled and held up her train ticket.

"Good morning," she replied, in English. "This is correct, isn't it?"

The first policeman looked at the second.

"Nice pair of tits," he said in Japanese, "but there's no way this girl could do anything useful."

"Depends what you mean by useful," responded the second officer. "Come on…"

225

When the train arrived at Narita, Tessa waited as long as she dared before getting off. She hoped another train would arrive so she could mingle with its passengers, but none did. Eventually she simply hoped the security staff would have relaxed after the other passengers had gone. She went up the escalator and handed her papers to the official at the security desk. He passed them to a colleague and directed her to another desk at the side.

As she walked over to it, she noticed a stylishly dressed man standing a short distance away. He was studying her carefully and gestured to see her papers. The officials behind the desk bowed and she sensed two policemen coming up behind her. Both were armed with long wooden staffs.

"Nariko, we would like to inspect your sword, please," said one of the officials in English.

"It clearly states in my RCL documentation that, unless you are accusing me of having committed a crime, I am not obliged to show you my sword," replied Tessa quietly but firmly in English, finishing with a smile. "You are of course welcome to check all my other baggage."

The man took her bag and handed it to a female assistant. She opened it and looked through, eventually nodding to indicate she had found nothing of interest.

An awkward silence followed as the officials appeared unsure what to do next. Meanwhile Tessa stood motionless with a firm grip on the strap holding her sword case over her shoulder. The silence was broken by the sound of a man coughing gently. Everyone looked round at the man in the suit. Much to her surprise, he indicated they should let Tessa pass.

"Sorry for the delay. You may go," said one of the officials behind the desk.

"Thank you," she replied with a slight bow.

She grabbed her case, crossed the hall and went up the escalators to Departures. She quickly found British Airways and went to the First Class Check-in desk. As she handed her papers to the clerk she sensed someone approaching her from behind. A moment later a man's voice addressed her in perfect English.

"Nariko, my name is Inspector Maeda. I would like to have a word with you, please."

Tessa turned round and smiled at the man in the suit who had been standing near the security desk.

"Of course, I'll just finish checking in."

"That won't be necessary," said Maeda, gesturing to the clerk to give him all her papers.

The two policemen she had seen on the train stood behind the Inspector. He motioned one of them to come forward.

"My colleague will take your sword case, if you don't mind."

An inexplicable wave of panic swept over Tessa as she realised someone wanted to take her weapon from her. She had never experienced anything like it before, and hadn't expected to. But she knew the last thing she wanted was to allow anyone to touch her sword.

"Actually I do mind, a lot," she replied. "What exactly is it you want?"

By now the crowds of people milling around were distancing themselves, but nevertheless pausing to watch. Maeda looked at her and smiled.

"There was an incident at Ueno station this morning. I would like to ask you some questions about it, in that interview room."

He nodded towards an alcove with a door in it, at the side of the Departures Hall.

"I see. Well, that's not far. Don't worry, the case isn't heavy, I'll carry it myself."

"That is not convenient," replied Maeda.

"It's very kind of you to be concerned, but I can assure you it is perfectly convenient," continued Tessa.

"Nariko, please don't make this unnecessarily difficult. We are going to the interview room. Your sword is coming with us, but you will not be carrying it."

She had no choice but to comply, if she wanted to avoid a scene.

"Hmm. In which case, that young woman by the X-ray machine may carry my sword case in front of me to the interview room. You can lead the way and your two able-bodied colleagues can follow me. Would that be an acceptable compromise?"

Maeda sighed, nodded and called the woman over. He gave her instructions and Tessa passed her the sword case. Then Maeda led their little convoy forwards with the woman nervously carrying the case. They entered a grey box of a room with a square white table in the middle. Maeda gestured Tessa to sit on the chair to the left of the door while he sat opposite her. The woman deposited the sword case behind the table to Tessa's left, equidistant from the two of them. She clearly wanted to beat a hasty retreat, but Maeda stopped her.

"Would you like a cup of coffee or something?" he asked Tessa.

"Oh, thank you. May I have some green tea, please?"

"Of course, that will probably be easier." In Japanese he asked the woman to bring them two cups of decent green tea before she returned to her post.

The two policemen took up position to either side of the door. There were no windows in the brightly lit room. Apart from the table and chairs the only furniture was behind Tessa, a drinking water dispenser in the corner to her left and a metal wastepaper bin in the corner to her right.

They waited in silence until the woman returned with the tea. When it arrived, Tessa noticed it was served in two beautifully decorated fine porcelain cups.

"Thank you," she said. "You must be very important to have tea served in such lovely cups."

Maeda smiled.

"Nariko, as I was saying, there was a most unpleasant incident at Ueno this morning. Five Japanese RCL holders were attacked by a blonde Caucasian woman. She drew her sword, forcing them to draw theirs to defend themselves. This incident took place at the time you must have been boarding the train."

"Really?" She delicately picked up her cup. "I presume you would like to know whether I saw anything?"

"Actually, I would like to know if you were involved. After all, you are a blonde Caucasian woman, of whom there are not that many in Japan; and you were the only person carrying a sword on that train. Perhaps I should remind you that when you entered Japan some ten weeks ago, you signed a declaration confirming that you understood drawing your sword in a public place without cause would constitute a serious offence."

"I remember. Suffice to say, I would never draw my sword anywhere

228

without very good reason. What provoked this incident?"

"We don't know all the details yet as only one of the men has regained consciousness."

Despite her best efforts Tessa couldn't stop a slight smile from creeping over her face, and she saw Maeda had noticed it.

"Were any of them seriously hurt?" she continued quickly.

"No. Some bruising, concussion and bad tempers are likely to be the only after-effects."

"I see. Well, presumably you have pictures from the surveillance cameras?"

"No, they were broken."

"So, you are suggesting this blonde Caucasian woman destroyed the surveillance cameras and overcame five licensed Japanese sword carriers without hurting anything other than their testosterone-driven egos? Don't you think it's strange she would pit herself against such odds?"

Maeda breathed out noisily.

"As I said, we don't have all the facts yet. But I do not intend to let anyone who may have been involved leave Japan. Especially if they are carrying a sword and may have committed an offence by drawing it."

"I understand. However, you said this woman is supposed to have drawn her sword and yet none of the men were cut?" Maeda nodded. "Well, if I had used my sword against them, they would all be seriously injured."

He looked at her sternly.

"Nariko, please don't make me lose patience. This is no joking matter."

"I wasn't joking, Inspector."

She quietly took another sip of her tea.

"This woman did not leave any fingerprints," continued Maeda. "Why are you wearing gloves, Nariko?"

"My hands are a bit sore, that's all," she replied uneasily.

"Let me see, please."

She painfully removed her left glove, exposing a horribly bruised black and blue hand. The two policemen gasped and Maeda looked taken aback.

"That looks painful. How did it happen?"

"Oh, just an enthusiastic work-out. I'm sure you appreciate it wouldn't look like this from a brief confrontation this morning?"

"Of course. I presume the other hand is the same?"

"Pretty much," replied Tessa, replacing the glove. She continued, keen to change the subject. "So how was this woman dressed? Did she travel alone?"

He smiled.

"The woman wore black leather and travelled with a Japanese man."

"Then I don't qualify on those counts either."

"I know. But I would still like to see your sword."

Tessa remained motionless.

"I would like to inspect your sword now, please."

She shook her head, refusing to let him open the case himself.

"I am willing to unpack my sword and present the blade to you."

"I think it would be foolish of me to take such a risk."

"Inspector Maeda," replied Tessa, indignantly, "you do me a great disservice. I was trained never to draw my sword unless I intended to use it. Suffice to say, I have absolutely no intention of using it now. You have my word of honour."

A tense silence ensued, broken by Maeda sighing again.

"Very well, Nariko, once more I will go the extra mile for you. Please unpack your sword."

The two policemen grumbled noisily, but he remained adamant and put on some white gloves before standing by expectantly.

Tessa got up and walked round the table to her sword case. She undid the catches and removed the sword, holding it horizontally towards him. He gasped when he saw the sheath decorations.

"Incredible!" he exclaimed. "An Amakuni sword, how did you get this?"

"A friend commissioned it for me. It is as much a part of me as my arms. Perhaps now you understand why I will not let anyone else handle it."

She pulled the sword open some fifteen inches.

"Oh, this is truly wonderful," marvelled Maeda. "It is one of the finest swords I have ever seen. The capabilities of these blades are legendary."

"Inspector, you clearly appreciate the unique quality of this weapon.

If I had used it against the men this morning they would not simply be bruised. So I cannot be guilty of the offence which you seem to be suggesting I have committed."

Tessa slammed her sword and hilt together.

"Hah!" chuckled Maeda. "I might even believe that if I thought you could use this sword properly. Prove that to me, and I will let you go."

"What do you mean?" exclaimed Tessa.

"You suggest you are so proficient with this weapon you could defeat five well-trained licensed Japanese sword carriers. Now it is you who does Japan a disservice," replied Maeda calmly. "But I am willing to give you the benefit of the doubt and let you prove your professed superior prowess... Don't worry, you can show me here."

Tessa stared at him in disbelief.

"Sorry, I don't perform to order, and I don't do shows," she said with unmistakable irritation. "I take the use of this sword extremely seriously. Besides, it would be against your laws for me to draw it here."

"Yes, yes, I wouldn't have expected any other answer. However, if you want to convince me you are telling the truth, and there is mounting circumstantial evidence to the contrary, then you have no alternative but to do as I ask. Surely being allowed to catch your flight is just cause for demonstrating to me that what you say is true?"

Tessa smiled. She liked him for calling her bluff, and if it meant she could still catch her plane and avoid what could otherwise be a lengthy interrogation, maybe it would be worth it.

"If I must," she sighed. "However, I would like it noted that I do this most unwillingly, and only at your express bidding. I presume you give me permission to draw my sword in this room?"

"Yes, of course," said Maeda, "but not to hurt anyone. So, how will you demonstrate your skills in wielding this sword?"

She scowled at him, but he smiled back. Meanwhile, the two policemen stiffened in dismay at the prospect of what he had initiated. Maeda picked up his cup of green tea and went to lean against the wall behind his chair.

Tessa looked at the two officers by the door. Both of them carried wooden truncheons.

"I presume the Japanese authorities can afford to lose a truncheon?"

231

"Er, yes," replied Maeda, puzzled.

"In which case, I will put my sword on, and then that man…" said Tessa, gesturing to the policeman on her right "… should throw his truncheon at the water dispenser. I will ensure only half the truncheon hits the dispenser while the other half goes in the wastepaper bin. If I do that, Inspector Maeda, my understanding is you will help me catch my flight and accept I am not accountable for the events at Ueno this morning?"

He smiled.

"If you do what you say, I will be most surprised and will indeed let you go … and not hold you responsible for the incident this morning. But, Nariko, I think you have struck a very poor bargain."

"Does your man understand what to do?" she muttered, as she put her sword on with a conventional belt. She didn't want to show them her shoulder harness in action.

Maeda repeated their agreement in Japanese and the policemen chuckled in disbelief. Tessa twisted round to finish adjusting her belt, but, fair or not, the policeman decided the time had come for him to throw his truncheon.

Tessa reacted instinctively and in a flash had drawn her sword. It started ringing, loud and confident. As she swung it upwards the blade struck the truncheon, cleaving it in two with an abrupt click. The top half of the truncheon sped upwards, spinning end over end, while the bottom half started down. She quickly brought her sword round and struck it with the back. It hit the water dispenser's glass container with a loud *clang*. Then she swung her sword upwards and hit the top half of the truncheon straight into the wastepaper bin. A tinny rattling echoed round the room as the bin vibrated with the impact. She re-sheathed her sword and turned to Maeda; his mouth had fallen open and he let his cup slip through his fingers. She drew her weapon again and swung it round. The proud ringing stopped abruptly as his cup landed on the end of the blade, a few inches in front of him.

"Careful, Inspector, it would be a shame to break such a pretty thing."

Maeda swallowed and carefully retrieved his cup. With a flourish, Tessa returned her sword to its sheath.

"Amazing," said Maeda. "I know of only one other person who

could have achieved such a feat of swordsmanship."

Tessa took off her sword and returned it to its case.

"I have done as you asked, so now it is your turn. You said you would help me catch my flight and not hold me responsible for this morning's events at Ueno."

Maeda nodded, but nevertheless decided to try another approach.

"Yes, but before you go, perhaps we could talk *hypothetically* about this morning's incident. What do you think *might* have happened at Ueno?"

"Ah. Well, speaking *hypothetically*, I would surmise the woman concerned was hoping to travel to the airport quickly, quietly and discreetly. But five men approached her from behind and started shouting abuse. One of the men probably threw a can of Coke at the woman's companion and a baseball at her. No doubt both objects would still be in the correct rubbish bins on the platform, with the man's fingerprints on them. I am sure the woman would have pleaded many times with the men to leave her and her companion alone. But two of the men could have taken mops form the cleaners' bags, smashed the security cameras, and started to attack her. When this happened, she would have had no choice but to defend herself. So, she would have overcome the men as best she could without drawing her sword or injuring them seriously."

Maeda thought for a moment, chuckled and looked up at her.

"I daresay that is a reasonable *hypothesis*, and if correct the woman concerned deserves an apology, and the men involved should have their RCLs revoked. However, no doubt you will agree, any such events involving potential Peacekeepers are deplorable and must be both reported and avoided in the future."

"I am sure the woman concerned would have tried everything she could to prevent matters from escalating. If the woman involved was provoked without reason then she cannot be blamed for defending herself. What's more, if she carried a sword, and did not draw it, then that would have shown exemplary restraint. Fortunately for me, since you have accepted I cannot be held accountable, there is nothing for you to report concerning me, is there?"

"No, there isn't. Nevertheless, if by chance you meet this woman, perhaps you could inform her of Japan's displeasure with such spontaneous incidents, and suggest she tries even harder in future to avoid confrontation. Otherwise she might not be regarded as a welcome visitor to our country."

"Inspector Maeda, I am sure the woman would feel such a pronouncement to be most unjust. If provoked without cause by men who posed a real threat, she had no choice. Far from making herself unwelcome in your country, she has done Japan a service by exposing inappropriate RCL holders. She deserves your thanks, not your recriminations."

He nodded.

"I understand, but if you were to see her, please tell her what I said. It is my duty to have said it."

Tessa relaxed.

"If I happen to meet her, I will most certainly pass on what you said."

"Good. Well, Nariko, thank you for your assistance with this matter. It looks as though we will be unsuccessful in our attempts to find the woman concerned. I am sorry to have delayed you, but you will still be able to catch your flight."

He put his cup down and in Japanese told the policemen to escort her back to the Check-in desk, to book her on to her flight and arrange for her sword to be crated.

"*Arigato gozaimas*," she said, continuing in Japanese. "However, I was hoping to purchase a rice cooker after I had checked in to my flight. I think there will still be time. Would that be … convenient?"

"You didn't say you spoke Japanese."

"You didn't ask," she replied, as the policemen who had looked down her blouse on the train shifted nervously from foot to foot.

"Indeed," laughed Maeda, staying in Japanese, "I think it would be better if my officers were to escort you to your plane, just to make absolutely sure you don't become embroiled in any unfortunate incidents. But they can take you to the Duty Free shopping area first."

He nodded to Tessa to pick up her sword case and they all returned to the Check-in desk. Tessa had her seat assigned and placed her sword in the secure Shipping Crate, again being given one of the two keys. Then the policemen led her to the shopping area, pushing a trolley with the shipping crate on it.

She found an electrical store and asked them to wait outside the store's narrow aisles. With the men quietly chatting by the entrance, she walked round the display of rice cookers. She nearly burst into laughter when she found Hayasaka crouching behind the stand.

"*Konichiwa*, Hayasaka-san. How did you manage to get in here?" she asked, checking her escorts didn't suspect anything.

"Family connections," he replied, grinning, easing her bag from her hand. "In addition to returning your leather suit, I am giving you some green tea. It is a small gift of my favourite brand which I hope you will enjoy. There is also some green tea infused with apricot. You might like the taste."

"Thank you, Hayasaka-san, you are most kind," she whispered, pretending to read the boxes in front of her.

"Now, I recommend you buy *that* rice cooker, it is very good. We have an earlier model at home," he continued, pointing. She immediately lifted one up.

"Also, I suggest you purchase this CD. I found it on the stand over there. It has Japanese music on it which I think you will find … memorable."

"Thank you, Hayasaka-san. Thank you for everything, and…" She paused, hesitating over whether it was appropriate for her to continue. "Please give my regards to Master Matsumoto."

"I will, and you are most welcome. If it is so fated, as I suspect it is, we shall look forward to seeing you again."

He disappeared behind another stand, leaving Tessa to take her purchases to the cash desk.

Ten minutes later, as she approached her departure gate, she was surprised to find Inspector Maeda waiting by another security check.

"I see you found a rice cooker," he said.

"Yes, thank you. I presume this doesn't concern me? My bags have already been searched."

Maeda smiled.

"Well, we wouldn't want to be seen to be making concessions. It's only a formality."

She shrugged and handed her bag to the woman behind the desk. With Maeda standing behind her, she felt it unlikely he would see her leather suit. The woman opened the bag and swung the lid up in front of Tessa. Maeda walked round and joined the woman in looking inside. He laughed as she removed the leather clothes.

"Now, isn't that interesting? A nice camellia cutting too." He gestured to the woman to replace everything and return the bag. "By the way, all five men involved in today's Ueno incident have regained consciousness and admitted to having initiated the conflict. They also confessed, somewhat reluctantly, to having received a comprehensive beating at the hands of the unknown Caucasian woman. Their RCLs will be revoked and their training school warned to tighten its vetting procedures. Have a pleasant flight, Nariko, I would be surprised if we do not meet again one day."

They bowed to each other, and parted. As Maeda watched Tessa board the plane, he muttered, "Well, Hachiro-san, you have an equal, at last…"

Twenty minutes later the plane took off, and not long afterwards Tessa fell fast asleep. She opened her eyes occasionally as someone approached her or the cupboard where her sword was stored, but only woke properly when the plane was an hour and a half from London. Then she enjoyed a breakfast of smoked salmon and scrambled egg, fruit and green tea.

At Heathrow Airport, she quickly retrieved her sword case from the shipping crate and caught a taxi home. Being back in the UK delighted her now, and by the time the taxi stopped outside her house, she was feeling positively euphoric.

She opened the front door, and, grimacing at the pile of mail, switched off the alarm system and opened the shutters. She heaved a huge sigh of relief and made herself some green tea. Then she did some research into camellias on the Internet, bought a book about them and, with considerable care and affection, planted her cutting. Back in the lounge, Tessa found the CD of Japanese music which Hayasaka had told her to buy. She frowned and put it in the CD player.

As the music started, she flopped down on her sofa, laughing. Not only did she recognise the tune, she knew it so well she could have sung the words from start to finish. She selected some other tracks and found she knew them all. She shook her head in disbelief; at least now she knew one of the things she had been doing during the past ten weeks.

Continuing to listen to the music with some green tea beside her, she started to sort through her mail. Having confirmed there was nothing of great urgency, she turned her attention to the e-mails.

There were a couple of short progress reports from Jones. She quickly read them and sent him an e-mail saying she had returned and would like to meet the following afternoon.

Then she read numerous messages from John Brown and was delighted to find her Bugatti was ready. She quickly sent a message asking whether she could collect it late the following day.

Shortly afterwards responses arrived. John Brown said she could collect the car at any time between 3:30 p.m. and 5 p.m., and Jones confirmed he and Sinclair would meet her in Antonio's at 2:30 p.m..

Tessa looked at the clock and decided to go for a run round Hyde Park. She suspected she had got used to a gruelling fitness routine and intended to continue it. As she ran, she wondered whether Lee knew she was back, but decided she wouldn't disturb him now, but would simply go to SKS the following morning.

When she eventually went to bed, she found to her dismay that what she had previously known as a very comfortable mattress, now felt unacceptably soft. She made a mental note to contact Sarah, an interior designer she knew. Then she rolled up some towels to use as a pillow, lay down on the carpet with her sword by her side and spread a duvet over herself. She fell asleep, wondering how closely she could make her bedroom resemble a room within a samurai house.

CHAPTER 25

Tessa woke early and automatically prepared for another run. She even put on her sword, only remembering to take it off as she opened the front door. At 4:30 a.m. she sped through the gates into Hyde Park. As she ran round the Serpentine listening to the dawn chorus, the sun started to rise, heralding the start to a fine autumn day. However, she couldn't help pining for the vistas she had grown accustomed to at Matsumoto Castle. But then her thoughts turned to how she might use her new skills to track down Penny's killers, and whether she would be attacked again... *Bring it on, guys, bring it on!* she concluded.

Sinclair and Jones had been conferring late into the night, deciding what to say to Tessa during their meeting. But they were also up early as Sinclair wanted to have a private meeting with someone in South Kensington. Eventually, he emerged from beside the auction house, crossed the road and joined Jones in the Starbucks coffee shop. For once Old Brompton Road was empty; it had been closed for resurfacing and everyone was avoiding it. They sat behind the dark-tinted window and surveyed the inactive roadworks which boasted a plethora of bollards and equipment but not a single workman.

"Morning," said Jones, as Sinclair sat down with a large coffee like his own. "Why exactly are we here?"

"Oh, Maeda's informal note about that tussle in Ueno and his interview with Dr Pennington got me thinking. I know Maeda well and he's not an easy man to impress. Anyway, since she's bound to go to SKS this morning, I thought it would be interesting to see how she looks after her ten-week *vacation*."

"I thought you knew what she was doing?"

"How could I?" replied Sinclair with a wry smile.

Jones lowered his eyes and gulped down some coffee.

"Well, the undercover cordon around her place won't be re-established for another couple of days. The local Police are resisting. Apparently it's skewed their crime prevention statistics; virtually nothing criminal happened in South Kensington while we were keeping a discreet eye on her."

Sinclair gestured towards the corner of Cranley Place, around which Tessa had just appeared.

After a quick breakfast, she had put on a black tracksuit to match her gloves and had left for SKS with her sword case over her shoulder.

Jones turned to Sinclair.

"Are my eyes deceiving me or does she look rather fitter than when we last saw her?"

"Fitter in what sense?" queried Sinclair, with a mischievous glint in his eyes.

"Just about every sense I can think of actually," replied Jones, grinning.

Much to her surprise, Tessa found Old Brompton Road deserted. She had seen the roadworks during her run. However, even with resurfacing equipment strewn everywhere, it was unusual for South Kensington to be completely empty at any time. Continuing towards Barnaby Mews, her suspicions were aroused by finding an empty car with its engine running. She had just reached the Moroccan restaurant where she had eaten with David once when a commotion erupted fifty yards in front of her. Two men rushed out of Floyds Bank, carrying heavy bags. One was armed with an automatic pistol, the other had a large wooden club. They rushed towards her as another man staggered out of the bank after them, with blood gushing from a head wound.

"Stop them!" he shouted.

"Oh, shit!" exclaimed Jones. He reached inside his jacket, noting the gentle vibration as his pistol's recognition system armed the weapon. He and Sinclair were amongst the few still licensed to carry guns in the UK. But his boss put a hand on his arm.

"It's too late for that. We'd make it worse."

"But we've already lost one lead in this case. We don't want to lose another."

"I know," growled Sinclair, "but what exactly do you propose we do?"

Jones double checked the distance to the two men, noting that his aim would be compromised by the resurfacing equipment. He said nothing, but kept a firm grip on the stock of his pistol, just in case.

Meanwhile, Tessa couldn't believe what was happening. As the two men sprinted towards her, she calmly stood her sword case on the pavement.

"Out the fucking way!" shouted the man with the gun.

"Sword case, stupid!" bellowed the other. "Shoot the bitch!"

As the man with the gun slowed to take aim, Tessa took two quick steps forward and dived to the ground to start a series of handstands forwards. Not only did she want to cover the ground fast, she also wanted to confuse their aim.

Jones was bordering on panic. Sinclair on the other hand appeared curiously relaxed.

During her third handstand, Tessa avoided a clumsy sweep of the club, and continued towards the man with the gun. Halfway through her fourth handstand, she brought her feet over towards his head and kicked up under his jaw. There was a loud *crack* as it slammed shut and snapped. Her kick was so powerful it lifted him off his feet. He started falling backwards, already unconscious. She finished her handstand with her feet landing either side of the collapsing man. She just had time to prise the gun from his right hand and flick the safety catch on before he landed motionless below her.

She quickly spun round on her left foot, bending down to form a 'T' with her right foot sticking straight out   A moment later it landed a vicious kick in the second man's stomach. There was a loud *thud*, and a groan as he doubled up, winded. She stood up straight and reached out with her right hand. Despite his firm grip on the club, she yanked it round and tapped him sharply on the back of the head with it. There was a abrupt *clonk* and he collapsed forward, leaving the club in her hand.

"Hmm, cool," she muttered with a satisfied smile.

She tossed the club into the entrance of the nearby Chinese medicine shop and ejected the magazine from the gun high into the air. Then she extracted the bullet from the breech and tossed the gun down next to the club in time to catch both magazine and bullet. She inserted the bullet in the magazine and, bending down, slid it along the ground towards the gun. Finally she took four long black plastic tie wraps from her waist bag. She used them to bind the men's hands and feet, putting them both in positions where they could breathe unrestricted. She did all this so quickly, she had already finished by

240

the time the man with the head wound arrived on the scene.

Jones looked at Sinclair and burst out laughing.

"Bloody hell!" he exclaimed. "I understand what Maeda meant now. You knew already, didn't you?"

"Better not let her see us," replied Sinclair. They moved away from the window, continuing to watch surreptitiously.

Tessa meanwhile was inspecting the wound on the newest arrival.

"Don't worry," she said reassuringly, "this isn't serious. All scalp wounds bleed a lot." She reached into her waist bag and positioned a dressing over his wound. "Hold this down hard and get yourself to hospital as soon as you can. You might be concussed."

"Thank you, I can't say how grateful I am," he gasped, gathering the bags with his free hand. "I'm sure Floyds will want to give you a reward. Just wait until I tell the Police what you did. It was fantastic!"

"Ah, yes, well, I'd prefer it if you didn't mention me. Say you didn't see me clearly, or something. I don't want any publicity."

"Really?" replied the man in surprise. "I'm sure something like this could help convert your licence." He gestured towards the RCL logo on her sword case.

"Quite possibly, but I prefer the quiet life. I have enough on my mind at the moment, thanks all the same. I'd better be off."

"As you wish. Why don't you come and see me next time you're in the area?" said the man, recognising her as one of the bank's more affluent customers.

Police sirens started wailing in the distance.

Tessa winked at him, turned and retrieved her sword case. In a moment, she had retraced her steps up Cranley Place and turned left into Onslow Gardens. Then she walked down Sumner Place and round into Barnaby Mews. She stopped abruptly in the darkness, even though she couldn't see or hear anything.

"*Ohayou gozaimasu*, Master Lee," she said, bowing. "How are you?"

"*Ohayou*, Nariko-san. I am very well, thank you. And so, it would seem, are you. That little demonstration of yours shows it is not only your Japanese which is impressive now. Welcome back!"

"Thank you," replied Tessa, pleased that he of all people had been watching.

"Master Matsumoto has indeed taught you much, and you have

learnt well. I am sure he will be very pleased to hear of what you have just done."

They continued towards SKS, talking quietly.

Sinclair and Jones finished their coffee and strolled across the road to the gathering throng of police. Flood came over to greet them.

"Good morning, sirs. These two tried to rob Floyds; they left a Calver Cats calling card while they were at it. But they only got this far. Someone, as yet unknown, downed the pair of them and left them trussed up like Christmas turkeys. A very professional job – they're still out cold. Anyway, a witness from up the road thinks it might have been a woman with a sword case, which is why I'm here. The bank manager has taken a knock to the head, but he'll be OK. He says he arrived soon after, but hasn't the foggiest idea who intervened. Needless to say that person has left the scene, which is a bit suspicious. Did either of you happen to see anything from the coffee shop?"

"Sorry, Flood," said Sinclair, "but we're not able to help you. I know leaving the scene of a crime is not good, however the intervention seems to have been both timely and public-spirited, and not without risk. On this occasion, don't bother to pursue the perpetrator. They've done us a favour and for some reason presumably don't want any recognition. The least we can do is to show our gratitude by leaving them alone."

"Really?" queried Flood. "That's quite irregular, and of course one sword licensee does live near here..."

"Yes, we know, just let this one drop," continued Sinclair, winking at him. "And tell Potter to leave it too if he gets involved."

"Ah, understood. No problem, sir," replied Flood, turning away.

CHAPTER 26

Tessa and Lee talked for the rest of the morning. She revelled in the opportunity to share what she had been doing with someone who could relate to her experiences. She even described what had happened at Ueno station and then in Narita. Lee listened patiently, nodding, smiling, and refilling her cup with green tea.

"You know, Lee," she said eventually, "it really is quite remarkable. It's just as Matsumoto said. I can't consciously recall very much of what he taught me at all. But, when I need some knowledge, it just seems to be there, as though instinctively. Both at Ueno and here, I knew I could handle the situation. It's very weird."

"Well, that is one of the many unique qualities of his teaching. He does it partly to protect what he knows, but also to stop people teaching his techniques to others who might not use them so wisely. Did you enjoy your time with him?"

Tessa paused to reflect on all the pain and discomfort she must have endured. Even if she couldn't remember the details, the after-effects were still evident. She surveyed her battered hands, and smiled.

"Yes, I did. It hurt a lot, in all sorts of ways, but for a while I didn't want to come home. However, it has changed me, and I'm not sure whether the change is for the good. Am I proud of what I just did? Yes. I'm even more amazed that I could do it. But am I proud I'm able to do it? I'm not sure ... and that part scares me a bit."

Lee chuckled.

"Matsumoto no doubt warned you that the consequences of learning with him would be far-reaching. But I am pleased to hear you enjoyed it, and to hear you say it so enthusiastically. You will have changed. All experiences change us, and very few are completely bad. Again, I would counsel you not to worry. The answers you seek will become clear in time."

After training for a while, during which Tessa quickly exhausted Lee, he asked her what she planned to do next.

"Well, this afternoon I'm meeting those two Private Investigators

I hired. I want to hear what they've been up to. They've had another ten weeks to find out who killed Penny, and why. Then I'm going to collect my new car... Come to think of it, I need to be off."

"Oh, what car did you get in the end?"

Tessa grinned.

"A Bugatti."

Lee roared with laughter.

"A Bugatti! That's hardly in keeping with your hallowed low profile."

"True, but I'm rather looking forward to getting it now."

"I'm sure you are. Perhaps I could borrow it one day?"

"Of course, any time," she replied, automatically reaching for her sword case.

"You can leave that here if you like?"

"I know. But I feel naked without my sword at the moment. I daresay I'll get over it, but for the time being I'm taking it everywhere."

Lee shrugged.

"You'll make people nervous."

"Yes, but it would make me more nervous not to have it," she replied, putting her gloves back on. "I'll try to get used to not carrying it some other day."

After a brisk ten-minute walk Tessa entered Antonio's. Effervescent as ever, he erupted with joy.

"Oh, Dr Tessa! It's-a so wonderful to-a see you. Where 'ave-a you been all-a this time? I 'ave a-missed you terribly ... we all-a 'ave. Oh, but you look-a fantastic, darling."

"Antonio," she replied dolefully, with a poor impersonation of his Italian accent, "my life has not been complete without you."

Soon they were laughing together... Finally, Tessa remembered why she was there.

"Anyway, Antonio, we will be three today. A business meeting."

He looked at her sword case and passed her the key to the cupboard behind the counter. He and Tessa had an unspoken routine with regard to her bringing her sword. He would automatically take her to a table near the oak corner cupboard and give her the key so she could use it to store her sword case out of sight.

"Let-a me get-a you a latté. A strong and sophisticated, rich Costa Rican perhaps?" he said, grinning.

"Hmm. I'll savour that image. But, well, actually ..." Antonio stopped in his tracks. "...I don't suppose you have some green tea, do you? Bitter preferably."

He reeled back in surprise, clasping his hand to his heart.

"No-a! Tell-a me you are a-joking?" he gasped. "You come-a to Antonio's to drink-a green-a tea? Oh, what-a terrible thing has-a happened to you?"

"I've just developed a taste for it, that's all."

He sighed.

"Darling, for-a you, anything."

He smiled and histrionically blew her a kiss.

Tessa was soon sipping her green tea and waiting for Sinclair and Jones. They arrived and came over to her table, noticing she was still wearing her gloves.

"Hello," said Sinclair as they sat down, "we were beginning to get worried about you. You said you would only be away for a few weeks, and it was ten."

"Well, everything's fine, thank you. Or it will be when you tell me you've found out who killed Penny, and why."

"Oh. So, I take it you don't want to tell us what you've been doing and why your return was so delayed?"

"Why should I? I hired you to find Penny's killers, not to admire my holiday snaps. Also, I told you before I left that I'd expect results on my return or I would consider my options. What have you found out?"

Sinclair chuckled.

"You are absolutely right. We were just curious, that's all." Their coffee arrived, and the three of them huddled closer as Sinclair lowered his voice. "I'm pleased to say we have made significant progress. Regrettably we still don't have the whole story, but we do have more pieces of the jig-saw."

Tessa responded much more quickly than he was expecting.

"What were your sources?" she demanded, staring at him.

Focusing her question on the sources rather than the information, and delivering it so abruptly, momentarily wrong-footed Sinclair. Just as she'd hoped, he responded without thinking.

"Well, mostly Special Forces..."

He immediately regretted having said that. Before he'd even finished speaking, Tessa's expression had changed. She couldn't resist smiling. Even Jones looked at his boss in surprise.

"I don't want to say too much as our sources are very hush-hush," Sinclair continued quickly. "However, we have now all but confirmed that a criminal gang called the Calver Cats played an important role in Penny's murder, although we're still not sure they carried out the killing themselves. I don't know whether you've been keeping up with the news, but there has been a war raging within New Crime. The Calver Cats gang has been in the middle of it and is set to emerge as the most powerful underworld organisation in the UK, and they're already expanding overseas. They are extremely well run, by someone who is clearly both capable and well connected. It seems they have information sources all over the place, and some of them must be in high places. They've proved very adept at foiling attempts to trap and apprehend them."

He paused expectantly and looked at Tessa, but she didn't react. She'd not been impressed by what he'd said; his historical update didn't seem like ten weeks' worth of progress to her.

"The Calver Cats appear to be structured much like a legitimate business. There is a boss, though as yet no one has any idea who that is, and a small cadre of cronies who manage day to day operations. From what we can gather, some of them have regional responsibilities and one leads the training and strong-arm operations. It seems the Calver Cats only have one group of heavies in the UK. It's about a dozen strong, all highly trained ruffians. There are a couple of guns, but the Cats seem more interested in making money out of black-market weapons than in using them. Most of their heavies are equipped with swords, and pretty handy they are with them too.

"The main activities of the gang now are drugs and weapons, but they funded their start-up from human trafficking and the sex industry, progressing into robbery and money laundering. If you name something illegal, the Calver Cats probably reign supreme over it in the UK. Needless to say, they won't hesitate to employ extreme violence to get what they want and we know this has included the *removal* of people. So they wouldn't think twice about eliminating someone like Penny. But goodness knows why they considered it necessary. As far as we can ascertain, all the other killings were strictly business, at least from their warped perspective. This looks like a crime out of context..."

"But even if one accepts all that," interrupted Tessa, "surely they wouldn't have gone to such lengths to kill her so brutally? I daresay these thugs are violent, but Penny's death doesn't seem like just another hit, it looks personal."

"Yes, you're right," agreed Sinclair. "I accept we don't have all the answers yet."

He paused and sipped his coffee. Tessa waited for him to continue.

"It was some new evidence that led us to focus on the Calver Cats. There were no witnesses when they snatched Penny outside BNYI. At least, no one has dared come forward. But we recently stumbled across an internal security camera in a city branch of Starbucks. You can credit Jones with that ... he wanted a coffee. Anyway, while we were there, we noticed the camera could just see where the kidnap took place. Apparently, it was thought to have been malfunctioning, but luck smiled on us and it took some pictures at just the right time."

Tessa leant forward again, her enthusiasm renewed.

"We couldn't make out precisely who grabbed her, but clearly a number of people were involved. There were lookouts around the bank's main exit, and others surrounded Penny as soon as she left. The van pulled up and she was quickly bundled into the back. She wouldn't have realised what was happening until it was too late. The whole operation was performed with almost military precision. But as the van moved off, it travelled towards the coffee shop. It is this shot which our friends in the Special Forces used to identify the driver." He paused for effect. "Now, it is generally accepted that a woman nicknamed The Barb is the gang member responsible for training and leading the heavy mob. The pictures are very poor but it seems likely she was driving the van."

"So, has this *Barb* been arrested?"

"No. Nobody knows who she is. She always takes care to disguise herself when on gang business so no one has been able to track her down... But for some reason, she has taken to wearing a rather distinctive jacket."

Jones slid a picture over to Tessa. It was impossible to make out the driver's face, but what was clearly discernible was the distinctive 'EB' logo on her black leather jacket.

"Wow, that's a Ettore Bugatti jacket!" exclaimed Tessa in surprise. "I've got one of them."

"Have you really?"

"Yes. But it's not me in the picture."

"We know that," Jones, assured her.

"Anyway," continued Sinclair, "The Barb has trained the whole gang in evading capture. Nobody knows their identities. They all wear blue jeans and a black fleece jacket with a three-hole balaclava when working. It's almost a uniform. But clever too. It keeps everyone guessing who they are and even what gender."

"What about the van they used?"

"Well, it looks remarkably like one seen leaving Sloane Square after you were attacked there, and the man who died was wearing a black fleece jacket."

"Hmm. Interesting..."

Tessa's mind was racing. Finally, some useful information. It seemed the Calver Cats were playing a central role in this saga. But why had it taken Sinclair and Jones so long to get this far? Surely CCTV pictures wouldn't have been archived for that long? More likely information was being meted out to her bit by bit, as slowly as they felt she would tolerate. Their numerous sideways glances at each other only added to her suspicion that they knew more than they were telling her. Maybe they had outlived their usefulness? But then she remembered Matsumoto saying, *"Brains not just brawn."* Tessa felt a rush of excitement as a plan formed in her mind. Perhaps the time had come for *all* her hunters to become the hunted.

"Well, I suppose that is marginally better than I was expecting after having read Jones' lacklustre reports," she said disparagingly. "But I've already read a lot about the Calver Cats in the newspapers. Nothing you told me was new. Let's just review where we're really at, shall we?" Sinclair and Jones looked blank, fearing the worst. "After all this time you have *nearly* confirmed that the Calver Cats organised Penny's death, and that they may be after me too. But we still don't know precisely who killed her, or why, and we're certainly no closer to apprehending any of those responsible. Is that an accurate assessment of the situation, or am I doing you both a gross injustice?"

"Well," stammered Jones, "it wasn't exactly easy to get this. We've had to work really hard … and it's dangerous too."

"Oh, so you want out?" asked Tessa, quickly.

"No, I didn't mean that!" he exclaimed, weakening under her determined gaze.

It was Sinclair's turn to smile.

"Your assessment is factually correct," he interjected. "However, you are doing us an injustice if you are suggesting we have not been working hard to get this far. It is also likely we will know *why* as soon as we know precisely *who*."

Tessa paused and drank some green tea.

"OK. I'll give you a short reprieve then," she said purposefully, "but this is the last one. The bottom line remains: you were hired to apprehend Penny's killers; you haven't, and I believe you should be further on by now. I'm putting you both on notice. You have three weeks from today to come up with something conclusive. If, at the end of those three weeks, you don't have anything which convinces me I should continue to retain you, then we will go our separate ways. I presume that's agreed?"

She looked at them both for assent. They said nothing.

"Good," she continued. "I'd like you to call another meeting as soon as you've heard from your friends in the Special Forces again, but don't wait until your three weeks is up. It seems you have some leads. Follow them up more quickly now so that we can bring this matter to a just and speedy conclusion. If this Barb is training a gang of a dozen or so, with swords, she's going to need a fair amount of space to do it, presumably near London. Surely that can't be too difficult to find?"

The atmosphere was tense. Sinclair and Jones had not wanted or expected her to react quite so harshly. They had hoped, by feeding her a little more information, to satisfy her for a while. It seemed they'd been over-optimistic.

"Understood," responded Sinclair. "We will chase our contacts and get back to you as soon as we can."

"Excellent. Well, thank you, gentlemen. See you again soon then," she said, signalling to Antonio for the bill. "I'm afraid I need to rush. I've an appointment to collect my new car."

"A new car? That sounds fun," said Jones, trying to lighten the atmosphere. "May I ask what you're getting?"

"It's a Bugatti, that's why I've got one of those jackets."

His mouth fell open in amazement.

"You're getting a Bugatti! A 260-miles-per-hour, four-turbocharger, ten-radiator, 1,000 bhp Bugatti?"

"Yep, that's the one," she replied, delighted he'd swallowed the bait.

"Wow! I'm envious. In fact, I'm very impressed and very envious."

Sinclair stood up.

"And we'd better be off too," he said. "Thank you for the coffee. One of us will be in touch again soon."

After they had left, Tessa retrieved her sword case and hailed a taxi to take her to Stanhope Gate. She was wondering how deep the investigators' links to the Special Forces ran. Meanwhile, back in their car, Jones turned to Sinclair.

"Phew! She's becoming very high-maintenance."

"Not really. I suppose there's quite a lot for us to clean up in her wake, but she's only being so assertive because she wants to do the right thing by Penny. We haven't exactly made it easy for her."

"You told her a lot more than I thought you would, and you didn't even ask why she's wearing gloves?"

"Yes, I know. And I noticed you crumbled too," replied Sinclair, grinning. "It's that look in her eyes which makes her so difficult to resist. I've experienced it with someone else, but I never expected to see it in her so soon... Anyway, I wonder what else she'll do."

"Well, we don't want her to have a go, do we? How would we protect her then?"

Sinclair looked thoughtful.

"Indeed. But three weeks is a long time; maybe something will crop up to distract her... Anyway, it's not only the Police who haven't been able to stop the Calver Cats, the Special Forces have been equally unsuccessful. I suspect there might be a mole somewhere. I know it's a bit unorthodox, but maybe we *should* cut her loose. She might be just the catalyst we need to get to the bottom of this..."

Fifteen minutes later Tessa was being greeted by John Brown.

"Sorry I'm late," she said. "My previous meeting dragged on a bit."

"Not a problem," he responded, looking at the sword case slung over her shoulder. "I see you brought it with you today. I bet that gave Anderson a shock."

Tessa laughed.

"Well, he didn't ask to see my ID this time."

"I'm not surprised! Anyway, we've given the car a thorough checking over. In all my years, I've never seen anything quite so phenomenal. Would you like to have a look at it straight away?" said the salesman, warmed by the thought of his commission.

"Oh, yes, please."

They walked through the showroom into the workshop, part of which was screened off. Inside stood just one car, Tessa's Bugatti. He pulled off its tight blue cover.

"There you have it," he said, gesturing with his hand. "The Bugatti PE."

"Wow! It's stunning."

"Isn't it just? And the first Bugatti PE ever bought by a woman! In addition to all the standard PE features, it has high-performance run-flat tyres, bullet-proof glass, armour-plating, and a whole host of defensive features – we'll program you as the sole user in a moment. And, of course, there's the obscuration system. It's the best we've ever seen. It's most effective in dusk or dark conditions. In full stealth mode one can barely see the car; there are even light-absorbent coatings on the wheels and glass. And, in partial stealth mode, it really does resemble an Audi TT. The system is powered from the main high-capacity battery, but if that runs flat, there's a small reserve battery to ensure the engine will still start. Also, there's the GPS tracking system; it's extremely sensitive. Here are your three tracking devices. If you need any more, just let me know. They are, of course, all laser-engraved with your RCL number. Their locations are shown on the car's map display."

"Oh, and I should tell you about the infra-red front and rear cameras. They can now be viewed on the new head-up display. It was an upgrade which became available in your absence. I hope you don't mind, but I took the liberty of having it included?" Tessa nodded her approval and walked round the car, grinning. "The only external indication the car is not standard are the PE badges. As I mentioned,

251

we are obliged to put those on to identify the vehicle to the authorities as, shall we say, special."

"Mr Brown, I'm speechless. It's wonderful! I'm petrified by how much it cost, but delighted. I do believe it takes my love of gadgets to an entirely new level. Why don't I settle up, and then you can take me through all the features more slowly?"

"Fine. But there's no rush and you're always welcome to pop back with any questions. We'd like to see it every six months anyway to make sure it's in tip-top condition. I'll put Simon on stand-by to explain the technicalities, he's our resident egghead."

Tessa cleared the final money transfer and the three of them spent more than an hour going through all the car's features. Eventually, the roller shutter on to Stanhope Gate was opened and, very carefully, she drove her new car home. She parked it in her garage and stood admiring it for several minutes.

"This should come in handy for tracking down the Calver Cats," she muttered. "I'll just have something to eat, and then practise…"

After a quick sashimi dinner, Tessa drove out of the mews, determined not to return until she could use every feature on the car without thinking. She particularly wanted to make sure she could drive it in the dark without lights, relying only on the infra-red cameras and head-up displays. It was early the following morning when she finally returned home, satisfied that the car performed every bit as well as she had hoped. She dozed for an hour before going for a long run and her usual practice session with Lee. They finished early so that he could admire her car too. They even went for a drive and she insisted he try it, which he was desperate to do.

That evening, Tessa received an e-mail from Blaise Collins-Clarke wanting to discuss an investment opportunity. She was amazed that the BNYI banker from whom she'd bought Penny's company would want to discuss anything with her again and replied that she was busy, but would get back to him. Then she spent several hours surfing the Internet, reading anything she could find about the Calver Cats. By the time she'd finished, she was in awe of the speed of their growth and apparent ruthless efficiency. However, she still could not understand why such a focused criminal gang would have wanted to kill Penny; and, apparently, were now after Tessa herself too.

CHAPTER 27

It had been two weeks since Tessa arrived back in London. She finished her daily training session and returned home to change and put her sword away. She was going to treat herself to a relaxing break in Antonio's.

After the usual greetings had been exchanged, she settled down with her green tea and started reading the *Financial Times*. Suddenly, she became aware of footsteps approaching. She recognised them instantly but remained stock-still, hidden behind her newspaper.

"Good morning, Tessa," said a familiar voice. "May I join you, please?"

She looked round the patisserie, barely moving her newspaper.

"There are plenty of empty tables. Why can't you sit at one of them?"

"Because you're sitting at this one. It would be much more difficult for us to talk if I sat elsewhere."

"I wasn't aware we had anything to say to each other," she replied curtly.

"Well, perhaps we don't have anything to say to each other. But there is something I need to say to you, and it would be a lot easier if I could sit with you while I say it. Please, Tessa, it's important."

She sighed and lowered the newspaper so she could look at David. He was as handsome as ever in a stylish pin-stripe suit. His perfectly pressed light blue double-cuff shirt was completed with a tasteful patterned silk tie, and gold cufflinks inlaid with cornflower blue sapphires. Tessa had chosen everything he was wearing. She couldn't resist the temptation to smile.

"Nice outfit."

"It is, isn't it?" he replied. "My favourite."

"So, will what you have to say take long?"

"Possibly not," replied David, with a smile which would have made her wilt if she hadn't still been so angry with him. Tessa motioned him to sit down.

"By the way, you look stunning," he said admiringly. "You've lost a little weight … not that you needed to … and you look fantastically healthy. That tan really suits you. You look as though you've, well, changed. What on earth have you been up to?"

"I've been wandering around the Far East. David, what is it you want to say to me?" she asked, worried she might have blushed in response to his compliments.

"May I have a coffee as well, or is that asking too much?"

She took a deep breath and caught Antonio's eye; he scurried over to them.

"Is-a this man a-bothering you?" he asked. "Just say-a the word and I have-a him e-jected."

She smiled.

"Tempting as your offer sounds, he's behaving himself at the moment. However, he would like a cup of coffee."

"…and I see your cup is empty," interjected David. "May I get you another latté?"

"I don't drink coffee any more, but another green tea would be nice, thank you."

"Wow, you don't drink coffee any more? That's … a surprise. So, one double espresso and one green tea, please, Antonio."

He nodded at Tessa, scowled at David, and walked off.

"He guards you well."

"Do I need guarding, David?"

"Certainly not from me."

Tessa purposefully folded her newspaper and put it to one side, making it abundantly clear she wanted him to say his piece.

"Right, here goes then… Tessa, to say I owe you an apology is a massive understatement. When you told me … well, you know … I reacted like an absolute ass. I shot from the hip, based on ignorance, prejudice and fear of something I didn't understand. I should have believed in the person I'd come to know, instead of what I didn't know. Tessa, please, please forgive a stupid man for what was said and done in foolish haste. I know I must have hurt you terribly and I can't apologise enough. Tell me what I've got to do for you to forgive me, and I'll do it. I'm really, really sorry, Tessa. I mean it."

She looked at him. The pent-up fury which she'd learnt to repress suddenly welled up inside her again. But other emotions were just as quick to surface. With David sitting in front of her, she remembered how immensely attractive she had always found him; bordering on the irresistible, in fact. For several seconds she didn't say anything.

"You hurt me, David," she murmured. She wasn't going to cry, she told herself, she definitely wasn't going to…

"I know. It was embarrassingly senseless of me. I'm so sorry."

"Stop saying sorry," she replied, raising her voice. "I've got that bit!"

He smiled apologetically. Then he glanced round to check the gangway was clear and noisily pushed his chair back over the quarry tile floor. He went down on one knee and looked up at her.

"Tessa, I have been a very stupid and foolish man," he said in a voice loud enough for everyone nearby to make out. Naturally, they all stopped talking so they could hear everything clearly. "I behaved like an imbecile and said things which must have been very hurtful to you. I sincerely apologise, from the bottom of my heart. Tell me what I must do to earn your forgiveness."

She looked round, wide-eyed. Everyone was staring at them in disbelief. A few people were holding up their mobile phones to try and take pictures, but Antonio dispatched his waiters to stop them. She looked at David and burst into laughter.

"Idiot! You can shut up and sit down for a start!"

David grinned sheepishly and made himself comfortable back in his chair. The background noise returned to normal and Antonio came over with a tray. Almost reverently, he placed Tessa's green tea in front of her. He then turned to David and banged an espresso down in front of him.

"Not-a bad, for-a starters!" said Antonio. "But if I-a were her, I be-a holding out for-a more. Much-a, much-a more."

"Thank you, Antonio," replied David, smiling, "especially for the drinks."

"You're-a welcome," he replied, winking at Tessa.

"Heavens," said David, "that'll teach me! But I meant what I said, Tessa. If it were possible, I would like to try again. Can you find it in your heart to forgive me?"

Earlier that day she had congratulated herself on the fact she appeared to have her immediate priorities well sorted. All of that had just flown out of the window.

"David, everything I said still stands. I needed to fix a birth defect and I'm not ashamed of what that meant I had to do."

"I understand, and there's no reason why *you* should be ashamed. You've proved yourself to be a damn' sight braver then I could ever have been."

"Fine. So what's brought on the histrionics?"

"Basically, I've done some much overdue thinking, and, like you, I've changed. But I knew I needed to do something extraordinary to convince you of my sincerity."

"Touché," she muttered. "Why is life always so complicated?"

"Oh, look, if you've found someone else, I quite understand. After all, why wouldn't you have? That's fine; I'll just leave you in peace. But I would feel a lot better if you said you'd forgive me first."

"No, it's not that. I'm unattached. It's just… well…" She paused before continuing. "This has all come as a bit of a surprise."

"I understand," he replied. "Actually, I hadn't realised I'd do the chair thing either, it was one of those on-the-spur-of-the-moment impulses. Got your attention though, didn't it?"

"In a manner of speaking."

"Seriously, is there any way we can start over? I've thought about it a lot. By the time I'd realised how daft I'd been, you'd already left the country. My life has been empty ever since. I've been trying to catch up with you for ages, but I didn't want to send you an e-mail or leave a telephone message. It had to be face to face, and this was the only place I thought I'd stand a good chance of catching you unawares. It's taken me ages, but I've been looking in here as often as I could, on the off chance. Would you let me take you out to dinner? Tonight … tomorrow … the day after. Whenever you like, wherever you like."

She drank some tea and tried to work out the logical course of action, but then her emotions seized control.

"All right, dinner," she replied, trying to sound unenthusiastic. "How about the day after tomorrow? You can choose where."

"Wonderful! Thank you," he exclaimed. "I know just the place. I'll collect you at four, evening dress. OK?"

"At four, for dinner!" Tessa replied, incredulous. "Oh, I suppose so."

"Excellent, I'll see you then," he said, gulping down his coffee and putting some money on the table. "Please excuse me for now. You want to finish your paper and I have some arrangements to make. See you the day after tomorrow. Tessa, I'm so pleased. Thank you."

He stood up, smiled and walked away with a spring in his step.

At precisely 4 p.m. on the day of their dinner, Tessa's doorbell rang. She had pulled out all the stops with a red strapless Dior dress, her best diamond jewellery and a diamond-studded Franck Muller watch. She opened the door to find David looking very dashing in a dinner suit. Behind him was a new maroon-and-grey Rolls-Royce. His chauffeur was holding the back door for her.

"Hello, David," she said with a smile. "Nice wheels."

"Wow!" he replied. "The belle of the ball. You look wonderful."

"Thank you. Where are we going?"

"Well, I thought you might like a night at the opera ... in Paris. There's an excellent interpretation of *Orpheus in the Underworld* which I thought would be fun, and afterwards there's this very nice little restaurant I know. I have a private jet waiting at Northolt, and a car at Orly Airport."

"Not bad, David, not bad at all," said Tessa, as she got into the back of the car. "Thank you," she added, as Andrew closed the door.

"You're welcome, ma'am," he replied, with a wide smile.

"When did you get the car, David? It's very swish, and ... armour-plated too," Tessa asked idly.

"Ah, yes, that's down to my SAS past. Not sure why they think I still need protection, but I got it anyway. It is a nice car though, isn't it? Andrew chose it. He's been keeping me in order for years, and gives the very best advice of anyone I know. Don't you, Andrew?"

"I do my best, sir," he replied, meeting his employer's eye in the mirror for a moment before discreetly looking away.

Tessa and David chatted in the back of the car as it travelled up the A40 to Northolt. It stopped in front of an executive jet, and, once they had boarded, they drank champagne as they were flown to Paris. The operetta was wonderful, and the dinner afterwards delightful...

It was 4 a.m. when Andrew finally held the car door open for Tessa, back outside her house. David got out and stood behind her as she went inside and switched off the alarm. She returned to the front door.

"That was lovely, David, thank you."

"You're more than welcome. Look, I know it won't be easy, but could we have another go? I'd love to see you again."

For a moment there was silence, then she smiled, leant forward and kissed him lightly on the cheek. "Call me," she said, and closed the door.

A smile spread across David's face. He turned and got back into the car, beaming.

"A successful night then, sir?"

"I believe so, Andrew. I think we've managed to rescue a situation which I thoroughly deserved to lose. Not a bad night at all."

For a while Tessa stood with her back pressed to the door and listened as the Rolls pulled away. She sighed. Then she saw the clock.

"Oh, no," she groaned, "it's time for my run!"

At 8 a.m. she had just finished showering when an SMS arrived from Sinclair. *We have something. Can we meet? 3 today, usual place?*

Hopefully they'd have something worth hearing; but even if not, she'd have an opportunity to put her own plan into action.

"At last," she exclaimed, and quickly replied, *Yes c u @ 3.*

Late that afternoon, she drove the Bugatti to Yeoman's Row near Antonio's. She left it in a residents' parking bay, well back from the meters where she hoped Sinclair and Jones would park. After exchanging the usual greetings with Antonio, she settled down to drink her tea.

Sinclair and Jones didn't keep her waiting long. As they sat down, she smiled warmly at them. They thought she was welcoming them; in fact it was because she'd seen Jones slip some car keys into his pocket.

"We have some promising progress to report," said Sinclair. "It's not everything we'd hoped to have, but it is a significant step forward. Not only have we now established, beyond reasonable doubt, that the Calver Cats organised Penny's death, we have also managed to locate one of their training grounds." He paused for a moment to bask in what he hoped would be some form of adulation. But Tessa was too busy marvelling at what a little pressure could do to galvanise them into giving her some worthwhile information. The possible awkwardness was interrupted by Antonio bringing some coffees for them and more green tea for her.

"Well done," she said eventually. "Carry on."

Sinclair smiled.

"It seems something was overlooked when Penny's body was found. The Calver Cats usually leave a calling card when they commit a crime. It's to make clear that they were responsible, and make others take heed. Well, they left one on Penny but the delivery driver who found her didn't realise what it was. He picked it up and put it in his pocket. His wife found it later when she took his jacket to the cleaners. She brought it in to the police."

"I hope they know how much investigative time has been wasted?" exclaimed Tessa, not sure whether the driver should really be held accountable or whether Sinclair and Jones had always had this information, but only chosen to divulge it now.

"Probably, but that's a police matter," replied Sinclair, dismissively.

"Where exactly was Penny's body found? You never said."

"I know, and we're still not allowed to. The Police have never released the precise location."

"Surely you can tell me?"

"No, sorry."

"Hmm. Are you going to show me this calling card, then?"

Sinclair smiled and nodded to Jones, who produced a photocopy from his briefcase.

"As you see, it's a sort of geometric flower with a tiger's head in the middle," said Jones, handing it to her. "It's still highly confidential, the media have agreed not to publish it, so please don't tell anyone you've seen it or we'll be in real trouble."

Tessa nodded and studied the complex motif...

Reader, please note: The Calver Cats logo is shown in the bottom left-hand corner of the back cover.

"How strange. Does it mean something?"

Jones shrugged.

"May I keep this?" she mused. "It's interesting ... I promise I won't go bandying it about."

Jones looked at Sinclair who nodded again.

"Thank you," she said, carefully folding it up and putting it in her handbag. "Now tell me more about this training area?"

"Well, it seems they're using some wasteland to the east of London," replied Jones, evasively. "The location is even more hush-hush than the calling card, so it's probably better if it stays that way. Anyway, we thought we'd check it out first. We wouldn't want you going over there and getting yourself into trouble."

Tessa glared at him.

"I don't pay you to be patronising. Where is it?"

Jones looked offended.

"He wasn't being patronising," interjected Sinclair tersely. "Gareth is concerned for your safety. It's only sensible we should check it out first."

"OK," replied Tessa, equally tersely, hoping that by appearing irritated she would make them more susceptible to her plan. "Is there anything else you are willing to tell me, or shall we just fix another meeting for when you've checked this place out?"

"We're hoping to go there in the next few days," continued Sinclair, "at least to confirm the gang is using the place. We'll give you a call as soon as we know what, if anything, is happening. But they're unlikely to be there every night, so it could take a while."

"I suppose that'll have to do. Just make sure you do keep me informed."

Sinclair nodded and Tessa relaxed.

"By the way, Jones," she continued with a bewitching smile, "I came by car. If you'd like to have a look at my Bugatti, it's in Yeoman's Row."

"Oh, yes, please," he replied, enthusiastically. "Ours is parked there too."

As they left Antonio's, Tessa discreetly secreted one of her car's tracking devices in her hand. They talked quietly until they had to cross the road to a brand new dark blue-grey BMW saloon.

"This is ours," said Jones. "We picked it up yesterday."

"Lovely car. I must be paying you too much."

Sinclair burst into laughter; Tessa grinned.

"You should have seen our old one," replied Jones, swiftly. "It needed replacing. Our cars take quite a beating, and it's nowhere near as smart as yours."

With both men still standing on the pavement near the middle of their car, Tessa walked round the back, as though admiring it.

Stopping by the nearside rear-wheel arch, she looked over at them and smiled.

"Well, it looks super. Nice colour too. Mine's just down there..." As she spoke she gestured with her hand, on purpose catching her handbag on the side of their car so that it spewed out a number of cosmetics. Obligingly a lipstick, eyeliner and mascara rolled across the boot while her powder compact fell on her side of the car.

"Oh, no!" she exclaimed, quickly bending out of sight by the wheel. Meanwhile, Sinclair and Jones were completely distracted as they went in search of her other cosmetics. As she picked up the powder compact, Tessa positioned the tracking device high inside the wheel arch. "Honestly!" she said loudly to hide the *clunk* of the device attaching itself. Then she stood up and started checking through her handbag.

"Sorry about that, gentlemen. Thank you," she said as they returned her cosmetics. "Anyway, as I was saying, mine's down there."

Sinclair and Jones went with her and admired the Bugatti. She took great pains to stand in front of the PE badges, and they pretended not to notice them. Eventually, they said their farewells and, as they walked back to their own car, she got in. She couldn't wait to switch on the tracking system, but decided to move off first so as not to make them suspicious. She drove past and waved; then stopped in a nearby side street to switch on the display. She held her breath as the screen came to life.

"Gotcha!" she whooped exuberantly, as a green dot representing Sinclair and Jones' car moved down Brompton Road. It passed through South Kensington, down Sydney Street and across Chelsea Bridge. After a few minutes, the car pulled off the main road past Vauxhall Bridge and stopped.

"Hmm, perhaps that's where they live," she mumbled.

She zoomed in on the dot to see if the map had any further detail on that location, but it remained blank. So she drove home, occasionally looking at the screen to see whether the dot had moved. She only hoped they would use that car to visit wherever it was the Calver Cats trained.

Tessa spent most of the evening dressed in a black tracksuit, sitting in her car in the garage, listening to music and watching the display.

At 10:30 p.m. her patience was rewarded when the dot on the tracking screen started to move eastwards.

"Lead on, my fine British bloodhounds," she murmured, sensing a confrontation. "Then step aside and leave it to the professional."

She checked her sword case couldn't be seen in the passenger seat, opened the garage door, and set off in pursuit. The tracking system was functioning perfectly, and they were well within its ten-mile range. She estimated she was about a mile away from them, but decided to stay on the north embankment rather than cross the river. If they were going to East London, then they would have to come over to her side sooner or later. Judging from their route, she thought they were likely to go over Tower Bridge. She switched the car into partial stealth mode.

She smiled as the green dot marking their car made its final approach to Tower Bridge. She would have liked to have confirmed Sinclair and Jones were inside, but felt it wiser just to go wherever the car went. As the green dot continued eastwards, she turned past the Tower of London into East Smithfield.

Twenty minutes later, she was half a mile behind them. The road was almost completely deserted and she began to worry the distinctive brightness of her car's xenon lights might attract Sinclair and Jones' attention. She checked no cars or people were around. Then, as she passed a side road, she veered off course slightly, as though turning in, and switched her car into full stealth mode. The engine noise disappeared completely, cancelled by an out-of-phase noise generator. All the lights went out to be replaced by an effectively invisible infrared glow and the head-up display burst into life, giving her a crystal clear image from the front and rear cameras.

"Girls with gadgets," she muttered, grinning. "I love it!"

The green dot continued along the A13 as it changed from Alfred's Way into Ripple Road. But then it turned off to the right. Tessa reached the same junction and drove on into complete darkness. Now barely a minute apart, both cars crossed a railway bridge and turned left into Tiger Lane. She followed them into a large rundown industrial area, which, according to the faded sign, was called Rippleside Industrial Estate. The green dot had stopped about a quarter of a mile in front of her. She was impressed that she had not seen any lights from their car after it had turned into the estate; presumably they were driving 'blind'.

Tessa reversed into an alleyway between two high warehouses, put on a black woolly hat and got out. She slung her sword case over her shoulder, locked the car and armed its defensive systems. After checking the coast was clear, she walked to the end of the alleyway, stopping at the base of a high railway embankment. As she glanced back at her car she smiled. If she didn't know where it was parked, she would never have been able to make out the barely discernible outline.

She glanced to her left and her right, but couldn't see or hear anyone. She scrambled up the embankment, crouching down near the top. The night was clear and still, and she had an excellent view. The embankment was heavily overgrown as it had clearly not been maintained since its single railway track had been removed. She looked round, listening. There was an unnatural stillness; no wild-life sounds, nothing. Only the monotonous rhythmic *whoosh-whoosh* of three huge wind turbines, illuminated by the lights from a far-off street.

About half a mile away there was another railway embankment, slightly higher and wider than the one she was on, and with several glistening railway tracks. A large, flat, triangular-shaped area of wasteland filled the space between the two embankments. Narrowest to her left, it widened to her right where, in the distance, she could just see the moonlight glistening on a narrow stream.

The only building in sight was a dilapidated office block near the opposite embankment, halfway along. A nearby tunnel though the embankment apparently gave access to the road behind.

The wasteland appeared to be covered with black cinders. It looked as though it had been used for freight storage since some rusty containers stood at the furthest end. There were floodlights around the edges, but only a couple were on.

Not a nice place, thought Tessa, but a great training area. She shivered, and wondered whether Penny had ever seen this lonely, forbidding place. Finally, as she strained her eyes, she saw Sinclair and Jones moving slowly and quietly along the embankment.

"Not too bad," she murmured, smiling, "for PIs."

With so little happening, Tessa decided to see if she could find a better place to secrete her car. She scrambled back down the embankment and started to pick her way along the back of the warehouses, further into the estate. She proceeded with caution, given that she was nearing the spot where Sinclair and Jones had parked their car.

The first acceptable alley turned out to be blocked by piles of wooden pallets. The next was much better. It had a narrow, but adequate, access from the road between two large warehouses, and broadened out nearer the embankment, providing more than enough parking space. Ideal, thought Tessa, making a mental note of what the fronts of the two buildings looked like.

She retraced her steps to the embankment and stopped to see if she could hear anything new. There was still nothing except the *whoosh-whoosh* of the wind turbines. She considered trying to retrieve her tracking device from Sinclair and Jones' car, but decided that would be taking an unnecessary risk. However, she knew she'd have to retrieve it sometime.

Taking care not to make any noise, she climbed the embankment again. She couldn't see the other two but felt sure they were still there somewhere since she had neither seen nor heard their car leaving. Tessa crouched down for a while, considering what to do. She could wait, on the off chance something would happen that night; but she wasn't terribly well prepared. Alternatively, she could leave now, increase her chances of getting away unseen, and prepare herself properly. Now she knew the location, she could come back whenever she wanted. She concluded it would be sensible to go, and crept back to her car. She confirmed that the dot representing Sinclair and Jones' car had not moved, and drove silently away.

The following day she trained with Lee as usual, but didn't mention what she'd done the night before. She had just arrived home when David telephoned.

"Hello, Tessa. It was a good evening in Paris, wasn't it?"

"Yes, it was."

"Well," he continued, hesitantly, "do you think we could have as much fun again without going to Paris?"

There was a pause while she tried to give the impression she was thinking about how to respond. In fact, she had already decided she would give him a second chance.

"I suppose we could try something else and see, couldn't we?"

"What an excellent idea. I would like that very much. Thank you."

Shortly afterwards Tessa received an SMS from Sinclair saying nothing had happened the night before, but that they would continue observing the place. He promised to arrange a meeting as soon as they had something to report. She sent a quick acknowledgement, and went to see Kono.

Tessa and David met next at Antonio's and talked for several hours. She drank green tea while he started on coffee, progressing to red wine as he relaxed. They brought each other up to date with what they'd been doing during the past few months; something which, surprisingly, they hadn't done during their trip to Paris. However, Tessa took great care not to mention her training with Matsumoto or the fact that she had a sword licence. She felt David still didn't need to know about that part of her life. Instead she described places in South East Asia she had visited in the past: Thailand, Burma and Cambodia. By the time they left, both were sure it would be possible for them to pick up their relationship again.

In the days that followed Tessa divided her time between SKS and meeting David. She knew that seeing so much of him distracted her from pursuing Penny's killers, but felt she couldn't afford to waste this second chance with him.

One evening, she took him to a Burmese restaurant on Edgware Road. She chose it because it was such a contrast to the opulent sophistication of the places he took her.

The Rangoon Restaurant was characterised by functional, rather than luxurious, furniture. It had a small cramped seating area with PVC tablecloths, like those often found in restaurants in Burma itself. Nevertheless, it boasted an unrivalled reputation for authentic cuisine. Tessa suggested it would be better if they dressed casually and travelled by underground rather than use the Rolls.

She laughed as David peered unenthusiastically through the restaurant's steamed-up window.

"Well, you plied me with posh, so I thought I'd balance things out. It may not look smart, but the food is fantastic and the people are really nice. Trust me, you'll enjoy it."

"If you say so," he replied, doubtfully.

Tessa smiled and went in. She put her hands together and bowed, greeting the owner in Burmese with a hearty *Mingalabah*. His face wrinkled into a wide smile of recognition and she and David were welcomed like old friends. They ate and drank extremely well, only leaving as the restaurant closed. David had to admit he had had a wonderful time. They caught a taxi and, fifteen minutes later, stopped outside Tessa's house.

"So, here we are," said David.

"Looks like it."

"May I come in? I think the flames of that last curry could do with some more dousing."

"Of course."

He paid the taxi and they both went inside and took their coats off.

"Water or something stronger?" asked Tessa, as she put some quiet music on the CD player.

"Oh, just water will be fine, thanks."

She returned a moment later with two glasses of water and they sat down next to each other on the sofa. They chatted, listening to the music. Then David moved closer, reached over and put his arm round her. She smiled at him and he put his hand under her chin and gently lifted her face until her eyes were looking directly into his. Then he kissed her passionately.

"How long do you think it will be before we can go to bed together?" he enquired.

She moved back slightly and looked at him mischievously.

"How long do you want it to be?"

He cocked his head to one side and smiled.

"Hmm, would ten minutes be all right?" he whispered.

"That's a long time to get upstairs... Are you sure?"

"Absolutely."

"Well, ten minutes it is then."

In reality, it took them much longer as they both showered and she put on a seductive red lace camisole and shorts.

"Wow," exclaimed David, as she came out of the en-suite bathroom.

"I'm not sure that outfit is good for my blood pressure."

"Well, you'd better help me take it off then!"

Neither of them got much sleep, but they both had a good time.

The following morning they had breakfast at Antonio's where they enjoyed smoked salmon, scrambled egg and champagne. There was no doubting they were an item once more. They spent the rest of the morning walking arm in arm round Richmond Park during which Tessa confessed she'd never had sex before. David kissed her passionately and insisted on treating her to a celebratory dinner.

Two days later Sinclair contacted her to set up a meeting. At last they told her what she wanted to hear: for the previous two nights they had witnessed the Calver Cats training. Sinclair and Jones confirmed they would continue their surveillance and were sure useful intelligence would soon be forthcoming. Not surprisingly, they also asked for more time. She agreed, provided they sent her a brief report each day. At first they refused. But eventually they relented when she said a quick SMS would suffice, unless they had something of real significance to tell her.

In fact, Tessa was already committed to taking matters into her own hands. She had developed a plan but, since she knew it would be risky, had decided to confide in Lee. She opened the discussion by showing him the Calver Cats calling card. He stared at it for several seconds, ashen-faced.

"Nariko-san, this is serious. I have no idea what the flower design means, but the tiger's head in the middle is without doubt the Amafuji mark. Just as your sword has a pouncing tiger on it, Amafuji swords bear a tiger's head. It means at least one of those involved with the Calver Cats has an Amafuji sword; and no one has one of those unless they know how to use it."

Although startled by his concern, Tessa remained undaunted and explained how she hoped to pick off one or two of the gang. But the more she described her plan, the less Lee seemed to like it. Especially when he realised it relied on him providing her with an alibi. So she asked him whether he could think of a better plan; he couldn't, and eventually agreed to play his part in hers.

Later, as Tessa walked home, she decided Lee hadn't been surprised at all by her planned intervention. Usually his protests were far more difficult to brush aside. This time he hadn't *really* tried. Ultimately, he'd simply implored her to be careful and promised to keep her plan secret.

A couple of days later, David went away on business. This gave Tessa an opportunity to act. She spent the afternoon double and triple checking her preparations for what she expected would be an educational, and possibly dangerous, excursion. She remembered what Matsumoto had said when she'd asked how she would know whether she had the knowledge and skill to handle a situation. *"Sprint if you're scared!"* was her abbreviated version of his wise words. So far, she didn't feel at all scared.

During their morning training session Lee had again ostensibly given the impression he objected to her going to Rippleside, but without making any concerted attempt to stop her. Instead he took great pains to emphasise the importance of covering her tracks well, especially if swords were used.

"The Special Forces will investigate all sword licensees in the UK very quickly if a fight has taken place, particularly those near London," he warned her. "You will need to ensure you can clean and hide everything as soon as you get back."

Respecting what he said, Tessa augmented her preparations accordingly. She understood all too well that if she was discovered carrying her sword uncased she would be in serious trouble. Furthermore, if she was injured then that would be unimaginably bad. However, she couldn't help chuckling when she realised that, assuming she was still alive, she would much rather face the wrath of Potter than admit her clumsiness to Matsumoto. There was no denying she was excited at the prospect of this adventure – and by the thought that she was closing in on Penny's killers at last.

Later that afternoon, she closed all the curtains and carefully cleaned her sword. This was the first time it had been prepared with a combat purpose in mind. For a while Tessa questioned her own motives. After all, she had always told herself she abhorred violence. But she felt strongly that on this occasion her actions were more than justified.

She would leave at 10 p.m. That would get her to the industrial estate well before Sinclair and Jones were likely to arrive, if they went at all that night. She needed to have a light dinner at about 7, change, relax and then limber up.

Preparing the fish herself, as she often did now, she had an early dinner of sashimi, miso soup, steamed rice and green tea. Then she went upstairs and changed into the new outfit Kono had made for her. It was essentially a dark bluish-purple leather catsuit – the traditional Ninja colour for night-time camouflage. The suit allowed her freedom to move in the way she would need to in a fight while also providing some protection as a number of tough steel wires had been sewn into the material. She put on some matching soft leather boots with flexible rubber soles, and, with a proud smile, the waist bag she had made at Matsumoto Castle. She put a selection of medical supplies in it, together with a matching balaclava hat. It would hide her face and blonde hair, hopefully making it difficult for anyone to see and recognise her. Finally, she put on thin leather gloves.

She looked in the mirror and smiled at the sight of herself.

"Trim, dangerous, and just a little bit sexy," she decided with a smile.

She returned to the lounge and meditated for thirty minutes, emptying her mind of superficial thoughts and rallying all her mental and physical strength for whatever lay ahead. Then she did some exercises to warm her muscles. By 9:30 she was ready. She checked everything one final time, and then, although it was slightly early, decided to leave.

She took a deep breath and went to the garage. There she put her sword and harness in the passenger well, covering them with one of several black sheets, and got into the car. She had already switched the garage lights off to ensure the mews would not be illuminated when she opened the door. Meanwhile the GPS tracking system confirmed Sinclair and Jones' car remained at its usual place on the south bank of the river. For a moment she wondered if she should go past it on the way out to see where they'd parked, but then decided it would be foolish to take the risk. She hoped they wouldn't go to Rippleside that night as she didn't really want to bump into them. But if she did, then so be it. After all, they were working for her.

CHAPTER 28

Tessa found London surprisingly quiet that night. Whenever possible she drove along backstreets in full stealth mode. But she knew her chosen route already avoided the traffic surveillance cameras. It was 11 p.m. when the Bugatti slipped unseen and unheard into Rippleside Industrial Estate.

She reversed into the alleyway she'd found before and parked between the packing cases. After waiting several minutes with the window open, she was satisfied the only unnatural noise was the *whoosh-whoosh* of the wind turbines in the distance. Furthermore, Sinclair and Jones' car still hadn't moved from Vauxhall. Since they were normally underway well before this, it seemed unlikely they would be coming tonight. She had arrived earlier than intended but felt it would be advantageous to have more time to re-familiarise herself with the surroundings.

She closed the car window and put on her three-hole balaclava, taking care to gather all her hair into it. Out of the car, she quickly donned her harness and slipped her sword in; she flexed her right shoulder to check it drew correctly. Then she armed the car's defensive systems and walked towards the railway embankment.

On the other side of London, in front of their now-dark office block, Sinclair and Jones were just getting into their car.

"You're late," grumbled Sinclair.

"Yes, I know. Sorry, I got tied up," replied Jones. "If you put your foot down we won't be much later than usual. Lamper can do something useful for once and sort out the speeding tickets. Besides, Potter and Flood were there the last few nights and nothing happened."

Tessa quietly clambered up the embankment; she wanted to confirm her mental image of the wasteland. Illuminated by the sullen glow of the moon and the light from the same few floodlights, it all looked distinctly unwelcoming, and deserted.

She scrambled back down and checked again that she couldn't hear anything suspicious. Then she turned and followed the track further into the estate. She continued until she found a secluded alcove, formed by two brick piers jutting out from the back of a large warehouse. It looked ideal and was not far from a rough track leading up the embankment. She stood with her back to the warehouse and settled down for what she expected would be a long wait.

After an hour of listening only to the wind turbines, she made sure the coast was clear and quietly climbed up the embankment. From the top, she had an unrestricted view of the whole wasteland. Several more floodlights were on, but what really brought a smile to her face was seeing all the lights blazing in the office block. Clearly preparations for something had started. Encouraged, she returned to her hiding place...

Meanwhile Sinclair had just driven silently into the estate. Their car had been travelling in full stealth mode with the lights off and the car's infra-red systems on. As he parked the car in their usual alleyway, Jones uttered a grunt of satisfaction as he finally managed to find the 'Security Settings' screen on their car's computer display.

"You know, this motor really is terribly clever... Hold on a second! That idiot Lamper hasn't set all the features correctly. Mind you, with his reputation for screwing up everything... Good grief, he hasn't even enabled 'On Board Security'."

Sinclair smiled; he was renowned for his dislike of gadgets.

"We're still here, aren't we?"

Jones worked through some more menus.

"There, that should do the trick. Here we go."

They both watched as the screen went blank for a moment and then burst back into life. It displayed a neat schematic of the car with a blinking red cross over one of the back wheels. An alert message flashed at the bottom of the screen in bold red letters just as a polite female voice announced, "*WARNING! Alien device detected! Rear-nearside wheel arch.*"

Instantly, Sinclair and Jones flung open their doors and rolled out of the car.

"I'll kill that imbecile," growled Sinclair. "What is it?"

"I'm not sure, but it's not a bomb," whispered Jones reaching up. "It's a tracker. Got it... Wow, it's a very nice one. State of the art."

He stood up and studied the device.

"It's filthy … must have been there for ages."

He rubbed some of the dirt off and peered at the markings on it, holding it up so he could see them more clearly. Then a smile spread across his face. He held the device up between thumb and forefinger and showed it to Sinclair.

"Recognise the design?"

Sinclair shrugged his shoulders in disinterest, realising that Jones was having difficulty containing his laughter.

"You know I don't."

"Well, you're not going to like it, but I warned you she was resourceful. Mind you, I have to admit, I hadn't expected her to go this far."

"What are you talking about?" rasped Sinclair in a low voice, rapidly losing patience.

"This is the most up-to-date device you can get. In fact, it's as good as ours; and that's because it's the same as ours. Furthermore, it has a serial number on it: 44000625/001 … recognise the number?"

"Oh, no!" whispered Sinclair. "Isn't that…?"

"Yep. I thought she was too relaxed about the stuff we were drip-feeding her. Do you remember at Antonio's, she dropped her handbag on our car? I bet she planted it then. No wonder she wanted us to look at her motor. I'm surprised our guys at work didn't find it; maybe they thought we had a spare. Anyway, that means she's been tracking us. I wonder how often she's been here. Maybe she's here now?" Jones desperately wanted to laugh, but didn't dare. "You've got to hand it to her, she's very good."

Sinclair looked thoughtful for a moment.

"I know that. But if we find her, we'll have to tell her who we really are and read her the riot act."

"Yes, I suppose so," said Jones, trying hard to look serious as he pocketed the tracker.

They checked their guns and engaged the user-specific recognition systems. Then they locked the car and armed its defensive systems.

Meanwhile, Tessa had noticed two men approaching along the track from her right. She knew they weren't Sinclair and Jones, not least since they were coming from the wrong end of the estate. Plus, she couldn't believe anyone other than two of the Calver Cats would advertise their presence so brazenly. If they carried on in this direction, they would pass directly in front of her; an ideal opportunity for her to intercept them and see what they knew about Penny's death. There was bound to be trouble, but with just two of them, she felt confident she could handle it. She smiled at her good fortune and flexed her muscles to warm them. She couldn't have wished for better circumstances.

Then her heart sank. Approaching from her left were Sinclair and Jones and the two pairs of men were on a collision course with her in the middle. She looked round for somewhere else to hide. She had always expected to be able to go either left or right. Now, both those options were out and it would be impossible to go up the embankment without being seen. Also, there was no way she could warn Sinclair and Jones. She opted to stay put and let events take their own course.

To her relief, the Calver Cats disappeared up the embankment. Sinclair and Jones clearly hadn't seen them since they continued walking slowly towards where Tessa was hiding. When they were a few feet away, she stepped out and blocked their path.

"Good evening, gentlemen," she said, in as deep a voice as she could muster. They both froze. Not only had they been completely unaware of her presence, they didn't recognise her either. Sinclair's hand started creeping towards his holster in which Tessa could see the hilt of a substantial pistol. However he'd barely moved before she had nonchalantly drawn her sword and positioned it by his neck. She briefly let the blade ring, to emphasise its menacing presence, then flexed her wrist to stop the noise. Jones stood a little way behind, trying to decide whether he should go for his gun.

"Don't even think about it, either of you," she growled. "Who are you, and what are you doing here?"

Jones answered.

"We're Special Forces, on surveillance. Lower your weapon and surrender. Reinforcements will be here soon."

There was a brief pause, then Tessa sighed.

"Well, I suspect the first part is probably true, but I very much doubt the rest. Tell me, do you make a habit of moonlighting to boost your salaries?"

Sinclair's heart was racing. But then he noticed the pouncing tiger emblem on the sword and relaxed.

"What the hell do you mean?" exclaimed Jones.

"I mean, how often do you accept generously paid commissions as PIs while working for the Special Services?" whispered Tessa, using her normal voice.

"Oh, dear!" muttered Jones.

"Quite," hissed Tessa, returning her weapon to its sheath.

"And what exactly are you doing here?" asked Sinclair.

"Unlike you, succeeding in remaining undercover. There were two tough-looking guys over there on a collision course with you."

"And?"

"Well, I came to see what was happening for myself because you were clearly not being honest with me. I hadn't expected to have to look after you though."

Sinclair and Jones glanced at each other. Tessa beckoned them into her alcove hideaway.

"Now," she whispered, "perhaps you could explain why you've been pretending to be PIs and didn't tell me you were Special Forces?"

"Both good questions," acknowledged Sinclair, "and, despite my inclination to do otherwise, maybe it is time we all came clean. I'll show willing by going first, but then it's going to be your turn."

"We took responsibility for investigating the Calver Cats after the gang's prominence increased. Initially the Police had been handling it, but they weren't making any headway and lost several good people. Shortly afterwards, Penny commissioned a Private Invesitgator friend of ours to investigate some suspicious events in her life. Our friend stumbled across a connection to the Calver Cats, and contacted us. We introduced ourselves to Penny as PIs and took over. We soon confirmed that there were links to the gang, but couldn't find out why. We were still working on that when, out of the blue, she was killed. We hadn't expected that, and still don't understand why it was sanctioned. We've never been able to establish a motive, and it just doesn't fit the gang's usual MO.

"Anyway, you arrived on the scene and retained us to continue the work. There was always the possibility that, with Penny dead, you would become the next target, and you were attacked. But we haven't found a motive for that either. So, one way or another, we thought it would be advantageous to maintain our cover and continue as before."

There was silence as Tessa thought this over for a moment.

"What have you been doing with all the money I've been giving you?" she asked.

"It's in a holding account. We knew we'd have to tell you sooner or later. You can have it back whenever you want."

"I see. Then you must have investigated me as well?"

"Of course," replied Sinclair, meeting her eyes without a flicker. "Though you can rest assured that the information on our files is restricted to a need-to-know basis. We had to find out everything we could about you, to ensure neither the investigation nor your safety would be compromised. We really did like Penny and hated losing her like that. Therefore we were, and are, doubly determined not to let anything similar happen to you."

He smiled at Tessa, and for the first time she realised that, ponytail or not, she was dealing with a true professional.

"But that's enough from me; now it's your turn," he told her. "Unless I'm mistaken, you only have an RCL so are not permitted to carry your sword uncased, let alone draw it. Tonight's little escapade means you've broken the law, not to mention scaring the living daylights out of me and Jones. I would also be interested to hear why you're dressed like a Ninja cat woman. Expecting trouble, were you?"

"Ah," acknowledged Tessa. "I came here to watch professional criminals in training. Surely you agree it would be foolish of me to come without being prepared for all eventualities? If I was seen, I wanted to be able to defend myself. Now, I know those two thugs didn't see me, but I'm not so sure they didn't see you two."

"Don't change the subject," countered Sinclair. "Presumably you wanted to try and find some stragglers and see what you could get out of them? We weren't born yesterday, you know. It looks as though we found you just in time. Anyway, we, not you, have work to do here, and we don't want to be worrying about you while we're doing it. We certainly don't want you drawing your sword again. If you stay, the chances are someone will get hurt, then we'll all be in serious trouble. I'm sorry, but I want you to go home now. Your continuing presence would only be a hindrance and could jeopardise the whole operation."

"What! You are joking, aren't you? From what I've seen, you two need me to keep an eye on you!"

"We have managed to survive so far without your help," replied Sinclair. "Need I remind you, we are legally entitled to be here; you are not. I'll do a deal with you, in order to keep your RCL unblemished. If you go now, we'll ignore the fact we saw you here with your sword. We can meet up tomorrow afternoon and discuss the rest."

Tessa was ready to explode. She glared at him in disbelief. Unperturbed, Sinclair stared back.

"I think this is totally unfair," she said through gritted teeth. "However, I am going. But consider yourselves fired!"

Sinclair smiled.

"Duly noted. We'll meet tomorrow."

Tessa nodded, checked the path was clear in both directions and left the alcove.

Five minutes later, fuming and deeply disappointed, she turned into the alleyway where the Bugatti was parked. She had watched the other two go over the embankment a short while ago. But as she prepared to unlock the car she heard a noise which made her blood run cold. It was the report of a gun, followed by the quick *swish swish swish* of a knife being thrown, and a shout from Jones. Professionals or not, they were in trouble.

She took a deep breath and ran back to where the Special Forces men had climbed over the embankment. In a moment she was near the top, crouching down to look over. Sinclair and Jones lay at the bottom of the slope, a short distance to her right. Sinclair was sprawled awkwardly and completely still. Jones seemed to be conscious but clearly in considerable pain. She could see two thugs walking towards them. They were in no great hurry, preoccupied with joking together about what they had just done. One brandished a pistol menacingly. Tessa heard the other say on a walkie-talkie that they'd downed two men, but that everything was under control; he requested that the airwaves be jammed.

Tessa smiled. She knew what to do. Still crouching, she ran down the embankment, standing up straight only when she reached the place where Jones was lying. She winced when she saw the large knife sticking out of his thigh. Sinclair's silence was even more ominous. She had to help them both, and quickly.

The two thugs stopped, clearly surprised and slightly bemused by

Tessa's sudden appearance. She tried to size them up. They looked like fighters: fit, alert and confident.

"You shouldn't have hurt my friends," she hissed.

Tessa could see Jones watching her intently. She glanced down quickly at the knife hilt and readied herself. The man with the gun started to raise it; then his colleague grabbed his arm.

"No, mate, don't waste a bullet on her. She's mine!"

He pocketed the walkie-talkie, drew another knife and threw it at her. His throw was good: well-aimed, strong and fast. But, for Tessa, this was child's play compared to what Matsumoto had subjected her to. She judged the trajectory and spin of the knife and leaned to her left. Then she reached out her right hand and caught the knife by the tip of its blade. She grinned broadly at the thugs … and threw it straight back. It struck the man with the gun in the centre of his forehead. Without making a sound, he keeled over backwards, tossing the weapon behind him as he fell. The second thug rushed back to find it.

Tessa knelt down by Jones, grabbed his hand, and pressed it down on his wound, two fingers either side of the blade.

"Sorry," she said, "keep pressing hard … this will hurt."

Then she grabbed the hilt and pulled the knife out. Before Jones had time to shout a protest, she had stood up and thrown it at the second man. He had just started to turn back to her, holding his colleague's gun. The knife entered his left eye and killed him instantly. But as he collapsed, the weapon fired three shots in the air.

Jones looked up, his face twisted with pain.

"I think I'm pleased to see you, but now we're all in the shit! Sinclair's out cold and I'm no bloody use. The others must have heard. They'll be here soon."

"Then we'd better be quick. Can you walk?"

"Probably, but I'm losing blood; the knife may have hit an artery. I think Sinclair's even worse."

"OK," said Tessa, handing him a wad of bandage from her waist bag. "I don't think the knife hit an artery, it's just a deep cut. Keep pressing this on the wound. I'll have a look at Sinclair."

She moved over to where he was lying.

"You're right, this is bad," she whispered urgently. "The bullet's gone right through, he needs a hospital."

Tessa took out two more wads of bandage. She added some of the blood-stemming moss and herbs Matsumoto had given her, and pushed the pads hard into each of Sinclair's wounds. Then she bandaged them tightly in place and laid him in the recovery position. She was amazed to see the bleeding start to reduce almost immediately.

"Jones, call for help," she instructed over her shoulder.

"Can't ... just tried, no signal, everything's jammed," he groaned. "Can you find Sinclair's gun? I threw mine back over the bank."

Tessa tried her *cbc*.

"My phone's not working either, and I can't see his gun..."

"Damn!" moaned Jones. "They're equipped with recognition systems. It won't be long before they're inoperable."

Tessa went back to him and knelt down. She sprinkled some more of Matsumoto's herbs and mosses on a fresh wad of dressing and started to bandage it to his wound. He gritted his teeth as she pulled as tight as she dared without restricting the blood supply to his leg. As she finished, they heard the sound of people running across the waste ground.

"They're coming. Go and get help," ordered Jones, "or we'll all die here."

"How many are there?" asked Tessa, finishing his bandage.

"About twelve, I think."

"Hmm. Could be worse," she observed calmly, glancing over her shoulder. "So how about if I do a deal with you now? I'm definitely not leaving; they'd kill the pair of you. Either we all die, or I'll save you. And, if we escape, the fact that I was here and with my sword will never be mentioned. I want your word on that, you can speak for Sinclair ... may I suggest you say *yes* quickly?"

Jones looked at her with an incredulous expression on his pale face.

"Don't be daft, you can't fight them all! They'll kill you like they killed Penny, if not worse! Then they'll come and finish us off. Just go and get help, then at least one of us escapes."

Tessa took another look behind her at the advancing horde.

"Actually, I think it's too late for that. So do we have a deal? No matter what happens, if we live, I was never here?"

As Jones looked at her, and then the gang, Tessa realised she felt completely relaxed and ready. She smiled reassuringly at him, noticing that his face was glistening with beads of perspiration.

"This is madness! Yes, you have your deal… Have you a plan?"

"Not yet. But a man in Japan told me that if the need arises one will come to me … and he's always been right so far."

Jones' eyes grew wider, and he shook his head in disbelief. Suddenly Sinclair groaned and started to speak.

"I heard that. You're mad, the pair of you… Nariko, are you scared?"

Tessa turned to look at him, and smiled.

"No, I'm not scared."

He tried to smile back.

"Then you go and get them!"

"Very well, gentlemen. Try not to bleed to death, I'll be back shortly."

Tessa strode across the cinder expanse towards the oncoming group. She wanted to put as much distance as she could between Sinclair and Jones, and the place where the confrontation would take place. She started considering different conflict strategies, quickly concluding it would be easiest if she could split the group. Eventually Tessa and the thugs converged. She counted thirteen; eight of them appeared to be carrying swords, two had long staffs, and one near the front was carrying what looked like a large aluminium club. She couldn't see the other two clearly.

The thugs all looked very tough and Tessa felt sure she ought to be scared; but she really wasn't, not even nervous. In a clear, strong voice completely devoid of emotion, she addressed the gang.

"Hello there. Whom do I have the pleasure of addressing?"

"We're the Calver Cats," growled one of them. "Who do you think, bitch?"

"Just checking. Sorry, about your colleagues, but they tried to kill my friends and paid the price for shoddy workmanship. Anyway, it seems you guys have hurt two of mine, and I've hurt two of yours, which means we're about even, doesn't it? If you could just answer a couple of simple questions for me, then no one else need get hurt and we can all go our separate ways."

"Who is this creep?" grunted another Cat in disbelief.

"Dunno, don't care. Let's just top the lot of 'em," responded the first.

"There's no rush," said a blonde woman from the back. "They're not

279

going anywhere."

She was slightly taller than the others and Tessa could now see that she carried a sheathed sword in her hand. In the distance a grey van, without lights, pulled away from the other side of the office block and disappeared under the bridge. It was just like the one in the picture Jones had shown her… The taller woman noticed the direction of her gaze and smiled.

"Take off your mask and tell us what you want," she called out.

Tessa shrugged, removed her balaclava and put it in her waist bag. Then she ran her fingers through her hair to unruffle it. "I'm a friend of Penny Reid whom I believe some of you murdered. I want to know who killed her and why. That's all."

"And those two?" continued the woman, confirming her position as leader of the group.

"They're Special Forces who are clearly on to you, which means their colleagues know about you too. So, one way or another, you're in trouble. It won't help to kill them; more will follow."

For a moment there was silence.

"You may be right, but two of our friends are dead. Someone has to pay for that."

"Or you could just answer my questions," retorted Tessa. "Then everyone lives to fight another day."

"We'll take our chances. I think you three came on your own or else the place would be crawling by now. So, I tell you what, if you live long enough to get to me, I'll answer your questions." She nodded towards the man with the club. "Move that smile to the back of her face. Permanently!"

The man grinned and broke away from the group.

"Oh, dear, is this really necessary?" drawled Tessa.

She didn't get a reply. Instead the man with the club waddled enthusiastically towards her. He was a big man, strongly built, but heavy; she doubted he would be quick on his feet.

The man stopped about six feet in front of her. With a flourish of his spade-like hands, he twisted the boss at the base of the club. There was a metallic clunk as four metal spikes flipped up near the top.

"Don't worry," he growled, "this won't hurt at all."

"Good," she replied, "I'd hate even a Neanderthal like you to feel anything."

With a roar the man took a pace forward and swung his club over his shoulder and down towards Tessa. He was quicker than she'd expected, but she was much faster. She darted to her right and the club whisked harmlessly by.

"You'll have to do better than that," she taunted.

A moment later he swung again. This time she moved to the left to dodge it.

"...and that."

But Tessa had noticed one of the group fall back from the others. He had a gun and was kneeling down to take aim at her. The man with the club leered and, twisting his body back to his left, swept the club round horizontally. This time she didn't move. Instead, just before the impact, she took a small step forward and turned to meet the club with both arms outstretched. There was a loud *clap* as the body of it hit her hands, well below the spikes. However, instead of trying to stop it, she simply rolled back and round to her left, redirecting the club's momentum up towards the man wielding it. His grip was for swing and he couldn't resist her determined change of its direction. The club came up and hit him in the face. There was an unpleasant *crunch* as one of the spikes sank deep into his skull and he fell back dead, leaving Tessa holding the weapon.

She quickly changed her grip and twisted the boss at the end of the handle to retract the spikes. Then she hurled the club at the man kneeling with the gun. He wasn't expecting a missile to be thrown at him and it hit him squarely on the head. There was a loud *crack* and he fell backwards, dropping his weapon.

Tessa looked at the rest of the group.

"What a waste. If you'd just answered my questions, you'd be two men up. But all of you can still go if you tell me what I need to know."

"No way," replied the woman, clearly annoyed. "You're as good as dead."

Tessa stood motionless in front of them, her expression set, determined and emotionless. She kept her eyes fixed firmly on the group.

Some instructions were murmured, and a few seconds later four fighters broke away and came towards her. Tessa responded by

281

backing away to her left. She wanted to position her foes so that when she'd finished with them she was again between the rest of the gang and Sinclair and Jones.

Tessa could see that two of the advancing men were carrying long staffs. The other two were armed with swords, although one carried a pistol too, on his left side. The two with staffs twisted a grip on them and knife blades sprang out from both ends.

"Hah! Bit primitive, boys," observed Tessa, "but strangely familiar."

The four of them approached in a crescent formation with those carrying the staffs to her right.

Finally, Tessa decided their positions suited her plan. Concentrating on the two men with staffs, she ran forward a couple of paces and started quick handstands towards the one on the left. He responded by pivoting his staff round to strike a stabbing blow at her. His colleague, to her right, closed in quickly with his staff still vertical. Just out of reach of the first man, Tessa stopped her handstands and did two neat cartwheels, ending up in front of the second man. She grasped the staff with her left hand and forced it back hard into his face. There was a loud crunching sound from his nose, and he gasped, but didn't let go of the staff. She tried to wrench it from his grip, but still he wouldn't release it. Then she imagined bursting a sack of wet sand swinging in front of her, and punched his chest. There was a resounding *thump*. Several of his ribs cracked and he staggered back, groaning. At last Tessa had his staff.

With a momentary smile, she spun round to meet the other staff holder. He was running now and threw his weapon at her, but she nonchalantly used hers to deflect it. Then she brought the staff horizontal and launched it at him, letting it fly through her hand. But as the end of the staff reached her right hand she clamped her grip around it. The other end was a couple of inches from the on-comer's chest. He reached up and grasped it, but his own forward momentum and Tessa taking a quick step forward were enough to plunge the blade deep into his chest. With a short moan, he staggered and collapsed. As she pulled the staff back, she heard the man she had punched draw a knife and start towards her. She simply launched the staff backwards. The blade at the other end crunched through his ribs and burst his heart; he died instantly. She retrieved the staff, gripped it firmly and pointed it at the fighter closest to her. His colleague moved round to her right. She was just about to attack when the man in front held up his left hand.

"Hold on, darlin', I'll tell you who topped your friend. But you'll 'ave to do what I say."

Tessa considered her options. To delay her attack would reduce her advantage, but she might learn something useful.

"What do you have in mind?" she asked, rotating her staff upright.

The man smiled and walked forward. He stopped about six feet in front of her, while the other man approached her from behind.

"First, I want you to chuck the staff. My brother will draw his sword so he can keep an eye on you, just in case you cheat. Then I'll tell you who killed your girlfriend, right?"

"That doesn't sound very fair to me."

He shrugged and Tessa heard a sword being drawn behind her. From the direction of the noise she pictured in her mind where the man was standing and how he held his weapon. She had noticed earlier that he was right-handed, which meant his sword would be aimed at her right kidney. However, the man standing in front of her was left-handed, and it was a left-handed cut which had killed Penny.

She smiled and discarded the staff.

"Good girl," sneered the man in front of her. "So, it took most of us to grab the blonde in London. Feisty bitch she was … struggled all the way. 'Course, by the time we got her 'ere she was a bit the worse for wear. Still OK, mind, but quieter like. We 'adn't been told to get any stuff from her. Our orders were just to make sure she died, slowly and painfully. And that's what we did."

"Who actually killed her, and on whose orders?" queried Tessa, focusing only on the words, the images they conjured up were too disturbing.

"Now, now, I only said I'd tell you who killed her. We all roughed her up a bit … well, quite a lot really, I suppose. Then me and my brother here, well, we enjoyed her company … know what I mean? She didn't seem to appreciate it. Strange that, I've never had any complaints before. Anyway, she managed to get hold of my sword. I think the bitch would have been quite handy with it if she'd been in better condition, but she was pretty far gone by then. Still put a gash in my arm though, but then my brother downed her. Not that she was dead, mind, but close."

"Anyway, being an obedient sort of chap, I remembered our orders and slit her stomach open. I'd never done that before, it's very messy, probably hurts like hell too. We can try it later, if you like?" He leered at Tessa as he spoke; but, despite being appalled, she kept her face completely expressionless. "Once she'd died, we dumped her body in London, just as we'd been told. End of story." He turned to wink at his colleagues, then his tone changed. "You know, you really shouldn't come to a place like this without a sword ready to draw. Carrying it over your shoulder looks great in movies, but it ain't much use 'ere, is it? Anyway, 'nough said. I told you what I promised, so our deal is done. OK?"

Already, Tessa's stance had subtly broadened; her weight had shifted and her right knee was flexed slightly.

"Are you sure you don't want to tell me any more?" she asked.

"Don't know any more."

"Oh, well, in that case, thanks. You've made this much easier."

"Good. Then we'll move on, shall we? You never know, maybe you'll meet your friend again. Soon."

His left hand moved to draw his pistol. But, like lightning, Tessa's right hand reached up. This prompted her sword sheath to shoot down and her sword hilt to be catapulted into her waiting hand. The blade immediately started ringing enthusiastically as she swung it over her shoulder. With a brief *whoosh*, she brought it down in a vertical stroke. The sword barely paused as it cut through both muscle and bone, effortlessly severing the man's arm just below the shoulder. Still holding the gun, his arm started to fall. But Tessa had already spun round to face the man behind her.

As expected, he was holding his sword in his right hand with its blade vertical. She brushed it out of the way with a relaxed sweep of her left forearm, taking care to face the blade with one of the reinforcing wires in her leather suit. Meanwhile her sword swept by her right side and continued its now upward course between the man's legs. As the sword started cutting deep into his groin, he yelped in excruciating agony. For a moment Tessa paused and the blade remained motionless. The man appeared to grow a couple of inches in his instinctive attempt to avoid her blade's cut. He dropped his sword and stared at her transfixed, eyes wide with terror. But once convinced she had all that remained of his attention, she simply winked at him and moved her sword rapidly upwards. There was a gurgling scrunching sound as the blade cut up through his body. Eventually, the tip reappeared from the man's chest and he lolled backwards, his body twitching. But she had already turned back to the first man. He hadn't moved, except to clamp his right hand over the stump of his bleeding arm.

"You cut my fucking arm off!" he yelled.

"Oh, dear!" she mocked, her sword hanging by her side. "Does it hurt?"

"What sort of a bitch are you?"

"Peace-loving, just like Penny."

"She was only a fuckin'..." He stopped abruptly. The look of emotionless professionalism in Tessa's eyes had changed to one of abject fury. With a flick of her wrist the sword began to ring again and, with a graceful sweep, she brought it up between the man's legs, following his right thigh. But when it reached his groin and started to cut, she turned it round, and brought it down along his left thigh. He sank to his knees, whimpering, clutching his crotch.

Tessa looked down at the man she'd wanted to meet since seeing Penny's lifeless body.

"It seems your *fucking* days are over," she said, keeping a watchful eye on the rest of the gang, "and pathetic whining won't help you now."

There was another brief *whoosh* as her sword swept across the man's throat, slashing his larynx. He moved his hand up to the new wound, gurgling helplessly.

The remaining Calver Cats were furious and eager to attack, but their leader held them back.

"Leave her! She's earned her revenge. She'll pay soon enough."

"Typical bully!" continued Tessa. "Only brave while you think you're in control. Anyway, as you said, it's time to move on."

She thrust her sword deep into his abdomen and cut horizontally, generating the same wound she had seen on Penny. The man gasped, clutching at his stomach as blood oozed out. Tessa wiped her sword clean on his shoulder and returned it to its sheath.

"That was for Penny," she said. "Go and be judged."

She stepped over to the man's severed arm and, with the hand still holding the gun, kicked it towards Sinclair and Jones. It came to rest some ten yards short. As she walked towards the seven remaining Calver Cats, their colleague's moaning weakened. Finally, there was a dull *thud* as his body fell forward.

"Well, it seems the odds have just moved further in my favour," announced Tessa calmly. "Now all I need to know is who ordered Penny's death. Tell me that and the rest of you can still leave."

The leader laughed, replying equally calmly.

"You know it doesn't work like that. None of us can stop now. You're surprisingly good, and fast, that much we've seen. But we're still too many blades for you."

She whispered orders to the remaining six Cats. Across the wasteland, Sinclair and Jones, both faint from loss of blood, followed the fight, enthralled.

"I hope Takara's watching," gasped Sinclair weakly, "it's payback time."

The four men and two women, all with swords drawn, fanned out and advanced in a line towards Tessa. They were clearly determined to get her this time, and were far more disciplined in their approach. Tessa moved left into open space, prompting those at the end of the line furthest from her to try and cut her off while the others started to go round her.

Tessa decided to attack before she was completely surrounded. She took two steps and then did quick handstands towards them. She aimed at the centre of the line curving slightly to the right as she went. During her fifth handstand, she saw the rightmost three tense up ready for the fight, while those on the left concentrated on encircling her. She completed the handstand and cartwheeled fast to her left, moving slightly backwards. When she stood up she had already drawn her sword and was only a few feet away from the two Cats at the left end of the line.

She swung her sword down and decapitated the first man. Sweeping her sword round as she side-stepped towards the second man, she delivered a fatal slash across his torso, severing his right arm as he attempted to bring his sword into play. There were yells of rage from the remaining four. They surrounded her, and stood in a square formation, each about eight feet away. The two men were in front of her, the two women behind.

Tessa's sword was covered in blood from the two men she had just dispatched. She raised it to eye level and whirled it round. It flung a haze of red across the eyes of the men in front of her, momentarily distracting them. She darted to her left and dived to the ground. As she rolled down, she felt a stabbing pain in her left shoulder, but ignored it. She half-unfurled just behind the man and woman to her left and brought her sword round with a strong horizontal sweep. It struck the woman on the back of her left shin, severing the leg. Screaming, she started to topple over. Lurching over on one knee, Tessa continued her sword swing round and up at full stretch. She cut a deep gash in the man's side almost through to his spine. He reeled from the fatal blow, dropping his sword as blood gushed from the wound. Tessa stood up over the woman whose leg she had just severed. Without hesitating she swung her sword round and thrust it into the woman's chest. Tessa flicked the blood off her blade and calmly walked towards the last two.

At first, they backed away, but then they stood their ground. They presented their swords with the blades pointing at Tessa's neck and prepared to fight. The only sound was the menacing ringing of the Amakuni sword and the *whoosh-whoosh* of the wind turbines.

The man to Tessa's left moved first. He swung his sword round at her and their blades met with a echoic *clang*. The woman joined in, both of them trying to draw Tessa's guard so one could strike the decisive blow. There was a lengthy exchange, but Tessa was far too fast and skilled for them. The woman assailant made the first mistake, and Tessa put a deep gash in her arm. She cried out in pain and staggered back. The man tried to take advantage of the situation and lunged at Tessa. But she viciously swept his sword aside, leaving him defenceless. Before he could recover, she brought her sword back and slashed him across the neck. He dropped his weapon, collapsed to his knees and fell forward, dying. Tessa turned to face the woman who, although wounded, had gathered her wits and come forward again. She stood, swaying slightly, with tears streaming down her face.

"Don't be stupid," said Tessa, "give up now. Enough blood has been spilled tonight. Discard your weapons and surrender to the men over there. There's no need for you to die too."

The woman sniffed and changed her grip on her sword.

"Imagine our roles were reversed. What would you do if I'd just killed your boyfriend?"

"I'm sorry, but I wouldn't commit suicide. You threatened me at South Kensington, didn't you?"

The woman nodded.

"But it wasn't you with the staff?"

The woman shook her head, took a deep breath and advanced. She aimed a sweeping horizontal blow. But Tessa simply took a step back and used her sword nonchalantly to deflect the attacking blade. Then she cut the woman's other arm.

"Please, don't do this," pleaded Tessa, "you can't win."

But the woman came forward again. There was a quick succession of *clangs* as Tessa's sword parried and brushed aside her assailant's attacks. Then there was silence. The woman looked down to see Tessa's sword sticking into her chest. As her own sword fell to the ground, she toppled backwards.

Tessa sighed, flicked her sword clean and deftly re-sheathed it. Then she turned to face the woman in charge. She was tall and attractive with her blonde hair gathered into a bun at the back of her head. She looked supremely confident. She smiled at Tessa and drew her sword, discarding the sheath on the ground behind her. She warmed up her sword arm.

"Well, you said you'd answer my questions if I got to you," observed Tessa. "Here I am."

"Good try," came the calm response. "I have to admit, I never expected to meet someone of your calibre here. Despite everything I'd taught them, the Calver Cats have been eliminated in minutes by just one person. Very impressive. And that's a fine weapon you have there too. But now you've got to beat me."

"Why? You could just tell me who ordered Penny's death, and we're done."

"I don't think so," replied the woman. "Your friends would want you to bring me in, and I can't allow that. No, we have to fight. What's your name? I like to know the names of those I kill."

"Getting ahead of yourself, aren't you? Anyway, what's yours?"

"Bryani."

"Nice name. Pleased to meet you, Bryani. I'm Nariko."

"Well, Nariko, I'm pleased to meet a Peacekeeper of consequence, for once."

"Hmm, Bryani … are you The Barb?"

"Yeah, that's right. Everyone who comes close to me, gets cut; including you. But Nariko isn't your real name, is it?"

"It's what I'm called when I'm out with my sword."

"Yeah, but I've told you my real name. What's yours."

"Tessa…" she hesitated. "Tessa … Pennington."

"Hah! Well, well," exclaimed Bryani. "Then there's more than one agenda at work here. And to think, even I didn't know..."

"What do you mean?"

"Beat me and I'll tell you!"

"As you wish. But first, it wasn't you who attacked me with a staff in central London, was it?"

"No, but I think I know who did. Shall we?"

"If you insist."

To the rhythmic *whoosh-whoosh* of the wind turbines, they started closing in. They stopped a few feet apart, studying each other in the sullen orange light.

"I tell you what," started Tessa, "why don't you…" But the words had barely left her lips when Bryani swung her sword into the traditional attacking position. Tessa responded automatically; for a moment both swords hung motionless, pointing at the base of their opponent's neck. Then, following the same strategy, they twisted their bodies to the right and quickly unwound, bringing their swords round, hard and fast. At the last moment they both flicked their weapons over. The blades met back to back with a resounding *clang*. Each was trying to break the other's sword, but neither succeeded. Instead, sparks flew out from the point of impact and they both took a step away.

"Wow!" observed Tessa. "Where did you get your sword?"

"Kyoto," replied Bryani. "I persuaded a renowned sword-maker to make me and my husband a matching pair."

"Well, I never. One of the last two Amafuji swords."

"That's right," replied Bryani. "So, where did yours come from?"

"It was forged by Kimi Amakuni. The friend you helped to kill commissioned it for me. They say there are no blades finer than those made by these two families. It looks as though this duel will have to be settled by skill and stamina alone."

"Sounds fine to me."

"Where's the other sword?" asked Tessa.

Bryani smiled.

"Too many questions. Are you ready to die?"

The fight resumed.

Sinclair and Jones had watched everything. Jones, in particular, had been grimacing every time Tessa dispatched one of the Calver Cats. Despite his own combat experience, he had still been shocked by the incredible speed and ferocity of the battle; the wasteland was now strewn with bodies. But they both knew they would only survive if Tessa won completely. However, they were wondering how on earth they were going to explain it all without mentioning her. Nevertheless, a deal had been struck and they intended to honour it. They only hoped she would be able to secure answers to her final questions. That should enable them to bring down the whole Calver Cats organisation, especially if The Barb could somehow be brought in for questioning…

Tessa and Bryani fought on. After a long, fast exchange, they paused while Bryani caught her breath.

"Are you sure you're up to this?" asked Tessa, grinning. Although she had beads of perspiration on her own brow now, she wasn't panting like her opponent.

"Oh, don't worry about me."

She looked questioningly at Tessa and raised her sword. The fight resumed, but while Tessa remained supple, strong and agile, Bryani was tiring. Her swings became weaker, less precise and more desperate. Tessa's strategy to wear her down was working.

With all her might, Bryani tried a particularly wild attack. Tessa stepped back and Bryani's sword flew harmlessly round to her left. For an instant it stopped, as she prepared to bring it back. But Tessa had chased it and, with a strong *thwack*, she hit it further away with her own weapon. The impact was so hard that Bryani struggled to hold on to the hilt. Her body twisted to the left as she maintained her grip, leaving her right side defenceless. Tessa quickly brought her sword back and slashed the top of Bryani's sword arm, severing her triceps, electing not to take her take the arm off. The wound wasn't life-threatening, but it was serious enough to render her right arm completely useless. She winced, but said nothing. She could no longer maintain a double-handed grip on her sword and folded her useless arm across her stomach. She was obviously considering fighting on, single-handed.

"I wouldn't try that, if I were you," warned Tessa. "Not if you want to keep all your arms and legs attached. It's over and you're still alive, so I hold you to your word. Who ordered Penny's death?"

"Congratulations," groaned Bryani.

Tessa still held her sword raised in her right hand. It rang menacingly. However, she stepped forward and reached across with her left hand to take Bryani's weapon. But the other woman made no move to give it up.

"Promise me *you* will look after my sword? Promise me you won't let the Special Forces take it?"

Tessa smiled.

"I will look after your sword. I give you my word."

Tessa ignored the distant murmurs of protest from across the wasteland and nodded to Bryani; with a sigh, she released her grip.

Tessa stepped back and lowered her weapon into a less threatening position. She kept Bryani's sword in her left hand, holding it like a dagger with the blade pointing behind her.

"Believe it or not, I'm glad it's over," said Bryani, weakly. She clasped her hand round the wound in her arm; blood oozed from between her fingers. "I just wanted to make some money fast, and re-join my husband. But soon the Calver Cats were being asked to do jobs I didn't like. I thought maybe it was just a phase, but it kept on getting worse… I never thought it would come to this, though. I can't let you take me alive … you do understand, don't you?"

"Let's worry about that later," said Tessa. "Answer my questions first."

On the other side of the wasteland, Sinclair and Jones, increasingly confident about their survival prospects, were sitting up. Sinclair surveyed the battlefield.

"Gareth, get that gun, quickly ... that guy she threw the club at, he's still alive!"

"Oh, shit!" exclaimed Jones, starting to drag himself forward, gasping with pain.

With his gun beside him, the thug was sitting up and looking round. He was surprised to find Tessa and Bryani talking, and no one else left standing. He picked up his weapon, took aim and squeezed the trigger. There was a pronounced metallic *click!* But the gun didn't fire; he'd flicked the safety catch on when he'd dropped it earlier. Swearing, he struggled to release it, but all of them had heard the noise and Tessa reacted immediately. But a moment later, the report of a single shot rang out.

Tessa felt the draught as the bullet sped past her left side, passing between her arm and her body. She knew it had missed her by only a hair's breadth. Then she heard the unmistakable sound of it hitting Bryani. Just as Jones finally took aim, Bryani's sword sank deep into the gunman's chest. Tessa had thrown it backwards horizontally. She hadn't turned to take aim, she didn't need to, she knew from the sound where the gunman was. With a foot of the blade sticking out from his back, the man collapsed sideways, dropping the gun. Bryani sank to her knees, groaning and clutching her stomach. Tessa quickly re-sheathed her sword and knelt down as Bryani slumped into her arms.

"Well, that's sorted," she moaned. "Now I'm definitely not going to be taken alive. Please, promise me again, you'll look after my sword?"

"Yes, yes, I promise. I'll get help…"

"Too late. In missing you, he did a good job on me."

Tessa looked at the wound, and knew Bryani didn't have long to live.

"Please keep your part of our bargain. Tell me why Penny was killed?"

"I don't know why … but our orders were very specific. To me the whole job stank, and suddenly it had to be done that afternoon. She was a brave bitch; fought to the end, never gave up. I'm sorry…"

"Who ordered her death?" implored Tessa, shaking her opponent slightly. Out of the corner of her eye, she saw Jones and Sinclair, supporting each other, staggering across the wasteland towards her.

"The calling card logo shows the initials and my Amafuji," gasped Bryani. "Two C's for Calver Cats and … fuck!" She looked as though she was about to pass out.

"Bryani, stay with me! Concentrate."

Tessa laid her flat and held her head.

"There's me and … he works in the City," she groaned. "One of those fancy places…"

"What's his name? Which firm? What building? Bryani, please!"

"B… B…"

She spluttered, opened her mouth to speak, and went limp.

Sinclair and Jones arrived just as she died.

"Damn!" panted Sinclair.

"So near, and yet so far," replied Tessa, gazing up at the wasteland strewn with bodies. "Good grief," she exclaimed, clearly appalled. "What part of me did that?"

Jones looked at Sinclair. They both realised she was genuinely shocked by what she'd done.

"You have no reason to feel guilty," said Sinclair, sitting down heavily. "It was them or us. You saw what happens if just one is left alive."

"Yes, but all those people… It's so strange, I was just concentrating on winning."

"Well, I don't know how you did it," added Jones, "but I'm very glad you did."

"Hmm. Perhaps I did go a bit over the top with the two who tortured Penny."

"I wouldn't lose any sleep over it," sighed Sinclair. "Are you all right?"

"Pretty much. I've done something to my shoulder, but I don't think it's serious. I still feel sorry for her, though," Tessa continued, motioning towards Bryani. "I think she was just drawn deeper and deeper into things."

"I'm not so sure about that," said Jones. "She's killed a lot of good people. I recognise her now. She's wanted in the US for assassination and armed robbery. Apparently she married some Asian guy … nobody knows who. It's rumoured they separated when he found out what she did for a living. Anyway, we need proper medical attention, and you should leave."

"What a mess," said Tessa, glancing again at the lifeless bodies spread across the wasteland. But she forced herself to snap out of it and found Bryani's mobile phone. "This one's not jammed," she said, passing it to Jones. "But let me sort out her sword first. I need to take it with me."

"Please don't," Jones entreated, "it'll make explaining all this much more difficult." He looked to Sinclair for moral support, but received only a non-committal shrug.

"Sorry, I have no choice; it was a death-bed promise, I've got to take it," said Tessa. "But hopefully I'll be able to hide the fact that a weapon has been removed."

She went over to the last woman she'd killed. She removed her sword, its sheath and her knife, and returned to Bryani. She wiped the sheath through Bryani's hands a few times before putting it on the ground in place of hers. Then she cleaned the sword hilt and pressed it several times into both Bryani's left and right hands, taking care to wrap the fingers correctly around it. Finally, she moved the knife through the wound on Bryani's arm. Then she walked back to the woman and placed the knife in her hand, continuing to the man who had fired the gun. She removed Bryani's sword and carefully slid into its place the one she had just taken from the girl. Satisfied with her deception, she went back for the Amafuji sword, slid it into its sheath and stood up.

"That'll never work," said Jones.

"We'll see," Tessa replied, kneeling down to adjust their bandages. "Sinclair, just lie still. And Jones, you should lie back too. That stuff I put on your bandages is wearing off."

"OK, but you'd better take this with you," replied Jones, sounding noticeably weaker. "Please don't bug our car again, it's against the law." He held out his hand.

"Ah, thanks," said Tessa, smiling as she retrieved her tracking device. "Sorry about that, but it's just as well I did come, isn't it?"

She stood up as Jones lay back and started pressing keys on the phone.

"*Au revoir*, gentlemen. Send me an SMS when you can. If you tell me where you are, I might even bring you some flowers. Oh, and you're still fired!"

Tessa jogged across the wasteland with Bryani's sword in her hand, grimacing as she passed the bodies. Two minutes later she reached her car and wiped as much of the blood off her tunic as she could.

She quickly changed into fresh sneakers and spread a large clean black sheet over the driver's seat. Then she put her boots and gloves in a polythene bag and wrapped them in another sheet together with both the swords. With the car in full stealth mode, she set off with adrenaline still coursing through her veins, listening to the can-can from *Orpheus in the Underworld*.

Shortly afterwards, the Rippleside Estate was swarming with Police and Special Forces. As doctors treated Sinclair and Jones, Potter came over to them.

"What on earth happened here?"

"No idea," replied Jones. "We were jumped at the beginning of what we thought would be routine surveillance. The next thing we knew, it was like this. Some sort of squabble must have broken out ... maybe over us."

"Hmm. More like a massacre."

Then, as Sinclair and Jones were lifted on to stretchers, it started to rain.

CHAPTER 29

Back in her garage, Tessa hurried to hide her involvement in the fight. She grabbed the swords and her dirty clothes and took everything into the kitchen. There, standing on a clean sheet she'd already spread on the floor, she stripped naked and washed her hands and face before putting on a fresh track-suit. Then she put her leather outfit, gloves and boots in a polythene bag which she hid behind a section of her kitchen plinth. Next, she placed everything else she had used in her washer/dryer, switched it on and telephoned Lee. She quickly described what had happened; that she had met Sinclair and Jones and that there had been a big fight, but she was fine. They agreed they should both expect a visit from the sword-licensing authorities soon. Her prearranged alibi was on course.

Then Tessa gave both swords a quick clean, took them into the lounge and opened the secret compartment of her sword safe. She removed the copy of her Kimi sword and replaced it with the two proper swords and the cleaning kit she'd used. She closed that safe and locked the copy in the front safe.

Finally, she sorted out the washing machine and went upstairs for a long hot shower. Afterwards, she inspected her shoulder and found it had some nasty abrasions and bruises, together with a single deep gash. Chiding her over-confidence in the heat of battle, she cleaned the wound and put some of Matsumoto's herbs and mosses on it.

Eventually, exhausted but convinced she had done everything she could to eradicate any trace of her adventure, she climbed into bed. Dawn was imminent.

She had been lying down for only a few minutes when she heard a car stop outside. Not long afterwards, her doorbell rang. She put on a short silk gown and checked her shoulder wound was not visible. Downstairs, she looked through the spyhole in the door. It was Potter, the man who had presided over her Proficiency Test. Next to him stood a neat-looking woman with auburn hair. Tessa opened the door.

"Hello, Mr Potter," she said. "How nice to see you. But isn't it a bit early to be making house calls?"

"Good morning, Nariko," he replied coldly. "We'd like to come in."

Tessa let them in and closed the door behind them.

"This is Constable Johnson," said Potter, gesturing towards his female colleague, who was studying her. "We're visiting all sword licensees to inspect their weapons. While I'm doing yours, Constable Johnson will search the premises."

"What … inspect my sword, search my house? What on earth for?" asked Tessa, indignantly. "I know I've got an RCL, but that doesn't give you the right to just barge in and… Don't you need a warrant or something? Why are you doing this?"

"I'm sorry, but there was an incident last night during which a number of people were killed, many with swords. We're interviewing all legitimate sword owners in order to eliminate people from our enquiries. It's only a formality and quite normal in the circumstances. I don't have a warrant but, if you insist, I will get one. Are you sure it would be wise to put me to that trouble?"

"Goodness, Potter! I suppose you'd better get on with it then. But don't make a mess. And if you're going to be rummaging through my drawers, could you both wash your hands first, please?"

Tessa found it hilarious watching them fastidiously washing their hands in her kitchen. But her mirth was short-lived as Constable Johnson soon went upstairs and Potter insisted on examining her sword. Tessa watched as he performed a swab test on her copy-sword to see if there was any blood residue on the blade; not surprisingly, there wasn't. However, he studied the sword for rather longer than Tessa would have preferred. Eventually he returned it, and quizzed her about what she had done the night before. She stuck religiously to the story she had agreed with Lee. Meanwhile, Johnson came downstairs and went into the kitchen, and then the garage.

"Did you use your car last night?" she asked when she came back.

"Yes," answered Tessa. "As did Master Lee from SKS. I went to his place, stayed there for a while and walked back. I wanted some fresh air. He used my car afterwards to run some errands."

Potter looked at Johnson, who nodded to acknowledge that what Tessa had said appeared to check out…

They left shortly afterwards and Tessa went back to bed, wondering whether her preparations for their visit had proved as comprehensive as she'd hoped. She heard their car leave and tried to get some sleep. But whenever she closed her eyes, images of the previous night's violence flooded back. She found herself deeply disturbed by what she'd done and decided to go for a run on the off chance that some exercise would help calm her.

When she got back, she showered again and prepared breakfast. She'd decided to treat herself to a cup of strong coffee. But while she was making it, her right hand started trembling so much she could barely hold the kettle. She sat down, took several deep breaths and told herself to get a grip. She was beginning to understand how debilitating post-traumatic stress could be.

Eventually, she relaxed sufficiently to eat her breakfast. She tried to rationalise her guilt, hoping her symptoms of stress would not manifest themselves again. Determined to get on with her life, she cleaned her real Kimi sword and Bryani's comprehensively, studying them both carefully. Her Kimi sword was completely unscathed and showed no sign of ever having been used. But the same was definitely not true of Bryani's. Although clearly a weapon of quality, it had endured a hard life. Its hilt was slightly damaged and there were a number of scratches on the blade. Although the cutting edge was still razor-sharp, the sword was in desperate need of a comprehensive professional refurbishment. Even the tiger's head emblem was barely distinguishable. Tessa made a mental note to ask Kono to see what he could do with it. She hid both swords again and walked round to SKS. She wanted to tell Lee everything that had happened the night before.

But she didn't have a chance to say much since he was adamant she should exercise as usual. She ended up interspersing her account with bouts of intensive training. He appeared pleased with the way she had handled the conflict, although he raised his eyebrows when she described how she had dealt with Penny's killers. When she'd finished, he reached over and put a friendly hand on her shoulder. Tessa yelped in pain.

"You said you weren't hurt!" exclaimed Lee, insisting she show him the wound.

"I wasn't," retorted Tessa, wondering what all the fuss was about. "I did this when I dived between two of the final group of four. I think I must have landed on a sharp cinder, that's all."

He inspected her wound. It wasn't serious, but looked very sore.

"This wasn't caused by cinders; it was something much sharper … glass maybe. I just hope the rain washed your blood away so they can't trace it back to you. Nariko, you shouldn't have dived down without looking! I understand why you did it, but it was a foolish risk. That single error of judgement could have cost you victory. Also, you didn't get control of the staff quickly enough; nor did you kill the man with the gun when you threw the club at him. He could easily have shot you instead of Bryani. And you are *lucky* she died … you told her your real name, that you must never do! Far too many mistakes. Any one of them could have cost you your life, and those of Sinclair and Jones, too."

Tessa was silent for a while. Then she swallowed, knowing what she was about to say would greatly disappoint him, but it had to be said.

"Well, I don't think I'll be doing anything like that again anyway."

"What do you mean?"

"At the time it felt good to use the sword to win justice for Penny, and to be able to save Sinclair and Jones, but … but when I looked back … all those bodies, the sounds, the blood… I really don't feel good about it. In fact, I feel downright ashamed. This morning, I nearly dropped the kettle because my hand was shaking so much. Matsumoto warned me about the guilt, and he was right. I'm not sure it's correct for anyone to act as judge, jury and executioner. I would still like to help Sinclair and Jones track down the rest of the Calver Cats and find out why Penny was murdered. But, with a bit of luck, I'll be able to do that without using the sword again."

Lee looked at her in exasperation.

"You have no reason to feel ashamed! I know you were there primarily for Penny, but you saved the lives of two Special Forces men too; that's no mean achievement. You have done a difficult and distasteful job for the first time. These things have to be done by someone; this time it happened to be you. Think of the people those Calver Cats terrorised in their turn. You have enabled them to rest in peace, and probably saved many others from a similar fate. You did what needed to be done. You saved those who needed to be saved, and stopped those who needed to be stopped. If you hadn't, they would have killed you. If she could, Bryani would have killed you; she wouldn't have given it a second thought." He paused and smiled at Tessa's troubled expression. "You must have known this was going to happen sooner or later? You were given special skills for a reason: to help others, not for your own personal indulgence. You were given the sword for a reason: not so you could sit comfortably in South Kensington cleaning it. Not to use your skills and your sword to their fullest extent, as a force for good, would itself be a criminal act."

Anger and frustration bubbled up inside Tessa, but she controlled them.

"Thank you for that. But remember, I have always said this is *only* a hobby for me, *not* a way of life. Look at the trouble we might both be in."

"Nariko-san," continued Lee, "go home and rest. You need it. If we get into trouble because you did the right thing last night, then so be it. I certainly don't mind."

"But I do!"

"I know. It is always deeply unpleasant when one is first involved in a real conflict, and so it should be. It is never wrong for you to feel sad for having ended people's lives, even wicked people. But your conscience has no grounds for unease. You simply did what you were meant to do, and I'm afraid that's not something you can stop and start whenever it suits you… I'm sorry if you've found me overly harsh, but tomorrow we should train as usual."

Soon afterwards, still feeling depressed, Tessa walked home. She had barely left Barnaby Mews when Lee telephoned Japan.

"Ah, Matsumoto-san," he began. "How are you? …Good, I'm pleased. Yes, we're fine, and Nariko is too. In fact, I think her transition from hawkish businesswoman to formidable fighter is almost complete. She's started! Fourteen down and a fifteenth beaten, but killed by someone else. Some foolish mistakes, but nothing the rest of her training won't fix. But what will intrigue you is that the fifteenth was Bryani, and she was using one of the last Amafuji swords… She bequeathed it to Nariko…! Yes, ironic, isn't it? I just wish we knew who had the other one. Anyway, that's not why I'm calling. You see, Nariko is … well, she's having difficulty with what she's done… Yes, I know you said she would. But listen, I have an idea. It's quite creative, and you'll need to have a word with Isamu…"

Despite everything Tessa managed to sleep well that night, and the next morning she did train as usual with Lee. Much to her surprise, he made absolutely no mention of the confrontation, not even asking about her shoulder. He simply acted as though nothing had happened and expected her to train as hard as he normally would, which was very hard.

Afterwards, she jogged home and changed into a pretty white dress. She had arranged to meet David for lunch at the Lancelot restaurant in Holland Park.

They had a wonderful meal and talked happily throughout. It helped Tessa push the events of the previous couple of days to the back of her mind. David's business meetings had gone well and he wanted to celebrate, so their extravagant meal started with champagne. Tessa happily joined in and drank alcohol for the first time for several weeks. After they had finished eating, they were both slightly flushed and talking about the future when her *cbc* vibrated. It was an SMS from Sinclair. *C&W Hospital. Ask for Rm X6. Any time.*

"Ah," she said, smiling at David. "I'm going to have to go; something has cropped up. Nothing serious, but I need to attend to it."

"No problem. We should probably finish up here anyway, there're a few things I should do too. Are you free this evening?"

"Yes, should be. I could come round to your place, if you like?"

"Super, see you later then."

Tessa kissed him goodbye and went downstairs. She found she couldn't stop grinning, she was so happy and relieved. Penny's murderers were facing a higher justice and she had a loving man in her life. She got into the waiting taxi and sat back almost hugging herself with glee.

"Chelsea and Westminster Hospital, please," she chimed. "But go via South Kensington underground station, I want to buy some flowers at Gilding the Lily…"

Twenty minutes later, she walked through the hospital's revolving door carrying two large bouquets of exotic flowers. She went to the reception desk and attracted the attendant's attention.

"Good afternoon," said Tessa, continuing more quietly, "Room X6, please. I'm expected."

"Name?" replied the woman, in a tone devoid of both interest and emotion.

"Dr Pennington."

The receptionist nodded and turned to where a burly man was leaning against the wall, ostensibly reading a newspaper. He was dressed in a poorly fitting creased grey suit. The receptionist caught his eye and tipped her head towards Tessa. He folded his newspaper and approached her.

"Come with me, please, miss," he said quietly.

He directed her to one of the service elevators. But after it had gone up only half a floor, he pressed the emergency stop button and the lift jolted to a halt.

"Who are you?" he asked sharply. Tessa studied the man with a playful glint in her eyes. He looked overweight and clumsy, with poorly styled curly brown hair and cheap shoes. It seemed his career had already peaked.

"Let me see your ID first," she replied, with a degree of assurance that made the man smile. Taking care not to move his gaze from her, he took a small leather wallet from his jacket pocket and gave it to her. It certainly looked like a legitimate Special Forces photo-identity card.

"Hmm, good likeness, Constable Kenyon"

"Thank you, miss."

"I'm Dr Tessa Pennington. Hold on, I'll find my ID."

She transferred her bouquets to one arm and handed him her driving licence, thinking it would be tempting providence to show her RCL identity card.

"OK, miss, so why are you here?"

"I want to visit the people in X6."

"And who would that be, miss?"

"Sinclair and Jones."

"Thank you, miss."

Kenyon inserted a key into the control panel, prompting the lift to judder as it continued upwards. He took out a walkie-talkie.

"I'm coming up with a Dr Pennington, female, for X6."

The lift reached the fifth floor, theoretically the top of the building, and travelled one floor further. It stopped and a woman constable beckoned Tessa to follow her.

"Dr Pennington, I need to search you and the flowers," she said mechanically as they entered a small room.

Tessa smiled, passed her both bouquets, and then held up her arms. A few minutes later, the constable led her into a large pleasant room which contained two beds. Both occupants looked pale, but were sitting up and smiling. On Tessa's right was Sinclair, who had just finished a telephone call, Jones was on her left.

"Ah, good afternoon, Dr Pennington, how nice to see you," said Sinclair, a trifle weakly.

"Likewise," replied Tessa, "and you, Jones. You're both looking remarkably well ... considering."

"Generally, we are, thank you," he acknowledged, "and apparently that is largely due to our guardian angel. According to Mr Perkins, if our wounds hadn't been so expertly dressed, we would be in a much worse condition now, if not dead. But with a bit of luck, we'll both be thrown out before the weekend."

Tessa smiled with a mixture of pride and embarrassment.

"That's good. And, to aid your recovery, I've brought you some flowers."

"Oh, those look lovely, thank you," continued Jones. "We don't get many visitors who bring us nice things, it's usually work." He gestured towards the papers strewn over his bed. "I think there are some vases under the basin."

Tessa walked over to the cupboard, took out two vases and busied herself with the flowers. She smiled as she realised that they were both watching her admiringly. But as she arranged the second vase, she swallowed nervously. Someone else had entered the room. She didn't need to look round; she recognised the sound of his footsteps. However, he had apparently mistaken her white dress for a nurse's uniform.

"Good afternoon, sir ... sir. I've completed my on site, preliminary investigation and can give you that summary you asked for. Also, there are a couple of follow-up actions I'd like to have approved."

"Sounds good, Potter, but give us the short version, please," replied Sinclair in a superior but friendly tone. "Oh, don't worry about her, just carry on."

Tessa looked over her shoulder. Beyond Potter's back, she saw Jones smiling at her.

"Right," said Potter. "The people who died were all core members of the Calver Cats gang. With a bit of luck, this will put a major dent in their aspirations, not least since Bryani, aka The Barb, was one of those who died. Furthermore, the chap who received the Calver treatment was wearing a sword whose signature matched the fatal wound on Dr Reid. We also found Dr Reid's *cbc* near the embankment. Now, first impressions suggest some sort of internal conflict. However, the more I studied the evidence, the less plausible that seemed, and not only because you were both spared. I believe those who died were simply overwhelmed by a single, superior force who subsequently left the scene. But, given the dead were by no means amateurs, their attack strategy was naïve; which suggests they didn't recognise or understand what they were up against. The forensic teams are still trying to find something to help identify the killer, but the rain hasn't helped."

Jones smiled at Sinclair, but still neither man mentioned Tessa's now flushed presence.

"It also seems likely that the perpetrator removed a weapon as the sword stuck through the chap with the gun does not match his wound. Furthermore, the sword found by The Barb is not of the quality which would have been needed to shatter Takara's blade. Why a weapon should be taken from the scene is unclear, but it is not uncommon for a warrior, as they die, to bequeath their sword to the victor. So, I initiated a country-wide check of all licensed sword owners. Most were fine, but two in London made me suspicious.

"One was a teacher in South Kensington called Lee. He's been an OCL Peacekeeper ever since it was possible, but he's no longer on active service." Tessa's eyes widened; she had not known Lee held an OCL. "The other is one of his female students, a Dr Tessa Pennington, aka Nariko. I adjudicated at her Samurai Proficiency Test about six months ago and she was incredibly proficient. I doubt Lee had any involvement in the conflict itself, but I think he might know who did, and Nariko's alibi relies on him. Therefore, I would like you to sign…" Potter produced a wad of papers from his attaché case… "round-the-clock surveillance orders for both Dr Pennington and Lee. I think a couple of weeks should suffice. Which of you shall I give them to?"

Sinclair took a deep breath.

"Excellent job, Potter, well done. So good in fact that I think we need to put you in the picture about a few things. But what I'm going to tell you is classified and needs to stay that way. Understood?"

Potter nodded, suspicious that what he'd expected to be straightforward was about to become complicated.

"I'm sorry we couldn't mention this earlier, but it could have compromised our investigation. As you know, Jones and I have been tracking the Calver Cats for more than a year, and not entirely on our own as we managed to convince someone else to help us. So you can put those surveillance orders away and say hello to the person standing behind you."

Potter hesitated, and then slowly turned round.

"Hi," beamed Tessa.

"Good heavens! Dr Pennington ... what on earth..."

"Potter," continued Sinclair, "you have carried out an exemplary investigation into this conflict which needed to be carried out, and needed to be seen to be carried out. This is a complex case which, unfortunately, is far from over. Dr Pennington has been assisting us for some time but after the death of her friend, we were concerned she might become a target herself. Her taking up swordsmanship was judged apposite as we wanted her to be able to defend herself. However, we also wanted as few people as possible to know about it. Anyway, I'm sorry we couldn't tell you this earlier, but..." He nodded to Jones who obediently held up a file of papers. "...Nariko became a full OCL Peacekeeper a couple of weeks ago."

Potter was stunned, and Tessa's own mouth momentarily fell open.

"An International Peacekeeper ... but ... I wasn't told," stammered Potter. "I'm meant to be the only person who can initiate the documentation for such a conversion. I presume the UK was the first country to propose her, but what was the second? And in what crimes did she intervene? There's nothing in my files."

He turned to look at Tessa, but she simply smiled coyly and shrugged her shoulders.

"No, there isn't, and I couldn't allow there to be," continued Sinclair calmly. "It has all been kept very much under wraps. To answer your questions, the proposing country was indeed the UK; the second was Japan. Inspector Maeda signed the papers himself. Concerning her interventions, there were three. One at Ueno station in Tokyo, which Maeda investigated. The others were a bank robbery in South Kensington and a gangland mugging in Stepney."

"Oh, I see. I did wonder why those events had been brushed under the carpet. Well, you've obviously done the main paperwork, but presumably the rest still needs to be done? Would you like me to organise that now?"

"Yes, you might as well. Just don't publicise it … at all."

"Right. Very good, sir," replied Potter. "I presume also that my investigations of the Rippleside crime scene may be brought to a close, concluding that they all died as a result of an internal conflict and there are no missing persons or weapons?"

"Yes, please."

"Well, thank you, sir. That about wraps it up for now."

Potter packed away his papers and turned to Tessa.

"So, Nariko, perhaps you would be kind enough to visit our offices in order to complete the OCL formalities. I work at the same place as Sinclair and Jones. Would tomorrow afternoon be all right?"

"Sure," she said. "How about three?"

"Perfect," replied Potter, with a disarmingly pleasant smile. "Bring your real combat sword with you, please. We'll need to perform a cutting test so we have its signature on file. Also, for the pictures, it would be helpful if you could come attired as you would normally expect to be to implement a Mission. You should plan for a process which will last about two hours."

"Fine, see you tomorrow," she replied, nodding.

"Well, goodbye gentlemen," continued Potter, "it's good to see you both on the road to recovery."

Sinclair and Jones looked at Tessa, apparently extremely pleased with themselves.

"I don't know what to say," she told them after an awkward silence. "I certainly didn't expect that. Er … thank you."

"It really is us who should thank you," replied Jones. "If you hadn't come back, we'd be dead. But we knew we would need to do something pretty fundamental to stop Potter. He's no fool … and removing the sword was bound to be problematic. But after having read the Bushido Code…" he pointed to a worn-looking book on his bed "…I do have a slightly better understanding of the situation. Anyway, as a Peacekeeper, you can register as many swords as you like. But it would probably be better if you didn't take the new one with you tomorrow."

"Of course. I'll only take my Kimi sword."

"Kimi sword? Maeda said you had a very special Amakuni sword?"

"Hah! He did tell you a lot. Yes, it is rather special. Unique in fact. Kimi Amakuni forged it in Japan, but I call it my Kimi sword for short. There's not a lot it won't cut through."

"We noticed. What's else is special about it?"

Tessa smiled, placed a vase of flowers by each of them, and pulled up a chair...

CHAPTER 30

By the time Tessa walked out of the hospital her smile had gone. The implications of what had just happened already weighed heavy. Ostensibly, Sinclair and Jones had done her a big favour in securing her an OCL; it had quashed Potter's interest in investigating either her or Lee. However, in other ways things couldn't be worse. She was already worried that the sword was controlling too much of her life and an OCL would bring with it all sorts of long-term responsibilities, nearly all of which she didn't want. She might even have to take on Missions. They would probably want her to sign up to one against the Calver Cats. While she still struggled with her conscience about having used her sword once, Sinclair and Jones had just licensed, and obligated her, to do it again and again!

She went into a café across Fulham Road, flopped down at a corner table and tried to get a cup of green tea, eventually having to settle for ginger and lemon. She cast her mind back over the strange series of events which had led her to this situation. Knowing she wouldn't want it, Penny had commissioned the sword without asking Tessa. However, somehow she had managed to find it. After that, Lee and her own conscience persuaded her to take lessons … and the rest was history. But now an OCL had been awarded her as a *fait acompli*, with Potter conveniently there when she was told so she couldn't object.

It seemed inconceivable that all, if any, of these events could simply be coincidences. But if not, by whom were they being orchestrated? All she needed now was to find out that David was involved! If so, she wouldn't have anything left in her life except her sword … well, swords. Her *cbc* rang.

"Hello, David."

"Hi. How are you doing? Are we on for this evening?"

"Absolutely, I'm all done. I could come round now, if you like? But you'll have to take me as I was dressed for lunch."

"I'll take you any way I can get you."

Tessa smiled, finished her tea and walked to Belgravia. She liked his

Georgian house with its imposing white stucco frontage; the inside was cosy and luxurious and much larger than hers. Later that night, they were lying in bed together.

"David…"

"Yes, darling."

"Have you got a middle name?"

"Embarrassingly, I have," he replied, stroking her shoulder. "Why the sudden interest?"

"No reason really, I just wondered since I haven't got one," she replied, laying her arm over his chest.

"Well, don't laugh but it's Dunmore. Understand why I don't use it?"

"Oh. It's not that bad … but David is easier."

A while later, she continued talking.

"Have you ever wondered how in control of our own lives we are? Of all the things that happen to us, how many do we really choose ourselves? How many are in fact chosen by others, or by fate, whatever that is?"

"Ah," said David, pulling her closer. "Now there's a question. I suspect we make far fewer of our own decisions than we would like to believe. Fate is no doubt active in the background, but I doubt it works at anything other than the most strategic of levels. So that would leave a whole load of things which happen to us as being orchestrated by others; whether we like it or not, and whether we know it or not."

"I suppose that's why these new Peacekeepers are supposed not to ally themselves to any shade of politics or religion, or the like. It would expose them to all sorts of manipulation one way or another. But as you know, in business, almost unwittingly one accumulates favours and obligations along the way which are likely to have to be repaid one day. I doubt life for Peacekeepers is any different. Whether that will be a problem, I don't know. But as an ideal, the concept remains intellectually attractive. Anyway, getting back to your question, I'm not sure it's ever possible to lead your life without being manipulated in some way or other… Why do you ask?"

"Oh, it's just that a few things that have happened recently have made me question whether it's really me who's controlling my life."

"Regrettably, I suspect that troubles most of us," continued David, gently kissing her. "Events follow their course, and to a large extent we simply have to go with the flow. Alas, we can't cherry-pick, we can only play the cards we've been dealt. Concerning others manipulating us clandestinely, the best we can hope for is that whoever it is has similar goals and does not wish us any harm."

"But that sounds like an excuse for all sorts of things," interjected Tessa, "including just sitting back and abandoning any attempt at self-determination."

"No, I don't think so. On occasion, for whatever reason, we're all pleased to let others make decisions for us. It could be that we simply don't want to do it for ourselves, or maybe we just aren't ready or able to do it. Either way, it's usually all about trying to work out who we can trust."

"Can I trust you, David?"

"Oh, yes. I would never do anything to harm you. Can I trust you, Tessa Pennington?"

"Yes," she said, propping herself up on one arm and looking into his eyes. "You can trust me."

He kissed her again.

"I know, and quite frankly that's the only sort of relationship I can handle. We are both independent people who need our own space. I have no problem giving space to someone I trust. We both have pasts and I'm sure there are details of our lives we still haven't told each other. But it doesn't matter if we trust each other, does it?"

"I suppose not," she replied, not entirely sure she agreed. "Good night."

Soon, in a close embrace, they fell fast asleep.

The following day they breakfasted early as David had a meeting to go to. He dropped Tessa off at her house on the way. She changed into a tracksuit and went to train as usual at SKS. When she told Lee about her OCL, he roared with laughter.

"I said you wouldn't be able to hold back the tides of change."

"Hmm, thanks. But this only serves to heighten my concern about using a sword. As far as I can tell, the only upside is that I can now register both of mine and carry them uncased."

Tessa returned home and phoned Kono. She told him she would be bringing an Amafuji sword for refurbishing, and that she wanted him to make a shoulder harness capable of holding two swords, one over each shoulder. Then she changed into her spare leather outfit for her appointment with Potter. She put on her harness and slid her Kimi sword into it. It was just like being back with Matsumoto.

Nevertheless she slipped on a cloak to make it more difficult to see she had a sword, although most of the hilt still projected above her shoulder. However, her attempt to be discreet failed dismally. She soon realised that travelling in London wearing a sword in public was not a comfortable experience. It was bad enough carrying a sword in a case, but a sword in the open had a markedly more dramatic effect. Pedestrians were petrified, motorists stared and policemen became weirdly obsequious. Finally she arrived at the Special Forces building in Vauxhall. It was an imposing brick building that was a sophisticated mix of contemporary and art deco styles. For Tessa, the privacy it afforded was most welcome. Although it was a hive of activity, nobody batted an eyelid at the sight of her sword. However, she was told by Security that she would have to stow it in one of their carrying cases.

"Ah, good afternoon, Nariko," said Potter as she entered his office. "Let's start straightaway, shall we?"

He then proceeded to ask lots of questions, explain endless regulations and point out innumerable obligations, all of which Tessa found excruciatingly boring. Not even Constable Johnson's bringing her a cup of green tea brightened her spirits.

"Right, now for the cutting trial," said Potter. "As I'm sure you know, every sword leaves a unique signature when it cuts, and we need to have details of yours on file. Here's a standard piece of test material which you will be able to sever easily enough. I know it's a bit informal but, to save us going elsewhere, we'll do the test here, if that's all right?"

"Fine," replied Tessa, standing up in front of him.

He turned to Johnson.

"Could I have a tripod, please?"

Then Potter heard a *whoosh* and the rod in his hand twitched. He looked back at Tessa, still standing in front of him. She reached up and caught the piece of test material which had been spinning in the air since she cut it. She handed it to him with a smile.

"Ah. Impressive! Rather glad I didn't see that. Right, well, now I need to photograph and measure the sword. May I have it, please?"

Unwillingly, Tessa handed it over. When he had finished weighing it, Potter picked up the unsheathed sword by the hilt and turned it over to admire it.

"I must admit, this is a very fine weapon," he mused.

"Indeed it is," replied Tessa, "but please be careful, the blade is unbelievably sharp."

"Yes, it must be, but don't worry I've been doing this for years," he replied confidently. Then he gently patted his right index finger on the edge of the blade as though testing a blunt carving knife for sharpness. He smiled as if to say *"I told you so"*, then looked down at his finger to see blood oozing from a deep cut. It wasn't serious but he was quite shocked to see how much it bled. Tessa bandaged the wound for him using their First Aid kit.

"Sorry, Potter, but I did warn you."

"I know. I think that's the sharpest blade I've ever been foolish enough to touch. Wow, it stings," he moaned... "Anyway, it's very important that no one can connect your Peacekeeper name with your real name and, of course, that applies to your address too. As such, no one is allowed to take photographs of you with your sword, and I would suggest you keep others to an absolute minimum. However, if ever you are attacked in any way, by anyone, you are permitted to defend yourself with whatever degree of force you feel is justified. But you mustn't knowingly instigate a conflict unless it is part of a Mission you have accepted. Your two Guardians, namely those who will communicate with you on a day-to-day basis, are Messrs Sinclair and Maeda. For a Mission to be valid, it must be signed by one of your Guardians, and an authorised representative from the primary country concerned.

"You are permitted to decline Missions, but, once you have accepted one, it is only possible to withdraw before completion if the signatories agree, or on medical grounds. When involved in a Mission, you will only be addressed by your Peacekeeper name, and all countries that have signed the International Peacekeeper Treaty are obliged to use their best endeavours to assist you. If it is proven that you have acted outside your Peacekeeper remit, the consequences are dire. Your OCL will almost certainly be revoked, possibly your RCL too. If you kill someone outside a Mission, without due cause, then you will be deemed to have committed murder. Similarly, if you commit a crime in a country which does not recognise Peacekeepers, you will be subject to the penalties due under its legal system. Do you understand?"

Tessa nodded, having had her worst suspicions about the OCL confirmed.

"Good. So, just the DNA test to go. Johnson will take you downstairs for the nurse to draw some blood; they'll inoculate you against HIV too."

Tessa didn't move. She had wondered whether he would want a blood sample; presumably to confirm her presence at a conflict site, or identify her body. But this test was the easiest way to expose aspects of her past which she wanted kept secret.

"Umm, Potter, is the DNA test really necessary? Could I perhaps opt out?"

He smiled sympathetically.

"I'm afraid it's mandatory. But I believe Constable Johnson and I both know what you're worried about, and it is of no consequence to us. We are only interested in the results insofar as they affect your OCL Peacekeeper identification. Beyond that, the entire contents of your file are classified as secret. Indeed only we two, Sinclair, Jones and Maeda will even know you're a Peacekeeper."

"Hmm, thanks. I suppose I'll have to do it then," she replied. Still uncomfortable, she followed Johnson, returning a few minutes later. Potter stood up and smiled.

"You'll be pleased to hear, Nariko, there's only one thing left to do. Congratulations! Here's your Peacekeeper Certificate. You've already more than earned it."

He handed her an elaborate document, written in both English and Japanese, confirming her election to International OCL Peacekeeper. Tessa took it from him, shaking his outstretched hand.

"Thank you, Potter, it's beautiful. What a shame I can't hang it up!"

"Yes, they are rather pretty. Hopefully, though, you'll be able to admire it in private for a long time. But as you probably already know, one of the consequences of being an International Peacekeeper is that you become a target."

Tessa nodded.

"I'll say. Just coming here wearing my sword gave me a good indication of how much one sticks out from the crowd."

"Quite, but I'm sure you'll be fine. At least now, if you find yourself in the middle of something nasty, you'll be able to do something about it *legitimately*... Oh, before you go," he added, "here's something we haven't distributed widely yet, but you're welcome to have one if you're interested. It's a prototype tracker watch; an effective and discreet means for the Special Forces to establish your location. You activate and deactivate it by pressing the light-on knob three times in quick succession. When transmitting, the second hand moves in one-second intervals, otherwise it moves in a continuous motion."

Tessa nodded and gladly took the watch; she never could resist a new gadget. Then she put her cloak back on and left, determined to get home as quickly as she could. Once back, she phoned Kono again to tell him she would visit the following morning with Bryani's sword, so he could start refurbishing it and make her a double sword case too.

CHAPTER 31

The next week proved refreshingly peaceful. Tessa and David met frequently, and for some time she didn't even go to SKS. She knew it was compromising her training but she didn't mind, even though Lee was clearly irritated.

One day she and David were having lunch in the City. Their meal, at one of David's favourite swanky restaurants, had been delicious and extravagant.

"By the way," he said absentmindedly, "a Director at BNYI, a chap called Blaise Collins-Clarke, has invited me to a function at the Guildhall. The Lord Mayor-in-waiting is being introduced … some sort of pre-installation dinner. Anyway, he'd like my presence to grace the proceedings; it'll be oozing pomp and circumstance, and probably horrendously boring. I was sent a single ticket, but I don't want to go without you."

"Hmm. I met Blaise once," said Tessa thoughtfully. "I bought Penny's company from him, in fact. I didn't like him very much."

"I doubt many do. I've had a few business dealings with him myself. They've gone OK, but I wouldn't seek him out. So, what do you think?"

"Well, I suppose it's a good excuse to get dressed up if nothing else. When is it?" she asked.

"A week on Thursday. I'll check the details and let you know."

Later that day, Tessa was shopping for an evening dress amidst the designer collections in Harrods when her *cbc* vibrated with a text message from Sinclair. *Could we meet, please? AP at 3 today?*

Tessa looked at her watch. It was 1:30 p.m. She could easily make it. However, it was with a simmering sense of foreboding that she responded: *OK.*

She selected a beautiful dress, left it for the hem to be taken up, and walked back along Brompton Road to Antonio's.

She was taking a sip of her green tea when Sinclair and Jones arrived. She smiled as they slowly approached her table. Sinclair always had a limp, however, today it was markedly more pronounced; Jones too was walking awkwardly.

"Good afternoon, gentlemen. It's nice to see you both vertical although I'm beginning to think a limp is mandatory for you guys!"

"Ha-ha," replied Sinclair, grinning. "We're still fragile, but recovering well, thank you."

They both ordered tea.

"No sword?" asked Sinclair.

"Definitely not! One soon learns that carrying a sword in public attracts far too much attention. Mind you, it is a good way to get a table in a busy restaurant … provided you don't mind everyone else leaving! But otherwise I think it's best left at home. Besides, I don't want David to be troubled with that part of my life just yet."

"Understood," replied Sinclair. "I presume Potter told you that I'm your UK Guardian?"

Tessa nodded, eyeing him suspiciously.

"And you no doubt realise that, as part of your OCL registration, you were obliged to provide Potter with more than enough information to place you at Rippleside."

She nodded again, fearing the worst.

"Well, the only way to ensure there will never be any repercussions from that is for you to have been there as part of a Mission. So here it is, in triplicate. Dated, shall we say, appropriately. I've already signed it, as has Inspector Maeda. We're lucky he's willing to play along with all this."

He handed her three sets of papers.

Antonio arrived with their drinks, but quickly scurried away when he sensed his presence was an intrusion. There was a moment's silence as Sinclair let Tessa absorb what he'd just said. She sighed. She'd expected something like this, but actually being asked to commit to a Mission made it a depressing reality.

"Isn't there anything else we could do instead?"

"I don't think so, but we're open to suggestions. All three of us are in a difficult position. We promised to keep you out of the firing line, but there are limits to what we can do with regards to normal legal process. Although I don't think Potter would say anything, there's no reason for him to get himself into trouble to protect any of us."

"Hmm. I suppose by signing, I undertake to bring to justice those

316

responsible for Penny's death?" asked Tessa, hoping it wouldn't go any further.

"A bit more than that, I'm afraid. Although we know now that the Calver Cats were responsible for her death, we couldn't previously have initiated a full International Peacekeeper Mission only to bring her murderers to justice. However, it would make sense if the Mission were to close down the Calver Cats. Hopefully, we'll be able to identify and detain the gang's leader soon, and then the Mission will be completed. Jones has the Mission detail referenced in the summary."

"Oh, dear!" she groaned.

"I'm afraid your intervention at Rippleside made this ... inevitable," replied Sinclair.

Jones rummaged in his briefcase and produced a thick file, handing it to her in silence. Tessa paged through it, but there was little she didn't already know. Then she turned her attention to the Mission Summary; it was clear, succinct and straightforward. At the end she found both Sinclair's and Maeda's dated signatures. Beneath them, in the middle, was a blank dotted line.

"Maeda's being very helpful, isn't he?" noted Tessa.

"Yes, he's sticking his neck out for you. But you impressed him, although he still won't tell us what you did."

She breathed out noisily and took a fountain pen from her handbag.

"Oh, well, I hope I live long enough to regret this."

"I hope we all live not to regret it," countered Sinclair.

They both watched her sign all three copies *Nariko*, in both English and Japanese, adding the date indicated by Sinclair. She screwed the top back on the pen.

"Nice pen," remarked Jones.

"It was Penny's. I suspect my catching it once started this whole thing off... Anyway, she's the one who should really be signing, so what better pen to use?"

Tessa took one final look at the Mission Summary, and returned two copies to Sinclair. She had formally committed herself to a legally binding international contract, enforceable for as long as it took.

Eventually Tessa broke the silence. "Sometimes I wonder who's really running my life. Is it me, my sword or somebody else?"

Jones looked pensive for a moment.

"Well, it's not clear that question can ever be answered in its entirety. To an extent, it depends upon whom one's favourite philosopher is, and what one considers to be the difference between random coincidence, serendipity, destiny, and, of course, free will. But if one applies a sort of generalised reverse logic and considers what one would have done otherwise, and whether or not that would have been more or less likely to result in a superior outcome…"

Sinclair and Tessa looked at each other aghast, and then back at Jones.

"Gareth, will this take long?" asked Sinclair, with a wry smile.

"Well, it's an intriguing question."

"Very," interjected Tessa, "but I'm not sure we have the time to contemplate all its ramifications. Maybe we should concentrate on completing the Mission first, then we can turn to more philosophical issues. So, what else have you got for me on this?"

Sinclair's smile held a tinge of sadness.

"For starters, here's an update to the file which includes recent events … well, most of them, but you know the others anyway. Then, given what Bryani said about the Calver Cats' logo being made up of initials, our people have been trying to work out which letters might be involved. We've come up with a name which fits … Nariko."

Tessa grimaced. He had called her that once at Rippleside, but she hadn't had time to pay much attention to it then. Now, though, it sounded distinctly ominous.

"The scenario we like most for the logo is three Bs round the outside with four Cs inside. Bryani said that two of the Cs stand for Calver Cats while the Tiger's head in the middle is for her Amafuji sword, whereabouts currently unknown. But we don't know whether Bryani, aka The Barb, counted for one or two Bs, or whether the remaining two Cs are linked to the Bs in some way."

"Yes, but there are lots of other letter combinations which would also fit. Ds instead of some Bs for example; or Os, or Cs … even Ps?"

"True," acknowledged Sinclair. "But one has to start somewhere, and we began by considering combinations that would fit people Penny knew."

"OK. So if Bryani accounted for two Bs, that would leave one B and two Cs." Tessa thought for a moment. "I can only think of one person

318

whose name fits those letters. But he's far too much of a wuss."

"We're clearly thinking of the same person then," interjected Jones, laughing.

"Not Blaise Collins-Clarke?" exclaimed Tessa. "Admittedly Penny did say she didn't get on with him, and I don't like him either. But I wouldn't have thought he'd be capable of masterminding anything like murder. He's an archetypal pin-stripe banker, not a hood or one ever likely to assume responsibility for bloodthirsty things."

"Ah, but if that were his cover," continued Jones, "it would be a very good one, wouldn't it? He's certainly well connected, and big banks like BNYI have access to all sorts of shady resources. So is it really such a far-fetched idea?"

"Well, I hear what you say, but I still struggle to believe he's that sort of a man. The Calver Cats are into guns, drugs, armed robbery and so on. An investment banker as their boss sounds unlikely to me... I suppose you've done some snooping? Has he secret foreign bank accounts, alibis and the means to run a violent crime syndicate? And why would he want to anyway?"

"Good pertinent questions," agreed Sinclair, "and we don't have any of the answers yet."

"So, will you bring him in for interrogation? Darkened room ... spotlight in his eyes?" asked Tessa, grinning. "Which of you would be the nice guy?"

"You've been watching too many movies," replied Sinclair, laughing. "No, we thought it would be better to adopt a rather more subtle approach."

"Oh, good, that counts me out then," she muttered.

Sinclair raised his eyebrows.

"You are correct inasmuch as we don't just want to *decapitate* the organisation – we want to close it down completely. With Bryani and the Calver Cats' heavy mob gone, someone will have to find replacements. That won't be easy, and they'll need to do it quickly if they're to keep the rest of their operations running smoothly. A good opportunity for us all to watch and collate any information that comes our way."

"Unless I'm mistaken, you just said all watch and collate. Am I meant to infer that you would like me to consider getting involved?"

"Hah! Getting the hang of this, aren't you? Yes, please, that would be helpful. After all, your acquisition of Schrauben & Mutter brought you and Collins-Clarke together in a business context. Could you arrange to meet him again, perhaps under the pretext of business, or socially if you prefer? Meanwhile, we'll do some more digging and see what we can find out."

"Socially! You must be joking. But, funnily enough, he wants to meet me."

"Really, why?" asked Sinclair, already suspicious.

"He sent me an e-mail the day I got back from Japan, saying he had a business venture to discuss. But I didn't follow it up."

"Could be a coincidence," said Jones.

"Even so, maybe it isn't such a good idea for you to go and see him," decided Sinclair. "It would be too easy for him to prepare in advance."

"I'm not worried," said Tessa. "It might bring things to a head."

"True, but without your sword you'd be vulnerable, and it would be difficult for us to protect you discreetly inside BNYI."

"Well, I'm going to meet him a week on Thursday anyway. He's hosting a function at the Guildhall. I'm going with David. It'll be very public though."

"That sounds much better. Public events have their advantages," continued Sinclair. "People tend to be off their guard. What is it?"

"Apparently the Lord Mayor-in-waiting is being introduced to the wealthy and worthy of London."

"Oh, yes," interjected Jones. "I saw a note about that. There'll be a lot of security. Not sure we'll get much, but it's certainly worth a try."

"But what can I say in front of everyone at the Guildhall? I can hardly ask him whether he's running the Calver Cats in his spare time? He might not give an entirely honest answer."

"You think?" replied Sinclair, sarcastically. "Actually, what quite often happens is that someone caught unawares in public is forced into a poorly constructed lie, which subsequently proves to be their downfall. All you should do is be polite and circumspect, raise the issue and see where the conversation leads. We'll get some relevant articles in the press for you to use as attention getters. Don't be too aggressive, just go with the flow."

"All right. But there's no way I'm going to be able to hide my sword in the evening dress I just bought!"

"Don't worry. If you're attending an event like that to meet our friend, we'll be there to watch over you and Lord Kensington. After all, we're under a legal obligation to help you. One last thing," added Sinclair, "since this is official business now, it would be better if we met at Special Forces headquarters in future. It's more secure."

Tessa nodded her acceptance as the final element of informality to their meetings was stripped away.

The following day, after a long training session, she took Lee for lunch at the sushi bar in Thurloe Place. It was one of her favourite fast-food venues, catering for takeaway clients and those who wanted to sit at the bar and choose from the sushi conveyor. She told him how Sinclair and Jones had effectively obliged her to accept a Mission to stop the Calver Cats. He responded by depressing her further. He waxed lyrical about how her OCL and the Mission simply gave others more reasons and opportunities to kill her.

"Thank you, Lee, that's just what I needed to hear!" she retorted. "But it's what you always wanted, isn't it? Me and my sword in the middle of the action?"

"Yes, it is, and I am sure you can take care of yourself. But you mustn't be under any illusions about your situation. You will live or die now according to your skills, primarily with the sword. You started this by hiring those Special Forces agents after Penny died. Admittedly you didn't know who they were then, but now it is they who have hired you."

Tessa sighed with exasperation.

"Yes, but in spite of everything, I'm still against violence, *mostly*."

Lee laughed.

"Of course you are." He looked round to check they couldn't be overheard. "How many Calver Cats was it that you dispatched at Rippleside?"

"That's precisely what I meant by *mostly*," she remonstrated. "It was them or me, and there were Sinclair and Jones to consider, and settling a debt for Penny. All mitigating circumstances."

"Nariko-san, there always are *mitigating circumstances*," continued Lee. "You might think you can choose when to use your special skills, but you can't. Eventually the day will come when, if you want to stay alive, you will have no alternative but to use your sword again. So, although there is no denying your skills are already considerable, you should not forget that you are only partially trained."

"Great!" retorted Tessa. "Previously, I was only depressed; now I'm well on the way to despondency! Anyway, I'd hate to disappoint you, so what exactly do you mean by *only partially trained*? Another of your clandestine traps in the making?"

"Not at all," replied Lee, smiling. "I told you before you went to Japan that Master Matsumoto teaches in at least two stages, with a break in between for practice and adjustment. You have spent only a relatively short time with him. You did well, he said so and I know so. But he could teach you much more. If you went back it would improve your chances of survival when the inevitable happens."

"Well, I'm not going back," she said, decisively. "I think I've done quite enough, thank you."

Lee shrugged.

"As you wish. How's the camellia?"

"Like me, thriving here and not lonely," she said, returning her attention to lunch.

The day before the Guildhall dinner, Tessa received an SMS from Sinclair. He wanted a meeting, in his office. As usual, the invitation was very polite, but Tessa couldn't help interpreting it more as a summons than a request, and that irritated her.

"Thanks for coming," he said, looking up from his desk when she arrived. "Sorry we're meeting here at such short notice, but we've uncovered something important and we're in a bit of a rush."

Tessa nodded, and smiled as Jones stood up to pull a chair over for her.

"It's about our BCC friend," continued Sinclair.

The conversation paused as a coffee and two green teas arrived.

"Did you know there was a major falling out between Penny's father and our banker friend? It took place just before her parents and sister were killed in circumstances which many at the time regarded as more than just a burglary gone wrong."

Tessa's brow furrowed and she shook her head.

"It seems Penny's father and Collins-Clarke were partners in a substantial business venture. But things didn't work out; Penny's father ended up very rich with full control of the business, while Collins-Clarke lost virtually everything. He narrowly avoided being declared bankrupt, and only got another decent job because he called in some favours on the old boy network. We're still trying to find out who it was that helped him. Anyway, years later, Collins-Clarke suddenly finds he's got Penny's company on his books ... then her company mysteriously runs into trouble and she is killed. But, as soon as you take over, its problems miraculously disappear."

"Heavens, you make it sound as though I orchestrated Penny's death!"

"No, I was implying that Collins-Clarke could have used this turn of events to settle a deep-seated grudge, and once he'd done that, it was no longer necessary for him to strangle Schrauben & Mutter."

"Hmm, so I provided a solution to the threat to his business reputation by obligingly bailing out Penny's company..."

"Precisely," agreed Sinclair.

"... which *would* make me partly responsible for her death!"

"No, you really mustn't think of it like that. If Collins-Clarke intended to use the Calver Cats to eliminate Penny, then he would have done so sooner or later. He could have wanted her to suffer the loss of her business publicly first, and you prevented that by intervening when you did. Don't forget, Penny's kidnapping took place right outside BNYI. How come they were waiting for her there? Presumably only a couple of people at the bank would have known about the meeting."

"Well, a few more if Blaise really intended to foreclose on Schrauben & Mutter. How do you suggest we play this then?"

"Well, you can certainly afford to be more provocative when you meet him. With a bit of luck, he'll blurt out something useful."

"Fine, I'll give it a go."

"Good. Now, here's a two-way earpiece for you to wear on the night." Sinclair handed her a small grey object that resembled a squishy overweight caterpillar. "Just sticking it in your ear switches it on. It's very discreet, no one will know you're wearing it. It will allow us to listen in to all your conversations and, if no one's watching, you can use it to talk to us. Unfortunately, its range is limited; one beep and it's acquired our signal, two beeps and it's lost it. The same applies as we switch in and out of your frequency."

CHAPTER 32

David's Rolls stopped outside Tessa's house at precisely 6:30 p.m. the following evening. She opened the door and was thrilled to hear his sharp intake of breath. She was dressed in a long flowing pink Escada evening dress, a tight-fitting, low-cut design with narrow straps and chiffon sleeves covered with tiny crystal beads.

"My goodness!" he exclaimed, taking a step back to admire her. "You look fantastic. That's an amazing dress, and I love your hair up like that. It makes you look completely different. Very nice."

"Thank you," she replied, blushing. "I'm especially glad you like my hair. I've never had it done like this before, it took ages."

She slipped on a matching pashmina and armed the house alarm. With the front door closed, David led her over to the car. His chauffeur held the door open for her.

"Hello, Andrew, how are you?"

"Good evening, ma'am," he replied with a smile. "I'm very well, thank you."

David and Tessa talked quietly in the back of the car as it picked its way across London. If David noticed her nervousness, he didn't say. After a while, Andrew started talking on his headset with the Guildhall reception staff to coordinate their arrival.

Thirty minutes later, the Rolls glided under a stone archway and across the paved courtyard towards the building's substantial neo-Gothic entrance. Two stewards wearing black long-tailed suits, top hats and white gloves walked towards them. Andrew brought the car to a gentle halt with Tessa's door directly in line with the steps leading up to the main entrance. The stewards, now on either side of the car, paused to ensure the passengers were ready; then David's door swung open. He sprang out, thanked the steward and walked round the back of the car. Tessa quickly put in her earpiece, and waited for her door to be opened. Then she got out with all the grace and decorum she could muster. She was very nervous. She had never attended a high-profile event with David before, and there was Blaise Collins-Clarke to worry about too.

A number of people had massed near the entrance and, although dignitaries in their own right, all looked round to see who had arrived with such aplomb. Tessa stood up straight, checked her dress, and took David's arm as the babble of conversation lowered markedly. She smiled at him, and he grinned back proudly. Then, in perfect time, largely because she'd insisted on practising the previous evening, they advanced towards the main entrance. As they approached, two more stewards moved aside to allow them into the vestibule where they stopped for a moment. This gave Tessa the opportunity not only to check that her dress was straight, but also to appreciate the grandeur of the building. With parts of it dating back to 1411, it was an impressive sight. However, as an even more noticeable hush descended upon the other people there, Tessa snapped back to reality and whispered to David.

"Heavens, is it always like this?"

"No, it's only because you look so absolutely stunning," he replied. She gave his arm a squeeze, and they prepared to join the queue waiting to go up the stairs to be introduced to the hosts. They were both surprised when everyone moved aside to allow them to go straight up.

"And why is this happening?" she whispered.

"No idea. Perhaps it's because they're convinced you must be somebody terribly important."

"What, because I'm with you?" she retorted, with a momentarily more relaxed smile.

"Hah! In both our dreams."

They continued advancing slowly and purposefully up the stairs. As they turned left to climb the second flight, Tessa paused briefly to steal a glance back. Sinclair and Jones had just come through the main entrance. They were both wearing double-breasted dinner suits and looked remarkably debonair. Jones carried a leather attaché case and was followed by two burly men. She recognised one as the assailant whose sword she'd broken during her Proficiency Test. As Sinclair and Jones stopped in front of the stewards, she could see various passes being flashed. Sinclair glanced up at her, smiled and touched his headset, prompting a *beep* in her ear.

"Good evening," he said. "You look very beautiful."

"By the way," said David, drawing her attention back to him, "just for something to wile away the time, here's the invitation. I thought you might like to see why we're here."

"Oh, and there I was, thinking it was simply so we could submit ourselves to very public scrutiny."

Beep, beep.

Tessa took the invitation, grateful for anything to distract her from all the staring faces. However, walking up the stairs gracefully in stiletto heels and a long flowing dress required considerable care. She wondered what she should do if she trod on her dress and tripped. Nevertheless, she glanced quickly at the elaborate invitation with all its embossed black, gold and red lettering. The event was the Presentation of the Lord Mayor (designate) pending formal inauguration two days later. Then her smile evaporated. Her eyes widened and she raised the card to check she had read it correctly. But there was no mistake. The name of the next Lord Mayor of London was none other than Beauchamp Caradoc Caille.

Tessa was so absorbed she forgot to concentrate on climbing the stairs, and staggered slightly. David paused to let her catch her balance.

"Everything OK, princess?" he asked, smiling at her.

"Yes, and no. Oh, David, what a fool I've been!"

"What do you mean?"

"Oh, nothing to do with you," she replied quickly. "It's the invitation, I should have looked at it earlier. It's made me think of something … horrible."

"I'm sorry about that, but may I suggest you think of something more agreeable for a while? We seem to have rather a lot on at present."

"I'll try, but I'm not so sure it was a good idea for me to come here."

"Oh, don't worry about all the people looking at us, they're just envious of me and curious to know who you are."

"I think they're about to find out," she mumbled. But David didn't hear. He'd turned away and was gently urging her forward.

As so often happens when least expected, Tessa's mind had rapidly linked a number of ostensibly unconnected pieces of information. In particular, the invitation with its bold Gothic script emphasised the first letters of the Lord Mayor (designate)'s names and suddenly there was an alternative suspect for boss of the Calver Cats. But her brother … surely not? He couldn't have known Penny, she would have said, so why would he have wanted her killed? Nevertheless, Tessa needed to tell Sinclair and Jones urgently. Where were they?

David led her up the last few stairs to where a grinning Blaise Collins-Clarke stepped forward to meet them. The three of them became the focus of everyone's attention.

Beep.

"David, old boy, how marvellous to see you," said Blaise, gripping his outstretched hand. He clasped his left hand over the top of his guest's as if to emphasise their familiarity. Tessa wanted to grimace as she sensed David's discomfort, but she didn't have time. Blaise had turned to her.

"Tessa my dear, for once in my life I am utterly speechless. You look radiant. I don't think I've ever seen you looking more lovely. I'm not surprised that no one can take their eyes off you."

As he advanced towards her he swayed slightly, suggesting he wasn't entirely sober. She quickly stretched out her hand to stop him coming too close; he kissed it theatrically. Even from that distance, she could smell the whisky on his breath.

"Good to see you too, Blaise," she replied. "It's been a while, hasn't it?"

"Alas, yes," he purred, wistfully. "But I'm pleased our last transaction worked out so well for you."

"Shame that Penny isn't around to enjoy it too, isn't it?"

"Indeed, terrible business … brutally raped and murdered, how awful," intoned Collins-Clarke. "And then her body being left in front of the Gherkin like that. Such phallic finality."

Aghast and deeply offended, Tessa glared at him; but before she could say anything a voice whispered in her ear.

"Don't react now but that is where Penny's body was found," said Sinclair. "He shouldn't have known – you didn't. Let's see what else we can get, we'll attend to him later. On the move now."

Tessa was ready to explode. But then David moved slightly, barring her way, and started talking to Blaise.

"All right," muttered Tessa, tersely, "but only because…"

Beep, beep.

"Oh, for…!" she hissed.

"Anyway," continued Blaise, in a superior tone, "there's a bit of a queue building up, so we'd better get you both inside. It shouldn't take long. Bill Chalmers is acting as an impromptu steward to help marshal everyone. He's Beauchamp's chauffeur. He's not meant to be involved really, but he's one of those tough-looking cockney types you don't particularly want to say no to."

David led Tessa towards the Great Hall. She looked round, bursting to speak to Sinclair again but smiling pleasantly at anyone whose eyes met hers. At last, she saw Sinclair and Jones coming out of the hall opposite and walking down the corridor towards her. They did both look remarkably good and for a moment she was distracted.

Beep.

She snapped to attention and checked no one was watching.

"About time, boys. Have you seen the invitation?" she whispered. "We've an alternative villain. Sorry I didn't think of him sooner, but it's a part of my past I'd rather forget."

"Ah, hold on a second, we had to gate-crash," replied Sinclair, prompting her to giggle.

They borrowed an invitation from another guest. Jones then looked at her with a puzzled expression on his face. Again fortuitously, David was blocking Blaise's view of her.

"He's my brother, his initials spell *BCC*, and his chauffeur is called Bill Chalmers," she murmured.

Jones slapped his forehead and muttered an expletive. Sinclair looked exasperated, then nodded.

"OK. No problem. Don't worry."

Beep, beep.

He started talking into his communicator. Tessa heaved a sigh of relief and slipped the invitation back into David's pocket. She felt guilty about being the cause of what was likely to be a very awkward scene in which he would inevitably be involved. But there was nothing she could do about it now. She just hoped Sinclair would have time to regroup before they moved into the Great Hall. She glanced back at Blaise.

Beep.

"…the pair of you have certainly chosen an excellent night to display

328

your … umm, relationship publicly," he continued. "Everyone who's anyone is here. It's the evening when those of us on the High Council meet to put our formal stamp of approval on the Lord Mayor's successor. He's a lawyer this time, a partner in one of the leading City firms. Thoroughly decent chap. His wife Caprice is with him, but she seems to be leaving the talking to him."

"Have you known him long, Blaise?" asked Tessa.

"Oh, yes, ages. We've done each other a favour or two in the past. You know how it is."

They paused at the impressive entrance to the Great Hall. There were a number of people at the doorway still being introduced. Tessa looked round and admired the stonework. It exuded a sense of time-honoured superiority which had long since faded from the collective psyche. She noticed Sinclair and Jones were already inside, engaged in earnest conversation with one of the other guests who was in uniform. The attaché case was open and all of them were feverishly paging through papers.

Blaise gestured them to go in.

"David, I'm really sorry," she whispered. "I do hope this doesn't go too badly."

"I'm sure it'll all work out just fine. Hang on in there."

He spoke to the Master of Ceremonies and told him what he and Tessa had agreed should be said to announce her. The Master of Ceremonies nodded and waved them forward; Blaise followed close behind. David momentarily flinched as Tessa tightened her grip on his arm. He assumed she was nervous or excited, or both.

The newcomers being greeted by the hosts moved away and the Master of Ceremonies coughed quietly into his gloved hand to clear his throat. Moments later, despite expecting it, Tessa was surprised by the volume and clarity of the announcement which rang out nearby.

"The Laird Kensington of Graemeshall, and partner."

Amazed, Tessa looked round at David.

"Graemeshall? You never said you had Orcadian connections."

"Oh, yes. We've been lairds there for centuries," he said, walking forward. "But how do you know where Graemeshall is?"

"Oh, it's a long story. I'll tell you later."

"Hah. What a fun evening this is turning out to be… Mind you, this will be the boring part."

"I wish," she muttered.

As David took the final few paces, Tessa fell back slightly while keeping one hand on his arm. He could feel that her grip had altered, but had given up trying to interpret all the subtle changes in her behaviour tonight. Meanwhile Blaise had moved up to just behind David. He looked round and found himself level with Tessa. She seemed to be straining to keep one hand on David's arm while remaining shielded from view behind him. But he had by now neared the host, so Blaise decided to step forward alongside him.

As he moved, it gave Tessa a clear view of a heavily-built man leaning against a wall nearby. He appeared to be half-asleep and clearly wasn't paying much attention to what was happening. However, she instantly recognised his distinctive chin strap beard.

"Excuse me, boys," she whispered. "That man leaning against the wall by the entrance … the one with the manicured facial hair … he's the one who got away from Sloane Square tube station."

"Well, well," acknowledged Sinclair, glancing towards the entrance. "Flood, he's yours."

Jones broke off from the meeting, and came closer to Tessa. She noticed a substantial bulge in his jacket. He was armed.

"Beauchamp," Blaise was saying. "I'd like to introduce you to a friend of mine, Lord Kensington, and his partner whom…"

"Evening, Graemeshall," interrupted Beauchamp with a silky smile. "How nice to meet you and your … er … *partner*." He too appeared to be slightly drunk and leered openly at Tessa as he finished talking. But his expression quickly reverted to a more plastic smile. "Let me introduce my wife C–"

"Charmed, I'm sure," interrupted David, equally smoothly, barely hiding his contempt for Beauchamp's discourteous greeting.

After some further stilted pleasantries had been exchanged, Beauchamp moved forward and to one side, so that he could see Tessa better.

"No need to be shy, you know, I don't bite … often. We sort of missed being introduced, didn't we?" he said, scanning her approvingly. Caprice quickly moved closer to him, but he'd returned his gaze to David. "Please, do tell me, who is this intriguing partner of yours?"

Tessa had heard enough. Checking Jones' location, she moved alongside David who rightly concluded she had decided to get involved. Beauchamp interpreted this as an invitation to address her directly.

"How nice to meet you. What's your name?"

David glanced at Tessa, sensing the intense coldness with which she was eyeing their host. Even the Master of Ceremonies realised something was wrong and decided not to summon anyone else into the Hall until the awkwardness passed. The tension was palpable, and Caprice was now desperately trying to attract her husband's attention. But he ignored her, the smile fading from his face as his expression became more guarded.

"Hello, Beauchamp," said Tessa. "I know it's been a while, but that was by your choice, not mine. I'd have thought you'd still recognise me, though."

"Er, I'm sorry," he said. "But … you mean we've met?"

Exasperated, Caprice looked angrily at him.

"You always were a bit slow when it came to the really important people stuff, weren't you?" replied Tessa disdainfully. "How many siblings do you have?"

"Just the one … but we're not that close," he replied dismissively.

"Hah! Bit of an understatement! You must be downright distant if you don't even recognise your own sister when she's standing in front of you."

There was a stunned silence as everyone breathed in sharply. Beauchamp swallowed and looked round in horror, hoping no one else had heard. But he soon realised they were all straining to listen. Like an echo, the word *sister* bounced around the Great Hall. David chuckled.

"Don't be absurd, I…"

"Careful, Beauchamp. Just because we haven't seen each other for a while doesn't mean I don't exist," continued Tessa, a note of controlled menace creeping into her voice.

"No, no, indeed not," he stammered, his glance moving to the man with the distinctive facial hair. Tessa's eyes followed his. She saw the large Special Forces operative approaching him. Then Jones walked round next to Blaise, while Sinclair moved nearer Tessa. She smiled.

"Well, you're no doubt delighted to meet me at last, aren't you? And in public too!"

"Yes, it's wonderful," said Beauchamp, beginning to perspire. "But obviously now is not a particularly good time for us to talk. Let my chauffeur take you both home, and we can catch up tomorrow. Why don't you come and have a look at my new offices? They're at the top of the Gherkin ... you'll love the views, they're fantastic. Bill!"

The heavy-set man, disturbed from his cat-nap, stood up, blinking – only to find the enormous bulk of Flood blocking his way.

"Hold on, Beauchamp, did you say your offices are in the Gherkin?"

"Yes, that's right"

Tessa paused as the penny dropped.

"Oh, good grief," she groaned. "Now I understand. I upset your friend, so he asked you to do his dirty work ... after all, just another favour on the old boy network. But then you had her body dropped outside your own offices, so you could savour my despair at first hand."

"What are you talking about!" exclaimed Beauchamp.

"I'm talking about the owner of Schrauben & Mutter."

"Don't be ridiculous," he retorted. "It's one thing to try and make a fool of me in public, but I'm not putting up with accusations of murder from you of all people."

"Who said anything about murder? But you knew precisely what I was referring to, didn't you?"

"No, I did not. It doesn't take a genius to work out you were referring to your friend's body which was dumped outside our offices."

"How did you know Penny was my friend?"

"Er ... Mum told me."

"No, Beauchamp, I know for a fact she didn't. And Penny would have told me immediately if she'd ever met you."

Blaise glanced around nervously.

"Look," hissed Beauchamp, "this is nonsense. You can't substantiate any of it, can you?"

"It's not up to me to prove anything. The experts will do that, and I don't think they're going to have any difficulty whatsoever. They've even got the flowers you asked Bill to deliver."

Beauchamp bit his lip and glared at his chauffeur.

"That's enough," whispered Sinclair in her earpiece. "Well done."

"Better get yourself a lawyer, Beauchamp," she warned.

"Don't be daft," he replied. "I'm about to be invested as Lord Mayor … let's settle this tomorrow. We'll get Mum and Dad along as well, just like the *good old days*."

Tessa had momentarily relaxed, but now her anger flooded back.

"Beauchamp!" she exclaimed. "There were no good old days for me while you were around, and Mum and Dad are ten weeks into a world cruise. You'd have known that if you and your family hadn't stopped talking to us all!"

For a moment Beauchamp didn't know what to do. He could see the Commissioner of Police approaching.

Tessa smiled.

"The truth will always out, Beauchamp. You of all people should know that."

"Just … go away," he sneered.

Sinclair suddenly noticed Tessa clench her right fist. Beauchamp was swinging his arm back ready to hit her. He quickly darted forward, almost bumping into David as he too moved to block Beauchamp.

"Wow!" said Tessa, amused by the near collision in front of her; she peered between the two men. "Well, it's been lovely seeing you again, Beauchamp, but I think it's time to let someone else look after you now. Rest assured, I'll give you just as much support as you gave me when I needed it. Goodbye."

Sinclair started to caution Beauchamp, while Jones dealt with Blaise Collins-Clarke and Bill Chalmers was led away handcuffed.

Frenzied conversation erupted throughout the Hall and the proceedings dissolved into chaos. David turned to Tessa, and smiled.

"Well, that was interesting. Are we all done now?"

She relaxed and took a deep breath. "I think so."

"Oh, good," he continued. "It seems the atmosphere here has grown a trifle intense. Shall we eat elsewhere?"

She grinned and linked her arm through his.

"What a lovely idea."

Ignoring the commotion, they started to leave. As they walked away, Tessa glanced back. Sinclair was still talking to Beauchamp, but for a long time afterwards, she remembered the piercing look Caprice directed towards her.

"It just so happens," said David, gently leading her away, "I only intended to make a brief but decisive appearance here – and we certainly seem to have done that. I've already made a reservation at Regulations in Maiden Lane. Would that be all right?" He reached into his pocket and pressed the button to summon Andrew.

"That would be perfect," she replied with a smile, squeezing his arm. "I do believe we have cause to celebrate. The orchestrators of Penny's untimely death have been caught at last."

David led Tessa back down the stairs and she surreptitiously removed her earpiece. If people had been curious while they were walking up, they were transfixed as the couple came back down again. But, on the landing between the two flights of stairs, Tessa stopped.

"Don't you want to know what that was all about?"

"If you want to tell me, yes. But if you'd rather not reawaken demons from your past, then that's OK too. I trust you, Tessa Pennington, and that's enough for now, isn't it? Anyway, it's quite clear your brother is a bit of a toad and deserves, as you put it, to be looked after. I presume you've been on a bit of a mission to get this resolved. I just hope it's over now, so that we can get on with our life together."

"Thank you," she said. "But you'll have to wait until we're in the car before I kiss you."

"As I keep saying, you've got to do those spur-of-the-moment things straightaway, otherwise they lose their impact."

"All right," replied Tessa. "What a girl's got to do, a girl's got to do."

She put her hands on his shoulders, reached up and kissed him.

"Hmm, thank you." David smiled and continued to lead her down. "Tell me, how is it you know so much about Orkney?"

"Oh, I don't know that much really. But I do know the laird's estate encompasses all of Holm and Deerness, and the vast majority of Burray."

"Yes, that's right. All but one parcel of land…" He paused. "No! Please tell me that's not you?"

CHAPTER 33

After an absence of several weeks, Tessa finally visited SKS again. Lee made no secret of his annoyance.

"Nariko, you are attending less and less frequently when you should be preparing to return to Matsumoto."

"I've told you," retorted Tessa, exasperated, "I'm not going back. Penny's murderers will be sentenced soon, which means I'm free to focus on other things … notably, living. I admit I still enjoy training. But I don't see why I should continue developing my skills with the same single-minded dedication as before."

"The world doesn't turn according to your rules, Nariko. There are other forces at work here. They will creep up on you unawares. You must be prepared."

"We'll see. I've worked hard to ensure David remains oblivious to my *hobby*, and I want it to stay that way. I'm sorry, but he is far more important to me than my OCL. So don't make me chose between the two."

However, despite her protestations, quietly, calmly and with infuriating persistence, Lee continued to implore Tessa to return to Japan. She ruled it out completely and was on the verge of threatening to stop training altogether when she decided to end the discussion rather than say something irrevocable. She didn't want to be unfair to Lee without whose help she would never have been able to bring Beauchamp to justice.

Later that day, she was summoned to a meeting with Sinclair and Jones. This time, eager to hear their news, she went to the Special Forces building with a lightness of step.

"We've made excellent progress," announced Sinclair. "We've enough evidence to put Beauchamp and Bill Chalmers away for a long time. Chalmers will almost certainly get the death penalty. He's got a criminal record as long as your arm, and his DNA was matched with the bouquet."

"Why wasn't his name thrown up earlier?"

"Good question, we're looking into that. Anyway, Blaise Collins-Clarke will be going down for a plethora of criminal charges resulting from a variety of financial manipulations, including acting against Schrauben & Mutter. Although he almost certainly instigated Penny's death, we're still struggling to prove it. But it's early days yet."

Tessa nodded.

"Beauchamp the head of the Calver Cats … I still can't believe it."

"I'm afraid there's no doubt. Anyway, the court hearings are being fast-tracked and, whatever the verdicts, that will mark the end of your Mission."

"Thank heavens. I just want to relinquish my OCL and be boringly conventional…"

Tessa left the Special Forces headquarters feeling ecstatic and convinced she was right to refuse further training with Matsumoto.

It was another week before events started moving again. As she was returning from her run one morning, she registered the sound of police sirens in the City, but didn't pay any attention to them. She'd agreed to train at SKS that day so changed into a black tracksuit and set off with her sword in its case. As she turned into Cranley Place, Lee was in the middle of a telephone call.

"…the situation has changed very much for the worse," he said.

Matsumoto sighed.

"I fear you are right. She is in grave danger and we have invested too much in her to have her killed by some inadequate nobody who strikes lucky. We have more important matters for her to attend to… I have bad news too. The Fujiwara are involved now. I don't know how the initial contact came about, possibly by accident, but the link is well established."

"That's all we need… Mind you, although that exacerbates matters, in some ways it simplifies them too."

"Yes, it seems destiny has merged all our feuds. You *must* persuade Nariko to come back here. While she is with me, she will be safe, and hopefully the Special Forces will put an end to her brother's feud with her. If they fail, she will at least be better equipped to survive, once her training is complete."

There was silence while they considered the seriousness of the situation.

"I don't think she'll leave here," continued Lee, gazing out of the window and considering how the tranquillity of his garden contrasted with what was happening in the world outside. "She's in a serious relationship and has had great difficulty in coming to terms with the deaths she caused. The last time I suggested she return to you, we came as close as ever to a complete break. I think she is even considering stopping training and returning her OCL."

"Oh, she won't do that," exclaimed Matsumoto. "Whether she likes it or not, she could never give up the sword now. Talk to her again. She must come back, and sooner rather than later."

"Talk alone will not be enough," mused Lee.

"Then challenge her, beat her, draw blood if necessary. Demonstrate your superiority and use that as justification for her further training."

"Hah! I can challenge her, but whether I can beat her, that is a different matter."

Matsumoto roared with laughter.

"My brother, surely you don't mean she's already better than you?"

"Quite possibly," replied Lee, in a voice strangely devoid of emotion. "I *used* to be her teacher, but you have assumed that role. Now I am merely the catalyst for her continuing development."

"Then be creative. After all, your last idea proved to be a great success, even if she doesn't think so. Meanwhile, I will do what I can to help. I will have another word with Isamu."

Lee put down the phone, looked at his wife and sighed.

As Tessa walked into Barnaby Mews, her comfortable day-dreaming stopped abruptly. Instead of being greeted by the sound of students training, there was a cold inhospitable silence. Not wishing to draw attention to her presentiment that something was wrong, she stepped into the shadows before opening her sword case. Her shoulder harness was still with Kono to adapt it to carry a second weapon. So, she slung her sword from a conventional belt.

She stopped by the large double doors; unusually, the door to her left was ajar. She put her sword case down and peered inside. It was pitch dark and completely quiet. She took a deep breath and went in, immediately stepping to her right to avoid being silhouetted against the light. She heard a rustling outside, and the door slammed shut. Lee's voice spoke out of the darkness.

"Nariko, I have listened patiently to your whining about the deaths you inflicted. I have listened patiently to your euphoria at having started a relationship, and I have listened patiently to your ramblings about stopping your training. As every day passes, this nonsense becomes more irritating. Whether you like it or not, there is no turning back. Your path stretches before you, and you have no choice but to follow it. So, I challenge you. We will fight for your future. We will fight until blood has been spilt."

"Don't be stupid," she retorted. "I'm not going to fight you. Such a challenge is demeaning." In the silence that followed, Tessa was suspicious; she knew he'd moved but wasn't sure to where. "Men and their endless melodrama," she said with bitterness. "Too much testosterone and not enough calm, honest communication."

His response was to throw a knife at her – she ducked and it missed. However, it had passed close enough for her to know it would have hit her had she not moved. She walked back to the door and reached for the handle, only to hear the lock being turned from the outside. Then another knife came whistling towards her and she rolled quickly away. The other exit was via the corridor to Lee's living quarters; but he was unlikely to have left that route open. She would have to use the main door, which meant she needed to disarm Lee without hurting him. Silently, she walked back to the door and tried it again to check it really was locked. She heard him approaching. As she stood back from the tiny ray of light streaking in through the keyhole, he audibly drew a sword.

"Lee, this is madness. I don't want to fight, I want to leave. Please, let me go."

"You have no choice but to fight. Otherwise you will die."

Tessa smiled.

"Are you sure?" she replied quietly. "I'm not scared."

"Neither am I."

He lunged at her. She dodged. He attacked again and again, driving her into a corner. Motionless, she waited in the darkness. They both knew she would have to draw her sword soon to protect herself, or trust that he wouldn't really hurt her. Lee swung his sword round with a loud *whoosh*; it slashed the front of her tracksuit, narrowly missing her skin. It was an extremely accurate, well-judged warning. Any lingering doubt she had that he was willing to hurt her, had most definitely been cut away.

He swung again, this time aiming for her body. She no longer had any choice. A confident ringing announced she had drawn her own sword and shortly afterwards a loud *clang* echoed round the room as their blades met. A rapid exchange of clashes followed, then another, then another. Tessa forced him back to the centre of the room. Despite the darkness, they both knew the precise position of each other's sword. Evenly matched, they fought ferociously. However, Tessa was younger and fitter. Nevertheless, she fought defensively, determined to prolong the conflict and wear him out. He already knew that to win, he would have to act quickly. The fight raged around the room. She remained fast and relaxed while he began to pant.

Suddenly, Tessa took a couple of awkward steps back, giving the impression she had stumbled. Just as she'd hoped, Lee lunged forward at full stretch. She twisted her body and spun round. With all her strength, she struck his sword with the back edge of hers, smiling at the tell-tale *chink* of his blade shattering. Metallic clattering reverberated round the room as metal fragments bounced on the floor. She re-sheathed her sword.

"I'm going now. Goodbye."

She turned and walked towards the door. But then she heard the swish of Lee drawing another sword. He had tricked her! He'd carried the first sword and worn a second, not the sheath for the first. As he attacked, she quickly somersaulted away and his blade just missed her. In a moment, she was standing again and had re-drawn her sword. Their weapons met and they fought on; again he was barring the way to the door.

She could tell Lee's second sword was of a much finer quality than the first. She doubted she could break it, but it was much shorter than hers. Presumably he hadn't wanted to be hindered by wearing a second full-length weapon.

By now desperate to end the duel, he stooped down to strike at her legs. But she ran forward and, putting one foot on his shoulder, leapt over him; driving him to the floor. She reached the double doors and, with all her strength, kicked the one to her right. There was a resounding *crash* as it splintered and broke. Only the upright remained, flapping on three large wrought-iron hinges. Light flooded into the room and she spun round to see Lee with his face covered in perspiration. He came after her and prepared to attack once more.

Tessa sighed and held her sword down in front of her.

"Very well, have it your own way, just see what it wins you."

For a moment he hesitated, then brought his sword round to slash at her waist. However, with lightning speed, she swung her own weapon up and flicked it over. The blades met with incredible force. Lee's short sword twanged violently in protest and shuddered in mid-air, but Tessa simply hit it again, driving it out to his right. As her sword rang menacingly, she slid the longer blade between his sword arm and his torso. If he tried to bring his arm back, it would push her blade into his waist.

"Yield!" she yelled.

Lee looked down and smiled.

"Such a challenge cannot end honourably until blood has been drawn. So, let this be an indication of how much I value your life, and how important it is for you to return to Japan."

Tessa watched in amazement as he brought his sword arm back. Still ringing, her blade barely paused as it passed through his tunic. A moment later, she saw a trickle of blood from the new wound in his side. Now, she couldn't move without making the wound deeper. She looked at him in disbelief.

"I thought it unlikely I would beat you," he continued. "But it is still very close. Maybe I'm just a little too old. Ultimately, you could never win because it is even clearer now that you must go back to Matsumoto. You still make mistakes. You made some when you fought the Calver Cats, and you made some just now. If you do not learn more, you will be killed for being only as good as me; and that is simply not good enough. In your heart of hearts, you must know you can never give up the sword. It is part of you, and you are no longer whole without it. If you try to give it up, you will only die one dark night at the hand of some cheap thug."

He relaxed his arm and Tessa retrieved her weapon. As he gripped his wound, blood dripped from between his fingers. Tessa flicked her sword clean, re-sheathed it, and walked through the shattered doorway, kicking debris out of the way as she went. She returned her sword to its case and looked back at him.

"I owe you too much to ignore what you say. But you have just done me a great disservice."

She turned away and marched up Barnaby Mews.

Lee's wife joined him and gently moved his hand to look at the wound. She shook her head, smiled sadly and offered him a dressing sprinkled with herbs and mosses. He nodded and she pressed the send key for the SMS he had written earlier.

Tessa stomped out of Barnaby Mews into the bright bustle of Old Brompton Road. As she strode between the nervous people, her *cbc* vibrated; a text message had arrived from Sinclair. *Come quick. Our place. Very urgent.*

"Oh, brilliant!" she muttered in disgust, and hailed a taxi. As one stopped, the driver looked nervously at her sword case.

"Don't say it" she growled angrily, climbing into the cab. "Just take me to Special Forces Headquarters in Vauxhall. Quickly, please."

"Yes, miss," replied the driver. "Sorry, I didn't mean to stare. It's just that I don't often pick up someone with a licence to carry one of those things." He turned to look at her. "You do have a licence, don't you, miss?"

"Yes, I do," she snarled. "Now will you get on with it, please? I'm in a hurry, *and a really bad mood!*"

"Yes, miss, sorry."

He swallowed, and turned back to the road. The taxi barged out into the swiftly moving traffic and, fifteen minutes later, stopped by the Special Forces security lodge. The guard looked at Tessa and smiled in recognition, waving the taxi through to the main entrance. She paid the driver and went in, immediately having to join a queue of people waiting to pass through the metal detectors. It was only a short queue but that didn't stop her hackles from rising.

"Ah, good morning, Nariko," said one of the security guards, glancing at her sword. "Major General Sinclair is expecting you. Would you mind transferring your sword to this case, please?"

"Oh! If I must," grumbled Tessa, resisting the temptation to ask why hers wouldn't suffice. She continued through the metal detector, making it buzz annoyingly, and went to the lift. But it had just left, so she ran up the stairs to the fifth floor. Nodding to Sinclair's secretary, she continued through to his office. Both he and Jones were there.

"Hello. That was quick," said Sinclair, putting down his phone. "I've only just been told you've arrived. Anyway, thank you for coming. I suggest we all go and see Lamper and hear it from the horse's mouth, so to speak. Perhaps we'd all benefit from an update."

Tessa could tell that something serious had happened, but didn't feel like asking what. She shrugged and followed Sinclair out. The three of them waited for the lift.

"You've an enormous hole in your tracksuit," observed Jones.

Tessa looked down. Lee had ruined her favourite tracksuit.

"An accident, nothing of consequence."

They went down four floors and walked towards an office displaying the nameplate 'T. Lamper, Manager UK Overt Security'. Not bothering to knock, Sinclair strode in, followed by Tessa and Jones.

Timothy Lamper looked up from behind his desk. He was a short, overweight man with a round face and ruddy complexion. His shiny head was obscured only by a few strands of black hair which had been greased and combed across in an attempt to conceal his advancing baldness. Tessa quickly decided she was studying a man failing miserably to appear dapper and in control. He started fidgeting anxiously when he saw who had entered.

"Ah, hello again, sir. Oh, and this must be, Dr Cai– Pennington," said Lamper uncomfortably. "I'm pleased to meet you. Have a seat. Make yourself comfortable. Can I offer you a cup of..."

"Stop blabbering, Lamper!" rasped Sinclair. "Tell her what's happened."

Tessa couldn't help smiling. Sinclair's outburst was so out of character for the taciturn serious man she had grown to know and like, she correctly concluded there was no love lost between these two.

"Right," replied Lamper. "Well, er, Dr ... I'm afraid I have some rather disturbing news. You see, a few hours ago we were transporting Caille from Paddington Green to the Old Bailey and, well, to cut a long story short ... he escaped. Most regrettable and rather embarrassing." He studied Tessa's face in an attempt to discern how worried he should be, but found no indication in her deadpan expression. "Hmm. Anyway, that happened, well, three hours ago now, and we think he may already have left the country. His escape was extremely well planned and executed." He paused, starting to perspire as blood rushed to his face, making it go even redder. "He left a message pinned to the dead body of one of his guards," he continued, looking at Tessa. "It's for you."

Tessa took it and read aloud her brother's words of hatred.

To my sibling freak,

No matter where you hide, I will find you. No matter where your friends hide, I will find them. After you have watched them all perish, you will die a slow and painful death. Only then will the debt between us be settled.

À bientôt,

B

In the pause that followed, Lamper nervously dabbed his forehead with a grubby handkerchief and Big Ben chimed in the distance. Desperate to break the silence, he started talking again.

"I'm sure we'll get them back. But … er … it might take a while."

"Lamper, you really are an idiot," interrupted Sinclair. "You didn't tell us about the note before. And what do you mean by 'get them back'?"

"Ah! Oh," he muttered, swallowing loudly. "Well, unfortunately, it seems Chalmers has gone too. He was in a separate convoy, of course… All we know at the moment is that an Asian woman with two swords oversaw both escapes."

Tessa shook her head in amazement. It didn't seem possible that her life could disintegrate so completely, so quickly. Sinclair appeared close to exploding.

"I don't believe it," he growled. "You didn't tell us that either!"

"I only just found out myself," whimpered Lamper.

"Lamper!" continued Sinclair, his voice adopting a blood-curdling tone. "Do you have any idea how dangerous these men are? Do you know how long it took us to catch them? All you had to do was to get them to court! How on earth… To lose one is incompetent; to lose two defies comprehension. And now you're telling us Beauchamp has found a replacement for The Barb too!"

"Er, yes. It was very well planned ... very clever. They had a lot of people, and vehicles too. I should have a preliminary report on my desk, well, very soon."

He turned back to Tessa.

"No doubt these unfortunate events will make you concerned for your own safety. I understand you have started learning to use a sword, but after all it is only a sword. So, in the circumstances, and despite the general ban on such weapons, I have taken the liberty of obtaining a Hand Arms Licence for you. I've requisitioned a pistol too; H&K with a thirteen-round magazine. It's a little on the heavy side but accurate and reliable, without much recoil. Just sign here and I'll get an expert to program it for you and show you how to use it."

He held up a large black-and-gold fountain pen and pushed some papers across his desk towards Tessa. Sinclair and Jones stared at him dumbfounded.

Tessa stepped forward and smiled.

"Mr Lamper, how considerate. But have you ever seen a sword at work? With your permission, I'd be delighted to give you a quick demonstration?"

"Oh, well, yes, that would be interesting," he replied unctuously, convinced he was making progress. "Feel free…"

Tessa opened the Security-issue sword case, and, before he had time to react, drew her sword and swung it round. She ensured it did not ring and all Lamper saw was a silver blur passing in front of him; but he did feel a draught across his hand. Then, as he watched Tessa close the sword case, he heard the clatter of the top half of his pen hitting the desk and sensed the wetness of the ink as it dribbled over his hand. He gulped noisily.

"Thank you for the offer of a gun," she continued softly. "But they're unsophisticated, cowardly and noisy, with a habit of hurting innocent bystanders. Just get Beauchamp and his sidekick back behind bars, please. Quickly."

With that, she marched out of his office.

Lamper sat wide-eyed. Her refusing the gun hadn't surprised him, but he'd hoped that offering it would absolve him of any responsibility for her inevitable death. However, he hadn't expected his own expensive fountain pen to be cut in two!

Jones turned to Sinclair and grinned.

"Hmm. Well, it could have been worse," he said, gesturing towards Lamper. "His head's still attached … I think."

Sinclair looked at Lamper with contempt.

"Jones is right. It seems Dr Pennington doesn't feel like cutting your head off, but I most certainly do! Stop playing politics for once. Get out of your office and get Caille and Chalmers back in custody *quickly*, like she said," he barked. "If not the consequences will be dire for many people – including you."

Lamper nodded weakly. Sinclair marched out, shaking his head in exasperation.

"I somehow thought you might end up needing this," said Jones, tossing a roll of gaffer tape on to Lamper's desk. "Unfortunate accident that, wasn't it? Silly of you to break your pen?"

Lamper nodded in disgruntled acceptance, and Jones quickly followed Sinclair out. They joined Tessa as she waited by the lift.

"Sorry about that," she said, "but his mind needed focusing."

"That's all right," replied Sinclair, with a smile. "He deserved that and some. I could quite happily throttle him myself. We will get them back, you know."

"Yes. But when … and what havoc will they wreak in the meantime? It sounds as though Beauchamp is rather upset. Do you think he meant that about killing all my friends?"

Sinclair gestured for Jones to leave them alone.

"I think it's a real possibility," he confirmed. "I doubt he knows about your identity as Nariko yet. Not even Lamper knows you're a Peacekeeper. But when Beauchamp does find out, and realises it was you at Rippleside, his fury and hatred will know no bounds."

"Hmm. The funny thing is," mused Tessa, "I still don't understand why he wants me dead."

"I asked him that. He ranted and raged for ages, but quite frankly I'm none the wiser. Certainly the shock you gave him a while back fuelled the fires, but they'd been burning for a long time."

"Well, I know I'm not perfect. I regret many things; some I did, and some I didn't. But I always tried my clumsy best."

Sinclair smiled.

345

"We all do. At the end of the day, although you may unwittingly have exacerbated the situation, I doubt you caused it, sibling rivalry apart. Beauchamp said he'd despised you from the day you were born. He even intimated he'd tried to get rid of you before, when you were very young. Psychologists would probably point to a scenario of an elder child never quite coming to terms with the arrival of another. But who knows? Unless you are able to have a calm conversation with him one day," continued Sinclair, "you may never find out what his motivation is. Maybe he doesn't know himself any more. A transient comforting thought has become a way of life… Anyway, I thought you should know, he did say he held Lord Kensington partly responsible for his public humiliation." Tessa's blood ran cold; it had never entered her mind that she might unwittingly endanger David. "And I'm afraid it gets worse. Beauchamp didn't see the court process through, so the Mission you signed to stop the Calver Cats has not been completed."

She looked at Sinclair in horror.

"Oh, no! You mean I'm still under an obligation to go after him? I don't believe this… Are you and Jones in danger too?"

"Probably, but that's not something you need worry about. It's what we get paid for. And besides, you sacked us, remember?"

"When I crawled out of bed this morning, all was well with my world. In fact, it was better than I thought it could ever get. But since then, my day, my life, my future, have all spiralled downwards."

"Well, you are legally obliged to pursue the Mission, but only if you're on active service. If, for example, you had already committed to doing something which at least one of your Guardians had approved, well, that would be a different matter."

Tessa glared at him, breathed out noisily and moved round to trap him between the banister and the lift. Then she opened the sword case.

"Hmm," he mused, "you can be quite intimidating at times."

"I wouldn't draw my sword without just cause. But if I thought one of my Guardians was manipulating me, an independent Peacekeeper, then that would be cause enough, wouldn't it? I suspected something had been going on behind my back, but didn't want to believe you were involved. However, you've just confirmed that it does, so you'd better tell me all about it."

Sinclair looked over her shoulder and saw a very worried-looking Jones about to call for help. He smiled, shook his head and looked back at Tessa.

"Sometimes it's very difficult being at the end of the tail that wags the dog."

"Trust me," she replied tersely, "it's far worse being the bitch whose tail it is! I'm waiting. And while you're at it, you can tell me where exactly you learned to tie your ponytail like that."

"Hah! I told him you'd notice. Well, as you've deduced, we have a mutual friend in Japan. I doubt I know him as well as you, but he has my respect and I trust him completely. So, when I was asked to help convince you to return for further training, I agreed. I received assurances it would be in your best interests, not only to improve your skills but also to keep you safe. I was asked to do whatever I could to find and detain your brother while you were away...

"I don't profess to understand everything that's going on, but I do think you should go back to Japan. If you stay here, just about every low-life in Europe will be on your trail, and possibly Lord Kensington's too. I would recommend you leave quickly because as a fugitive Beauchamp will try and strike as soon as he can. While you're away, I will do my best to get him and Chalmers back behind bars. I will also keep an eye on Lord Kensington ... discreetly, of course. But it will probably help him immensely if the two of you are not seen together for a while."

Tessa shook her head in anger and frustration.

"When did you meet Matsumoto?"

"Years ago. Lee introduced us, after which I spent a few weeks with Matsumoto in Japan. It had nothing to do with you or this Mission. I went with a specific purpose in mind. But I didn't give him enough time and left before my training was complete. Because of that, I failed in my task and ended up with this limp."

Although glad that her hunch about him had been proved correct, his advice that she should leave sickened her.

"Is Tessa such a bad person that even you want to see her disappear?"

"No, of course she's not," countered Sinclair. "You shouldn't view this so pessimistically. There's nothing wrong with Tessa. But her future changed fundamentally the day Penny died. Tessa isn't disappearing, she's evolving, maturing. These are turbulent times; the world is a rapidly changing place. We must all constantly adapt to survive. This is simply Nariko taking over from where Tessa left off. Nariko is the Tessa of the future. The good in her, and there's a lot, will persist if you want it to."

"Hmm, good answer," she replied, prompting a shrug from Sinclair.

"I can understand your not wanting to leave but I really do think it would be better if you did. I will do everything I can to sort things out while you're away. Then, when you get back, you'll be able to get on with your life. Hopefully, we'll all be able to get on with our lives."

Tessa went over to the banister and gazed out over the atrium to prevent him from seeing how distraught she was. She wanted to cry, but couldn't; not here. A single tear escaped and trickled down her cheek. She quickly wiped it away, despairing, inconsolable and furious.

"At least do me the courtesy of not telling *anyone* we had this conversation – and I mean *absolutely no one*, not just Jones."

"Of course," replied Sinclair, nodding. "Beauchamp's escape is a serious setback for everyone's plans. However, I'll do you a deal. If we've got him behind bars by the time you come back, I'll make sure you're not offered any other Missions."

"Hah! I suppose that's the best deal going, because it seems to be the only damn' deal going; everything else is a done deal. I'm just the last person to find out about it…"

Sinclair smiled, convinced she was agreeing to go. Then Tessa spun round, eyes ablaze. He took a step back in surprise.

"Damn it, Sinclair, I'm fed up with all these blasted pre-determined deals. I object to being coerced into doing things I don't want to do! I'm not going; I refuse to let Beauchamp continue ruining my life. He's done that for long enough."

"Perhaps now is not the right time to make such an important decision," he replied, shocked by her vehemence. "But please believe me when I say that every day you spend here only increases the risk."

"Really? Or is it just because you, Lee and Matsumoto want me to go?"

Sinclair sighed.

"If you stay, you'll have to be on your guard every second of the day, carrying your sword at all times. Eventually, maybe they'll decide they can't get you that way, so they'll come after you with guns, and it will continue escalating until they do get you... I can understand your being wary of what I say, but I would never knowingly do anything to endanger you."

"I know that," she acknowledged, calming down, "but you haven't exactly played fair with me, have you? And neither have the others."

"No, you're right, and for my part I'm sorry... Look, I can delay things for a day or two, but tell me you'll think about going at least?"

"OK," said Tessa, nodding.

Sinclair gestured Jones to rejoin them.

"Right," he said, looking at them both quizzically. "I presume, Nariko, you understand we'll have to resume the Mission?"

"Yes and no," replied Tessa. "You see, you two told me the Mission was all but over, so I set some long-term plans in motion. I need to see whether I can wriggle out of them. I'll be in touch."

"What?" exclaimed Jones. "But..."

"Sinclair will explain," she continued. "Oh, before I go, could you do me a favour, please? Could you ask Potter to add a second sword to my OCL? I found one; must have been a family heirloom."

"Ha! And whose family would that be?" asked Jones, glancing at his boss for the approval he needed... "Fine, I'll take care of it."

"Thanks," said Tessa, peering over the banister to check it was clear below. Then she neatly vaulted over the railing, landing with barely a sound on the marble floor below. Soon through Security, she broke into a run and disappeared from view.

"What on earth was all that about?"

"That," replied Sinclair, "was somebody fighting their own destiny... I wonder if Beauchamp realises what he's creating?"

"Well, although the actions of others affect us, they don't make us who we are."

"I know," mused Sinclair. "But at crucial times, when our defences are down, isn't it all too easy to be swayed by the actions and arguments of others?"

"True. But that doesn't excuse us from responsibility for making the final decision. What I would say is that if their paths do cross again, I doubt they'll both walk away. I wonder who the victor will be?"

"Indeed. But I suspect what's worrying Nariko is what she will have to become to have even a chance of surviving… Anyway, she needs some time to think, so let's make sure she stays safe. Have her watched, twenty-four/seven. I don't want her out on her own."

When he reached his office, Sinclair spoke to his secretary.

"Get me David Kensington again, please. He should still be at Burrody Castle. Tell him it's urgent … and I don't want to be disturbed while I'm talking to him."

CHAPTER 34

Thirty minutes later Tessa was standing outside SKS. The carpenters rebuilding the splintered door looked at her reproachfully.

"Hah!" exclaimed one. "You guys are never around when you're needed. Look what some bastard did to this door."

"Hmm. Looks like a strong door too," mused Tessa. "Must have been a good kick."

"It was a very good kick," acknowledged Lee, emerging from inside. "You haven't come back to demolish the other one, have you?"

"No. I thought we might have some tea, if you have time?"

"Always," he replied, gesturing for her to come in.

As the carpenters stared at Tessa, she instructed them to leave her the bill. Then she followed Lee inside. He looked pale and walked slowly, clearly in some discomfort. As they passed though the practice room, it momentarily fell quiet; both she and Lee looked round angrily, and the activity immediately resumed.

In his private room, Lee's wife brought them some tea. As usual, she smiled at Tessa, but said nothing.

"Lee, I'm sorry about…"

"Nothing for you to be sorry about," he interrupted, raising his hand. "I couldn't think of a better way to try and persuade you to do what I felt was important. But I had forgotten you must be allowed to make your own decisions."

"Chance would be a fine thing," she replied bitterly.

As they drank the tea she recounted what had happened, albeit omitting any mention of her private conversation with Sinclair.

"…So it seems I must at least consider going back to Matsumoto. For the good of everyone else, if not myself, although I still don't know how to explain it to David. It's all so unfair."

"Well," said Lee, "you already know that I want you to go. There is no doubt further training will leave you much better equipped to overcome whatever challenges confront you later. If these Special Forces men cannot stop the Calver Cats in your absence, you will

351

need to be more skilled than you are now in order to survive and protect your friends."

Tessa looked downcast, but said nothing. She had always wanted to make sure those responsible for Penny's death were brought to justice. But she had never expected her efforts would drag her so far away from the peaceful, loving life she yearned for.

"What a waste."

Lee frowned.

"What do you mean?"

"All that time I devoted to succeeding in business. All the pain, prejudice and sacrifice I endured to become who I really am. I always knew there would be consequences, but I never expected this; to be despised by my own brother, and have to wield a sword to keep myself and my friends alive…"

Her words petered into silence against the sound of water streaming over rock outside. Lee sighed.

"Every aspect of your past, including your brother's cruelty to you, helped make you what you are today. True, your path now appears very different from the one you expected, but that is no reason to be ashamed of what you have achieved. It is because of *everything* you have done that you are able to right some wrongs which affect you, and many others too. That is probably what you were always intended to do."

"But, Lee, I've had a glimpse of another life; a better life, a life full of love. And early this morning, I thought it was within my grasp… I don't want to be known as a terrifying Peacekeeper whom nobody dares to cross."

"Unfortunately, you cannot deny your skills, Nariko-san; the sword is not a possession, it is a part of you. Perhaps your past expectations *are* fading, but maybe they were always unrealistic. Life is never easy, and often lonely. Sometimes one is most lonely when surrounded by friends. Although our ultimate destinies are decided by a higher power, I do believe we are free to shape them, at least temporarily. But there is always the danger that postponing the inevitable will simply make matters worse."

Tessa took a deep breath. She could never forgive herself if David became entangled in this sordid mess, just because of her. Furthermore, she feared Lee was right and she couldn't give up the sword. And, perhaps most confusingly of all, she knew there was part of her that *wanted* to go back to Matsumoto. She'd felt the pull for some time, but didn't want to admit it, even to herself. It was the prospect of life with David which had held her back.

"I fear for my future if I go, but I fear even more for David's if I stay," she said sadly. Her eyes were watering, but still she refused to cry. "Why me? Haven't I done enough?"

"I'm sorry," commiserated Lee. "I understand your path is a sad and difficult one at present. There is nothing I can do to alter that."

"Well, I've got a couple of days," said Tessa, standing. "I'll think about it."

CHAPTER 35

The following morning, Tessa left home early for her run. As she turned out of her mews into Cranley Place, Crick joined her, dressed in running gear. They hadn't met since Tessa's Samurai Proficiency Test, but Crick's short bleached hair was very distinctive.

"Hello! What are you doing here?" asked Tessa, spotting the *Urgent Assistance Required* transponder in her hand.

"The boss said you weren't to be left alone, and I drew the short straw so I'm running. But go easy on me, please, twenty-five squared."

Tessa laughed and slowed down so that they could talk as they ran. She soon recognised that there was a lot to like about the Special Forces woman. She was well informed, worldly and clearly kept very fit. It wasn't long before they were both enjoying each other's company and had agreed to have a sushi dinner together that evening.

Meanwhile, a black SUV stopped in Hyde Park, near a path leading down to the Serpentine.

"Goodbye, Beauchamp," said Caprice. "Are you sure you don't want my gun?"

"No, too quick," he replied, shaking his head. "I'm taking that wretched *thing* with me ... alive."

"Well, I hope you succeed... But whatever happens, don't let them catch you."

"I won't, darling, don't worry. Bill's already on his way. I'll miss you..."

"I know, but it's too dangerous for you to stay in the UK. I'll be fine."

He smiled, kissed her and got out. Then he watched until the car had disappeared from view and slowly walked down the path.

Tessa and Crick were already down by the lake. As they neared the tunnel under the road, Tessa heard rustling in the bushes and the unmistakable whine of a Taser gun charging.

"Ambush!" she yelled. Crick instinctively pressed the emergency transponder but was immediately hit by a pair of Taser darts and collapsed, shaking uncontrollably from the electric charge. Tessa swerved and just managed to evade more darts. She found two burly men confronting her. The one who had fired at Crick kept pulling the trigger, causing her to twitch horribly. The other man fumbled with a fresh Taser. Tessa sprang forward, reaching him just as he aimed the gun. She grabbed his wrist with her left hand and punched him hard in the face with her right. As his nose crunched, she yanked his arm round, aimed the Taser at his colleague, and jammed her finger into the trigger guard to make the gun fire. The darts struck their target and the other man collapsed, dropping his weapon. Crick relaxed and pulled out the darts, but stayed on the ground, badly disorientated.

Then the man Tessa was holding tried to head-butt her. She quickly moved away to avoid his attack, but in doing so, had to release her grip on his gun. He swung a wild punch at her; she ducked, and his fist only lightly brushed her shoulder. She responded by kneeing him in the groin. As he doubled up in pain, she cupped her hands together and hit him hard on the back of the neck. He collapsed unconscious.

By now the other man had recovered from his brief electric shock and drawn another Taser. He fired as Tessa ran towards him, but she weaved and he missed. She grabbed his outstretched hand and yanked it round, twisting it up behind his back. Then she clamped her right arm around his throat, intending to render him unconscious. But a third man appeared, dragging a woman jogger. He was holding a knife to her neck.

"Let go of him," he yelled.

"You let go of her first," replied Tessa.

"Suit yourself," he sneered, cutting the woman's throat and tossing her body aside. Then Tessa's prisoner bent forward, lifting her off the ground. He started to twist round to make her a better target for his colleague. But Tessa immediately changed the grip on her prisoner's neck and it snapped with an unpleasant *crack* just as the other man threw his knife. It was a fine throw; but she still had time to catch it and throw it back. It sank deep into his forehead. She sighed and turned round to face her brother.

"Aren't you the violent one?" purred Beauchamp. "And using knives too, I didn't know you could do that."

He had his left hand on Crick's throat. She was lying on her back, glaring up at him. He lobbed some tie wraps to Tessa.

355

"What do you want, Beauchamp?"

"You, of course. I told those bungling idiots you knew Karate, but they wouldn't listen. Not to worry, this'll work. Now, do as I say or she dies."

Police sirens could be heard in the distance, together with the sound of a helicopter approaching.

"Take him!" yelled Crick, but Beauchamp simply pushed down on her windpipe, choking her.

"Strap your ankles and your wrists, loop the ties together," he ordered. "I'd do it quickly, if I were you. I think she'd like to breathe."

Tessa picked up the tie wraps.

"I'll do it if you let her go."

"Hah!" he said, drawing a knife. "I'll count to three, then she's dead."

"You'd lose your leverage."

"One, two, …"

"OK, OK. Just don't hurt her!"

Brandishing his knife, Beauchamp relaxed his grip on Crick's throat; she gasped for breath.

Tessa sat down and engaged a tie wrap round her ankles.

"That's better," sneered Beauchamp. "By the way, it was very entertaining watching that thing you called a friend being raped. She died well, eventually. And got off lightly compared to what I intend to do with you…" Tessa froze in revulsion. "Go on, or this one will die too."

Tessa was just about to tighten the tie wrap when Sinclair yelled down from the bridge. "Beauchamp Caille, you're under arrest!"

Crick took the momentary distraction as an opportunity to escape. She shoved Beauchamp back and rolled away, but he followed and stabbed her in the chest, killing her instantly. As he yanked out his knife, a helicopter swooped down from overhead with a rope ladder dangling below. Beauchamp waved it away from the bridge and looked at Tessa, trying to decide whether to throw the knife at her or not. She stopped freeing her ankles, hoping he would.

"Hmm. Catch you later," he said, sheathing the weapon. He laughed at her frustration, and dived into the lake.

"You murdering bastard!" yelled Tessa.

Finally free, she ran to the water's edge and … stopped. She wanted to go after him, but didn't dare. Beauchamp reached the ladder and started to climb. He shouted back, mocking her.

"What's the matter, *freak*, still scared of drowning? I wonder why!"

As the helicopter banked and sped away, Sinclair appeared at the parapet with a rifle. He fired three shots, but without material effect.

Tessa knelt down by Crick's lifeless body, and held her hand as once she had held her friend's. Sinclair joined her shortly afterwards.

"Why didn't you go after him?" he asked.

"I don't do water," replied Tessa. Sinclair raised his eyebrows in surprise. "Beauchamp knows. It's a long story... Oh, Crick, I'm so sorry, this should never have happened ... but I promise you, your death and so much more will not go unpunished."

The story continues in Vol. 2, Bitter Justice...

(see over for Bitter Justice Chapter 1, and The Glossary)

BITTER JUSTICE

(sneak preview)

CHAPTER 1 ~ Friday 13th April 2025

Global Times - Calver Cats threaten us all:

"The UNWP has finally been forced to admit that the Calver Cats pose a significant threat to world order. Originally UK-based, the gang has expanded rapidly. It now controls much of the world's illegal arms and drugs trade from operations in such far-flung places as Bogotá, Chicago, Shanghai and Tokyo.

The Calver name is derived from the Japanese technique of gutting fish alive, and many of the gang's victims have suffered a similar fate. British Calver Cats chief, Beauchamp Caille, was detained once, but escaped in a bloody ambush which left twelve dead. A UK-led multinational offensive against the gang has proved inconclusive prompting calls for a different approach..."

Japan News - Calver Cats Peacekeeper slaughter continues:

"The Calver Cats gang has consistently targeted International Peacekeepers to hamper Special Forces and dissuade new recruits. Particularly in Japan, Peacekeepers have been ruthlessly hunted down and killed. It is believed only a handful remains, but the secrecy surrounding these anonymous, licensed-to-kill, individuals makes verification difficult.

Calver Cats boss, Beauchamp Caille, also wants to settle some personal debts. Not only is he hunting the UK Peacekeeper who annihilated the original London gang, but also his own sister whom he holds responsible for his temporary incarceration. However, she has not been seen in public for a long time and rumour has it that she is already dead..."

GLOSSARY

Throughout the Samurai Revival Trilogy, references to street or road names are fictitious, even if the name does exist. Furthermore, all references to brand names are intended to be complimentary.

Also, the author would like to thank the various public domain databases used while preparing this Glossary, in particular, Wikipedia.

A13 a major road in England leading radially east out of London, linking the City with east London and south Essex.

A3 (Bundes)autobahn 3 is a German motorway that links the border to the Netherlands in the northwest to Austria in the southeast, passing Düsseldorf and Köln (Cologne) amongst many other key locations.

(Royal) Albert Hall is a London concert hall situated to the north of South Kensington. It was opened by Queen Victoria in 1871.

Alfred's Way part of the A13 leading eastwards out of London.

Amafuji See Amakuni

Amakuni ('Arm-a-koon-ei') a Japanese sword-maker of around 700 AD reputed to have made the first sword/katana which proved reliable in battle (i.e. did not shatter). Amafuji followed about 50 years later.

Arigato means 'Thank you' in Japanese (see Domo arigato).

Arita a town/district in Saga prefecture on the island of Kyushu in southwest Japan. It is area renowned for high quality porcelain.

Balaclava a form of cloth hat that covers the whole head and face, usually only leaving the eyes, or eyes and mouth, exposed.

Balmoral Castle a castle on a large country estate in Aberdeenshire, Scotland. It has been owned by the British Royal family since 1852.

(The) Barb the nickname for a fictitious character responsible for training members of the Calver Cats gang to use a samurai sword.

Barnaby Mews a fictitious Mews leading off Old Brompton Road near the underground station in South Kensington.

Beauchamp ('Bee-cham') is a boy's name with French origins, literally meaning beautiful field.

Belgravia a part of Central London straddling City of Westminster and the Royal Borough of Kensington & Chelsea; one of the wealthiest districts in the world and is known for its extremely expensive houses.

Blackwall an area to the east of London, situated in the London Borough of Tower Hamlets on the north bank of the River Thames opposite Greenwich.

BNYI a fictitious international bank and stands for Beijing New York International.

Bokken a Japanese wooden sword used for training in place of a real weapon; although a bokken, when used by an expert, can also be lethal. In these books, bokken is interpreted more broadly to include long martial arts staffs more correctly called 'jo'.

Bryani a girl's name with English and Greek origins referring to a flowering vine used in folk medicine.

Bugatti an automotive company (originally Italian now owned by VW) associated with cars at the epitome of exclusivity, luxury, elegance, style and extraordinary automotive design (see EB).

Burray a small island in the south of the Orkney archipelago between Mainland and South Ronaldsay, joined to each by the Churchill Barrier causeway.

Bushido derived from 'Bushi' (warrior) and 'Do' (way) it is usually interpreted as 'The way of those that keep the peace' and is associated with a chivalrous and honourable samurai life.

Calver (Cats) fictitious violent criminal gang. The name is derived from 'calvered' as applied to salmon that is cut up alive.

Can-can see Orpheus in the Underworld.

Caprice a girl's name (pronounced Ka-preese) of English, French and Italian origins meaning whimsical, playful or fanciful.

Caradoc ('Ka-ra-dok') a Celtic boy's name meaning dearly loved.

Caroline Charles one of London's most respected designers of womenswear and an international business she founded in the 1960s.

Castrati a castrato (Italian, plural: *castrati*) is a man with a singing voice equivalent to that of a soprano, mezzo-soprano or contralto, more usually associated with a female. The voice is produced by physical castration of the singer before puberty, or an endocrinological condition.

cbc (*cloud based communicator*) a fictitious invention intended to be a highly sophisticated successor to today's smart mobile.

Chelsea an area of West London bounded to the south by the River Thames and running along Chelsea Embankment and Lots Road.

Chinthe a leogryph (lion-like creature) often seen at the entrances of pagodas and temples in Burma (e.g. the Schwedagon Pagoda in Rangoon and Mandalay Hill) and other Southeast Asian countries.

Die Entführung aus dem Serail is an opera in three acts by Mozart (K. 384). Translated from German as *The Abduction from the Seraglio* (or Serail – the sequestered living quarters for wives and concubines in an Ottoman household), the plot concerns the attempt of the hero Belmonte, assisted by his servant Pedrillo, to rescue his beloved Konstanze.

Dior a haute couture fashion house founded by Christian Dior in Paris, France during 1946.

DNA stands for deoxyribonucleic acid. It is a nucleic acid containing the genetic instructions used to develop and operate virtually all known living organisms. The DNA segments carrying this genetic information are called genes.

Domo arigato 'Thank you very much' in Japanese. If 'gozaimasu' is appended, the thank you even more generous and polite. It is pronounced ('Doe-moe Ah-ree-gah-toe Go-zah-ee-mahs').

EB the logo (when correctly stylised) is associated with Ettore Bugatti (1881 - 1947), an important member of the Bugatti family instrumental in the family company's rise to automotive stardom.

Echigo-Yuzawa a train station operated by Japan Railway East, located in the resort town of Yuzawa in Niigata Prefecture, Japan.

Emperor of Japan is the symbol of the Japanese state and currently the only remaining monarch in the world reigning under the title of Emperor.

He is a ceremonial figurehead under a form of constitutional monarchy and is head of the Japanese Imperial Family whose lineage is also the oldest in the world with the Empire having been founded in 660BC.

Escada an international luxury fashion group in women's designer clothing, founded in Munich in 1978.

Franck Muller (born July 1958) and is noted for the Swiss Watchmakers he founded, making high quality, sophisticated timepieces.

Fugu the Japanese for pufferfish, which can be lethal due to the strong neurotoxin it contains (no known antidote). Restaurants that prepare fugu are strictly controlled by law in Japan and several other countries; only chefs who are especially qualified may deal with the fish.

Fukagawa Seiji a pottery near Arita. The items made are renowned for their high quality, almost transparent white porcelain and beautiful deep blue designs.

Fuzzy logic rice cooker(s) have computer chips that direct their ability to make adjustments to cooking time and temperature. Whereas basic rice cookers complete tasks in a single-minded, linear manner, fuzzy-logic cookers are able to make judgment calls similar to those a person might make, ensuring proper cooking.

Gäststatte a small German hotel, frequently family run.

Gilding the Lily a well-known quality flower stall near South Kensington underground station.

GPS stands for Global Positioning System, a satellite navigation system, developed in 1973, that provides location and time information anywhere on or near the Earth, where there is an unobstructed line of sight to four or more GPS satellites.

Guildhall, London (c.1411) was where the Lord Mayor of London and the ruling merchant class held court. Today, some 800 years later, the Guildhall is still the home of the City of London Corporation and frequently acts as location for glittering banquets.

Guten morgen German for 'Good morning'.

H&K Heckler & Koch is a German manufacturer of fine guns.

Hachiro a Japanese boy's name meaning eighth son (see '-san').

Hakutaka   The Hakutaka is a limited express train service jointly operated by Japan Rail West and Hoketsu Express. It operates between Fukui, Kanazawa and Echigo-Yuzawa.

Hamon   a visual effect (wavy line) created on a sword blade by the hardening process (from the Japanese meaning 'blade pattern'). It is the transition between the region of harder martensitic steel (edge)and the softer pearlitic steel (body) of the blade.

Haneda   Tokyo International Airport, usually called Haneda Airport, is one of the two main airports serving Tokyo (see Narita). It is located in Ota, some 14 km south of Central Tokyo.

Hanko   a personal seal/stamp used on official documents in lieu of a signature in Asian countries, including Japan (See *Reason and hope*').

Hayasaka-san   the informal form of the Japanese surname Hayasaka. A key (fictitious) character throughout the Samurai Revival Trilogy.

Harrods   an upmarket department store on Brompton Road in the Royal Borough of Kensington & Chelsea, renowned for being able to supply virtually anything.

Hida-Takayama a city near the northern Japan Alps of Gifu Prefecture. It is famous for its well-preserved quarter with Edo-style streets rivalled only by those of Kanazawa. It is often visited en-route to *Matsumoto*.

Higashi Chaya a chaya (teahouse) is an exclusive type of restaurant where guests are entertained by geisha who perform song and dance.

Hikone Castle (c.1600) is one of only 12 castles in Japan with its original donjon/keep. It is on a hill by Lake Biwa, northeast of Kyoto. At the base of the hill, and across the inner moat, is the extremely beautiful Genkyu-en garden which was laid out in 1677.

Honmaru   *Maru* (baileys) are the enclosed area (usually three) around a castle's donjon (main keep). The main bailey is called *honmaru*.

Iga Ueno   formed in 2004 when Ueno, a city in Mie Prefecture, Japan, was merged with Iga and some other small towns.

Iwakuni   a city in Yamaguchi Prefecture, Japan famous for its graceful wooden arched bridge, originally constructed only using wood.

Kanazawa   (lit. 'marsh of gold') is the capital of Ishikawa Prefecture on the northwest coast of Japan, flanked by the Japan Alps. With a prestigious history, Kanazawa is renowned for its beautiful Kenrouken Park, the (restored) castle, its Samurai quarter and three geisha districts.

Karate a martial art, developed in the Ryukyu Islands (Okinawa) in the 19th century. Karate is a striking art using punching, kicking, knee and elbow strikes, and various open-handed techniques.

Keitaro ('Kay-Tah-Roh') a boy's name meaning 'blessed'.

Kenjutsu a Japanese martial art ('the method of the sword') started by the samurai class of feudal Japan to practise sword fighting without using (banned) metal swords. In these books it is understood to include the use of long staffs (see *bokken*).

Kenrouken Park (*Kanazawa*) was built during 1676-1850 by Maeda Tsunanori and others. It is one of the most picturesque gardens in Japan.

Kimi ('Kee-mee') a Japanese girl's name meaning righteous, honourable (see '*-san*').

Kimono a Japanese traditional garment, often elaborate, worn usually by women and children. It is T-shaped, with hems to the ankle and long wide sleeves. It is wrapped around the body (left side over the right except when dressing the dead for burial) and secured by an *obi* (see '*obi*').

Kintai Bridge a beautiful arched wooden bridge at Iwakuni.

Konichiwa 'Hello' or 'Good afternoon' in Japanese.

Kono-san the informal form of the Japanese surname Kono.

Kyoto a beautiful city in central Japan. The imperial capital from c.794 to 1869, it remains a very important and historic city.

Macha is a special finely milled green tea powder. Originating in China, it was brought to Japan in 1191, becoming popular amongst the samurai during the Edo period, and remaining widely so.

Matsumoto Castle a magnificent structure (c.1600) in Matsumoto. Also called Crow Castle due to its black walls and roofs like spreading wings.

Matsumoto a Japanese surname and key (fictitious) person in this trilogy (see '-san' and 'Matsumoto Castle'). Also, a city in Nagano Prefecture, some 170 km northwest of Tokyo.

Matsuo Basho   (1644-1694) was born in Iga Ueno. Famous during the Edo Period, he is still recognised for his haiku poems which traditionally comprise 17 phonetic units in phrases of 5, 7 and 5 respectively.

(Max) Shinkansen (the 'Bullet Train') is an high-speed railway network (c.2,500 km) operated by Japan Rail. Fast (300 km/h), efficient and popular.

Meiji Restoration was a chain of often bloody events that ultimately restored imperial rule to Japan in 1868 (Emperor Meiji) prompting major political and social restructuring.

Mingalabah   'Hello' in Burmese.

Miserere mei   full name '*Miserere mei, Deus*' ('Have mercy on me, O God') is a choral setting of Psalm 51 by Italian composer Gregorio Allegri. Probably dating from around 1630, it is sung during Matins in Holy Week.

Miso soup   a traditional Japanese soup consisting of a stock into which softened miso paste (produced by fermenting rice, barley and/or soybeans) is mixed; there are many regional and seasonal variations.

MO   the abbreviated form of the Latin 'modus operandi', ('method of operation') — describes someone's habits or way of working.

Nara   the capital city of Nara Prefecture in the Kansai Region on Honshu, Japan's largest island — the capital of Japan from 710 to 784.

Nariko   a Japanese girl's name (see '-san') generally agreed to mean thunder. It is pronounced 'Nah-ree-koh'.

Narita   a city in Chiba Prefecture, Japan best known for Narita International Airport, the main international airport serving Tokyo.

Ninja   mercenary covert agents/assassins in 12th-15th century feudal Japan. They were a stark, and clandestine, contrast to the Samurai.

Nishikigoi   (commonly called koi) are ornamental varieties of domesticated carp kept for decorative purposes in outdoor ponds/gardens. Colours include white, black, red, yellow, blue, and cream.

Nurqwoy   a traditional Orkney surname.

Obi   a sash for traditional Japanese dress, such as the uniform (keikogi) worn for Japanese martial arts, but is more widely known as the wide 'belt' used on a kimono.

OCL Open Carrying Licence. A fictitious construction to indicate a licence to carry a samurai sword, uncased, in public.

Ohayou gozaimasu 'Good morning' in Japanese. The abbreviated form, 'ohayou', is the less formal form.

Olympic Park an east London sporting complex for the 2012 Olympics.

Orkney Islands (sometimes 'the Orkneys', a name disparaged by locals) comprise some 70 islands of which 20 are inhabited, Kirkwall is the capital. They are 16 km northeast of mainland Scotland.

Orpheus in the Underworld is an operetta by Jacques Offenbach. The Infernal Galop from Act II, Scene 2, is famous outside classical circles as the music for the often riské dance, the 'Can-Can'.

Rangoon Restaurant a fictitious Burmese restaurant in London.

RCL Restricted Carrying Licence. A fictitious construction to indicate a licence to carry a samurai sword, cased, in public.

Reason and hope – tools of dignity the translation of the Kanji characters comprising the author's Hanko pronounced as Rheagan Greene.

Ripple Road part of the A13 leading eastwards out of London.

Rippleside Industrial Estate an industrial estate to the east of London used entirely fictitiously in this trilogy.

Ritsurin-koen ('chestnut grove garden') is a famous and beautiful historical garden (built c.1625) in Takamatsu on the island of Shikoku.

Sake is an old Japanese alcoholic drink made from fermented rice. More like beer than wine, sake is produced by a brewing process and typically has a higher proof than wine or beer.

Samurai the military nobility of pre-industrial Japan ('those who serve'). By the end of the 12th century, the samurai (c.10% of pop.) followed the *Bushido* rules of conduct; these are still popular.

SAS the Special Air Service is a corps within the British Army constituted in 1950. The *Special Forces* in this trilogy are fictitious.

Sashimi is a Japanese delicacy of thinly sliced pieces of very fresh raw fish (occasionally meat).

Satsuma-Chōshū Alliance (or Satchō Alliance) was an uneasy military alliance between the feudal domains of Satsuma and Chōshū, in southern Japan, formed to overthrow the Tokugawa shogunate.

-san a common honorific signifying respect and formality (similar to 'Mr', 'Mrs' or 'Miss'), usually masculine, denoting familiarity if used with a first name. *NB Japanese honorifics are complex, so they have been simplified in this Trilogy to just '-san'. Apologies to Japanese purists.*

Sayonara ('Si-o-na-ra') Japanese for 'Good-bye'

Scapa Flow a natural anchorage amongst the Orkney Islands and one of Britain's most historic stretches of water.

Sinclair a surname derived from the French Saint-Clair, associated with Orkney since Henry Sinclair, Earl of Orkney (1345 - 1400).

Skyliner Express train service from Tokyo to Narita Airport (see *Ueno*).

SMS Short Message Service is a system that allows short text messages to be sent/received from mobile phone devices.

South Kensington a London district within the Royal Borough of Kensington & Chelsea, loosely defined as around the underground station.

Starbucks the author's favourite coffee house and where much of the Trilogy was written.

Sushi nigirizushi ('hand-formed sushi') is a Japanese food comprising an oblong mound of rice (mixed with vinegar, sugar and salt) usually with some wasabi and a thin slice of fish/meat on top.

Takara ('Tah-kar'ah') a girl's name meaning 'treasure'.

Tatami is a traditional Japanese floor mat made of rice straw with a covering of woven soft rush. Mats are made in standard sizes, with length twice the width and brocade usually finishing the long edges.

Tatsuya ('Tat-soo-yah') boy's name meaning 'accomplished one'.

Tokugawa Shogunate a feudal regime in Japan established by Tokugawa Ieyasu following the pivotal battle of Sekigahara (c.1600). The next 250 years are the Edo Period (Tokyo's name before the Meiji Restoration).

Torii a traditional Japanese arch typically consisting of two pillars and one or two lintels (possibly joined midway), the topmost of which may be curved. They are usually found at the entrance of or within a Shinto shrine to mark the transition from the profane to the sacred.

Tower Bridge (built 1886–1894) an iconic bascule bridge over the River Thames, near the Tower of London. It consists of two steel framework towers, clad in Cornish granite and Portland stone, joined at the top by two horizontal walkways to withstand the forces exerted by the bascules.

Tsuba is usually a round, or rounded-square, disk between the hilt and the blade on Japanese weapons, such as a sword (or katana).

Tübingen a traditional German University town in Germany situated some 30 km south of Stuttgart, the state capital.

Ueno a district in northeast Tokyo, well known for its large Japan Rail station which is a major commuter hub and the terminus for many long-distance trains from northern Japan. Nearby is Keisei-Ueno Station/terminus where the Keisei Skyliner serving Narita Airport stops.

Vauxhall is an inner city district of central London within the London Borough of Lambeth on the south of the River Thames.

Vauxhall Bridge a steel arched bridge in central London, opened in 1906. It crosses the River Thames from Vauxhall.

Yoshino a Japanese girl's name meaning respectful, good. It is pronounced 'Yo-shi-no'.